and no Riel Montclair. Dashing on light, quick toes, she gained the door to the sumptuous guest quarters. The door handle felt smooth and cold beneath her clammy hand. Trepidation pounded in her heart. What if he was inside?

He isn't. Stop being foolish.

Heart fluttering like a bird, Lucinda opened the door and slipped inside.

The letter. Where was it? She must find it, and quickly, for he could return at any moment.

Lucinda swiftly checked his sea bag. Nothing there. Feeling a little warm, she regained her feet and scanned the room. Where might he have put the letter? Provided it wasn't tucked in his jacket this very moment.

The bed. She knelt and peered under it. Nothing there, either. Lucinda gripped the mattress with two hands and shoved it up with all of her strength. Her fingers fluttered, searching...searching... They brushed paper.

Spirit soaring with elation, she snatched out the folded parchment. Sure enough, Father's flowing script read, "Mr. Chase."

She'd found it. Lucinda sat back on her heels in triumph.

A red wax seal secured it, as Riel had said. Now that she'd found it, should she read it? Or quickly destroy it?

A small click sounded at the door. Lucinda's pulse exploded in fright, and she whipped a glance over her shoulder. Riel! Sure enough, the door knob turned.

With horrified, shaking fingers she shoved the letter into her bodice, trying to work it down so he couldn't see...

"Lucy." Displeasure thundered in the deep voice.

She sprang to her feet, still turned away from him, struggling to fix her bodice.

A hard hand jerked her around to face him. "Why are you in my room?"

"I...I came to see that all is to your satisfaction..."

Alarmingly, his dark, pirate eyes fell to her bodice, still askew. Worse, a small corner of the parchment peeked out.

The
Pirate's Desire

JENNETTE GREEN

DIAMOND PRESS

THE PIRATE'S DESIRE

A Diamond Press book / published in arrangement with the author

Scripture quotation taken from the New American Standard Bible®,
Copyright © 1960, 1962, 1963, 1968, 1971, 1972, 1973,
1975, 1977, 1995 by The Lockman Foundation .
Used by permission. (www.Lockman.org)

ISBN: 978-1-62964-010-5

Library of Congress Control Number: 2014933239
Library of Congress Subject Headings:
Love stories
Romance fiction
Historical—Fiction
Man-woman relationships—Fiction
Mate selection — Fiction
Aristocracy (Social class) — England — Fiction
London (England) — Fiction
England — Social life and customs — 19th century — Fiction

Diamond Press
3400 Pegasus Drive
P.O. Box 80043
Bakersfield CA 93380-0043
www.diamondpresspublishing.com

Published in the United States of America.

*"The LORD'S lovingkindnesses indeed never cease,
For His compassions never fail.
They are new every morning;
Great is Your faithfulness."*

LAMENTATIONS 3:22-23 NASB

Chapter One

England
June, 1812

"*FORGIVE ME IF I FIND* it difficult to believe you." In the soft twilight, Lucinda suspiciously eyed the man requesting entry into her centuries old home, Ravensbrook. He wore no uniform. In fact, he looked the worst sort of blackguard. And yet he professed to be a messenger from the Royal Navy...from her *father*.

The stranger stared implacably back at her. He was a big man, but this did not intimidate Lucinda. Neither did the fact he looked like a Barbary pirate, what with that faint, disreputable beard shadowing his jaw, and his unfashionably long black hair drawn back in a careless tail. All he lacked was a gold earring. In fact, was that an indentation where an earring used to be, there in his left ear? A shiver slid down her spine. The man exuded raw danger.

Lucinda told herself to stop being fanciful.

His clothes looked clean. And he didn't smell. This was a dubious point in his favor. The black broadcloth covering his broad, obviously muscular shoulders was made of the finest quality. His boots, however, had seen better days. And his beige pants appeared of uncertain origin. Quickly, she averted her eyes from this involuntary, fleeting inspection.

A subtle, threatening sense of power emanated from him, like thunder in a gathering storm. It deeply disturbed, and even, if she were honest, frightened her a little. It further convinced her that he was dangerous.

Although he made her feel uneasy, Lucinda refused to let him see it. She met the stranger's hard, dark brown eyes and lifted her chin a bit. He wore no cravat with his linen shirt, which left the deeply tanned column of his throat exposed. She surveyed his face again, which was composed of a blunt jaw, a straight nose and brow, as well as a firm, unsmiling mouth. If she didn't know better, she'd think he didn't want to be here.

Maybe she should grant his wish, and send him on his way. Unfortunately, he seemed determined to speak his piece. And, ruffian or no, if her mother were alive, she'd expect better manners from Lucinda than to escape up the stairs and slam the door in his face.

Too bad he had hailed her while she was out walking, otherwise the butler would have dispatched him.

Lucinda offered a polite smile. "If you have anything further to add, I am listening."

After this effort to be courteous, she straightened her shoulders, and tried to make the most of every one of her five feet six inches. It helped she stood two steps above him. It also helped to know she looked passably pretty in her lemon and cream, finely tailored silk dress that was the height of fashion this past Season. It complemented her blond hair and blue eyes, and did its best to divert attention from her freckled nose and tanned skin.

No need for this man to know she was only seventeen. For all purposes, she was the mistress of the house, since her father was a commissioned officer in the war. Never mind the housekeeper, who thought she ran things. Well, maybe she did, but this stranger didn't need to know that, either.

He rumbled, "Perhaps you will invite me inside. Our discussion will best be made in private." He spoke with a faint accent. French? Or somewhere more exotic?

Did he truly think she'd let him inside her home? Lucinda swallowed a small gasp of fear at the very idea. Who was he, to demand entry, with no calling card, nor letters of introduction? She would be an utter fool to let him into her house.

Soft flutters beat in her stomach, and she wondered how she could send him on his way. If only Wilson would come to the door!

A movement caught Lucinda's eye, and the man's sharp gaze followed hers. Abigail, the scullery maid, stared at the stranger with wide eyes, clutching a basket of groceries in her arms.

Quick relief flooded Lucinda. "Abigail! Please fetch Wilson."

Although the butler was over seventy, between the two of them, surely they could send this stranger away. Abigail swiftly bobbed her head and scuttled inside.

Lucinda returned her attention to the man. "Whatever you must say can be said out here." Ignoring the unease coiling within her, she pressed her lips into a firm line, as she had often seen the housekeeper do when displeased with Lucinda's behavior.

Lucinda pinned the man with an unwavering stare. "If you please, be quick. I have duties awaiting me." Such as arranging the flowers for the supper table, but this man need not know the details.

He placed a booted foot on the bottom step, which levered his massive frame disconcertingly closer. Her heart beat faster, like a frightened bird's. "You will be more comfortable if we speak inside."

Lucinda stiffened her spine. "I will be more comfortable when you leave," she snapped. "You say my father has sent you in his stead, but I find this harder to believe by the moment. Present your credentials, or be on your way."

The black brows drew together like a thundercloud. With a terse movement, he pulled two folded parchments from his pocket. "For you."

"Letters? Why didn't you say?" Lucinda's quick pleasure at receiving any sort of missive—presumably from her father—quickly faded. Why would this man carry a letter from her father? Her unease deepened.

All the same, she plucked the letters from his fingertips, which were calloused, with a bit of dirt under the nails. She flipped the parchments over, wanting only to finish this unpleasant encounter and send the stranger on his way.

One was from her father. She recognized his flowing script. He had been a Captain in the Royal Navy before he'd retired ten years ago, and after that he had become a part-time professor of war history at Oxford. When his friends at Command Headquarters in Portsmouth had written him, telling of the great need for seasoned officers for the prolonged war with France, he had immediately rejoined the British Navy. That had been two years ago. It had been months since she had heard from him. From his last, cryptic letter, she suspected he'd been recruited to head up some secret mission.

Now, it was all she could do not to rip open the note this moment and eagerly devour the contents. And assure herself of his safety.

But of course she could not do that with this man watching her. The other letter... Her hand suddenly trembled when she saw the seal of the Royal Navy and her own name, Lady Lucinda Hastings, written across the front.

The Royal Navy. Why would they write to her unless... unless...

She swayed slightly, and a firm hand gripped her arm. "Would you like to go inside?" His tone was gentler.

With a small, choked gasp, she jerked free. It could not be true. "Tell me how you came to possess these letters."

He did not answer.

This was some sort of a trick. It had to be. Who was this man? Surely he was an imposter, and not from the Royal Navy at all. Grief shut down her logical thoughts.

"They're forgeries. I know they are." Her voice wavered. Lucinda dropped both to the ground, suddenly blinded by tears. The horrified fear twisting her insides could not be true. It could not.

She mashed her delicate satin slipper onto the parchments, twisting them, splitting them.

"Go!" she gritted, and pointed to the drive. "Go, and never return!" Picking up her skirts, she fled up the stairs, for the entrance to Ravensbrook...for safety...and for its sheltering, comforting arms. Everything would be all right once she was inside, she thought incoherently. The man would go. And all would go back to normal.

"Lucy!" The deep voice reverberated down her spine and shivered to her toes.

Shaking, she stopped. No one ever called her Lucy. No one except for her father.

She cast a wide-eyed, horrified glance over her shoulder. The stranger remained where she had left him; only now compassion flickered in his dark eyes. "Lucy," he said again. "Perhaps we should talk inside."

He had retrieved the scuffed, torn letters.

She didn't want to touch them again. A sensation like worms creeping over her skin assailed her, and Lucinda felt nauseous and faint. "No." Her voice sounded thready and weak. Not like herself at all. "No!" she said, louder, and felt pleased by the authoritative ring in her voice. "Leave at *once!*"

She fled again, but grief swirled after her like a speeding shroud. With a tiny wail she ran faster up the remaining stairs for the house, but it was no use. Tears blinded her, and she pressed her hands to her face to catch the raw sobs. Running blind, her toes caught in the hem of her gown and she tripped and fell hard on the steps. Pain exploded through her shin and her hip.

She sensed movement and then strong arms lifted her and cradled her against a broad chest.

"Put me down. Put me down at once!" She struggled against the hard muscles confined within the fine broadcloth.

No answer. Just dimness as they entered her home.

"Oh my heavens, what happened?" The housekeeper's voice rose in fright.

"Lady Lucinda has received a shock, madame. Where may I take her?"

"Her room is just up these stairs..."

"No. Mrs. Beatty!" Lucinda struggled for freedom, and the man allowed her to regain her feet.

"Lucinda," the short, plump housekeeper said sternly. "Who is this man?" Worry sharpened her tone. "What has happened, child?"

"That man claims Father sent him. He...he has a letter. Two of them." Grief clogged her throat, and Lucinda swiped her eyes with her sleeve. Perhaps it wasn't ladylike, but the unconscious gesture was a remnant from childhood, when she'd run wild and free on the grounds with her best friends, Amelia and Tommy.

"Letters? What do the letters say, Miss?" the housekeeper asked.

"I do not know. I don't wish to know!" Her voice broke.

Above her, the man's voice sounded like the rumble of thunder from the bowels of a storm. "Please sit down, Lady Lucinda."

"Yes, miss, do." Mrs. Beatty took her arm and gently led her to a faded chintz couch in the parlor. "I'll fetch some tea."

When she left, Lucinda was alone with the man. Without invitation, he sat on the chair beside her. He sat forward, forearms on his knees. Lucinda felt him watching her, but could not look at him. Illogically, she felt if she did, it would make her worst fears become real. But they couldn't be. This must be some sort of mistake.

"Would you like to read the letters?" he asked quietly.

Lucinda bit her lip and plucked at a stray bit of lace on her sleeve. Fear knotted in her stomach. She didn't want to believe the horrible certainty filling her mind, but running would not change the facts. First, she had lost her mother to the dreaded pox twelve years ago. Now Father...?

A painful, growing ache in her throat made it difficult to speak. "Did Father truly give you those letters?"

"He gave me one. Command Headquarters gave me the other."

Helpless tears welled. "Why *you?*" she whispered. "Why would he give a letter to you, a stranger?"

"Your father and I served together. We became friends, and he trusted me."

Trust*ed*. Past tense. Lucinda's jaw ached from willfully clenching it. She refused to break down in front of this man. But tears swam in her eyes and she knew she could read no letter right now. "Tell me the truth. Is Father...is he dead?"

A second ticked by and the man expelled a short breath. "Yes. Your father fought valiantly and died among friends. His last words were for you."

"No." Lucinda felt unable to breathe. Her chest felt tight; unbearably, painfully so. Her beloved father, noble, honorable, and gentle for a military man—a man scholarly and full of high ideals—was dead. She would never see him again. He would never come home again.

"No!" She gasped out a high, keening wail, and hot tears wrenched out, boiling her soul in torment. Grief, long forgotten but bitterly familiar, ached through her. Grief for the hole in her life that would never be filled again.

"I am sorry." The stranger's words sounded rough, as if he did not know how to deal with a storm of emotional weeping.

"La, miss." Mrs. Beatty had returned, and the tea tray clattered onto the coffee table. A comforting, motherly arm went about her. "Now, then. Let's get you up to bed. Effie!" she called for Lucinda's maid. "Come help, if you please."

"I will carry her." Through her incoherent sobs, Lucinda heard the faint rumble of the stranger's voice.

Mrs. Beatty released her without protest, and the man scooped Lucinda into his arms again. When she was deposited in her bed, Effie and Mrs. Beatty fussed over her, drawing the sweet smelling sheets to her chin, leaving her a glass of water, and closing the curtains. Then, blessedly, she was left alone. Lucinda sobbed in broken, unbearable misery. Her father was dead. *Dead.*

Nothing would ever be the same again.

Nothing would ever be all right again. Forever, she would be alone now. She was an only child, with no parents...and only a few distant relations scattered far and wide across the world globe.

Then fright filled her. What would happen to her now? She had not yet come of age, and she was a woman, with no property rights. Would she be thrown from her childhood home while it was given to another...some distant relation she had never met? Fear mixed with the agony in her soul. Whatever would she do now?

ৰ্ভ ৰ্ভ ৰ্ভ ৰ্ভ ৰ্ভ

Gabriel Montclair had been unprepared for the girl's anguished, almost violent sobs. He had also been unprepared for her beauty, with her blond hair springing free from her rolled coif, and bright blue eyes the color of a summer day—a stormy summer day. A spitfire. She had distrusted him on sight.

Riel ran a palm over the rough whiskers on his jaw. He'd been in such a hurry to arrive before the shocking delivery of her father's coffin tomorrow that he hadn't taken the care with his appearance that he should have.

Not that it would have made a difference. Lucy appeared to have disliked him on sight. Perhaps she'd guessed the reason for his appearance on her doorstep. Perhaps she would not take kindly to anyone bearing the news of her father's death.

He hoped that was all it was. After speaking with the housekeeper, he'd clean up and finish speaking his piece to Lucy at supper.

Lucy. He should call her Lady Lucinda, but Commodore Hastings, the Earl of Ravensbrook, had always referred to his daughter as Lucy, and so Riel had come to think of her that way, too.

Peter Hastings had warned him that she was a handful; headstrong as they came, and with a will of iron. He'd said, "Lucy will either be the making of a man or the breaking of one. Lord only knows if there's a soul strong enough to handle her."

Grief tightened in Riel's chest for the man who had treated him like a father and a friend, even though Commodore Hastings, more than anyone, knew the worst about him. Peter had looked down on no one. It remained to be seen what sort of character his daughter possessed. Would she be able to handle the remaining news he must give her?

Riel's gut told him the upcoming scene would be unpleasant. Best to set a battle plan in mind now, for he would not leave until Peter Hastings' last wishes were carried out—no matter how long that might take.

✺ ✺ ✺ ✺ ✺

Lucinda awoke slowly. A lamp spilled light across her bed, and the smell of roast pork drifted upstairs. Her stomach gurgled.

She felt wretchedly tired. Her head hurt and her mouth felt like cotton.

Slowly, she sat up. Although her mind felt numb and dull-witted, she managed to summon the energy to move to the wash basin and splash water on her face. Her hands trembled. Father was dead, but life must go on. More tears welled, but she blinked them back. She must face the servants and pretend all would be well. Now—at least for a little while—she truly was the mistress of Ravensbrook.

At least the stranger would be gone by now. His dark presence had deeply disturbed and even frightened her, although logically she could not say why. Because he looked like a barbaric pirate? Because he'd come bearing awful news?

Yes. But it went well beyond that. He wore power effortlessly, as if it were as raw and natural to him as breathing. Lucinda was honest enough to admit she did not react well to authority of any sort. Father had been mild-mannered, which had helped to defuse the worst of her early adolescent rebellion, but she hadn't seen him in two years. Perhaps her behavior was not as meek and mild as a lady's should be these days; even though she'd tried hard to change into the mature young lady she should be. It was so difficult. Tears slipped out again, and she dashed them away.

If only she could be more like her beloved father. He would never have considered sending a stranger away from Ravensbrook, like she had itched to do. Instead, he would have immediately welcomed him. Logically, she should have done the same.

Emotionally, however, something had warned her to be wary of the stranger. For she'd sensed, from the first split second those dark brown eyes met hers, that an ineffable darkness lurked inside him. Certainly, not a man she could comfortably trust.

Thank heavens he was gone now.

Lucinda stared at herself in the mirror. Red circles underscored her dull, sad eyes. She bit her lip as more tears welled. *Time enough for crying later,* she told herself. Now she must gather strength for the servants' sake. Otherwise, they would worry about their livelihoods. She would do her best to reassure them. But soon she would need to speak to her father's solicitor and learn what was to become of them all; and exactly what would become of her.

Lucinda swallowed another lump of grief and rang for Effie to help her dress for dinner. All must go on as normal. It did not matter if her world had shattered and she was alone now. She must make everything right, if she could. No one would help her, or comfort her and tell her that everything would be all right. It was up to her to think of a plan to save them all. Otherwise, Ravensbrook would fall into the hands of another, and life as she knew it would soon end.

After dressing in a lime green, satin gown with ivory flounces, and after her hair had been carefully swept up into coils and curls atop her head, with tendrils kissing her cheeks, Lucinda slowly descended the stairs to the dining room, keeping her chin level. She tried to find a smile for each servant she passed. *All is fine,* she silently tried to comfort them. *Do not worry.*

If only she could believe it herself.

The footman hurriedly swept open the dining hall door before her.

Lucinda stopped dead in her tracks. Sitting at the head of the table, in her *father's* chair, was the stranger.

The man unhurriedly rose to his feet as she entered. Again she felt, like a fist punch to her stomach, the sheer shock of his physical size. He must be well over six feet, and she'd felt the muscles that encased those thick, broad shoulders. More hard musculature defined his trim hips and long legs.

He gave a small bow. "Lucy."

Her fists clenched in horrified dismay. "Pray, what are you doing here? Why hasn't Mrs. Beatty shown you out?" Perhaps her words were inhospitable, but this was a most unpleasant surprise.

"She invited me to stay for supper."

Lucinda swung her gaze around the room, looking for the housekeeper, but the two of them were alone. Unease pinched her. "Why? I was not notified, and I am the mistress of this house."

"We were unable to finish our conversation. Perhaps we can do so now." Again, she noticed the man's faint French accent. He had also shaved off his scruff of a beard. He looked more civilized...but only just.

"Sit," he invited, resuming his chair.

Presumptuous, arrogant man. How dare he invite her to sit, as if this were *his* dining room and she, the guest? With a tense arm, she pulled out her chair and sat. "You forget your place, Mr..."

He smiled, surprising her. Laugh lines crinkled from the corners of his eyes. "I apologize. We have not been properly introduced. I am Gabriel Montclair, Baron of Iveny."

The uncomfortable sense of wariness, which she'd felt from the first, inexplicably returned with full force. Although Gabriel Montclair's body language appeared relaxed, the innate, dangerous power that exuded from him indicated he would not leave until he was good and ready. Regrettably, this affected her much the same way a red flag did a bull.

If it wouldn't be unconscionably rude, she would ask Wilson to escort him immediately from her home. But clearly the man would not leave until after he had spoken his piece. It rankled, like burrs in a stocking, that he'd taken over her dining room and set down his own parameters upon which he'd leave. Lucinda did not like it. She frowned, and unfortunately spoke barbed words as a consequence. "I have never heard of Iveny. What country are you from, Lord Iveny?"

"France. And you may call me Riel. Or Montclair—whichever you prefer." He pronounced his given name as Ree el', with the accent on the second syllable; a name she had never heard before. "Titles were abolished in France in 1790, as perhaps you've heard. Although, of course Napoleon has reinstituted many titles at his discretion. Not the title of my family, however."

So that explained the accent. "You are our enemy?" Apprehension flared higher.

"I am half English."

So he was a disenfranchised French noble. His drop in social status did not seem to bother him overly much, which seemed unnatural. Suspicious, even.

"Hmm." Was he truly a noble? She found it impossible to drop her guard, for truly, she knew nothing about him. As a result, she did not know how far she could trust him.

"Since you insist upon staying to supper, we might as well eat." She signaled for the servants, and the first course, which consisted of piping hot rolls, served with steamed vegetables, arrived. She chewed the delicious food rapidly, wishing she could speed the meal along, and thus thrust her disturbing guest out the door as quickly as possible.

"Do you not say grace before you eat?"

Lucinda stopped chewing. Truth be told, she used to pray before meals, but had forgotten to continue the tradition after her father left home. It troubled her that it took this rough man to remind her of this basic propriety.

"Of course," she murmured, and bowed her head. "Thank you, Lord, for this delicious food." A thought entered her head. Her father was in heaven with God now. Of this, she had no doubt, for he had been a man of strong faith. On impulse, she whispered, "God, please tell Father I love him." A sob clogged her throat, and tears welled.

Stop it. Lucinda swallowed hard. She would not break down in front of this stranger. Not again. She would not.

"Would you like a handkerchief?"

"No," she said fiercely. "Leave me be."

He fell silent, and slowly her knot of grief dissolved into manageable portions. Guilt then assailed her conscience. Would her father be pleased by her treatment of his ambassador? He was her father's friend, or so Riel—Mr. Montclair—alleged.

She slid a glance at him out of the corner of her eye. "You say you were my father's friend." She placed the slightest emphasis upon the word "say."

His lips tightened and his dark brows edged together. Mildly, he said, "Yes. Perhaps now you are ready to read his letter?"

Why not? The sooner she read the letter, the more swiftly she could dispatch him from Ravensbrook. "Very well."

He pulled the folded parchment from his coat pocket and placed it into her waiting hand. It felt warm from his body heat. An unexpected flush crept up her neck, and she turned away from his dark eyes.

She opened the ripped, dirtied parchment.

Lucinda now deeply regretted the way she had mashed her father's letter into the ground. What had she been thinking?

She had not, that was the problem. Sometimes she acted before she thought through matters. It always got her into trouble. Always, she regretted her impulsive actions, and now, more than ever before.

Lucinda smoothed the letter open upon the table, and lovingly ran her fingers over the words her father had penned. His last letter to her. The script looked strong, letters perfectly formed; not shaky, as a dying man might write. Further suspicion flared.

"When did he write this letter?"

"A few months ago. It was only to be delivered in case of his death."

Lucinda turned her attention back to the paper, but tears blurred her eyes. She blinked several times, and read.

My dearest Lucy,

If you are reading this, I have passed on. I do not regret serving my country, but I regret that I will not see you again in this life. I love you, my daughter. Please never forget this. I also want you to rest assured that I have set safeguards in place so you will never need to worry about being evicted from your home. Ravensbrook will be yours when you marry.

With a small, choked sound, Lucinda pressed a hand to her mouth.

Most of the paperwork has already been filed with my solicitor. Besides the management of Ravensbrook, only one problem remains. You are still young, and unmarried. Since I cannot be there to watch over you, and make certain you make the right choices—including approving the man you will marry—I have asked a friend of mine to fill my shoes in this regard. He has been good enough to agree, and will begin his duties as soon as he can decommission his ship. He has also agreed to take my place and manage Ravensbrook until your marriage. My solicitor will be informed of my final wishes. Your guardian will be

Lucinda turned the page. She gasped.

Gabriel Montclair. Riel saved my life three months ago, and he is the most honorable man I have ever met. I trust him completely, and you may do so, as well. Lucy, listen to him. Choose wisely, too. Promise me you will not marry until you are at least twenty. You have a good head on your shoulders, and I trust you to find a man worthy of you.

Now and for always, I remain your loving Father.

Grief combined with a sick feeling of horror. Surely, this must be a mistake. This stranger was to become her guardian? He would take up residence in *her* home and act as if he were lord of her house? She drew an unsteady breath.

Until she could marry. And speedily she would do that! But still two years and four months to wait. It was unconscionable. This could not be happening. How could Father do this to her? How could he entrust her very life to a complete stranger? And one whom, if the truth were told, unnerved and intimidated her, as well.

But it was here, in Father's own handwriting.

Lucinda struggled to logically understand the reasons behind her father's decision, but the exercise did not help. Her heart could not accept it. Her world, which had already shattered into pieces upon news of his death, now seemed to crumble to powder and run unchecked through her fingers. She retained no control over anything any longer. With a few strokes of her father's pen, she had lost control of her life, her home—her entire existence—to this man.

How could she endure it? How could she live under this complete stranger's thumb for two whole years? She could not. Everything within her revolted at the thought.

Trembling, Lucinda slapped her hands on the table and stood. "Father's wishes will be done," she stated. "But understand one thing right now, Mr. Montclair. You will not rule over me. I am a grown woman, and I know my own mind. I will make my own choices. You may stay, since that is what Father wants, but your role here will be insignificant.

"Furthermore, I will continue to run Ravensbrook. Father was unaware that your help would be unnecessary. You may choose your pursuits, but let me make this clear: the less we see each other, the better you will like it. For peace, Mr. Montclair, I am sure you will be happy to accept these terms."

An unknown expression flickered through his dark, pirate eyes. No matter his claims of a title or the fact that her father had trusted him so implicitly; Lucinda just could not. After all, her father's kind heart had been wrongly led to trust more than a few times in the past.

One particularly frightening incident sprang to mind. When she was twelve, during a horrific rainstorm, a frantic knock had sounded at the door of Ravensbrook. Lucinda stood behind her father as he spoke to the beggar outside. Wind and rain lashed down, and the low growl of thunder electrified the air. The man had begged for shelter, and her father told him to take cover in the barn. Lucinda, however, had noticed that the man's hard, shifty eyes looked younger than his gray beard suggested. And a plump belly bulged beneath his tattered cloak. What hungry vagrant possessed a fat belly?

She'd warned her father of her observations, but he'd said it didn't matter. "Kindness counts, Lucy. We are to help those in need." While she agreed with her father's sentiments, even at that tender age perhaps her heart was too cynical to harbor the kindness that had exemplified her father's life. She'd wanted, both then and now, to be more like her father. She'd tried to believe that Father was right about the homeless man. Unfortunately, the next morning their best horse had vanished, along with the vagrant. Later, they'd learned a murderer from two towns over had escaped from jail the previous night. It was the same man. Luckily, he had harmed no one at Ravensbrook.

Her father's heart had always been in the right place, but he'd been duped before. It could have happened again.

Lucinda knew next to nothing about Montclair, except for what her father had penned, and what Montclair himself had told her. It wasn't enough. At all costs, she must protect Ravensbrook. The future and security of the estate and its servants lay in her hands. With her father gone, making the right choices now was not only her responsibility, but her imperative duty.

Frankly, she felt she was being generous, allowing Montclair to stay in her home. Of course, once the solicitor received this letter, she would not legally be able to turn him out. Briefly, she considered burning it. Then horror bumped through her. How could she destroy her father's last words to her? She could not, no matter the misery it might inflict upon her later.

Montclair's cool, shrewd gaze regarded her. "You misjudge me, Lady Lucinda, if you think I will break my word to your father."

"Ravensbrook needs no manager, Mr. Montclair. And I need no guardian. I have lived without one for the last two years. I will survive for another two, as well."

"It is my understanding you stayed with a friend during the Season in London."

"And a satisfactory solution that was, too."

"Except your friend is to be married, and her mother no longer plans to return to London."

How did he know that? She frowned. "Other arrangements can be made for next Season."

"Other arrangements have already been made. I have a townhouse in London. You will live with me."

Lucinda gasped. "That would be *most* inappropriate. Unless you have a wife..." Somehow, she sorely doubted this. His next words confirmed it.

"No. My great aunt, however, will serve as chaperone both here and in London. She will arrive on Wednesday morning."

The presumption of the man! He clearly had made these arrangements the moment her father had drawn his last breath. And, from his disheveled appearance earlier, he had made haste to gallop to Ravensbrook, as well. Why? Was it because he wished to get his hooks into an estate as grand and profitable as Ravensbrook as speedily as possible?

Fear prompted her next, sarcastic words. "Only your aunt? Have you no other relations who lack a roof over their heads?"

The bridge of his nose pinched white. Uncharitably, she was glad. In some warped way, it only seemed fair that he be as miserable with this arrangement as she. Perhaps he would decide to leave. Her spirits lifted at this happy thought.

His dark eyes bored into hers. "I understand that you have received a shock, Lucy. But being rude to me will accomplish none of your goals."

"Do *not* call me Lucy." Anger surged at his impertinence, and at the walls closing in around her. The man clearly possessed a will of iron. "Only Father called me Lucy. You do not have that privilege."

"I understand that you are unhappy. You are grieving your father..."

"Don't patronize me!" Lucinda trembled where she stood. "I am Lady Lucinda, and I will thank you to leave my house this instant. I cannot countenance your presence!"

Now he did stand. "Lucy—"

"Do *not* call me Lucy!" Fury flared higher, and anguish, too. She did not want to accept any of this. Her father's death. This...this disturbing man moving into her home, telling her what to do...none of it. Without coherent thought, she grabbed the roll from her plate. "I want you *gone!*" She flung it at him. "I want you gone now!"

The roll glanced off of his forehead, and for a split second Riel stared at her in shock. Pleased, Lucinda grabbed for another one, which lay beside her knife, but before she could throw it, something sharp and feral flashed in his eyes.

Lightening fast, he seized her wrist, twisted it, and forced her to drop the bun. She found her arms wrenched up behind her and felt a knee in her back, forcing her to the floor. She gasped in shock and pain. Her arms hurt, twisted up as they were.

"What...what are you *doing?*"

Just as swiftly, his grip on her arms loosened. He put a hand under her elbow to help her up. "*Pardon.* I am sorry," he murmured roughly. "I did not intend..."

She twisted free of his touch, breathing hard now with shock and indignation. "How dare you? I want you gone this instant! You *are* a barbarian, just as I thought from the beginning. Mrs. Beatty!"

"No." His hand shot out for her wrist, but he checked the movement before making contact. It was a wise decision, for Lucinda just might have kicked him. Although, when she remembered the look in his eyes moments before, she may not have, after all. The man *was* dangerous, as she'd sensed from the very first.

She heaved a breath, fighting for calm. Perhaps she had been hasty, throwing rolls at his head. But now she knew for certain with whom she was dealing. A dangerous, brutal rogue. One she must evict from Ravensbrook immediately, at all costs.

"Let me explain," he said in a low voice. His dark gaze now looked troubled.

Mrs. Beatty appeared in the doorway. "You called, miss?" She frowned when she saw them both standing. "Is there a problem with the food?" Her gaze fell to the roll on the rug, and her gaze unerringly went to Lucinda. "Is something amiss?"

Gabriel Montclair spoke first. "A misunderstanding."

"*No,*" Lucinda hissed. "I understand you perfectly now."

"I apologize. I acted without thinking."

Mrs. Beatty entered the room with a frown. "What happened?"

Lucinda cried out, "What happened is he *attacked* me..."

"After you threw a roll at my head and reached for another," Riel put in. "As I tried to explain, I reacted without thinking. In battle, it can mean the difference between life and death."

"But this is not a battle!" Lucinda fluttered her hand at the washed silk walls of the dining room. "You are in a civilized home, with..."

"Apparently, an uncivilized young lady." Mrs. Beatty said. With two fingers, she plucked the roll from the floor.

Lucinda gasped. "You can't take his side, Mrs. Beatty. He manhandled me. He twisted my wrist most painfully!"

Mrs. Beatty frowned. "Why were you throwing rolls at your guest, Miss Lucinda?"

"He is not my guest."

"No. He is your father's," the housekeeper replied. "Mr. Hastings left a letter for me, as well. I am sure he would be shocked to see you treating his guest so discourteously, Miss Lucinda."

Why was Mrs. Beatty taking Montclair's side? Couldn't she see that he was not to be trusted? That he was a dark, primitive heathen? Lucinda glared at Gabriel Montclair, who now regarded her with a steady, implacable look. Impotent frustration welled in her. What could she do? With the housekeeper siding against her, how could she ever get this man to leave her home?

Mrs. Beatty withdrew to the door, her lips pressed tight. "Are you ready for your next course?"

With a frown, Lucinda sat. "Yes, Mrs. Beatty." Perhaps she was going about this the wrong way. Losing her temper had not been smart.

More reasonable thoughts finally entered her head. Her behavior had been childish, too, which chagrinned her. Over the past year, she'd endeavored so hard to grow into the sort of young woman of whom her father would be proud. She'd wanted to surprise him with her newfound maturity when he returned home.

Now he never would.

Tears stung her eyes. Lucinda still wanted to make her father proud. Regardless of this goal, however, somehow she must convince Montclair to leave Ravensbrook. At once.

A tomb of silence ensued until the next course of pork chops and scalloped potatoes arrived. Riel picked up his knife and sliced into his meat. "Clearly you do not like me, Lady Lucinda."

At least he had stopped calling her Lucy. A small victory. She gave him a thin-lipped smile. "How clever you are, Mr. Montclair." In fact, he possessed only one redeeming quality; his unwelcome presence prevented the agony of her father's death from completely taking over her mind.

"Why?"

"I am a lady, and will not be rude. However, know this: Ravensbrook is my heritage. I will not entrust it into the care of a stranger. Furthermore, I will allow no one to rule over me, either. Least of all you, a complete stranger. Regardless of what you told my father, I have never heard of a Baron of Iveny."

Riel took a bite. "I assure you, I own land in France and a townhouse in London, as well as a ship. Facts beyond that are no business of yours."

"So you *are* hiding something."

"Do you wish to know my entire past history?"

"Tell it all," Lucinda agreed. "I would like to know the complete truth of your background...if, indeed you will tell me."

The black brows met again like a thundercloud. He did not like his honor questioned. Perhaps he would tell her the full truth, after all.

She waited, tapping her fingers on the table, pretending impatience. Never could he sense, even for a moment, that she truly wanted to discover every bit of information about him. This realization disturbed her, until she told herself it made prudent sense. After all, the more she knew, the better she could discern his weaknesses and assess the threat he posed to both Ravensbrook and herself.

And he was a significant threat, as she already knew quite well. His brutish behavior when he'd manhandled her had proven it. She must gather ammunition to boot him out of Ravensbrook before it was too late—no matter what her father had wished. Montclair must have duped her kind-hearted parent. Why else would Father put such a dangerous man as lord over her? The barbarian had hurt her! Her wrists still stung, and one thumb mark still reddened her skin.

If he could do so much damage in an instant, she shuddered to consider the damage he could cause to Ravensbrook—and to herself—during the next two years.

Riel spoke in a low voice. "I was born in Roué, France, twenty-eight years ago. My mother was English, my father French. My father squandered the family fortune in games of chance, and he lost our house in a poker match. When I was fourteen, I went to sea on a merchant ship."

He looked down and rubbed his nail—clean now, she noticed—into the design on the fork. "Conditions were bad," he finally said in a rough voice. "We sailed to the Barbary coast. I did not realize..." After a moment, he went on. "I escaped when I could. At seventeen, I jumped an English ship bound for the Mediterranean. It wasn't much better. I will spare you the details. One thing led to another, and I now own my own ship. In addition, I have been working closely with the Royal Navy for the past two years."

That wasn't the whole story. Lucinda sensed he withheld information. But what? Was it that dark something she'd sensed from the beginning? She looked into his black eyes and found no answers.

Still, she did not know how to respond to his tale. It rang with truth. She could well imagine him living rough years on the high seas, and on the Barbary coast, too. The area was known for slave trading and pirates.

So, she'd been right from the first. He was a pirate...at least, he'd likely served upon a pirate ship at one point, or perhaps for several years. That would account for the rough edge she'd sensed in him, tempered, however, by the thinnest veneer of civility. Also, it would account for his brute strength and quickness to react when threatened. As she'd suspected, he'd learned none of his savage behavior from his association with the Royal Navy. Instead, likely on a cutthroat ship.

She cleared her throat. "You said your father lost all of your family land. How can you own land in France, then?"

"A relative passed away. It is not a large estate, but it pays for itself, with a little extra to keep up my house in London."

Lucinda thought through all she had learned, and tried to figure out how to best lever each bit of knowledge to her advantage. "You must love the high seas, then. You've been sailing for what, fourteen years? And you help the Navy."

"I am happy to use my knowledge of ships for good, rather than evil, if that is what you mean."

It wasn't, but Lucinda grasped this new information and plunged on, determined to wiggle her foot into this door of opportunity. "Don't you want to keep working with the Navy, then? And save the world from evil-doers?"

He frowned faintly.

"I mean," she said more clearly, "I see no reason for you to leave your ship just to be a guardian to me." A flash of inspiration arrived. "You say your great-aunt is coming. She can do the job just as well."

"My aunt is in frail health. Besides, your father asked me to watch over you and protect you. That is what I will do."

"But why?" she said in a reasonable tone. "If it is a promise to my father that is holding you back, I release you."

"My word was to him, not to you. I will fulfill my promise."

"But why? Why on earth would you agree to be my guardian in the first place?"

A long pause elapsed. "I owe your father," he said quietly.

"Why? What did you do?"

"More like what he did for me. The fact remains, Lucy, I will stay here. I will be your guardian, and take care of Ravensbrook. I must return to my ship at the end of this week, however. It will take two weeks to make repairs and put her in dry dock. Then I will return here for good, and I'll stay until you are safely married."

He had called her Lucy again. Lucinda crossed her arms, not caring that she might look like a belligerent child. "I require no guardian, Mr. Montclair. You will quickly discover this is a complete waste of your time."

A smile glimmered. "I hope that is true. Then my next two years will prove agreeably pleasant."

Lucinda frowned. His next two years would prove entirely *un*pleasant if she had anything to say about it. In fact, the next week would be so disagreeable that he would sail away, never to return!

A faint smile crept to her lips. By hook or by crook, Gabriel Montclair would flee from Ravensbrook before the week was out. Painful though it might be, she already knew the first step to eradicate him from her life.

Her plan was almost laughably simple. The solicitor would receive no letters from her father. She would make sure of it, and then Riel would possess no legal grounds to stay. He would have no choice but to depart from Ravensbrook for good.

An end to this current, unfortunate episode could not come quickly enough for Lucinda. And if somewhere in her conscience doubt niggled, she ignored it. She was doing the right thing. Definitely. Lucinda did not trust Montclair one inch, and already she itched most fervently for his dangerous, disturbing presence to vanish from her life.

But first, she must discover more information. "Mrs. Beatty said Father wrote her a letter, as well. Did he send any other letters with you?"

He regarded her shrewdly. "Another for his solicitor. I will pay him a call tomorrow. Mrs. Beatty has been kind enough to tell me how to find him."

When the solicitor received that letter, there would be no turning back. She would need to act quickly.

Riel said, "One matter remains to discuss."

"Hmmm?" Lucinda pulled her mind away from the delicious, exciting plot roiling in her head. It had been some years since she'd attempted anything so daring. Her heart pumped faster, just thinking about it.

"Your father. His body will arrive tomorrow afternoon. I assume you will wish to make arrangements for his burial?"

Lucinda's thoughts fell to earth with a thud. "Yes... Yes of course. I will need to speak to Pastor Bilford in the village."

"You can ride to town with me tomorrow when I see the solicitor."

Lucinda did not relish the thought of traveling anywhere in Gabriel Montclair's close, disturbing presence. But she did need to see Pastor Bilford. Better yet, if all went according to plan, Riel would never visit the solicitor at all. Instead, he would immediately return to his ship.

However, her former optimism failed to return. Her heart felt like a lead weight in her chest. Lucinda had never planned a funeral before. She had been five when her mother had died. Perhaps Mrs. Beatty could give her advice. That was a good plan, for she needed to speak to the housekeeper on another subject, as well. If handled delicately enough, the conversation might prove quite fruitful indeed.

Lucinda signaled for the next course she did not want to eat. Riel Montclair did, however. He ate all of his food—a great deal of it—with obvious appreciation and enjoyment.

Enjoy it while you can, she thought. *Ravensbrook will not feed you for much longer.*

Chapter Two

AFTER SUPPER, LUCINDA found Mrs. Beatty in the kitchen, banking the fire in readiness for the next morning. Riel Montclair had retired to the parlor with a small snifter of brandy, and one of Father's books. Happily, he was unaware of her plot.

"Mrs. Beatty, supper was delicious."

The housekeeper sent her a sharp glance. "I trust no more rolls ended up on the floor."

"Of course not." Lucinda could have felt offended, but the housekeeper had been like a mother to her for the past twelve years. Besides, she deserved the gentle rebuff.

Mrs. Beatty straightened, and dusted her hands on her apron. "Why don't you like the Baron, miss? Your father sent him to watch over you and Ravensbrook. A blessing that is, to be sure."

Lucinda didn't want to get into an argument with the housekeeper. Perhaps to Mrs. Beatty's way of thinking, Father's solution would seem like a relief. A man would continue to run things until Lucinda was married. However, Mrs. Beatty had not experienced Montclair's rough hands on her wrists, and she was also blissfully unaware of the man's probable pirate associations. Lucinda could not allow him to run Ravensbrook.

At the crux of it, Lucinda wanted to know *why* Riel had offered to manage Ravensbrook in the event of her father's death. Had her father asked him, or had Montclair volunteered himself? Unless Lucinda could discover firm, unassailable evidence to Riel's good character—an unlikely prospect—his motivations remained suspect. Therefore, he must go, and speedily. At all costs, she must protect Ravensbrook.

On a more personal note, she also could not bear the thought of Riel—or any other man, if she were honest—ruling her life, or most especially dictating her choice of suitors. She would marry for love, whether the man was "worthy" or not, according to *ton* strictures. Her father had always been able to see the value in people, no matter who they were—title or not. Who knew what sort of guidelines Riel might try to institute for her suitors, and for every other aspect of her life?

She shivered. After living in utter freedom, as she had done for the past two years, and frankly, for most of her life, Lucinda could not countenance the thought of a stranger—particularly a savage, she reminded herself, rubbing her faintly sore wrists—wielding a scepter of authority over her head. No. And that was why she was here now.

"Mrs. Beatty, did you say Father wrote you a letter, as well?"

The housekeeper reached into the front pocket of her apron and pulled out a parchment similar to Lucinda's own. Only not trampled, of course. She gently ran her fingers over it. "Yes, he did, miss." When she looked up, tears glistened in her eyes. "And thankful I am for it, too."

Tears clogged Lucinda's throat. "You'll miss him, too."

"I will, miss. I've worked for your father for nigh on thirty-three years, did you know that? He took over Ravensbrook as a lad of twenty when his own father died. A better employer I could never have had."

Tears slipped down Lucinda's cheeks, and an answering one rolled down the older lady's face. "Oh, Mrs. Beatty." Voice breaking, Lucinda flew into her comforting arms, as she'd often done as a child. "I can't believe he's gone. I don't want to believe it!" She choked on a sob.

"Now then, child. We'll all miss him, we will. He was a fine man. Not many like him."

Lucinda finally pulled back, wiping her eyes. "Everything will be all right, Mrs. Beatty. Don't worry."

"Why would I worry, child? He's sent Mr. Montclair to watch over us. If your father trusted him, I have full confidence we can, too. Your father was a good judge of character."

Unfortunately, Lucinda found she could not fully agree with the housekeeper's trusting words. She was a good judge of character, too, and Mr. Montclair was not entirely what he appeared to be. A raw edge lived in that man; an untamed side that had told her to beware of Gabriel Montclair from the first moment he'd planted his massive boot on the bottom step of Ravensbrook.

In addition to the logical reasons she'd found to distrust him—namely, his brutish manhandling of her person—a sixth sense whispered that somewhere, perhaps dredged deep in Riel's past, lived something dark. Perhaps a secret her father had known nothing about. This was more than possible, and unfortunately, another disturbing memory about how her father's kind heart had been duped in the past flew to mind.

Three years ago, a young man and his pregnant wife had arrived at Ravensbrook, and begged for food and shelter. The woman's baby bulge had looked suspiciously lumpy to Lucinda, and she'd had a bad feeling about the "husband" all along. The dirty, hungry couple had insisted on working for food. Pleased, her father had agreed, and let them sleep in a guest room in the house. In the morning, the two were gone, along with the family's silver.

No, as much as Lucinda loved her father, she just could not trust Gabriel Montclair.

"Did you need something, Miss Lucinda?" Mrs. Beatty dabbed her eyes with her apron. The letter fluttered in her hand.

Lucinda looked at the note, and then at Mrs. Beatty's sad face. The letter meant the world to the housekeeper, just as Lucinda's did to her. Her hastily concocted plan to burn all the letters her father had sent, thereby destroying all evidence that Riel Montclair was supposed to be her guardian, puffed out like a candle.

Although she could sacrifice something of her own to ac-complish her goal, she would never dream of asking for, or destroying, something the housekeeper cherished.

A sick feeling welled in Lucinda's heart. "No. Thank you, Mrs. Beatty," she said softly, and swallowed back an ache of disappointment.

Now, how would she get rid of Riel Montclair? "I came to tell you that Father's body will arrive tomorrow afternoon. I plan to speak to Pastor Bilford tomorrow about a service."

Mrs. Beatty straightened her plump shoulders. "I will plan a reception here, miss. You need only say the day."

"Let's see. Today is Monday. Perhaps Wednesday evening?"

The housekeeper nodded her approval. "If you agree, I will send a few lads to the village to spread the news. Letters will need to be sent to the prominent families round about, as well as notices to his friends in London."

"I will write those tonight." Lucinda knew the handful of aristocratic families to whom Mrs. Beatty referred. They lived nearby, but would expect a personal invitation. The rest of the townspeople would know they were welcome. Her father had been a generous man; giving freely to those less fortunate, offering jobs, lending resources to those starting a new farm...and listening to anyone who had a problem. He'd never met a stranger, and social station meant nothing to him. He was well loved, and his funeral would be well attended.

Tears sparkled in Mrs. Beatty's eyes. "You are growing up to be a fine lady, Miss Lucinda. I'm proud of you, and I know your father would be, as well."

Lucinda hoped that was true.

"Thank you, Mrs. Beatty." With a teary smile, she hugged her old friend, and retreated across the hall to her father's study, which was paneled to the ceiling with shelves of books. A shabby, blue oriental carpet covered the wooden floor beneath the polished, dark teak desk. She needed to find his address book.

Her father had been meticulously organized, thanks to his many years in the Navy. When he'd retired from the service ten years ago, he had decided to pursue his love of war history, and had ended up becoming a part-time professor at Oxford. His naval career and then his teaching profession kept him away from Ravensbrook much of the time, and Lucinda had eagerly looked forward to the summer months when he was home full-time. She'd often joined him in this study, helping him dust and sort the old tomes. He'd shared his favorites with her, and because he loved history so much, she loved it, too.

Now she sat at his desk and pulled out the top right drawer. The drawer slid smoothly, as she'd known it would. A dark leather book lay on top. A lump welled in her throat, thinking of the many times she'd seen him sitting here, just like this. "Lucinda," he'd said once, "do you see that dark green volume on the top shelf? Fetch it for me, would you? Have you ever heard of the Boer War?" And that would be the start of an impromptu lesson.

Lucinda brushed at the tears trembling on her eyelashes. Her jaw ached from trying to hold in her grief. But she couldn't fall apart here, not where the servants might see her. It would frighten them. At all costs, she must appear serene, and try to keep things running smoothly, as Father had done. It was the least she could do in his memory.

The leather book held the addresses of his closest friends. The list was well over two hundred, she suspected. Tonight, she'd write up the most urgent notes, for the people who would actually be able to attend the funeral. Later, she'd hire the printer to engrave notices and send them to the others.

She pulled out parchment and quill, but her fingers stilled over the letter paper. It had been her father's desire that Riel Montclair be her protector. Could she deny her father's last wish?

While she did want to please her father, anxiety seeped into Lucinda's heart when she considered submitting her life to the authority of the man in the next room. Fear punctuated the dark feeling. Everything within her recoiled at the thought. She pressed her hands to her face.

"Father," she whispered, "why did you do this to me? I know you thought this would be best for me, but he's the wrong man for the job. Why didn't you see that?"

She imagined her father in the room, sitting at this very desk. What would he say? In a flash, she knew. With those intelligent gray eyes, hidden behind his glasses, he'd ask, "Why don't you like him, Lucy? Is it because you know you won't be able to goad him into behaving like you wish? That's why I chose him, you know. Choosing a marriage partner is the most important decision you'll ever make. I trust Riel to help you choose wisely. And I trust him to run Ravensbrook."

More tears wet her palms. "But I don't like him, Father," she gave a miserable sniff. "I don't trust him. Why did you?"

"Why don't you trust me, Lucy?" Riel's deep voice made her jump.

Hastily, she wiped her eyes. "I did not invite you in, Mr. Montclair. Kindly take your leave."

"I will soon be running Ravensbrook. Perhaps tomorrow you will show me the accounts and ledgers."

Lucinda gasped. The cheek of him. "I most certainly will not! Mr. Chase, our solicitor, is in charge of the books. He will remain so until I can learn to do them myself."

"Your father told me that a stipend from a trust is paid out each month for the maintenance of Ravensbrook. Is that true?"

Suspicion again reared its ugly head. Was this what Riel was truly after—Ravensbrook's fortunes?

"Yes. What of it?" True, her father had set up the estate so Mr. Chase could easily disburse monies into their standing merchant accounts while he was gone. Essentially, with this bit of effort on Mr. Chase's behalf, the estate could run by itself— except for dealing with tenants and daily practical matters, which she had done. And it meant nothing that Gabriel Montclair knew of these arrangements. Her father could have mentioned it to anyone. It certainly did not mean Montclair could brashly come in and usurp Ravensbrook's financial reins.

He said, "It was his desire that I relieve Mr. Chase of that burden. I understand the running of an estate, as I own one myself. I am qualified for the job, Lady Lucinda."

"I don't care if you're qualified to juggle melons, Mr. Montclair. You will not touch one pence of my father's money. Strike that. *My* money."

A muscle tightened in his jaw. "Mr. Chase will decide that."

Incensed, Lucinda rose to her feet. "Father's letter to Mr. Chase states this?"

"It does."

She pounced. "You've opened it, then."

"No. He told me what he wrote."

"Did he?" More suspicion flared, followed quickly by anger. "Or did you *force* him to write it, Mr. Montclair? What other liberties will you pretend he granted you? Perhaps in the event of my death, the entire estate will fall to you. Is that it?"

To his credit, he looked shocked. "No."

"Prove it." Swiftly, she swept by him, and then waited, arms folded, out in the hall. "Show me the letter Father wrote to Mr. Chase."

"It is sealed."

Lucinda smiled. "And if the seal is broken, your claims will prove worthless."

For a long moment he watched her steadily, his breaths even. "You have quite an imagination, Lady Lucinda."

"No more outlandish than you showing up on my doorstep with all of these outrageous claims. Suddenly you, a stranger, are to become guardian to me and trustee of the entire estate. I don't know you from Adam, Mr. Montclair. Excuse me if I don't take your word as gospel."

"Come with me tomorrow when I visit the solicitor. You may read your father's letter as soon as Mr. Chase is finished."

He sounded so calm, so reasonable. "I will read the letter, you may be sure of that. But just because my father penned the words doesn't mean they were his wishes."

Impossibly, his midnight gaze blackened still more. "How could I force your father to write a letter?"

"How am I to know? You crewed on a pirate ship—isn't that what you said?" She didn't give him time to respond. "At the very least, you sailed the Barbary coast on a barbaric ship. You admitted that already. I have no doubt you learned all sorts of torture devices while on that unsavory scow." Another disturbing detail flashed to mind. "You said you're half French. Perhaps you are part of the French Navy. You captured my father and...and forced him..."

"To appoint me guardian of a belligerent, unmannered girl? Truly, that is an assignment I have always wished." Black sarcasm cut through his words.

She flushed. "No. But to gain control of his estate..."

Riel gave an abrupt bow. "I will take my leave before I say something I regret. Good evening, Lady Lucinda."

Muscular shoulders tense, he brushed by her, and strode down the hall. He took the stairs two at a time, and then Lucinda heard the hard clomp of his boots overhead.

Quick breaths still heaved in her bosom. She felt a little ridiculous, standing there. Perhaps she had gone over the top, accusing him of belonging to the French Navy. Nor did she truly think he'd forced her father to write those letters.

On the other hand, could he have tricked her father into trusting him? Yes, indeed. Father had been sharp and quick, but his kind heart was his weakness.

It was bad enough, the idea of Riel becoming her guardian and ruling her life. But him taking over Ravensbrook and all of its finances, too? No. It was too much. *Never.*

Lucinda realized that she'd been mistaken to think she had to burn all the letters her father had sent. Only one must be destroyed—the sealed missive to Mr. Chase. With that dispatched, Riel Montclair would have no claim to Ravensbrook, whatsoever.

Simple, then. Mr. Chase's letter would mysteriously disappear. And then so would Riel Montclair.

Chapter Three

LUCINDA AWOKE EARLY the next morning. Knowing her father's body would arrive that afternoon brought fresh, aching misery. She did not want to get out of bed. However, she must. This morning, she must send Gabriel Montclair packing.

With Effie's help, she washed and dressed in her only black crêpe dress. Unfortunately, more black frocks would be required for the mourning period. Lucinda made a mental note to speak to Mr. Chase about advancing her clothing stipend for the necessary garments.

Lucinda hated black, and more so, the idea of spending her limited clothing allotment for the unbecoming garments. But for her father, she would do nothing less than give him the honor of a full black mourning time.

"Do you want breakfast in your room, Miss Lucinda?" Effie asked, hovering at the door.

"Yes, please, Effie." She opened a drawer and plucked out a handful of folded and sealed parchments. It had taken her an hour last night to write the dozen invitations to her father's funeral on the morrow. She handed them to her maid. "Please give these to Mrs. Beatty. And when you return, please tell me the whereabouts of Mr. Montclair."

"Very good, miss." The door softly clicked shut. While Lucinda sat to wait, plans flitted through her mind, like buzzing bees seeking the brightest flower. Depending upon Effie's report, she was ready to spring into action.

With a light knock, Effie returned. Lucinda found that her palms were damp with nervous perspiration, but she adopted a calm demeanor. "Thank you, Effie. Did you locate our guest?"

The maid poured tea into a delicate, rose patterned china cup. "He's 'aving breakfast, he is."

"Perfect. Thank you, Effie. I believe I will take a leisurely meal. No need to return for an hour."

"Of course, miss. Thank you." Effie flashed a small grin and hurried out the door, no doubt eager to spend her extra free, precious moments with her friend Henry, who worked in the stables.

After a moment, Lucinda peeked into the hall. All clear. Good. No servants, and no Riel Montclair. Straightening her shoulders, she swept into the passageway as if she had every right to be there...as, of course she did, Lucinda reminded herself, swiping damp palms against her dress.

The hall opened up a few steps later into a small rotunda arching over the circular grand staircase. Lucinda peeped over the railing and listened to the faint clank of dishes in the far off kitchen. No footsteps approached. No one was about to witness her underhanded deed.

Dashing on light, quick toes, she gained the door to the sumptuous guest quarters, located just on the other side of the rotunda. The door handle felt smooth and cold beneath her clammy hand. Trepidation pounded in her heart. What if he was inside?

He isn't. Stop being foolish.

Heart fluttering like a bird, Lucinda opened the door and slipped inside.

The open, dark blue curtains allowed in a stream of sunlight. The room was the exact image of her own, with three great windows straight ahead, a neatly made bed, flanked by bedside tables, and an armoire on the left wall, just beside the door. Instead of being decorated in yellows and creams, however, this room was more masculine, with a palette of dark blue and heavy, mahogany furniture.

Carefully, she edged into the room and cast a quick glance around the side of the armoire. *As if he would be hiding back there,* she chastised herself. Instead, she spotted his worn canvas sea bag. Was that the only piece of luggage he owned, or would more be arriving?

She then realized another disconcerting fact about her unwelcome guest. He had no valet. All nobles retained a valet. *Was* he a noble at all? Or was that merely a fabrication?

The certainty that she should not trust him intensified. Lucinda felt more determined than ever that she must succeed in her mission right now.

The letter. Where was it? She must find it, and quickly, for he could return at any moment.

Lucinda swiftly checked his sea bag, and felt embarrassed when her fingers ran over every article of his clothing. Thankfully, no one was about to witness her disgraceful actions.

Nothing there. Feeling a little warm, she regained her feet and scanned the room. Where might he have put the letter? Provided it wasn't tucked in his jacket this very moment. *Please, God, no.*

Of course, perhaps the Almighty wasn't listening to her. He couldn't be too pleased with her behavior. And what of her father? What would he think?

Lucinda tried to ignore these prickles to her conscience as she circled the room, searching in the drawers of a small desk, atop the bedside tables, and on the fireplace mantle above the smoldering fire; everywhere, even the top of the armoire. Finally, she put her hands on her hips and surveyed the room. Either he carried the letter with him now, or he'd hidden it. Either way meant he distrusted her.

She frowned. Riel Montclair would not win. He would not gain control over herself or Ravensbrook. If he had hidden the letter, she would surely find it!

She knelt beside the bed, checked under it, and then gripped the mattress with two hands and pushed upward. It was heavy, and barely budged.

She put her shoulder to the mattress and shoved upward again. Good. It rose a few inches. Speedily, her fingers slipped under the drooping bed coverings and searched for the letter.

Nothing. She moved down the bed, and heaved it up again. When she reached the far side of the bed, perspiration dampened her skin and her carefully coiffed hair straggled in tendrils against her cheeks. Effie would wonder what she'd been about.

No matter. This was the last place to check. Surely he didn't have the letter on his person.

With all of her strength, Lucinda shoved up on the mattress. Pain skewered like a knife down her back. Her muscles were unused to such exertions. Her fingers fluttered, searching...searching... They brushed paper.

Spirit soaring with elation, she snatched out the folded parchment. Sure enough, Father's flowing script read, "Mr. Chase."

She'd found it. Lucinda sat back on her heels in triumph.

A red wax seal secured it, as Riel had said. Now that she'd found it, should she read it? Or quickly destroy it? A longing to read her father's words warred with her need for haste. Perhaps if she hid the letter in her bodice, she could carry it to her room and read it there.

A small click sounded at the door. Lucinda's pulse exploded in fright, and she whipped a glance over her shoulder. Riel! Sure enough, the door knob turned.

With horrified, shaking fingers she shoved the letter into her bodice, trying to work it down so he couldn't see...

"Lucy." Displeasure thundered in the deep voice.

She sprang to her feet, still turned away from him, struggling to fix her bodice.

A hard hand jerked her around to face him. "Why are you in my room?"

"I...I came to see that all is to your satisfaction..."

Alarmingly, his dark, pirate eyes fell to her bodice, still askew. Worse, a small corner of the parchment peeked out. "What have we here?"

"Nothing! Unhand me at once." She struggled, but his grip held her immobile. Worse, the tanned fingers of his other hand reached for the corner of the parchment. She slapped his hand away.

"How dare you!"

"Then give the letter to me."

"Never!" she gasped, and struggled in a sudden, wild fury to free herself. She must escape now with the letter, or she'd be chained to this man for the next two years. "Get your hands off of me!"

She twisted hard to the right, and suddenly found herself slammed back hard against him. His rock-solid chest imprinted her back, as did every angle and plane of his body. She gasped still further, and a hot blush rose up her skin. "Unhand me at once, you...you barbaric pirate! I cannot believe you would treat a lady in such a manner!"

"A true lady would not behave as you are." The arm he'd clamped around her waist held both of her arms immobile, as well. She felt his warm breath on her neck and unaccountable shivers raced down her skin. In her ear, he said, "Now I will retrieve my letter."

"No." She struggled, but to no avail. In helpless frustration she watched his fingers swoop for the parchment, which poked up beyond the edge of her bodice. His tanned knuckles brushed her sensitive skin, and Lucinda shuddered, feeling that she might die of embarrassment. She reared back, away from his touch, but unfortunately, that only pressed her more closely into his solid, muscular body. Tears welled in her eyes. "You monstrous beast," she hissed. "Unhand me at once!"

The parchment slipped free, and in that instant she found herself free, as well. She whirled, flushed with temper. "How dare you touch me in such a manner? And...and *steal*..."

"Do not speak to me of stealing," he said in a dangerous tone. Was that a flicker of amusement in his gaze? Impossible. Nothing about this situation was funny.

Lucinda trembled with finely controlled rage. "Fine. Keep the letter. But know, Mr. Montclair, that I will protect Ravensbrook and my servants with my life, if necessary. I will *never* allow this estate's monies to pass through your covetous hands."

Any suspicion of amusement fled. "You care nothing for your father's last wishes, then."

"My father trusted too easily. He has been duped before."

"He was too quick to see the good in someone, you mean?"

"Exactly! So you admit you deceived him?"

"I see he did not perceive his daughter to be the selfish, spoiled young lady you are." He slipped the letter into his jacket pocket. "Have you always behaved like this, Lucinda?"

She did not like the dark way he said her full name. "I am merely trying to protect myself and everything I hold dear. I wish for you to leave. I can handle everything well enough on my own."

"You have made it clear to me that you are an immature young woman who lacks respect for others. Peter was right. You do need a guardian. Unfortunately for both of us, I am his choice. I will be your guardian, Lucinda, you may be sure of that. And you will come to treat me with respect."

"Respect is earned, Mr. Montclair."

"It is also learned, Lady Lucinda."

She did not like the steady, hard look in his eyes, and decided it was time to make her exit.

He spoke softly, just before she closed the door. "I will leave for the solicitor in one hour. If you wish to come, you will be ready."

Lucinda jerked the door hard, and its slam reverberated down the hall. The gall of the man! The utter cheek. Trembling, she stalked to her room and slammed that door, too.

She stood there, shaking. She had lost. Worse, she felt embarrassed and humiliated. An ache gathered in her throat. She'd been right from the start. He *was* a savage, through and through. What would he do to her—or to Ravensbrook—once he gained full control of both?

In an hour, the solicitor would read the letter and her fate would be sealed.

Tears welled and she stumbled to the bed. It wasn't fair! None of it. Father's death, living under Riel's boot for the next two years... Why did it have to be? *Why?*

Lucinda wept softly, in abject misery. Father's death was bad enough. She could not suffer through Riel's domineering rule over her life, too. And Ravensbrook. What did he intend to do with Ravensbrook, once the full financial reins fell into his hands?

ళ ళ ళ ళ ళ

Riel wondered what he had gotten himself into. He owed Commodore Hastings his life, but becoming a guardian to his daughter seemed like a stiff sentence to pay in return. Lucy was as fiery and strong-willed as they came. Clearly, she did not want him to be her guardian. Worse, the idea of him taking over Ravensbrook's finances seemed to have pushed her over the edge. She distrusted him completely. But why? Why would she hate him, when she barely knew him?

He thought through their confrontations; two of which he had resolved by force. A technique which had clearly inflamed her hatred for him. But what else could he do? Allow her to run off with Peter's letter and burn it?

Never. His jaw tightened. With his last breath, the Earl of Ravensbrook had begged Riel to watch over Lucy. To protect her. Riel had sworn on his life that he would. Lucy was mistaken if she thought she could run him off.

He frowned, and analyzed each of their confrontations again. Perhaps he was handling her the wrong way. Instead of telling her the way things would be, perhaps he should suggest the ideas first. Instead of treating her like an unruly new sailor, he could treat her like his first mate. He could listen to her views.

Lucy was upset about her father's death. Maybe that, in addition to all the changes in her life that Riel represented, was too much for her to handle right now.

As Riel gathered the necessary items for the visit to the solicitor, he decided he'd try to be more understanding. If Lucy agreed, they could go about his guardianship as a partnership. Provided, of course, she agreed to behave like an adult.

He would make Lady Lucinda realize that cooperation would be much more pleasant than war.

�� �� �� �� ��

Lucinda rode soberly to town in Montclair's black carriage. Riel glanced at her several times, perhaps wondering why she rode so placidly across from him.

Probably waiting for her next histrionic fit.

Lucinda averted her face and silently looked out the window. A sick knot clenched in her stomach as she slowly accepted the fact she could do nothing to change her future. Riel would become lord over her. And how would he treat her, after the way she'd just treated him? It didn't bear thinking about. He'd proven how dangerous he could be; twice, in as many days.

He could not become her guardian! Lucinda swallowed, and tried hard to prevent her distress from showing. Riel could not suspect how frightened and hopeless she felt right now. She could not bear it.

Even worse, what would become of Ravensbrook and her beloved servants? What did he intend to do with her family's home during the two years he would be in charge?

How could her father leave her fate and that of Ravensbrook in the hands of this man?

The carriage drew up in front of the solicitor's house. If only she could stop this meeting from taking place! But short of ripping the parchment from Riel's pocket, Lucinda could think of nothing she could do to stop it.

Her gaze slid to that jacket, wondering if the note still resided in the same pocket.

"After you." Riel stood aside, so she could enter the house first. His black gaze held hers, as if he knew what she was thinking. Flushing, Lucinda looked away and followed the butler into the stately mansion.

"In here." The servant bowed, and Lucinda entered a lushly appointed office. A Persian rug covered the floor, the chairs were of the finest black leather, and the desk shone. Law books filled the floor-to-ceiling bookshelves.

"Lady Lucinda." Portly Mr. Chase stood up behind his desk, beaming. His smile wavered when he took in Lucinda's unhappy face. "My dear." His hand closed around hers, a shade firmer than his usual, tepid shake. "I am so sorry for you loss. Your father was well loved and respected in this community."

"Thank you," she said quietly. From an unknown source, she summoned enough strength to straighten her shoulders. "As you know, that is why I am here today."

"Of course, my dear." Mr. Chase's gaze swung to Riel, and he put out his hand. "I am Thomas Chase. You might be..."

Riel's hand engulfed the other man's in a firm shake. "Gabriel Montclair, Baron of Iveny."

"Pleased to make your acquaintance. Why don't we sit?"

When Lucinda sat, she realized her chair and Riel's touched arms. A silly thing to notice, but it disturbed her, as did everything about her enforced relationship with the Baron...if indeed he was a Baron. Baron of Barbary perhaps, she thought darkly. Or perhaps Lord of the Pirates would be more apt. Although clean shaven this morning, he still wore his long black hair in a tail, and now that she was nearer to him, she could clearly see the faint indentation in his ear lobe where an earring must have hung, long ago.

His dark eyes caught her staring, and she narrowed her gaze. Much as he might fool everyone else, he would not fool her. Not ever. She knew very well what sort of a man lived beneath his finely tailored clothing. Truly, a brigand of the worst sort. Hadn't he treated her roughly? Hadn't he physically forced her to succumb to his wishes? *Twice*. Never mind her own questionable behavior. A true gentleman would never have responded in such a manner.

Averting her gaze, she sat ramrod straight and folded her hands in her lap. "Mr. Montclair has a letter addressed to you from my father."

"A letter?" With alacrity, Mr. Chase accepted the parchment.

"I was with the Earl when he died," Riel said in a low voice. "The letter states his final wishes."

The solicitor frowned. "His final wishes? I have his last will and testament on file."

"As I understand it, that document will remain the same. This is an addendum until such time as Lady Lucinda marries, and can take over running Ravensbrook on her own."

Mr. Chase nodded, and broke the seal. Silence ensued, except for the loud ticking of the grandfather clock in the corner. Each tick sounded like a hammer striking a nail into Lucinda's coffin. Why did she have the dreadful, absurd feeling that her father's letter would bind her to Riel for eternity?

Surely, she was being fanciful. Melodramatic, as Mrs. Beatty had often chastised her in the past.

It was only for two years. Right? Lucinda wished her stomach would stop roiling.

"I see." Mr. Chase lowered the letter and adjusted his glasses.

"May I see it?" Lucinda requested.

"Of course, my dear." When the solicitor handed it over, she quickly read the note.

Mr. Chase,

Please add this letter as an addendum to my will. In the event of my untimely death, Gabriel Montclair has agreed to assume guardianship of Lucinda until her twentieth birthday, or until she is married, whichever comes later. As you know, I love Lucinda dearly, but she can be a headstrong young lady. By this, I mean occasionally hot-headed and impulsive. She needs a steady influence and guiding hand to help her choose a suitable husband. Riel is that man. I trust him with my life, and I also trust him with Lucinda's, as well as with the responsibility of running Ravensbrook until Lucinda is married.

Please forward the monthly stipend to his hand to distribute as he sees fit for the running of Ravensbrook and everything that entails, including Lucinda's wardrobe. If extra monies are needed on occasion, Lucinda and Riel must petition you together for them. If it seems prudent to you, advance those sums to Riel, as well.

After Lucinda is married, my original last testament will take over.

Thank you, my good friend, and God bless you.

Peter Hastings, Earl of Ravensbrook

Tears filled her eyes as she read her father's last wishes. Truly, he had trusted Riel Montclair completely. Why, however, she still could not fathom.

And he had loved her very much to the end.

Still, it did not take away the sting of his descriptions of her being hot-headed and impulsive. Lucinda was honest enough to admit they were true; at least, on occasion. And thus Riel was to be her guardian. Her father had supposed he would be a steadying influence in her life.

But Riel did not steady her at all. He unsettled her, and had from the first. And her father hadn't seen her in two years. She was nearly eighteen, and had matured a great deal in her father's absence.

Her behavior to Riel being the exception, of course.

She certainly did not need a guardian. The panicky, sickly feeling boiled up again as she cast a quick glance at Riel's profile. The blunt angles of his face looked cut from stone, and his personality reflected an equally unyielding nature.

She bit her lip. This was wrong. *All of it.* It should not be happening. Her father should not be dead. This...this man should not be taking over her life.

At least her father had put a limit on the amount of Ravensbrook's money that Riel could access. Still, each month he'd fully control how the monthly stipend was spent. Could he be trusted to use the money as her father had intended? At least his possibly grander, fortune-hunting desires would be squelched; unless he had some other plan afoot that she could not yet imagine. Still, she did not know how he would run Ravensbrook, or treat its servants...or herself.

The lurches of her stomach made her feel sick.

"Very well." Mr. Chase cleared his throat, and Lucinda's thoughts returned to the gleaming study, which smelled faintly of orange oil. She realized he wanted the letter back. With reluctance, she returned it.

"All appears to be in order, Mr. Montclair. I will take care of the necessary paperwork. Perhaps you will return at the end of the week and sign the documents?"

"That would be fine," Riel said.

Lucinda did not reply. But a small, unexpected bit of hope bloomed. Apparently, the agreement would not go into effect until Friday. But on Friday, when Riel signed those documents, her fate would be sealed. She would be forced to submit to his leadership in every aspect of her life...including his guidelines for a suitor. In fact, for all intents and purposes, Riel would choose her husband.

She bit down hard on her inner lip to keep from moaning in protest. Three days of freedom remained. Surely, within that time she could discover a way to escape from her impending doom.

"At that time," Mr. Chase continued, "I will deliver the monthly stipend into your hand, Mr. Montclair, so you may pay estate expenses." He smiled. "Frankly, I will be glad to see an end to that task."

"May I have the account books in advance? I leave for my ship at the end of the week, and would like to understand how the estate runs before then."

"Of course." Mr. Chase retrieved several leather bound ledgers. "When will you return, Mr. Montclair?"

"Within two weeks. I need to oversee repairs, and then ready my ship for dry dock."

"You own your own ship, Mr. Montclair?"

"Riel. Yes, a merchant ship."

"You would put your livelihood on hold to care for Lady Lucinda?" Mr. Chase gave a jovial laugh. "That is most self-sacrificing, Riel."

"I owe the Earl a deep debt. It is the least I can do."

"Very well. I will see you on Friday."

"Mr. Chase." Lucinda sat forward on her chair. "Father's funeral will be tomorrow evening at Ravensbrook. If you can come, I would be most pleased."

"Of course. Of course." Mr. Chase nodded once, as if bestowing a great favor upon her.

"Also," her fingers smoothed her black crêpe dress with suddenly nervous fingers, "I will require an advance on my clothing stipend to pay for more black gowns." The last thing Lucinda wanted to do was beg Riel for dresses. She hoped Mr. Chase would give her the money now. In the past, he had been amenable to any requests she had made. All reasonable, of course. She had no wish to squander her father's money...*her* money, now.

"Certainly. I have saved a bit from last Season, and will advance that to Mr. Montclair, as well."

Lucinda slid a dismayed glance at Riel. "Please, may I have the money now? I must commission the gowns immediately."

The solicitor glanced at Riel. "Very well." He pulled a metal box from a drawer and counted the money it contained. "Forty pounds. Enough for a dress or two, eh?" With a chuckle, he handed it to Riel.

Lucinda gritted her teeth in annoyance. Apparently, she would have to beg Riel after all. Adopting a small, pleasant smile, she turned to the man beside her.

"If you would be so kind, Mr. Montclair? Please. Give the money to me." She couldn't help the faint, hostile note in her voice. "I will give it to the seamstress in the village so she can begin work today."

How she hated begging him for money. And this was just the beginning. Her spirits sank still further. He had all but gained his objective. In three short days—unless she somehow discovered a way to extricate herself from this distressing quagmire—he would win the permanent victory.

What triumph he must be feeling. What satisfaction.

Lifting her chin, she forced herself to meet his dark, pirate eyes. But instead of the triumph she'd expected to see, she saw soberness. As if he fully realized the great responsibility he had taken on.

He rumbled, "How many black gowns do you have?"

"This one."

He nodded. "One more can be made."

"One!" Lucinda sat a little straighter. Here it was. The beginning of his authoritarian rule. "One will not suffice. I need at least two. Preferably more."

Mr. Chase laughed loudly, clearly feeling uncomfortable. "I'm sure you can come to an agreement later." He stood and extended his hand. "I'll see you both on Friday, then."

A clear dismissal. Equally clear, Mr. Chase would be no champion for her. He wanted to wash his hands of the mess and return to his comfortable life.

She followed Riel into the bright sunlight and the awaiting carriage. She settled herself inside, properly arranged her skirts, and waited until the driver shut the door. Anger and frustration seethed in her bosom. A jerk, and they moved toward the seamstress's house.

"Is this the way it will be?" she said grimly.

"What do you mean?"

"I *mean* are you relishing this? From now on you can squish me under your thumb, and deny my every wish."

"Is this only about the dresses?"

"No! And well you know it."

His dark eyes held hers. "Rest assured, you will be provided with all you require."

She glared. "I cannot live off a few garments in a canvas bag."

"I understand that you will need more black gowns, Lucy. But one extra will serve for now. You will need new dresses for the upcoming Season, as well. Your mourning period will be finished by then."

"I realize that," Lucinda managed to speak in a reasonable tone. "However, I do not think two new black dresses would be extravagant. I have no intention of spending all of my clothing allowance now." In truth, the idea that buying too many gowns now might crimp the number of gowns she could purchase for the Season had not entered her head.

It would have, however, once she'd given it more thought.

"We will commission one gown for now," Riel told her. "Then I will study the ledgers and see how many more can be made."

The man was unbending, and it scraped on her last nerve. "Very well." Lucinda crossed her arms. "I would like to see the ledgers, too. I want to learn everything about Ravensbrook's finances."

To her surprise, Riel gave her a steady, considering look. "All right," he said. "In two years you will be responsible for them. It's a good idea for you to learn about them now."

Lucinda felt a flush of pleasure...and a flare of unease, too. Learning about the books meant she'd have to work closely with Riel. But perhaps that would be a blessing in disguise. Three days remained to discover the chinks in his armor. The time spent together, learning how to run Ravensbrook, would provide her with ample opportunity to discover his weaknesses and use them to her best advantage.

If all went well, not only would she learn how to run the estate, but she'd discover a way to convince him to leave before he signed the final documents. Lucinda settled back, feeling her first flicker of hope in hours.

Chapter Four

HAPPILY, THE VILLAGE MODISTE had a length of black bombazine silk on hand. She agreed to sew it into a dress immediately. Since she knew Lucinda's measurements, the fitting did not take long. She promised the dress would be ready in time for the funeral tomorrow.

Twenty pounds remained when Lucinda and Montclair headed for the parsonage attached to the village church. Lucinda had stuffed the money into her reticule, after snatching it from the seamstress when she'd held out the change to Riel.

"If it is all right, I will leave you here to speak to Pastor Bilford," Riel said, offering her an arm to step down from the carriage. For the sake of polite courtesy, her fingertips touched his proffered arm for the briefest moment possible. Even in that fleeting touch, she felt the raw strength of him. It disturbed her. He said, "I need to visit the mercantile."

"Very well. I am pleased to take your leave, Mr. Montclair." She turned away and headed down the pebbled path to the parsonage. Guilt for her dreadful manners assailed her conscience, and she bit back the apology that rose in her throat. Had her rude comment bothered him? No sound came from behind her, as if Riel watched her. And then the sound of boots on gravel reached her ears, and the carriage rolled down the country lane.

Unfortunately, the idea of prickling under Riel's skin elicited a wicked feeling of pleasure. Definitely not a good thing, Lucinda thought with a further sting of remorse, and glanced at the church. If only he wasn't such a thorn in her side. If only he would go away, then she would not have to behave like an annoying fox hound.

An unexpected thought crossed her mind. If she behaved badly enough—if she managed to infuriate him so frightfully that he couldn't stand to be near her—would he run from Ravensbrook? What was the saying in Proverbs? Better a corner of a roof than living in a house with a quarrelsome woman?

Well, maybe not quarrelsome. That did not appeal. Neither did acting like a harridan.

But if it worked... Would it be worth the cost, she wondered. Could she stomach behaving like a vixen for the next three days? The self-inflicted wounds to her self-respect might prove difficult to mend. Especially since she had struggled so hard over the last year to try to conform to the mature requirements of a young lady. This plot might erase all of her gains.

In truth, the plan did not appeal at all, but as of right now, she could think of no other way to convince Mr. Montclair to leave.

She climbed the step and rapped on the parsonage door.

Mrs. Bilford, a thin, sprightly woman with coiled iron gray hair and snapping black eyes saw Lucinda and said merely, "Lucinda," before wrapping her in a tight hug. "My child. I am so sorry. Won't you please come in?"

Lucinda blinked back tears. "Thank you." She followed Mrs. Bilford into the crowded front parlor. A secretary desk sat in one corner and a large wooden wardrobe in another. The room also contained a horsehair couch and an armchair. All sorts of knickknacks were scattered on every available surface.

"Please sit down. I will fetch the tea and send in Mr. Bilford."

Lucinda had always thought it funny the Bilfords called each other Mr. and Mrs. Bilford. A faint smile touched her lips as she sat on the slippery couch, but it vanished as she waited. What would she say to the pastor? How did one go about arranging a funeral service?

Mr. Bilford hurried in with his wife, who carried the tea tray. "Lucinda." He pressed her hands between his own. His kind eyes, behind round spectacles, looked concerned, and his bushy gray brows furrowed together. "I am so sorry. Your father was a good man."

"Thank you," Lucinda whispered, and bit her lip. Mrs. Bilford looked on, worried lines crinkling her forehead. The kindness and concern in both of their eyes was suddenly too much, and Lucinda burst into tears. Flustered, she fumbled in her purse for a handkerchief, but Mr. Bilford pressed one into her hand, instead.

"It's good to cry," he said gently. "You miss him very much. So will we all."

"Y...yes," Lucinda sniffed, and tried to blot the tears from her eyes. Unfortunately, they wouldn't stop.

Mr. Bilford gave her a fatherly pat on the shoulder and sat in an adjacent chair. "Take all the time you need."

Lucinda did not like to weep in front of others. She'd much rather cry in private and keep her deep emotions to herself. It felt strange and frightening that she couldn't stop crying. At long last, however, her sniffling sobs shuddered to a stop.

"There." Mrs. Bilford pressed a clean hanky into her hand.

"Don't be surprised if you weep often in the next few weeks," Mr. Bilford said kindly. "Little things will set you off. Take advantage of those times and cry. You need to grieve."

Lucinda nodded, but couldn't speak.

"And pray to God when you feel down, Lucinda. I'd be remiss if I didn't tell you this. He cares for you and will give you comfort."

"I'll try," she said in a small voice. Goodness knew, she didn't pray enough. Hadn't Riel been the one to remind her to pray at dinner last night?

Pastor Bilford said, "And always remember this; your father is in heaven. It's a wonderful, glorious place, and some day you will see him again."

Lucinda's mind flashed to all of her misdeeds; many of them recent. "I hope I will," she mumbled.

Pastor Bilford chuckled. "Faith pleases God, Lucinda. If you've committed transgressions, repent and move on."

What if she planned more transgressions? Lucinda felt uncomfortable, and decided to change the subject.

"We're having Father's funeral tomorrow evening at Ravensbrook. Will you be able to conduct the service?"

"I would be honored. If you wish, I will arrange the burial as well. In your family plot?"

"Yes." Grateful tears hovered, but she managed to blink them back. "Thank you. And I wondered about a grave stone."

Pastor Bilford motioned to his wife, and she immediately turned to the desk and withdrew a paper, quill and ink. "I will commission one made. Write what you would like engraved on the stone."

Lucinda accepted the items. But her quill hovered, unmoving, over the paper. Part of her could not believe she was about to write words that would commemorate her father's grave forever. It seemed a momentous task. Her words would be read for centuries to come.

She drew a breath, and tried to marshal her thoughts. Above all, she wanted everyone who read the epitaph to know a little about her father. She did not want him forgotten. Not ever.

After a long hesitation, she dipped quill into ink and wrote, "Peter Hastings, Earl of Ravensbrook, Commodore in the Royal Navy, professor, well loved for always. 1759 – 1812."

Hands trembling, she handed the sheet to Mr. Bilford. He smiled when he read it. "Very good. The stone should be ready in about three weeks."

Lucinda reached into her reticule and pulled out the twenty pounds. "Will this be enough? Or will it cost more?"

Mr. Bilford accepted the money. "A few pounds more, but don't worry. We can collect it in the future, Miss Lucinda."

A knock sounded at the door, and every intuitive fiber in Lucinda said it was Riel. She stood, clutching her bag. "It's time for me to go."

Mrs. Bilford welcomed Riel inside. Montclair looked very large standing in the doorway, with his black clothing accenting the lean, muscular lines of his body. He bowed over Mrs. Bilford's hand and introductions were made. Neither the pastor nor his wife seemed put off by Riel's long hair, pulled back in a tail, nor his unfashionable preference not to wear a cravat.

"I've just finished," Lucinda said, clutching her reticule tightly. She wanted to go. She didn't want Riel to guess at the tears she had shed here, nor the vulnerable emotions that still threatened to engulf her.

His black eyes ran over her face. "All is well?" he asked quietly.

Lucinda bit her lip and glanced at Pastor Bilford. "All is arranged."

"Is more money required for the stone?"

"Yes, but Mr. Bilford said it can wait. Perhaps until Mr. Chase gives you the monthly stipend."

"I will pay it now." Riel pulled a money clip from his inner jacket, and when Pastor Bilford named the remaining sum, he paid it in full.

Pastor Bilford's gaze met the younger man's and he offered a firm handshake. "You will take good care of Lucinda." It sounded like both a question and a command.

Riel returned the shake. "I will, sir."

Pastor Bilford smiled. "Good. I will see you both tomorrow night."

Lucinda followed Riel to the carriage and settled herself inside. "You did not need to do that." For the first time, uncertainty gripped her. Surely a dishonorable man would not have paid her debt with his own money. Of course, he could replace it later. But still.

"I like to pay debts in full. I do not like owing anything to anyone."

Lucinda nodded slightly. A policy her father had championed, as well.

She glanced at him, and then away. The man unnerved her, and on more than one level. She didn't want to admire anything about him. It disrupted her sense of purpose.

At Ravensbrook she hurried inside. She had plans to make. Plans she must carry out, for the good of everyone on the estate. More than that, she needed to rest. Her father's coffin would arrive this afternoon and she must gather her strength.

✿ ✿ ✿ ✿ ✿

Later that afternoon, wagon wheels rattled down the lane to Ravensbrook. With trepidation, Lucinda slid aside a curtain and looked out. Sure enough, an open wagon with a wooden coffin bumped into view. Grief gathered into an aching lump in her throat. Father was home for good. She bit her lip, but refused to cry. It felt as if she'd cried enough for one lifetime already.

A British soldier, clothed in dark blue, accompanied the wagon driver. Following them was a dun colored horse and a rider with long, scruffy blond hair smashed beneath a black, bicorne hat. From this distance, it was hard to guess his age, but his clothes looked worn. Definitely those of a commoner. Who could he be, and why was he accompanying her father's body to Ravensbrook?

Lucinda gathered her skirts and rose to her feet. She must welcome her father home for the last time.

Blinking quickly, she descended the wide, winding staircase and discovered Mrs. Beatty waiting at the bottom, wringing her hands. "He's here, miss," she whispered.

A knock sounded at the door. Riel appeared from Father's study and strode to open it, but Lucinda lifted her chin and hurried abreast of him. Her father had arrived, and she would welcome him home.

"Excuse me." With a scampering double-step, she achieved the front door ahead of him. Wilson, the butler, swept it open before her.

"Lady Lucinda." A tall British soldier bowed. "I am Lieutenant Simmons. I...I am sorry for my duty this day."

She nodded. "Do come in. Perhaps my father could rest in the parlor."

"Of course." He bowed again, and Lucinda, Riel and Mrs. Beatty stood aside as two soldiers carefully carried in the large mahogany box.

It did not seem real that her father lay within that sealed box. Lucinda turned back to the soldier, her vision blurry. "You have had a long journey. Would you like tea, or perhaps refreshments?"

"Thank you Lady Lucinda, but no. We will refresh ourselves in the village. I also have a flag for you, and a tribute written by Admiral Smythe." He pressed both items into her hands, and then, with another bow, he and the wagon driver made their exit.

Lucinda looked into the parlor, and then anxiously at Mrs. Beatty. She whispered, "Should we leave the door open, or shut?"

"Whatever makes you feel comfortable, miss."

Lucinda blinked quickly. "We will leave it open. It's Father's home. He's welcome, and he belongs here."

"Very good, miss. But perhaps you would like a spot of tea in the kitchen?"

"Yes, thank you." Gratefully, Lucinda latched onto this excuse to move away, at least for a few moments, from the coffin holding her father. It was too much to bear, to know he was in the next room, but would never speak to her again in this lifetime. Sorrow billowed up and tears slipped down her cheeks.

Still, as Mrs. Beatty disappeared, Lucinda glanced back, feeling guilty and remiss in her duty. She should say something to her father, and be with him for a minute, instead of running away like a tearful coward.

Yes. Her father deserved nothing less. Slowly, Lucinda returned to the parlor. "I love you, Father," she whispered, and touched the box. "Welcome home."

Tears overflowed, and she sat on a chair and let them come, sniffing and sopping them up with the handkerchief she'd begun to carry with her. Mr. Bilford had said to cry whenever she needed to.

She sniffled into silence. A low rumble of voices tickled her ears. They came from the next room, which was her father's study. Riel. She frowned, puzzled. To whom was he speaking?

The man on the dun colored horse. Could it be him? She hadn't seen him enter Ravensbrook, but then again, she had only focused upon her father when the soldier arrived.

Rising to her feet, Lucinda slipped close to the waist high bookcase which was pushed flush against the wall that adjoined with her father's study. Sure enough, she heard another man's coarse voice. Not Wilson, the butler's, for it sounded far too rough. Curiosity and suspicion arose. If he was indeed the man on the horse, why would Riel speak to such a disreputable-looking stranger?

Unless, of course, the man was no stranger to Riel at all, but one of his crewmen. Unsavory, too, by the look of him.

From the first, she had suspected Riel possessed a dark secret. Now could be her opportunity to discover it. A plan sprang to mind. Unfortunately, she knew quite well that her father, lying silently behind her, would have heartily disapproved of her intended course of action.

Lucinda tried to ignore this fact. She pulled out a thick book and found the round peg imbedded in the back of the bookcase. She pushed it hard, and the bookcase shifted left. Quickly, she withdrew her hand and slid the rolling bookcase left. A small, dark opening appeared, about three feet high and two feet wide. It was the only secret passageway Ravensbrook possessed; at least to Lucinda's knowledge. She'd loved playing in this one as a child.

Stooping, she slipped inside, and swiped at spider webs drooping from the ceiling. A soft, filmy one caressed her face, and she shuddered, although she knew it had to be an old web, for it wasn't sticky. Not to say there weren't new ones, and new spiders lurking nearby.

Lucinda shivered again and silently minced four steps to the right inside the secret passageway. No need to announce her presence. Hopefully, if the men heard her, they'd think she was a mouse scuttling within the walls. Lucinda swallowed a gurgle of revulsion and prayed no rodents ran over her toes.

Her fingers skimmed over the wall. And then again...and yet again, searching. It had been years since she'd done this.

Here. At last, she found the recessed lever. A gentle push, and the panel slid—thankfully noiselessly—inside, and to the right. Before her, a floor-to-ceiling tapestry concealed her hiding place from the men in the room. Dust motes tickled her nose, and she hastily pinched it shut so she wouldn't sneeze.

Now she could hear clearly, and she remained still and listened.

"It's worse'n you think, guvnor," a raspy voice said. "The Brits say they'll seize *Tradewind* if y'don' comply. Yer to be there Friday."

Heavy boots paced the floor. "The Admiral said that? In so many words?"

"I've a note. Here."

The crisp snap of a letter opened, and silence ensued. "He breaks his word." Riel sounded grim.

"What right have we to deny 'im? As you say, if y'don' want waves, don' sail in a storm."

"I'm aware of our predicament. But I cannot leave here yet. Documents must be signed before I can return."

"Kin you handle the gel?"

"I can handle her." Again, the words sounded grim. "But I won't leave until all is settled."

"Legal, or otherwise?"

Riel did not answer.

"Last thing yer want is to raise suspicion, Cap'n."

"As I know well."

Suspicion? Lucinda drew a soft, startled breath, and stopped pinching her nose in order to breathe better. Why would the Royal Navy possibly become suspicious of Riel and his crew?

Her heart pumped faster, and dangerous prickles of excitement danced over her skin. Riel must be running—or hiding—from something. Just as she'd thought. But what could it be? And how could she find out? She leaned closer to the old tapestry in order to hear better.

"Is it worth it, guvnor?"

"What do they intend, Haskins? You must have heard a rumor."

"All I know is the Admiral means business. To keep yer squeaky clean rep and boat, you've got to come."

"When will this end?" Frustration edged the deep voice.

"Until Bonny's banished, Cap'n."

Heavy boots strode in the direction of the desk. A quill scratched on paper. "Take this, Haskins. Tell him I'll be there on Monday."

"Aye, Cap'n."

"And Haskins, tell the crew I've not forgotten my promise."

"We don' need extra coin for sailin' the ship, Cap'n. Brits' infernal henpecking or no. We're your crew."

"You deserve it. I'll have money coming in soon. At the end of this week, in fact. I'll bring it when I return to the ship."

Money coming in soon? At the end of *this* week? Lucinda softly gasped. On Friday Mr. Chase would pay Ravensbrook's monthly stipend into Montclair's hand!

"Very well, Cap'n. Thank you. I'll be off."

Lucinda peeked around the end of the tapestry and saw the unkempt scoundrel exit. Her mission had proven quite fruitful.

Now, she needed only to escape from her hiding place without detection.

Her cheek dusted the tapestry as she drew back, and suddenly her nose itched most alarmingly. She must have stirred up dust. Lucinda grabbed for her nose again, unmindful that her hand would cause a noticeable ripple in the tapestry.

"Ah *chuh!*" Stifled though she'd tried to make it, the sneeze exploded like shattering china.

Lucinda scrambled to find the closing lever. Haste made her fingers clumsy. As a child, she could have closed it in two seconds flat.

Now two seconds stretched to three, then five...and with each one she heard boots clomp closer.

Her fingers closed on the latch. Finally! She jerked it down just as Riel swept aside the tapestry. Horrified, she stared back at him. His dark, shadowed face looked more like a pirate than ever before, and his black brows winged upward in surprised displeasure.

"Lucinda!" he thundered as the panel slid shut. Breaking free of her frozen horror, Lucinda bolted down the short hall, and then out the hole by the bookcase. She whipped a glance over her shoulder. No Riel. Shaking, she shoved the bookcase back, and it clicked into place just as her guardian's large frame filled the doorway.

"Lucinda," he said again, but with no more pleasure. His black brows looked ominous.

Trembling, she gripped the bookcase behind her. How should she play this? Pretend it never happened? That he'd seen a ghost who looked like her within the wall?

"Riel."

Flustered, she realized she'd called him by his first name. Attempting to adopt a modicum of dignity, she pulled out the hanky she'd tucked inside her sleeve. Glancing at her father's coffin, she dabbed her eyes. "Have you come to pay respects to Father?" She didn't have to fake the tremor in her voice.

Riel stepped into the room. "You have cobwebs in your hair, Lady Lucinda." His soft voice sounded dangerous.

"Oh!" Her fingers fluttered to her hair.

"Perhaps you will allow me." He stalked closer, and she shrank back.

"No. I...I will thank you to keep your distance, Mr. Montclair."

"You are frightened. Perhaps because you heard words that weren't meant for your ears?"

Lucinda lifted her chin and swallowed, fighting for courage. "Have you things to hide, Mr. Montclair?"

"I have private business to conduct. Business that is none of your concern."

"But you are very much my concern. I must understand what sort of a man you are, if you're to take over Ravensbrook." Her mind worked quickly, trying to decide which bits of information to provoke from Montclair first.

"You can trust me."

"Oh? Because you say so? I am not a feather-brained ninny. Tell me what your business was about." Her insides felt shaky, like a poorly set pudding, but outwardly, she struggled to project a visage of cool calm.

Here was her chance to discover the full truth about Riel Montclair. ...If he would tell her. And once she found out, how could she best use that knowledge to evict him from her home? Lucinda wished she had more time to plot her strategies.

A long moment ticked by. "Tell me what you heard."

"I heard it all," she said rashly. "I know the Royal Navy wants you to return to your ship. If you don't, they'll seize it and likely throw you in the brig." Of course, she'd embellished the last part, but she was fishing for information now. It was part of her hastily improvised plan of attack.

His fingers twitched at his sides. Because he wanted to throttle her? Or because she'd backed him into a corner and now he'd have to fight—or bluff—his way out?

"The Navy wants me to run a mission."

"Why?"

He paced closer, but she refused to cringe back. "It's top secret. I cannot give you details."

"Pooh," she said. "You want me to trust you. Then you must trust me first."

"I cannot say more."

Lucinda changed tactics. "Why, then, would the Navy be suspicious of you?"

Shadows darkened his eyes. "The Brits have no reason to distrust me. I have helped them for the past two years."

"Truly?" One brow arched. "I thought you owned a merchant ship. How could a merchant ship be of use to the English Navy?"

"Again, I would rather not say. It could be dangerous for you."

"Dangerous for *me?*" Surprise quickly devolved into suspicion. He was trying to scare her and throw her off the scent. Temper sparked. "I am not a fool. You have a dark secret, Mr. Montclair. I know it. And when I discover what it is, I'll personally invite Admiral Smythe here so he can cart you off to the Tower of London!"

Unknown emotions flickered across his face. To her surprise, he chuckled. "You have quite the imagination, Lucy."

Lucinda wanted to stamp her foot. She had learned exactly nothing about his nefarious doings! She snapped, "Who was that man, and why was he here?"

Laugh lines crinkled from the corners of his eyes. "You heard it all, did you?"

"Answer my questions!" She glared.

The smile eased back into a straight line. "Haskins is the first mate on my ship, the *Tradewind.*"

"A merchant ship."

"Yes. A privateer. Which means I own my ship, but in time of war we are authorized to attack enemy ships. The Royal Navy has commissioned me to work on their behalf."

"Oh." Lucinda reassessed the facts. The Royal Navy had an assignment for him. A secret mission, perhaps? A thought flew to mind. Her father had recently been on a secret spying mission, or so she'd guessed. "Was...was my father on your ship when he died?"

"Yes. We were under cannon fire. A cannon ball hit the stern railing, and your father was too close. We made him as comfortable as possible during his last minutes."

"I see." She swallowed the sudden lump in her throat. Now things were beginning to make sense. Riel and her father had met on the *Tradewind* and become friends. But how had Father grown to trust him so implicitly? They hadn't known each other long, had they? "How long was Father on your ship?"

"Seven months."

A good amount of time. And her father had never known a stranger. Seven months confined on a ship could probably make even enemies bosom buddies. But none of this explained what Riel was currently trying to hide from the English government. Truly, he didn't want them to become suspicious of him—she'd heard him admit as much to his man, Haskins. What was he hiding?

Then the other suspicious bit of information she'd overheard returned to mind. What about the money he'd claimed to be receiving soon? At the end of *this* week—coincidentally, when Mr. Chase would deliver Ravensbrook's monthly monies directly into Montclair's hands.

The idea that Riel might be planning to pilfer Ravensbrook's money for his own personal use made her see red. In fact, she opened her mouth to confront him on that subject, too, but then she bit her tongue. He would tell her nothing. Especially if he did plan to steal from Ravensbrook.

No. She shouldn't tip him off to her suspicions. Far better to catch him in the act—if, indeed, that was his nefarious plan.

So, she'd learn how to keep the ledgers. Hopefully she'd be able to prove his unsavory deed, should that be his scurrilous intent, and bring the evidence to Mr. Chase later. A good plan.

Unfortunately, she had little faith in her ability to prove mismanagement of funds, and even less faith in Mr. Chase's willingness to expend any effort to help her. As well, Riel would be leaving soon. He may not even write in the ledgers until he returned. What, then, would happen to the stipend Mr. Chase planned to pay him on Friday? What a confused mess this could become! No. The best plan would be to get rid of Riel now, before he signed the papers on Friday. Before he could touch a pence of Ravensbrook's money. Before it was too late.

Riel's big body appeared relaxed, but it belied the guarded look in his eyes.

Lucinda decided to pretend satisfaction with his answers. Clearly, he would reveal no deep, dark secrets to her. However, now she trusted him even less than before.

In the next few days, she would continue to ferret out facts and expose them to the bright light of day. Perhaps then Riel would be revealed as the rat he probably was, and scuttle off to the darkest cave...a dungeon, perhaps...and leave Ravensbrook in peace. No need to tip him off to her plan, however.

"Very well," she said. "I will take your leave."

His fingers gripped her arm as she brushed by, which forced her to stop very close to him. Her heart beat faster when she looked up at him. It was late, almost time for supper, and a dark beard shadowed his jaw. He was a powerful man. And dangerous. She again felt this rush of truth to her very marrow. Certainly not a man to trifle with. Much as he appeared civil now, if she pushed him too far, what would he do?

"Yes, Mr. Montclair?"

He released her arm. "Do not spy on me again, Lucy."

"I will thank you to call me Lady Lucinda. And you may be sure I have no intention of being found in such a position again, Mr. Montclair. If you will excuse me."

His faint chuckle further stoked her irritation. Drat the man!

All at once, she realized the full implications of the Navy ordering Riel to return to his ship. He would leave soon. Perhaps he would never return.

Her quick hope at this happy thought swiftly faded.

His mission would not last for two years. She still must find a way to get him out of Ravensbrook for good. A man of his questionable character could not gain control of her money or her ancestral home. Not even for one day.

Only two full days remained until he signed the papers on Friday morning. It was unlikely that she would discover any of his secrets in that short amount of time. However, during the time in the secret passage, she'd concocted the outline of a plan to oust him from her home—permanently. It may not be the most prudent scheme. But she believed it would convince Riel to leave Ravensbrook willingly. And better yet, at a fast gallop.

৵ ৵ ৵ ৵ ৵

Riel watched Lucy sweep away, her shoulders straight and regal. The faintest hint of irritation tilted her chin. She was as beautiful as a yellow rose, and just as prickly.

Something else had bothered her just now, at the end of their conversation; something she'd bitten back and kept hidden. He couldn't imagine what it could be, and the puzzle disturbed him.

His mind returned to their earlier conversation. She hadn't heard everything Haskins had said to him, although clearly she was quick to believe the worst. His gut told him if she knew the full truth of his past, which he did not intend for the British Navy to ever discover, she would not see it the way her father had. The dislike she felt for him would deepen into contempt.

Self-disgust twisted in him, for in truth, he felt the same way. How long would his past haunt him? For how long would he feel the need to make amends for what he had done? Forever?

He believed in God's forgiveness, and he'd asked for it, as Peter Hastings had advised, but still, Riel could not forgive himself. He felt certain Lucy would not forgive him, either. No, the truth would provide fuel for her to evict him from her life as speedily as a skiff with the wind at its back.

No, he thought grimly, Lucy must not find out. He must fulfill his promise to her father and protect her. A deathbed promise.

He'd made it five days ago, when Peter lay on the deck of the *Tradewind* with his life's blood seeping from his chest. Face as pale as death, his eyes had opened and stared skyward. "Riel." The scratchy whisper drew his attention.

"I am here."

Peter's eyes, dilated in agony, focused on him. "Riel." The older man's hand gripped Riel's arm with surprising strength. "My daughter..."

"Lucy."

"Yes," he gasped. The Earl's eyes looked heavenward, as if seeing something far off...a truth beyond the constricting barriers of time and space. "Protect her...from the wolfff..." The last word slurred, so Riel couldn't tell if Peter had said "wolf" or "wolves." Either way, the meaning was clear enough. The hairs prickled up on the back of his neck. Peter saw something that could—or would—happen in the future.

The Earl's eyes widened suddenly, looking wild. Clearly and sharply, he ordered, "Tell me you will do this!"

Riel gripped the older man's shoulder. "I will protect her with my life. I swear it."

Peter relaxed. A faint smile hovered. "I know...can count...you." Seconds later, his life slipped toward the heaven he had just seen.

Now, Riel's heart beat hard with the same urgency he'd felt then.

Lucy was a beautiful, wealthy girl. Peter was right. She would be choice prey for the wolves of London. At least until she married.

So Lucy would not chase Riel off, although clearly that was her fiercest desire. He would fulfill his promise to Peter and remain her protector and guardian; at least until he saw her safely married to some unwary nobleman. Then he would be on his way.

Amused pity flashed when Riel contemplated the man Lucy would snag with her beauty, but pierce with her thorns. Peter was right about something else, too. Lucy would either need a strong man—and he'd better love feisty confrontations, Riel thought with a faint smile—or a weak one she'd trample beneath her lovely feet.

Perhaps Riel would take pity on the most naive of her suitors and warn them off before they became too smitten. Or perhaps not. His oath bound him to Lucy until she was securely married.

Hopefully by the time of her last Season, Napoleon Bonaparte would be vanquished, and Command Headquarters would release its grip on the *Tradewind* for good. Riel longed for the day when he could sail free, with no fear of his past or the Royal Navy breathing down his neck.

Freedom. The taste of the wind in his teeth and his destiny ruled only by the cut of the sails. Riel knew it was his life, and his only future. His past ensured he could never have more. Love and marriage belonged to innocents like Lucy. Such pleasures of hearth and home would never be his, and he had accepted that. He was lucky to have his freedom...he was lucky to have a life at all. And within those boundaries he would remain content.

Chapter Five

"*MY GREAT-AUNT SOPHIE* should arrive late tomorrow morning,"
Riel told Lucinda that evening. He forked up a bite of succulent
roast.

"How splendid for you. Now I will be outnumbered in my
own home."

Inwardly, Lucinda winced at her horrible, rude words. Her
father wouldn't have tolerated them, and truthfully, it made her
feel sick to utter the wretched statements. But for Ravensbrook
and for her own sake, she must stay her newly chosen path.
Hopefully, she would be able to stomach herself in two days'
time.

Irritating Riel beyond measure was the only plot she'd been
able to devise that might convince him to wash his hands of her
and gallop for freedom.

Riel lay down his fork. "Do not take your quarrel with me
out on my aunt."

Of course, Lucinda would never worry or distress a frail
older lady. But Riel didn't know that. Not yet. Here was her
opportunity to goad him still further: to provoke him to
abandon his oath to her father. "Perhaps you should have
thought of that *before* you invited her without my consent."

He went very still, and eyed her. "You would not."

Encouraged by the warning in his low tone, she said,
"Truly? Know one thing, Mr. Montclair. Each of your decisions
concerning Ravensbrook will reap a consequence. If you want
my cooperation, discuss your wishes with me first."

Long, silent moments crept by. Lucinda sensed a dark thundercloud gathering behind Riel's unreadable features.

He rumbled, "Agree to treat her as a welcome guest, Lucinda." The hard inflection in her name sent a shiver through her. She almost preferred that he call her Lucy. At least then he sounded faintly amused and tolerant. But wasn't this her goal? To frustrate him beyond measure so he'd cry off guardianship duties before signing the final papers?

"I will do as I see fit," she promised.

"Your father raised you to be a lady."

"Of course. And that is what I am."

"Then you will behave like a lady with my aunt."

She offered her best, dimpled smile. "I see. You want me to soothe your ears with sweet promises. I'm sorry. You will have to live without them."

With uneasy satisfaction, she noted that his knuckles turned white around his crystal glass. Pretending nonchalance, she cut another bite of meat and popped it in her mouth. A heavy silence elapsed, which Lucinda endeavored to ignore. After clearing her plate, she signaled for the last course. Strawberries with cream, she was happy to discover.

Was the conversation with Riel finished? Had she won?

Biting into a sweet, luscious strawberry, Lucinda swept a glance from under her lashes down the table. A mound of strawberries, with a thick dollop of cream, lay on a fine china plate before him, but he made no move to touch it. His hard brown eyes caught hers, denying escape.

"You know I must return to my ship on Monday."

"Yes!" She injected a chipper note into her voice.

"That means I will need to leave here on Friday. I do not know when I will return."

"Even better."

Another long moment elapsed. "My aunt has a weak heart, Lucinda. While I am gone, I trust you will not upset her."

Concerned, Lucinda spoke without thinking. "Could she die?"

A flicker of satisfaction gleamed, and vanished. "The doctors have predicted her death for the past eight years."

"So, she is stronger than they think."

"No. She just has an indomitable will to live."

"Will she need special care? A nurse?" Lucinda suddenly realized that instead of fighting with him, she felt anxious to learn how she might help care for his aunt. She crossed her arms and sat back in her chair. "You are a clever man."

He smiled. "Aunt Sophie refuses a nurse. And Mrs. Beatty assures me a good doctor lives in the village." Softly, he said, "So. You agree, then."

How neatly he had cornered her. "I would never harm a frail old lady," she said abruptly.

"But you wanted me to believe you would."

She looked away. "Yes."

"Why?"

"I would be happy to be candid with you, Mr. Montclair. But I ask for equal frankness in return."

He settled back. A wary look darkened his gaze. "What do you wish to know, Lady Lucinda?"

So formal. Bluntly, she said, "What are you running from? What are you hiding?"

He did not answer.

"How can I trust you, Mr. Montclair, if you will not answer my questions?" It had been worth a try, but she hadn't truly believed he would reveal his secrets.

That black gaze shuttered. "I am fully qualified to be here. That is all you need to know."

She blew out a breath. "Check."

"As in chess."

"Yes. We each possess something the other wants. For me, I want to know if I can trust you completely. Provide me with the answers I require, and I will promise to behave myself with your aunt."

"Already I know you will, Lucy."

She frowned. "I have promised nothing."

He smiled. "Your tender heart betrayed you. You are worried about Aunt Sophie, and you haven't met her yet. I have full confidence that you will behave like the lady your father raised you to be."

How had he won so easily, yet again? Frustration surged, and she jumped to her feet. "Good evening, Mr. Montclair," she snapped.

He rose with unhurried grace and offered a short bow. "Good evening, Lucy. Perhaps tomorrow morning we can begin on the account ledgers."

Lucinda glared. Lips thinned with irritation, she spun and walked fast out of the room. That arrogant, obnoxious man. How dare he trick her into admitting compliance with his wishes!

Her goal to frustrate him out of hand was not proceeding according to plan.

Upstairs, Effie helped her change into a long white night rail, and then, at last, she was alone. Lucinda sat on the window seat and stared into the night.

Vexing Riel may prove more difficult than she'd thought. Her plan to be such a thorn in his side that he'd throw in the towel and gallop off in a fury wasn't going so well. She'd continue to try, but had doubts about its final outcome.

Unfortunately, she didn't see Riel giving up—not on anything. In fact, she unhappily suspected he was the sort of man who, after setting his mind to something, persevered no matter the storms that blocked his path. He was a man who accomplished his goals.

Depression licked through her spirit.

What should she do? If she failed in her quest, what would happen to Ravensbrook? To herself? What sort of a man was Riel Montclair? True, he had a dark secret, but without proof of an unknown, evil deed, or proof that he planned to steal from Ravensbrook, of what benefit were those suspicions to accomplishing her goal? What could she do?

Her gaze traced the outlines of the far trees across the meadow. How she longed to gallop into the darkness and leave all of her grief and cares behind. To feel the cool breeze on her face, to hear the thundering hooves and see the ground flying by... What joy, what freedom, to embrace the wild hope that she could truly escape...perhaps to a faerie land, as she'd imagined as a child, and live a whole new life. One free of worries and responsibility, and instead filled with bright adventure and love.

The clump of Riel's boots in the hall rudely wrenched Lucinda from her fanciful, half-remembered dreams.

No faerie lands awaited her. And it was too dark to ride. The full moon remained days away. So that temporary escape would be denied her, as well.

Unhappily, she climbed into bed.

That black-eyed pirate must go. Tomorrow, she would do her best to vex Riel at every opportunity. It would prove to be an exhausting day, for she must also get through her father's funeral, too. Not to mention welcome Riel's aunt to Ravensbrook.

Lucinda pulled the covers over her head. Tears seeped from her eyes. Somehow, she would accomplish her goal. She must. Everything would be all right. It would.

ৰ্শ ৰ্শ ৰ্শ ৰ্শ ৰ্শ

After breakfast the next morning, Lucinda asked Mrs. Beatty if she had aired out a suite of rooms on the first floor for Riel's aunt. Of course the efficient housekeeper had already accomplished this necessary task, so Lucinda reluctantly next went in search of Riel.

He had mentioned that he'd show her the ledgers this morning. Much as she would prefer to avoid him, Lucinda girded up her courage to set her unsavory plan in motion. In truth, she did want to understand the ledgers, so she could take control of Ravensbrook's financial obligations as soon as Riel departed.

She found Riel in her father's study, sitting at his desk, studying an array of open ledgers. For a second, she observed him before announcing her presence. He wore all black today, and it made his large frame appear even broader in the small study. Certainly, his sheer physical presence and size eclipsed the memory of her father sitting in the same seat. Her father had been slim like herself, of a medium build, and with thinning gray hair and spectacles. How she missed him.

A tight knot gathered in her throat. Today she would bury him. He would never again sit in this study. Only this man would, until she married—or until she somehow banished him for good.

She cleared her throat. "Mr. Montclair. Hard at work, I see."

He looked up and rubbed at the frown between his brows. After the barest hesitation, he stood. "Lady Lucinda." His gaze ran down her black dress—the same one she'd worn yesterday—and flicked back up, over the golden curls perched atop her head. "Good morning."

"Such formality," she said in mock surprise. "Finally, you pretend proper manners."

A smile glimmered. "Sit down, Lucy. Here." One broad, tanned hand pulled a straight-backed, softly cushioned Queen Anne chair next to his. "We can begin your lesson."

He'd called her Lucy again. However, she knew the hopelessness of arguing with him about it. Instead, she'd pick fresh battles; battles she was certain to win.

"Have you forgotten all etiquette, Mr. Montclair?" She cast the proffered chair a dubious glance. "It would be most unseemly for us to sit so close together."

He shot her a look of amusement. "You may sit on the other side of the desk, if you prefer. But I do not recommend it, unless you can read upside down."

Lucinda swept her skirts aside and tugged the chair a foot clear of his. "That is not what I meant, Baron. If you hadn't spent so many years at sea, perhaps you would know the basic proprieties."

A smile flickered across his straight mouth. "Perhaps you would be so good to teach me."

She met his steady, amused gaze, and a disturbed flush warmed her cheeks. "I am sure your dearth of knowledge is too abysmal to remedy." She glanced pointedly at the ledgers. "May we begin?"

Riel slid a ledger before her. "I believe I understand how your father set up his books. Mine are not too different. Look..." He launched into an explanation of debits and credits and payments and income that left Lucinda's head reeling. Clearly, Riel relished the task before him, for he spoke with passion. It also became evident that he possessed a quick, precise mind.

Lucinda was sharp—she'd been one of the top students at Miss May's School for Young Ladies—but this was too much, too fast. Her mind soon glazed into a state of panicked bewilderment. She didn't like it. She was in over her head, and she didn't understand what he was talking about.

The only thing she grasped was that simple addition and subtraction seemed to be involved—thankfully, a skill she'd mastered. But as far as setting aside monies here and there, and totaling them all up so they didn't exceed the budget...it was too much.

"Stop," she said faintly.

Riel glanced at her. A frown twitched his brows together.

With a shaky hand, Lucinda closed one of the books. "That is enough for today." She made to get up.

"Lucy?" His warm, calloused fingers curled around her wrist, gently stopping her flight. "What is wrong?"

Tears swam in her eyes. "Are you trying to confuse me on purpose?"

"No." He appeared genuinely taken aback. "Perhaps I have gone too fast. Sit down, and we will start again."

Lucinda pulled her wrist free and edged away from her chair. "I think not. I...I think perhaps I'm not ready to learn right now."

"I am sorry." Now he stood, too. "Perhaps I was mistaken, thinking you've helped your father with the books before?"

Drat it, a tear hovered on her lashes, ready to plummet down her cheek. "I have never seen a ledger in my life." The admission cost her a great deal of pride.

"I am sorry," he said again. "Please sit. We will start again, but slower this time."

With reluctance, she slid back into the chair. Clasping her fingers together in her lap, she leaned forward to pay close attention to every word Riel said.

To her relief, first he explained what the different lines and columns meant on each page. From there, he taught her rudimentary accounting principles, so that when the clock chimed an hour past, Lucinda was surprised to discover she was beginning to understand...at least a little...what the ledgers were all about.

"That's enough for now." Riel closed the books. "Aunt Sophie will arrive soon. You will wish to refresh yourself."

"Of course. Thank you for being so patient with me." The words of appreciation escaped before Lucinda could censor them.

Riel's dark eyes met hers. "You are welcome, Lucy."

He was much closer than she'd realized, and faint warmth stained her cheeks. His arm brushed hers as he gathered up the books. Her heart beat faster, and she watched his broad shoulders shift as he put the books to the side. Rays of sunlight filtered through the lace curtains and cast the blunt angles and planes of his face into fascinating textures of tan and bronze. Riel was a handsome man.

Hastily, she gained her feet and swept for the door.

"Lucy." His deep voice stroked like velvet over her jittery nerve endings.

Affecting a calm nonchalance, she turned back.

"If you are interested, I will continue to teach you the books each morning until I leave. I do not think, however, that you will be ready to keep the accounts while I am gone."

"Mr. Chase won't be happy to get the job back."

"You can learn from him. Or, if you prefer, you can wait until I return, and I will teach you myself."

Lucinda licked her lips. "I will speak to Mr. Chase."

"As you wish."

She speedily made her exit and hurried upstairs. What was wrong with her? For the entire morning she'd lost sight of her mission to vex him at every point possible. Instead, she'd docilely sat beside him, and then even thanked him nicely at the end. Even worse, she'd noticed—for the briefest second— that he was a handsome man!

He was *old*. Ten years older than herself. And her unwanted guardian.

She couldn't trust him, she reminded herself. He still possessed that deep, dark secret he hid from the Royal Navy. A man like him shouldn't be within a furlong of Ravensbrook...let alone perusing its ledgers, or discovering the breadth of the estate's wealth.

No. She still must evict him, and speedily.

Then why did her will seemed weakened in this regard? Lucinda rang for Effie. Riel was proving much more dangerous than she'd ever imagined. Did he possess charm? Was that it? Whatever the case, she would not succumb to his wiles like her father had.

Resolve strengthened, Lucinda sat quietly while Effie helped her freshen up for Aunt Sophie's arrival. This afternoon, after his aunt was settled, she'd set Riel on his ear again. He must go, and soon. Before it was too late.

✧ ✧ ✧ ✧ ✧

A black carriage arrived just before lunch, and Lucinda swept down the steps to welcome Riel's great-aunt to Ravensbrook. Riel stood at her side as the driver opened the carriage door.

A frail older lady appeared, bone thin and with white hair scraped into a loose bun. A network of fine lines creased into her cheeks, and radiated out from her mouth and the corners of her eyes. She wore a pale blue gown of classic lines, and white gloves. A shaky hand accepted Riel's arm and helping hand down.

Concern again rose in Lucinda. It appeared that a stiff breeze might knock the older woman over. Was she strong enough to be outdoors? Had traveling been a good idea, considering her health?

An older, sturdier looking woman descended next from the carriage. Presumably Sophie's maid.

"Lucinda," Riel's voice interrupted her thoughts. "I would like to introduce you to my great-aunt, Lady Sophia."

Although his aunt rummaged in her small clutch reticule at the moment, Lucinda said softly, "I am so happy to meet you."

Sophia extracted a dainty, beautifully embroidered handkerchief and looked up. Startlingly bright blue eyes twinkled at Lucinda. "So happy to meet you too, my dear. I am so sorry for your loss."

"Thank you, Lady Sophia."

"Please call me Aunt Sophie. It will make everything simpler." Birdlike hands clasped Lucinda's own. The pressure felt firm, to Lucinda's surprise, and a measure of relief eased into her soul. Sophie was stronger than she looked. And Lucinda could tell, just by looking into those bright eyes and her ready smile, that she was going to like Riel's aunt.

She smiled. "I would be honored to call you Aunt Sophie."

"Good. Now that that's out of the way, I would love a small glass of lemonade, if you have it. The trip has parched me."

"Was the trip long?" Lucinda asked.

As they all moved slowly toward the steps, Sophie relayed a few stories from her two day's journey, lightly garnished with flashes of humor. Alarmingly, though, she gasped for breath by the time she gained Ravensbrook's top step, and blue tinged her skin. She held tightly onto Riel's arm and stood very still outside the front door, trying to catch her breath.

Anxiously, Lucinda hovered close by. "May I get something for you? A chair, perhaps?"

"Never mind me," Sophie wheezed, but offered a ghost of a smile. "Need a minute."

Her skin regained its normal pale hue within a matter of minutes, and then she prodded Riel's arm, directing him to lead her inside. Amazingly, she took up the conversation right where she had left off. "I love your countryside immensely, Lucinda. My only quarrel is with the roosters who cackle at the first glimmer of dawn. Do you have chickens?"

Riel pulled out a chair at the dining table for his aunt.

Lucinda assured her that Ravensbrook did not have chickens nearby, and felt relieved that now the older lady appeared to be fine. She said, "The far reaches of the estate are used for farming, but you cannot see them from here. The forest provides privacy for Ravensbrook."

"And beauty, as well. Do you ride often, Lucinda?"

"Whenever I get the chance."

"I rode in horse shows when I was a girl. Genteel ones, of course, where we paraded in a circle with our horses groomed until they shone, and their tails braided and bows galore." The old lady giggled. "I would have been just as happy to gallop over fences with the boys."

"Aunt Sophie is not a conventional gentlewoman," Riel said, with an affectionate smile.

Lucinda smiled, too. "Perhaps we will get along very well, then."

Sophie's bright gaze assessed her. "I am sure we will, child."

Lucinda slid a look at Riel. He hadn't yet had a chance to recount any of her outrageous behaviors to Sophie—such as searching his room for the solicitor's letter. Would he? Somehow, she couldn't bear for Sophie to look on her with disapproval.

Riel sipped wine, but when his gaze caught hers, a trace of amusement glimmered. Almost as if he'd guessed her thoughts. He would enjoy recounting her disgraceful conduct, of course, but would he? A faint frown pulled at Lucinda's brows as she settled the napkin on her lap.

The first course arrived, along with Sophie's lemonade and the hot water she had also requested. The older lady retrieved a small bag of tea leaves from her purse and stirred them into the hot water. After a few sips, she said, "Has my great-nephew been treating you well, Lucinda?"

For once at a loss for words, she glanced at Riel. "It has been an adjustment to have him here."

"Tell the truth, Lucinda. You dislike me," he said calmly, but still with that glimmer of amusement.

"Is that true?" Sophie seemed interested.

It was time to goad him, but gently. "He is rather high-handed. In point of fact, he has swept in, determined to take over my entire life."

Sophie said nothing, but glanced at her nephew.

"I made a promise to your father that I will keep."

"But happily you will be leaving soon. I hope for many such respites."

Riel turned his attention to his aunt. "You see what Lucy thinks of me."

The old lady divided a glance between the two of them. "I see very well, indeed."

Lucinda wondered what that was supposed to mean. But she turned her attention back to Riel. Here was her opportunity to antagonize him still further, so he'd sail away, never to plague her again. However, when she opened her mouth to do so, she found she could not. It was bad enough she must act like a brat to Riel. It was quite another to do so before his aunt. One person thinking the worst of her was reprehensible; two would be unconscionable.

She bit her lip. Quietly, she said, "Please pass the rolls, Mr. Montclair."

Riel's eyebrows rose. However, he did not comment upon her uncharacteristically meek behavior.

For the remainder of the meal, Lucinda asked many questions about Sophie's life in London, and in the country. She learned Sophie had wanted a change in her life, and that was why she had agreed to come to Ravensbrook. She also discovered that Sophie would not stay for the entire two years. Instead, she'd only stay for a few months at a time, and she'd also stay at Riel's townhouse during the Season.

Luncheon was pleasant; surprisingly so. Lucinda felt Riel's dark eyes upon her more than once. He even chuckled once or twice, in a quiet, deep rumble that sent a tickle through her stomach. In addition, his manners were impeccable and charming.

She endeavored to ignore him. It was becoming more apparent with every passing hour that he was a dangerous man in innumerable ways. On the disturbingly positive side, he was smart, and could be quite charming, as well. No wonder her father had liked and trusted him. If she hadn't overheard his secret conference with his scruffy henchman, she, like her father, would be unaware of Riel's unknown, unsavory secret that he wanted to keep hidden from the Royal Navy. Not to mention the questionable manner in which he planned to "come into money" at the end of this week.

Although it was true she had no proof yet of wrongdoing on Riel's part, if the Royal Navy should not trust him, then she should not trust him, either, nor should she trust Ravensbrook into his care. And certainly not her choice of a husband, either.

No, despite the temporary truce at this luncheon, peace with Riel was not possible.

Chapter Six

AFTER LUNCH, SOPHIE retired to take a nap. The rest of the household trotted into high gear, readying for the Earl of Ravensbrook's funeral that evening. Servants set up chairs outside on the grassy lawn, and Mrs. Beatty instructed a platoon of serving girls, hired for the day from the village, to prepare the cold meats, cheeses and fruits for the reception afterward.

Lucinda's dress arrived; a rich, black silk. It fit perfectly. As the hour drew near five o'clock, a knot twisted tighter and tighter in Lucinda's stomach.

She was about to say goodbye to her father forever. And yet in many ways, she'd already said goodbye. Why did the coming funeral seem like such a momentous occasion? Perhaps because the coffin represented the last remaining part of her father—a part she could still touch. Soon it would be lowered into the ground, never to be touched or seen again.

She would never see her father again. Hot tears welled in her eyes and scorched her cheeks.

Would she weep throughout the entire funeral? She'd look dreadful, but did it matter? This evening was for her father, to remember him, honor him and grieve him with friends. No extended family lived close enough to come, and that was for the best, since few of them had known him well.

Through her bedroom window, Lucinda saw Pastor Bilford arrive. Two pairs of strong young men from the village carried her father's casket to a small grassy clump in front of the carefully placed chairs.

She looked at the clock on her bedside table. One minute until five. Time to go. Alone, she would meet throngs of people expressing their sorrow. Would they expect her to be strong? To raise her chin and put on a brave front? Perhaps even comfort others who mourned?

Lucinda didn't think she could do it. More tears glimmered as she stood in front of her closed bedroom door. She didn't want to go out there. She wanted to stay safe in her room and weep for her father...the best father in the world. A sob shuddered in her chest.

A knock came at the door. "Lady Lucinda."

Riel, and very formal, too.

With reluctance, Lucinda put her hand on the knob. She supposed she must go out sometime. After blotting her eyes, she opened it and looked up at her guardian. He still wore all black, but now he wore a cravat and a fashionable, tailed coat that fit his muscular shoulders to perfection. With the blunt angles of his face, and his black hair drawn back in a tail, he was the most striking, handsome man she had ever seen. She blinked up at him; for a second, at a loss for words.

He extended his arm. "I have come to escort you downstairs."

Lucinda felt a flash of gratitude. She gripped his arm, and felt the thick, corded muscles beneath the superfine jacket. She could do this. "Thank you," she whispered, but wasn't sure if he heard.

"My lady." He indicated for her to descend the stairs with him, and a glance upward proved he had heard, for a warm smile lurked in his dark brown eyes. He'd never smiled at her before, not like that, and it unexpectedly warmed a small, unhappy place inside her.

Holding tightly to his arm, and with her chin lifted, as if about to face the guillotine, she descended the stairs and slowly crossed the hall to the back door, which led to the garden.

She did not want to be here. She did *not* want to be here. Lucinda swallowed back a soft sob as Riel placed his hand on the knob.

"You are ready?" The deep voice was quiet, and even gentle.

She heaved a small, fortifying breath. "Yes. I suppose."

Riel opened the door and they descended the stairs to join the throngs of people dressed in black.

As soon as her nearest neighbor, Lady Sisemore, gripped Lucinda's hands and tearfully wailed, "Lady Lucinda, we are so sorry for your loss." Lucinda began to relax. Others—many others—had loved and revered her father, too. In a strange way, it comforted her that she wasn't the only one who grieved.

By Riel's anchoring side, she traversed the rows of white chairs, greeting townspeople and neighbors and offering a tearful smile to a friend or two. She wished her best friend Amelia had been able to come, but she and her family were visiting in northern England. Riel saw her settled in her seat, and then moved aside to talk to Pastor Bilford.

A short time later, Riel escorted Sophie to sit beside her, and the service began. Pastor Bilford had prepared quite a speech, and after he finished, others spoke as well, including Riel.

Lucinda listened closely as the familiar, deep voice introduced himself. Riel had been with her father when he had died. Would he say more about the events surrounding his death?

"The Earl of Ravensbrook was a fine, honorable man," Riel began, meeting her gaze for a long moment. "We became acquainted long ago, and that friendship solidified as he served the Royal Navy aboard my ship.

"Commodore Hastings always saw below the surface, to the true heart and worth of a man. I was seventeen when I first met him, and barely a man, but he made me a better one for having known him. I am grateful for his intervention in my life. By accident, we met again two years ago and he convinced me to use my merchant ship to help the Royal Navy. I was glad to agree.

"Commodore Hastings served for seven months on my ship. A braver, more honorable man I have never met. I deeply respected Commodore Hastings, and he died with courage and fortitude, serving this country. The world is a lesser place without him in it. I will miss him."

More tears filled Lucinda's eyes. Riel took his seat.

"Lady Lucinda?" Pastor Bilford cleared his throat. "Do you wish to speak before we close the service?"

"Of...of course." Lucinda clutched the letter the Admiral had written and rose to take her place.

Feeling nervous, she faced the small crowd gathered on the lawn. Nearly all of them were close friends, and most looked on with deep sympathy.

"My father was a wonderful man, as all of you know," she began in a wavering voice. "My mother died when I was five. Father took over then as both father and mother to me. I could not have asked for a more loving, wonderful parent." Tears clogged her throat. "I could go on all night remembering our happy times together, but instead I would like to close with words written by Admiral Smythe." With a crinkle and a trembling hand, she unfolded the letter. "He says,

> *Commodore Hastings served His Majesty's Royal Navy for twenty-seven years with honor and distinction. A finer officer and man I have rarely met. His courage and wisdom in battle saved countless lives, and his sharp insight proved decisive in many victories for England. He is matchless in peer and station, an outstanding hero and he will be sorely missed.*
>
> *– Admiral Smythe*

Tears overflowed then, and Lucinda quickly regained her seat.

The next two hours passed in a blur. Men carried Father's casket to the wagon, and horses slowly plodded to the family plot nestled at the foot of the forest. Pastor Bilford spoke more words over the coffin, and then the young men lowered it into the grave.

After a short prayer, Pastor Bilford sprinkled dirt on top. Through it all, Lucinda stood with her arms tightly crossed, and wept silently. She felt so alone.

Lucinda remained there, alone, as dusk fell and the others trickled back to the house. Her thoughts felt disjointed, and she felt incapable of moving from the spot. As well, the peace and beauty of the burial spot soothed her soul. She crossed her arms again, hugging them to herself, shivering a little in the cool evening. The young men shoveled the remaining dirt over the coffin. Lucinda remained stationary. She did not feel that she could leave until they were finished, and her father finally at rest.

"That'll do it." A lanky lad shoved a sleeve over his forehead.

"You are ready?" Riel's voice spoke behind her, and Lucinda jumped.

"I...I thought everyone had gone."

"I have been here the whole time."

She saw the steadiness in his eyes, and the compassion and sadness, too. At last, she believed her father and Riel had been good friends. Only a friend would feel the grief etched into Riel's face.

She offered him a small, wobbly smile and took the arm he offered.

Riel pulled a clean white handkerchief from his jacket pocket. With a sobbing laugh she accepted it. "My own is a bit soggy."

In silence, they walked together across the grassy field and back to the house. Once again, Lucinda felt grateful to Riel for thoughtfully accompanying her when she felt most alone.

Perhaps her father had been correct about some details of Riel's character. Not that Lucinda wanted him to become lord over her now. Oh, certainly not. But perhaps he was not quite as dastardly as she had begun to wonder. Surprisingly, that thought cheered her a little.

As soon as they arrived, it became clear the reception party was in full swing. People chatted and laughed, and filled their crystal glasses with lemonade and punch. Already a line formed at the buffet table. Candlelit tables had been set up in their absence, ready for the guests to sit and partake of their meal.

"Lord Iveny." Lord Humphrey, a plump man with a balding pate, accosted them within moments of their arrival. Lucinda did not like him much, and neither had her father. She suspected he lived an idle, bored life. Perhaps that was why he stirred up strife at every point possible.

"You own a privateer?" he said, sipping his red punch.

Riel's stiffened a little. "Yes. A merchant ship."

"But a privateer," Lord Humphrey insisted with a sly half-smile.

Riel's guarded look hardened into something else entirely. "You are correct."

"Mmphh." With a pleased smile, the viscount strolled away. Riel's narrowed gaze followed him.

Lucinda wondered what had transpired between the two. Clearly Lord Humphrey had made Riel feel uncomfortable. She wondered how.

"Lady Lucinda." The dowager Traynor gently patted her arm. "I am so sorry, my dear. I knew your father when he was a mere boy..."

Lucinda talked with many more guests as dusk deepened into night. Lanterns on poles brightened the grassy area, and always on the periphery she was aware of Riel's dark figure circulating among the guests. With apparent ease, he smiled and made small talk with the many strangers.

Before long, Lucinda helped Aunt Sophie find a table and fixed a plate for her, and then returned to the buffet line to prepare one for herself. A few feet ahead of her in line, Lord Humphrey grumbled, "Barely enough for a crow."

With a side glance at Lucinda, his wife quickly said, "But such a shame about the Earl."

"Yes, yes," Lord Humphrey mumbled. "More a shame he left Ravensbrook in the hands of a scoundrel like Montclair."

"Whatever do you mean?" murmured Lady Humphrey.

He snorted. "He owns a privateer. Pirate ship, is more like it. I've heard plenty about those scoundrels. They get a letter of marquee from the government and it licenses them to pirate the Frenchies without fear of the gallows. If the French capture them, they're considered prisoners of war." He snorted again. "Opportunists is what they are."

Sick enthrallment made Lucinda listen harder, but Lord Humphrey now complained about the rolls. Although she knew eavesdropping was unseemly, Lucinda followed her neighbors to the dessert table. There, Lord Humphrey perched one of each morsel upon his plate. Unfortunately, he said no more about Riel.

By now, however, Lucinda simply had to find out more about privateers. If she discovered evidence that proved Riel was an unscrupulous privateer, and therefore unfit to run

Ravensbrook, didn't she need to know? Shouldn't she find out everything she could?

Too bad she'd have to learn of it from a blatherskite like Lord Humphrey.

Lucinda quickened her pace. "Excuse me, Lord and Lady."

The Humphreys turned, their surprise palpable. To her credit, Lady Humphrey pinkened with embarrassment. "Lady Lucinda. The service and reception have been splendid. You have done your father proud."

Mrs. Beatty and her legions of helpers had done her father proud, but Lucinda did not belabor the point. She had matters of more import to discover.

"Thank you. Excuse me, but I heard you mention something about privateers, Lord Humphrey. I didn't mean to eavesdrop, but I find the subject most fascinating. I would be in your debt if you would enlighten me about it, for I have little knowledge on that subject." For good measure, she demurely fluttered eyelashes. Her first Season had taught her that the quickest way to get what she wanted was to stroke a man's ego.

Lord Humphrey chuckled, but cast an uncertain glance at his wife. "Why, of course, Lady Lucinda. What do you wish to know?"

"What is a privateer, my lord? Is it merely a merchant ship?"

He snorted. "Not likely. Privateers can board enemy merchant ships and steal their cargos. Snakes, the lot of them!"

Disbelief crept into Lucinda's heart. Much as she had wanted to believe the worst about Riel, and had actually accused him of being a pirate in the past, part of her had begun to think she might have been wrong about him.

But Riel *was* a privateer—he had admitted as much. And he'd also said the Navy had commissioned him to work for them for the last two years. Legitimate work, she'd thought, and perhaps it had been, when her father was on the ship, but before that, what had Riel done? Had he attacked enemy merchant ships, stolen their goods and reaped the profit for himself? And surely those French ships did not give up their cargos without a fight. So he and his men had killed, and all for greed...

A cold sensation, like icy stream water, slid through her veins. Lucinda felt faint. She gripped the back of a nearby chair for support.

"Are you all right, Lady Lucinda?" Lady Humphrey's voice seemed to come from a great distance.

"Yes. Yes, I'm fine." Lucinda forced a false smile to her lips. "The evening has been a bit much. I...I need to rest." She did not hear their reply. Thankfully, as she lurched away, her thoughts swam back into focus.

She spotted Riel standing a few yards away; a tall man with broad, muscular shoulders, all in black, with his hair in that pirate tail. Because he *was* a pirate!

With suddenly nerveless fingers, Lucinda set down her plate on a nearby table. That must be the secret Riel wanted to keep from the Royal Navy. He was a pirate. He had never stopped being a pirate. He killed people for gain.

With shaking steps, Lucinda headed for the corner of the house. It was too much. The service, the funeral, and now learning that the worst she had feared about Riel was, in fact, true. She must escape. She had to be alone.

ﺤ ﺤ ﺤ ﺤ ﺤ

Riel kept an eye on Lucinda as he circulated among the guests. He spent a few long moments with Mr. Chase, advising him of his soon departure. Mr. Chase agreed to continue administering the accounts on Ravensbrook's behalf, and also agreed to teach Lucinda to take care of the petty monies so his work load would be reduced.

By the time that necessary conversation concluded, Riel had lost sight of Lucy. He scanned the dimly lit throng for her bright head and then found her, delivering a plate of food to his aunt. As he watched, she leaned close to Sophie and spoke to her, obviously inquiring if she needed further assistance.

Surprise and appreciation flickered through him. He had been remiss, talking so long with Mr. Chase. He should have attended to his aunt, but Lucinda had done so.

His gaze followed his charge as she returned to the buffet to assemble her own plate. Lucinda astonished him at every turn. Although exasperating and ornery, to be sure, she also revealed glimpses of finer, deeper emotions that kept him guessing at her true character. Here, she'd cared for his aunt as though it was the most natural thing in the world to do, and clearly, she'd also deeply loved her father. Vulnerability flashed through her at unexpected times, which appealed to him.

Lucy was a study in contrasts. Sometimes she appeared to like him a little, and others she seemed hell-bent on antagonizing him, obviously hoping he'd wash his hands of her. Nothing would make her happier than running him off her property.

Yet Riel had sensed her gratitude, too, when he'd escorted her downstairs, and then back from the burial. Almost as if she couldn't make up her mind about him. Just as he could not decide what to make of her. A spoilt, rebellious, sharp-tongued girl? Or a sweet, vulnerable, caring one? Perhaps both. Sugar and spice.

Riel knew one truth—Lucy was a complicated young woman. But in their battle of wills, he would win. Riel would sign those papers on Friday, and he would be her guardian. It was no longer just because of his word to Peter. Lucy needed him, whether she'd admit it or not. Without a level head to guide her, she would likely take foolish, impulsive risks with her life. Much as he had done at her age.

He gulped back a hard swallow of punch. Riel would not allow that to happen. And he would not allow the ravening wolves Peter had foreseen to devour her, either. Riel had sworn to protect her, and he would; with his life, if necessary.

As Peter had been there for him, Riel would be there for Lucy. He would see her safely married to a fine young man, and then he would permanently return to the *Tradewind*. The intervening two years would prove a challenge. An inadequate description, he suspected.

Riel smiled. He thrived on challenges at sea, and in life. Lucy would probably be dismayed to learn that he liked her feisty confrontations. Hopefully the Navy's mission wouldn't keep him away for long. He didn't want Lucy to get into trouble while he was gone—although he believed she would be safe enough within the protected walls of Ravensbrook.

Riel scanned the crowd. Then again. Where was she now? Alarm kicked through him when he couldn't find her.

Finally, after a heart thudding minute, he spotted her talking to the pasty-faced Lord Humphrey and his wife. Lucy suddenly blanched white, and clutched the back of a chair.

Riel frowned.

With barely a parting word to the older couple, Lucy walked fast toward the far corner of the house.

Where was she going? Riel put down his drink and swiftly followed her into the lonely black night.

৺ ৺ ৺ ৺ ৺

Once she was around the corner of the mansion and no one could see her, Lucinda ran for the stables. Soft black night enveloped her. The quarter moon barely peeked above the forest, so the earth before her was dark, but Lucinda knew every inch of Ravensbrook, and ran without stumbling for the sanctuary of the quiet stables.

Since learning of the death of her father, Lucinda had neglected her horse, and now she longed for the quiet peace of the animal's affectionate, undemanding presence.

No grooms were about at this hour of the night, so she slipped into the stable without being accosted. The scent of fresh hay and warm horseflesh filled her nostrils. A tiny part of her relaxed when she at last reached her old friend.

Old Ben snuffled her hair and gave a low whinny of welcome.

"Benny!" She hugged his neck tight, and stroked his nose. "Let me see if there are apples."

There were, in a sack on the wall, as she'd known there would be. The stable lad always kept it replenished for special treats for the horses.

Old Ben's lips curled around the apple and he crunched it loudly in her ear.

"You like that, don't you?" Lucinda whispered. Tears crept down her cheeks. "You're lucky you're a horse. As long as you can have an apple, you're happy." She pressed her cheek into his neck.

"I hate it all, Benny," she whispered. "I'd begun to think Riel might be... Oh, I'm such a fool! I wish I could escape. I wish Father was alive, and he'd come home soon, and for all of this to be some awful nightmare."

Old Ben whickered softly in her hair.

More hot tears slid down her cheeks. Ooh, she was tired of crying! But her life had changed. No turning back. She was truly alone. Except for Riel.

Riel. Her fingers clenched into fists. He'd pretended such kindness this evening that her armor against him had finally cracked. She'd begun to believe, just a tiny bit...

Hurt and anger simmered in her. He *was* a pirate. He must be, for he met all of Lord Humphrey's descriptions of those despicable, greedy privateers. And yet Riel had tried to trick her into thinking he did legitimate work for the Navy. Why had she believed him, even for a moment? Especially after overhearing that suspicious conversation with his disreputable-looking first mate.

What had her father been doing on a pirate ship? Or perhaps for that brief span Riel had done actual, bona fide work. But the basic truth of the matter was, Riel was a privateer. Self-admitted. And therefore, most likely a pirate.

Then Lucinda realized a far worse truth. The British government *sanctioned* his activities. Why else would they order him to work for them? Therefore, in the eyes of the British government, his despicable exploits would not disqualify him from being her guardian, nor lord over Ravensbrook. The English government championed him, for he rid the seas of innocent French merchant ships.

The French. He even dared to plunder his own countrymen! What sort of a man was he?

A grasping, greedy monster—if truly he was one of the pirates Lord Humphrey had described so vividly. If so, it wasn't a stretch to believe he would plot to steal from Ravensbrook, too.

Swallowing back a soft gasp of distress, Lucinda impulsively yanked open the stall door and led Old Ben out. With quick, fumbling movements, she fit on his bit and bridle, and then urged him to the door. Outside, the moon shone faintly behind the trees. It was dark, but that did not stop her. Nor the lack of a saddle. She'd often ridden bareback. Although it was most unladylike, she hadn't cared at ten and she didn't care now, either.

What did following rules and social proprieties get her? Nothing. Certainly nothing that mattered, like her father back alive. Or the right to expel Riel Montclair from Ravensbrook.

She found a stool to stand on, and anchored her fingers in Old Ben's mane.

"Lucy."

Riel. His tall, broad body loomed in the darkness. Now, knowing more clearly the type of man he must be, his black presence felt dangerous; just as it had when she'd first met him on the steps of Ravensbrook.

Lucinda chose not to answer. Grasping Old Ben's mane more securely, she sprang upward, but Riel gripped her waist, stopping her. With a gasp of surprise, she stumbled back onto the stool. It wobbled alarmingly, and with a cry, she fell.

Strong hands dragged her up against a hard chest. Lucinda shoved at Riel, in a panic trying to free herself. To her surprise, he let her go.

"What are you doing?" His French accent sounded faintly ominous in the dim light.

Lucinda stepped backward. "Going for a ride, can't you tell?"

"At night?" He sounded faintly disbelieving.

Lucinda found Old Ben's bridle and urged him to stand next to the stool again. "I often ride at night. Not that it's any of your business." Of course, usually she rode under the full moon, when bright light illuminated the landscape.

He said nothing for a minute, but watched her carefully. "It is not worth the risk to your neck, or to the horse."

Lucinda gritted her teeth. "You are a fine one to talk about risks. Forgive me, but I would think a man such as yourself would live more...dangerously."

"What is that supposed to mean, Lucinda?"

Lucinda. She felt a spark of triumph. She had prickled under his skin. Perfect.

Not bothering to answer, she hopped back up onto the stool and worked her fingers into Ben's mane again.

"Stop."

"Or what?" Anger surged. "Will you spear me through the heart with your cutlass? Or do you save your finest blades for achieving spoils of a more valuable nature?"

"You speak in circles." Frustration edged the deep tone. "Come down."

"No." Again, she bent her knees, readying to spring up, but a large hand closed around her wrist, forestalling her.

"I cannot allow you."

Frustrated beyond all reason, Lucinda twisted to free herself. "You can't stop me." She twisted harder. "Let me *go,* you barbarian!"

"I am responsible for your safety."

She hated his calm, reasonable voice. A voice smooth and slick with lies. "I don't *care,*" she spat through her teeth. "You will let me go now, or you will know the consequence."

An eternal moment of dangerous silence elapsed. "Are you threatening me, Lucy?" His soft voice didn't fool her. Now his true, black nature would emerge. And she knew from past experience he might respond with brute force. If he lost his temper, would he hurt her?

She should be frightened, and she was. But pushed beyond all reason, she taunted, "Now will your civility molt away? Will the true snake you are emerge at last? How will you make me suffer if I do not submit to your will?"

"You do not know what you are saying."

"*I do!*" she suddenly screamed at him.

Old Ben trotted sideways.

"You are frightening your horse."

"Let me *go!*" she sobbed out.

Suddenly, it was all too much...Riel, continually calling her Lucy...learning he must be a devious, cutthroat pirate...her father irrevocably dead... She twisted again, harder, and then she reared back and kicked him with all of her strength. To her satisfaction, she heard his indrawn breath of surprise. Hopefully pain, too.

"Let me *go,* you dastardly pirate! Unhand me this very minute."

"No." Hands curled hard around her waist, he dragged her off the stool again. Her feet touched solid earth. His grip loosened, moving to her arms, but she knew if she tried to escape they would become like painful, iron shackles.

"You are a brute. A fiendish *brute*," she hissed, shaking with rage.

The pale moonlight illuminated the dark lines of his face. "Explain your words to me."

"I need to explain nothing." She twisted again, not caring how fruitless it was.

"You have called me all manner of names. A brute. A barbarian, a snake and a fiend."

"Don't forget *pirate*," she said, glaring. "That's the most accurate description of all, isn't it?"

An uncomfortable moment ticked by. "Why?"

"Because that is what you are. Admit the truth at last, Riel."

"I am no pirate."

"You *lie*." She struggled again, hard and viciously. It surprised him, for she slipped free. It was also so unexpected that she stumbled to her knees. She sprang to her feet again, but he was already before her, blocking her path.

"Don't touch me," she whispered, backing away. "I cannot bear it. You tricked my father! How could he have trusted you?"

"Who has told you lies about me? Lord Humphrey?"

"The only lies told are the ones said by you! You say you do legitimate work for the Navy, but that is a lie too, isn't it?"

"You think your father boarded my vessel and took part in pirating activities?" Disbelief cut through his harsh voice.

"No. But before my father boarded your ship, what were you? A privateer. You admitted as much yourself."

"Yes." His tone sounded guarded. "But I do not..."

"Lord Humphrey remedied my ignorance about the nature of privateers. Apparently, they are greedy opportunists. Under the full champion of the British flag they devour French merchant ships. All who dare try to stop their plundering are killed. And their cargos...French cargos...are stolen and used to fill the coin coffers of the privateer owners."

"I have done none of those things."

"So you say." How could she possibly believe one word he said to her? She *knew* he kept secrets. How could she possibly trust him? "Do you know what I find most despicable?"

He did not answer; hopefully reeling from her well-placed blows to his crumbling fortress of lies.

"You are French," she hissed. "How could you attack and steal from your own countrymen?"

"I fight against Napoleon. He is no friend of my family."

"Your English family, or your French family?"

"Neither!" His voice whipped. "Did you know Napoleon sided with the Jacobins during the Reign of Terror?"

"Yes." Lucinda knew a little about that bit of history. "But he did not take part in the killings, did he?"

"It does not matter. He favored the blood bath in the name of 'order.' My grandfather and uncles were executed then. If you want to point to a bloody opportunist, look to Napoleon. He is no friend of my family. He is a war mongering dictator, and with the help of Joseph Fouché instituted a police state in France. I could say more," he said grimly. "But that is enough."

So that explained why he fought on the side of the British. It did not explain, however, his activities aboard his privateer ship. "I understand. Still, it remains that you are little more than a pirate. Perhaps that is why you can afford a townhouse in London. And how you can own your own ship."

"I do not steal..."

"Never? Tell me you have never stolen in your entire life."

He did not answer.

Lucinda felt a sickened stab of victory. Surprisingly, it hurt, like a knife through her own heart. "I have proven my point. Stop pretending to be a man you are not. I know the truth."

He closed the distance between them. "I am *not* a thief, nor a pirate." His harsh voice shook with suppressed emotion. "You speak of things you know nothing about, Lucinda. You slander my character based on a few words from a weasel such as Humphrey."

"He merely stated facts..."

"Facts that do not pertain to me!"

Lucinda's heart pounded, and for a minute she did not know what to say next. He had refuted every one of her arguments. He said he was not a pirate. Or a thief. Was she to believe him now? Part of her did believe him, heaven help her. *Was* he telling her the truth?

It didn't matter. Too much was at stake. She could not trust him with Ravensbrook, for an error in judgment on her part right now could dearly cost not only herself, but Ravensbrook, and everyone else on her estate.

Much as it sickened her to twist the knife home when she was uncertain of her facts, now was her final and best opportunity to drive him off for good; to make him hate her as she surely should hate him. Guilty or not, he would despise her next words. "I will not believe you until you provide proof."

"How am I to provide proof?"

"It is impossible, isn't it?" She let that sink in. "Just as it is impossible that I will allow a man such as yourself to run Ravensbrook. Leave now, Mr. Montclair. Let this be the end of our unsavory acquaintance."

She sensed, rather than saw his hands clench into fists. She stood still, waiting. He could hit her, or he could leave. The first was an extreme measure she steeled herself to endure. Either way, a triumph.

Long seconds ticked by. Trepidation, and also an unwelcome pinch of shame coursed through her. She could well be falsely accusing him of deeds of which he was innocent. And yet here she was, levering possible untruths to pry him out of her life. Did the end justify the means? In that moment, she just did not know.

Finally, his voice came quietly through the night. "Stable your horse, Lucinda."

Uncertainly, she wavered, trying to read his expression. Was he giving up? Was this his last request to her? At last, without a word, she did as he bid.

After Old Ben was safely in his stall, she discovered Riel waiting for her. The sliver of the moon, now shining above the trees, gilded his powerful black frame in silver.

He said, "Promise me you will not take your horse out again at night."

Lucinda stood very still. Who was he, to be making demands? "I promise you nothing."

"I am not leaving Ravensbrook, Lucinda." Determination bit through that low tone. "And if you ride your animal at night you will know the consequence. I will not let a foolish girl be the death of herself or her horse."

Each of his words hit her like a punch to her heart. She had failed. He was not leaving, after all.

"No documents have been signed, Mr. Montclair. You are not lord over me yet. By Friday you will be gone."

"We will see, Lucy. We will see."

He walked beside her back to the mansion; a dark, unsettling presence. Anger simmered in him. She sensed it as palpably as her own heartbeat. Yet still he had not snapped. Still he insisted upon staying. Why? Why would he choose to remain?

Except to keep his word to her father.

An honorable act.

When they neared the house, Lucinda hurried ahead of Riel, not wanting to see him any longer. She felt disturbed—even ashamed by her accusations. Was he innocent, after all?

On the other hand, he was angry with her. Hadn't she achieved her ultimate goal, then? To infuriate him more and more—step by step—so he'd ride off and never return?

Lucinda hadn't known her small bit of victory could feel so empty. Her acquaintanceship with Riel Montclair was tearing her up inside; more with every passing hour. The end could not come soon enough.

Chapter Seven

THURSDAY MORNING Lucinda awoke late. The reception had gone on past midnight last night, and she had collapsed in bed exhausted, both physically and emotionally, at one a.m.

The funeral was over, and her father buried.

Pressure built in her eyes, but she did not cry. Last night she had cried enough for a lifetime.

After a long while, she rang for Effie to help her dress.

A disturbing idea, half-remembered from her restless dreams, returned as she readied for the day. She considered it, and then expanded upon it. Hope flickered, but mixed with a healthy dose of fear. Yes. It was the perfect plan to rid herself of Riel Montclair forever. Today was her last chance to convince him to leave.

Lucinda had no desire to see Riel this morning. Not yet. He was the chief reason why she'd gone to bed so distraught last night. The man disturbed her every second she was near him. For the remainder of the evening, she had sensed his gaze upon her, watching to be sure she didn't run off and attempt any more foolishness. It irritated the part of her that cherished her independence and freedom. The part that did not want a guardian of any kind.

And the guilt she'd felt over attacking him—perhaps unjustly—did not help matters, either. But the truth remained; he *was* hiding something from the Royal Navy. She didn't know what it was, but it couldn't be good.

Did he plunder enemy ships? Did he plan to plunder Ravensbrook? Much as part of her did not want to believe these things, logically, she just did not know the truth. And that meant she must move forward with her final plan, no matter how disturbed and uncomfortable it made her feel.

Lucinda ate a long, lingering breakfast in her room, and then reluctantly exited to face the day. To face Riel. For she still had a job to do, much as the discomfort of it tempted her to give up. But she would not. She had a plan now. At the perfect time, she must put it into motion.

Drawing a fortifying breath, she carefully considered from every angle the awful plan she'd formed. Without a doubt, it would antagonize Riel so utterly that he'd abandon Ravensbrook at daybreak tomorrow, and never return. Just the thought of putting it into action made her feel slightly sick. As well, her despicable behavior would not only emotionally distress her, but might end up physically harming her, as well. Would it be worth it?

Yes, she told herself. Better a little pain now, than years of it later.

After spending a few enjoyable minutes chatting with Sophie, whom she found sitting in a comfortable chair on the terrace with a book, Lucinda stiffened her spine and approached her father's study.

Tomorrow morning Riel would sign the guardianship papers. So today her behavior must eclipse yesterday's worst by tenfold, if she wanted her plan to succeed. She'd start slow, however, and build momentum until the final act this evening.

She could do it. Much as it would certainly sicken her at various points.

Riel sat at her father's desk, his broad shoulders leaning forward as he studied the ledgers.

"I am here for my lesson," she announced.

He looked up. Tension tightened his features, and unfriendliness flattened his black eyes. Good. She tried to ignore the prick of unhappiness that his clear dislike caused. He was still upset about last night. Now only to build upon that foundation, and learn how to decipher the ledgers at the same time.

Girding up her courage, she lifted her chin higher than usual and entered the room. "You *do* plan to keep your word and teach me the books, don't you?" She injected a cold, regal note into her tone.

He eyed her for an uncomfortable moment. "Mr. Chase has agreed to teach you how to manage the petty monies while I am gone."

That did not answer her question. Although Lucinda felt a quick stab of pleasure at the small token of responsibility he had afforded her, that alone would not accomplish her greater goal. She forced herself to finish the distance to the desk. "Will you keep your word?" she demanded.

Lucinda didn't like the hard words spilling from her mouth, and even less the dislike that flashed in his eyes. She didn't like anyone hating her. Even Riel. This was going to prove harder than she had thought.

"Sit." With a flick of his wrist, he slid the Queen Anne chair beside him again.

Lucinda lowered herself gingerly.

Tightly coiled displeasure simmered in him. She had succeeded in stoking his ire still further. She should feel pleased, not distressed. Wasn't it her goal to be rid of him?

Yes. She must persevere. If she kept the pressure on, tonight he'd snap, and she would gain her most important goal.

A slither of unease accompanied that thought. Truly, a dangerous game.

Did she want him to leave? Or not?

Yes. She *did*, she assured herself. This evening's plan would surely tip him over the edge, and he would leave tomorrow. Right now—during the day—she must only keep him wound up so tight that this evening his tenacious self-control would finally crack.

One of two things would happen then. Either he'd strike her, which she would report to Mr. Chase, who would surely champion her cause...or Riel would finally gallop off in a fury, unable to see the back of her fast enough. With the first, the solicitor would never allow Riel to sign guardianship papers if he saw a bruise upon her person. He'd call the constable, who would permanently escort Riel from Ravensbrook's premises.

Either way, she would achieve her objective. However, unease and fear quailed within her.

Riel watched her, his black eyes hard. She swallowed.

Gathering her wits and courage, Lucinda reached for the ledger and found the place where they had left off yesterday. "Explain what these monies are used for," she ordered, her voice cold. Unfortunately, it trembled, ever so slightly.

"Give it up, Lucinda," he said softly.

She met his gaze. "I do not know whereof you speak. Teach me the ledgers. Now, please."

Footsteps shuffled in the doorway. "Lemonade?" Mrs. Beatty carried a tray bearing a pitcher and two glasses. "Lady Sophia thought a cool drink might refresh you."

"Thank you," Lucinda and Riel said at the same time. She cast him a quick, uneasy glance. After delivering the drinks and leaving the pitcher, the housekeeper left.

Mrs. Beatty's appearance had interrupted Lucinda's focused mindset. She struggled to reacquire her resolve to behave like an icy brat. "If you would be so kind," she said haughtily. Looking down her nose, she pointed to the ledger.

To her shock, Riel snapped the book shut on her finger.

"How *dare* you?"

He gave her a thin-lipped smile. "Now the true Lucinda comes out."

"I will thank you to teach me..."

"I will thank you to behave like a civilized young woman. Do not treat me like a servant, and do not stare at me as if butter won't melt in your mouth."

She glared back. "You agreed to teach me the ledgers."

"And so I will." He leaned back in his chair and sipped his frosty drink. Though he pretended to be relaxed, his white knuckled fingers gripping the glass belied it.

Lucinda struggled for an answer. She wanted to antagonize him still further, but she also truly wanted to understand how the ledgers worked. Perhaps accounting was not a lady's typical occupation, but the money was hers. Before she ceded control of Ravensbrook to anyone, including her future husband, she wanted to understand how her father had run it. She wanted to make sure Ravensbrook would be cared for properly, and the only way to achieve that goal was to understand it thoroughly herself.

"Teach me, then," she commanded.

He lowered his glass with a soft click and flipped shut another book.

"Stop!"

But he continued to close ledgers.

She flew to her feet. "Fine. I'll study them on my own!" She made a wild scrabble for the books, and gathered them all into her arms. To her surprise, Riel did not stop her.

He leaned back in his chair and watched as she hugged the ledgers tightly to her bosom. A smile that was not a smile curved his lips. "Enjoy your studies."

Teeth gritted, Lucinda swiped up her drink, not caring that great splotches spilled on her dress. "That is exactly what I shall do. Good day, Mr. Montclair."

Whirling, she stalked from the room, her back as stiff as a poker. She longed to slam the door, but had no free hand. As she crossed the threshold, she heard a faint sound behind her. Was that a *chuckle?*

Lucinda ground her teeth. She would show him. She would learn it all without his arrogant, condescending help.

And then Lucinda realized a horrible truth. *She* was the infuriated one. Not Riel. Darkly, she remembered this evening's plot. She would win the ultimate victory over him then. It could not come quickly enough for her taste.

That ruffian had to go, and now.

ക ക ക ക ക

Lucinda spent the afternoon struggling to make sense of the ledgers. She even tried to enlist Sophie's help, but the older lady laughed and dismissively fluttered her fingers. "I wouldn't know the first thing about it, child. Ask Riel. He understands all of those bothersome, tedious facts."

"You never wanted to understand?"

"Why would I? My husband took care of it for fifty years. And now I have Riel. Why should I bother myself? Iveny is run splendidly." Sophie sipped her tea. Tiny tea leaves swirled in the hot liquid. Lucinda had noticed that Sophie always spooned in dried leaves from a small pouch she kept close at hand. Perhaps a special blend.

Her mind turned to other questions. Iveny. She had thought the Baron's land was in France. But wasn't Sophie from England? "Does Riel—Mr. Montclair—own your estate?"

"Yes, but he still considers it mine. My husband and I agreed it would pass to Riel when my husband died. Riel is the only of our remaining relatives we could stand. I love him dearly."

"Iveny is in England?"

"Yes."

Lucinda mulled over this fact. "But I thought he said he owns an estate in France."

"So he does. I'm his aunt on his mother's side. He also owns property in France through his father's relatives."

"But he's taken Iveny's title."

"Because titles were abolished in France." Sophie's bright blue eyes twinkled at her confusion. "If he chose to use his French title, he would be the equivalent of an English Duke. The Duke of Montclair."

Shock rippled through her. Riel, a Duke? Disenfranchised though he was...but still.

"Does it make a difference, dear?" Sophie asked, her eyes sharp.

"Of...of course not. I'm just surprised."

"Riel is a man full of surprises. One need only take the time to unwrap them."

To that, Lucinda could attest. Unfortunately, she felt certain many of his surprises would not come up smelling like roses, like his aunt believed. Lucinda admitted she was uncertain about his pirating activities. But she still sensed something dark in Riel Montclair. Much as he might try to claim honor and truth, he *was* hiding something. She knew it. What had his man Haskins said? They didn't want to make the British suspicious of them.

Not only that, but where did Riel plan to get his promised bounty to pay his crew? A prize he'd receive at the end of this week, no less. *Tomorrow*, more specifically.

Yes. Riel was not a spotless lamb. These were just two of many reasons why she must drive him from Ravensbrook with all speed. The fact he irked her beyond measure was only the icing on the cake. He would go tonight.

৵ ৵ ৵ ৵ ৵

At supper that night, Lucinda made polite conversation with Sophie. But in the back of her mind, her secret plot roiled. She tweaked and tuned it as she forked up dessert, which was a delicious raspberry trifle. By turns, she felt excited and sick with nerves.

Lucinda managed to finish the meal without speaking to Riel more than once. A social faux pas of the highest order. Did he notice the snub? Or had her rudeness failed to anger him still more? Frustratingly, she could not tell.

Sophie put down her napkin. "Good night, dears. I must thank Mrs. Beatty for the delicious meal. Will I see you before you leave tomorrow, Riel?"

"We'll meet Mr. Chase at eight o'clock, but I should return about nine and leave shortly after. Will you be up by then, Auntie?" A surprising twinkle gleamed in Riel's dark eyes.

Sophie patted his hand with an answering twinkle. "You naughty boy. You know my weakness and never cease to flaunt it." To Lucinda, she said, "I am a most awful lie-abed. I cannot seem to rouse myself before nine o'clock. But for you, dear boy," she returned her attention to her great-nephew, "I will get up at eight o'clock sharp."

Riel smiled and lifted Sophie's hand to his lips. "Your sacrifice is appreciated."

Sophie giggled like a schoolgirl and retrieved her hand. "Enough of this foolishness. Goodnight, Lucinda."

"Goodnight. ...La," Lucinda gave a fake yawn, "I believe I will retire, as well." She stood with Riel as Sophie slowly shuffled from the room. Lucinda gave Riel the barest of nods. "Mr. Montclair." She headed for the door.

"We will leave for Mr. Chase's house at seven-thirty." His mild voice stopped her in her tracks.

With a faint frown, Lucinda turned to him. "How good of you to inform me."

"Will you be ready?"

She narrowed her eyes. "I will be ready, Mr. Montclair. Of that you may be certain."

"Good. Before you retire, please return the ledgers to me. I want to study them before returning them to Mr. Chase."

"Perfect." She could not squash her gleeful smile. Now she knew where he'd be all evening. Then Lucinda realized her slip. "I mean," she said quickly, "I will fetch them immediately."

Lucinda felt his hard stare following her. She had left the books in the conservatory, and quickly retrieved them. Riel met her in the hall outside the study and relieved her of their weight. "Did you understand them?"

"What?" Lucinda had been so busy rehearsing her plan that it took a moment to comprehend what he was talking about. When she did, however, she refused to answer. He knew she had understood little of the ledgers, and likely wanted to rub her nose in it. Never mind. Soon he would pay. Satisfaction curved her lips.

His gaze rested on her face. "What are you plotting, Lucy?"

Lucy again. Had he already forgotten her unspeakable behavior this morning? Not to mention this evening? Hopefully not. Not if her plan was to succeed.

"My head is dancing with sugar plums, Mr. Montclair," she said archly. "Sweet dreams beckon me."

His dark brows lowered. "Sweet as roses? Or wicked, like their thorns?"

She grinned, unable to help herself. "Risk makes their nectar all the more sweet. I plan to harvest a bushelful of roses tonight, Mr. Montclair. I hope you will do the same." She would leave him with the thorns, that was for sure.

With that oblique taunt, she lightly ran up the stairs. Finally. Time to execute her closing act. Her heart pounded with anticipation. Had she suddenly developed a penchant for danger? Or had their latest confrontation only fueled her desire to best him in their battle of wills?

Neither was a good motivation, she mentally chastised herself. The plan was dangerous. She had orchestrated it to be so.

But perhaps she could enjoy ruffling his feathers a little, too.

Well, that might be possible for a while... Until the end.

∽ ∽ ∽ ∽ ∽

Lucinda waited until utter darkness cloaked the house, and the hall clock chimed ten o'clock. Experience told her Mrs. Beatty would work in the kitchen for an hour longer. She counted upon this fact for her plan to succeed.

Gathering her courage, Lucinda finally slipped into the silent hallway, wiggled out of the upstairs hall window and speedily descended the latticed trellis to the ground. It had been seven years since she'd last attempted it, but she remembered the broken slats, and thankfully additional ones did not break beneath her increased weight.

So far, so good. A sign, perhaps, that her plan would succeed. Lights still glowed in the kitchen, and she spotted Mrs. Beatty preparing dough for tomorrow morning's rolls. A peek in the study window proved Riel was hard at work studying the ledgers. She smiled to herself and made haste for the stables.

Lucinda quickly saddled Old Ben and led him into the faint moonlight. She hated taking even a small risk with her beloved horse, but in her defense, she planned only to trot across the lawn before the study window until she felt sure Riel saw her. The lawn was level and safe. Then she'd gallop off and hide among the trees in the forest for a good long while, just to give Riel time to bubble into a good rage. And then she'd return to face the music.

Her throat felt dry, and she swallowed. Mrs. Beatty would surely protect her if things went too far.

Her heart pounded harder. Maybe this wasn't the best idea.

Of course it was. She could do this. She *must* do this. No pirate would gain control of her home, or her life.

Old Ben trustingly walked beside her until she reached the house, and then she hoisted herself into the saddle and trotted back and forth on the lawn in front of the study window. All the while, she kept her eyes trained for any change in Riel's expression. Then she would flee.

Her muscles felt unbearably tense. She found it difficult to relax in the saddle and enjoy the leisurely ride.

A good many minutes passed, and Riel still did not look up. Lucinda felt a little sick now with anticipation, and her palms sweated in the cool evening. She had to get Riel's attention before Mrs. Beatty went to bed.

Time to take drastic action.

She dismounted, gathered up an array of small stones in her fist and mounted her steed again. Lightly, she tossed the smallest at the window frame. Nothing. She reined Old Ben to a stop and threw another pebble, but harder this time. *Crack!*

Hopefully it hadn't chipped the window, she thought uneasily, and then her blood surged, for Riel glanced up. He saw her. Those black brows came together like a thundercloud and he bolted to his feet.

With a choking little gasp, Lucinda dug her knees in Old Ben's sides. Startled, the old horse lurched into a wild gallop across the lawn. Lucinda let him have his head, for the lawn was smooth and safe. Once she was out of sight of the house, however, she pulled up on the reins.

"Whoa, boy," she whispered. "Don't want to break a leg." It wasn't pitch dark, not with the stars and sliver of moon hanging overhead, but it *was* difficult to see.

Lucinda urged Old Ben slowly into the forest. If she hadn't played on these lands since she was a child, she would be quickly lost. As it was, her knowledge played directly into her hand.

Now to let Riel stew for a while. She glanced overhead and gauged the position of the moon against the tallest tree. She'd let it move an inch or more, and then return home.

Long moments crept by, and goose flesh prickled up on her arms. Lucinda wished she had brought a cloak. For a summer night, it was surprisingly chilly. Still, it could not be helped. Better a little discomfort now, than two years of it later.

Lucinda allowed Old Ben to amble as he wished near the tree line. His ears perked to and fro, listening to the sounds of the forest. He seemed to be enjoying the adventure. Probably more than she was.

"Good boy," she whispered, keeping an eye on Ravensbrook, just to make sure Riel did not exit or try to track her down. Far more likely, though, he'd wait in the house in the study. Long minutes ticked by.

Not much longer, now.

Lucinda's heart pounded in sickening thuds. She was about to gain her heart's desire, if she had the guts to stick to her plan. Did she?

She closed her eyes and prayed for strength.

ৰ্গ ৰ্গ ৰ্গ ৰ্গ ৰ্গ

Lucinda shuddered with cold by the time she rode home. She stabled her horse, and then circled the house, heading to the back door—conveniently located near the study, and next to the kitchen, too. Inside, Mrs. Beatty wiped down the table with an old rag.

Good. Lucinda took comfort from the close proximity of her old friend. But she couldn't let Mrs. Beatty know what she was up to just yet. No, she had to face the music on her own, and accept the ultimate punishment...and the ultimate prize for her flagrant, willful disobedience. Mrs. Beatty would hear her, though, when she screamed.

Lucinda's fingers trembled as she grasped the familiar iron door handle. *It will be all right,* she told herself. *You can do this.*

Her heart pounded like a runaway horse when she entered the dimly lit hall, and she felt sick. Nerves prickled into her skin like tiny, torturous needles as she made her way toward the study. Toward Riel.

Breathing quickly and shallowly, and tongue feeling as dry as fall leaves, she approached the last corner. A scurry would take her past the study's open doorway and lead to the stairs and the sanctuary of her room. With a tiny, gulping swallow, she turned that last corner.

Only to find the study dark and empty.

She stood stationary for a minute, heart still racing, trying to come to grips with this unexpected development. Where was Riel? Had he gone to bed? Had he decided to let her willful disobedience slide...at least until he officially became her guardian?

Lucinda trembled, feeling let down, angry, vexed...and truly, more than a little relieved. When she clasped her hands together, she realized they were visibly shaking. All of the adrenaline...all the planning...all for naught.

So, no confrontation tonight. Riel had won. He would become her guardian after all. And lord over Ravensbrook.

She had lost.

Still trembling, Lucinda headed up the stairs. Her legs felt shaky, like half set gelatin molds, as she climbed the stairs to the upper hall. All was silent and dim up there, too. Riel must have retired for the night. She couldn't believe it. She had planned it all so carefully. She had been so *certain* he would not let it slide...that he would explode like a box of gunpowder.

The silence in the hall did not soothe her nerves, nor did it calm the trembles still shaking through her body. She would only feel safe in her room. Suddenly, that was where she wanted to be, and immediately. She bolted over the last few feet and swiftly closed her bedroom door behind her. She pressed her back to it and a long breath of relief filled her lungs. She was safe. It was all over.

The armoire on her left blocked her view of most of the room, but ahead a lamp burned high and bright on the dresser, casting flickering shadows on the walls.

She frowned. Hadn't she left the wick burning low?

For the first time, she sensed something was out of place in her room.

Heart accelerating yet again, Lucinda uneasily inched past the wardrobe and cast a quick glance about her room.

Adrenaline kicked up her heart rate when she saw Riel. He sat in a chair in the corner. He wore all black and almost blended into the shadows.

"Riel!" she gasped.

He rose to his feet; an alarmingly dark presence. "I see you have returned."

"What are you doing in my *room?*" This was not in her plan. Not at all. Mrs. Beatty was nowhere near. "Get out at once!"

"You refuse to heed my words, Lucinda."

Lucinda. His voice was even, but she was not fooled. He was angry, just as she had planned. Unfortunately, now would be her reckoning, and no one would witness it, or save her. Lucinda lifted her chin, fighting for calm and courage.

In a low, dark voice, he asked, "Where have you been?"

Although her fingers trembled, Lucinda nonchalantly pulled off her bonnet. "Out. I want you to leave. It is most inappropriate for you to be here."

"Riding in the forest?"

"Yes, if you must know." She turned partly away to place her bonnet on the dresser. He took one step closer while this transpired, making her feel even more tense. A tendril of fear crept down her spine. She faced him. "Leave my room immediately."

"We will finish this now, Lucinda. No more games."

"I play no games." She was pleased by how firm her voice sounded. Inside, however, she scrambled, struggling to figure out how to best take advantage of this situation. Although the confrontation was not playing out how she had originally planned, he *was* clearly angry. If she possessed the guts to play her hand to the full, as she had planned to do in the study, then her plan could still succeed.

But she was alone with him. The barest tremor slid through her. *Stop it,* she told herself fiercely. *Seize this opportunity.* She must grip her courage and play her role to the hilt. For Ravensbrook. For her own future.

He growled, "I have let you play me again and again. A mistake. I thought you were grieving. I believed that explained your belligerent behavior. I see I was wrong."

"Leave if you are not pleased, Mr. Montclair. No one is binding you to Ravensbrook. Return to the docks, if life here is so unpalatable."

A muscle clenched in his jaw. "An insubordinate lad aboard ship would have received thirty lashes by now."

Fear trickled like cold water down her skin. "I am not a lad, nor am I aboard your barbaric ship, Mr. Montclair."

"What method should I employ, then? Words do not work with you."

She stiffened her spine against the implied threat. Coldly, she stated, "I do not respond well to orders. I thought you had learned that lesson."

Something black flashed in his eyes. "I am not giving *orders,* Lucinda. I am concerned for your safety, but you will not heed my words."

"You mean obey you? I'm not a child. I'm a grown woman..."

"Then act like one!" he thundered.

She jumped a bit, despite herself. "I've done nothing dangerous. I know Ravensbrook blindfolded."

"You defy me on purpose."

How clever he was. With a small, mocking smile, she said, "Tell me, how has it worked?"

"I am staying, Lucinda," he said, his voice like black silk. "And you will listen when I give you instruction."

"Or what?" she returned, and managed to construct a sneer. "No. *I* will decide what's best for me. Not you. I will not listen to you. Not now, nor ever. So when you leave for your ship, don't bother to return. If you think these past few days have been unpleasant, know they're only a taste of what will come."

His face darkened. "You act like a willful child who needs a good swat."

She had never seen him so close to the edge of snapping before. Her heart bumped faster with fear. Was this it? Perhaps her next words would be the straw that broke the proverbial camel's back.

Yes, if she played her cards right, now she would free herself from his presence forever.

With deliberate precision, she curled her lips into a condescending sneer. "My father was a gentleman, born and raised. Not like you. He *never* raised a hand to me."

"It is what you need now!" His tense body looked cast in stone. Tightly checked anger vibrated, pulsing through the room, enveloping her senses. Lucinda felt a swift, piercing stab of fear.

He could do it, she knew in sudden fright, seeing the dangerous glint in his eyes. He could easily bend her to his will and humiliate her in such a way.

This was not in her plan. How could she show Mr. Chase those bruises? Her face flamed.

"Don't you dare lay a finger on me," she breathed. Panic fluttered like a tiny, agitated bird in her breast. "I will hate you *forever!*"

"You already hate me." Riel stepped closer.

Lucinda trembled. "No. Don't do it."

"Then behave like the civilized young woman your father believed you to be. He was proud of you, Lucy."

Her father had boasted of her to Riel? Her breaths came faster...agitated, confused and frightened.

What would her beloved father think of her now?

It wasn't hard to guess. He would be shocked and dismayed by her behavior. Instead of welcoming his friend into their home, she had deliberately provoked Riel. Instead of loving and respecting her father, she had ignored and rebelled against his last wishes. All to save Ravensbrook; but, if she were brutally honest, also to selfishly save herself, and her freedom and independence. Her father, without a doubt, would be deeply disappointed in her right now.

But, she quickly reminded her faltering resolve, her father had not known about Riel's secrets, nor his self-serving, greedy plot. For Ravensbrook, and for her father, she *must* retain her courage. She stiffened her spine.

"Tell me then," she said in a low, controlled hiss. "Should I trust my home to a man who plans to *steal* from it?"

"What?" His frown flashed like hot lightning.

"I know the truth, Mr. Montclair. I heard you tell your henchman that you will come into new cash at the end of this week. Cash to pay your crew. Cash that you plan to steal from Ravensbrook!"

Shock darkened his face. "I would *never* steal from Commodore Hastings. After what he's done for me... Never! How could you think such a thing?"

"*How?* You refuse to admit your secrets. You behave like a brutish pirate. You are a privateer. What else am I to think?" Her temper soared. "Truly, with all of these facts at my disposal, what *am* I to think?"

"You trust your father's judgment so little?"

"I trust his tender, trusting heart too *much*."

"I have told you before. I am no thief."

"Tell me, Mr. Montclair, what will you do with Ravensbrook's money?"

"What money?"

She gasped at his sheer bravado. "Truly? Mr. Chase will give it to you tomorrow."

"No. He will keep it. I told him that last night. He will continue to manage Ravensbrook until I return from my voyage. As to the money I'm expecting, a buyer owes me payment for a shipment. I will pay my crew with that money."

Flustered, Lucinda said nothing.

His words rang with truth. She'd been wrong, then. At least about that one issue. That relieved her, to a small degree. However, the hard tension in the lines of his body still frightened her. He had threatened moments ago to swat her. By the look of it, he was still angry enough to carry through on that threat.

He growled, "I understand that you want to protect Ravensbrook, Lucy." A bit more gently, he finished, "You are a strong young woman, just as Peter said. He loved you very much, and was proud of you."

"Truly?"

Suddenly, it was all too much. Lucinda put a hand to her face. If she did not need to protect Ravensbrook from Riel, then her reasons to want him gone were purely selfish. Why put herself in harm's way for such a selfish goal? Although this reasoning did not make his impending guardianship more palatable, still, what choice did she have?

Something inside Lucinda crumpled. She felt so distressed, weary and heartsick. And the last thing she wanted was to be a disappointment to her father, or to further deny his wishes. "He told you he was proud of me?"

"At every opportunity."

With that one last pin prick, her determination to oust him from Ravensbrook deflated. How had Riel known just the thing to say? It frustrated her beyond measure. She lowered her eyes.

"Lucy, is this the end of it?"

Lucy. By one question he demanded two things—the right to call her Lucy, and capitulation on her part to stop creating trouble. To accept his guardianship and rule over Ravensbrook for the next two years.

Every part of Lucinda hated the idea of submitting to him, but what other choice did she have? Did she want to shame her father? Did she want Riel to beat her? No. The horror of this last idea shuddered through her. So, in truth, she had lost. He would not leave, not ever, for he was more hard-headed than she was.

It was a bitter pill to swallow, to accept that he had won. Tears welled in her eyes. "Obey you, or receive a beating? Those are my choices?"

"I have not laid a hand on you, Lucinda."

"But you will!" she flared. "Isn't that what you're threatening? To beat me into submission?" Tears slipped down her cheeks.

"Lucy..." The note in his voice changed, but she would listen no further.

"Fine, you great brute! But know your pretense of civility doesn't fool me. You are a barbaric pirate, and *never* will I believe anything different. Yes, I will follow your rules. But steer clear of me in the future, Mr. Montclair. Your very presence sickens me!" To her dismay, a tormented sob escaped, and she pressed her hands to her face. "Go! Go at once. I never wish to see you again!"

After a small hesitation, she heard a whisper of movement and then the latch clicked as the door opened. Another moment of silence passed, as if he stood in the doorway, contemplating speaking to her, and then the door softly closed.

With a sob, Lucinda flung herself on her bed. She wept stormily. She couldn't bear to think about her future. What was more, she hated herself, and she hated him. Her fists curled tightly into the quilt, her body trembling from the agonizing defeat.

ক্ষ ক্ষ ক্ষ ক্ষ ক্ষ

Riel heard the wretched sobs through the closed door and felt like a villain. True, for one split second he had felt the overwhelming urge to turn her over his knee and give her one hard swat.

Never.

He had sworn he'd never allow fury to rule him again. Long ago, he'd almost forfeited his life by reacting like a hot-headed fool. A man had died. By rights, Riel should have swung from a noose.

Never again.

The scene in Lucy's bedchamber seared his mind. He shouldn't have been in there in the first place. But when Riel had seen her gallop off into the night with that backward, gleeful look at the house, something inside him had snapped. Instead of chasing after her, he'd sat in her room, waiting for his anger to cool down. It had. In fact, he'd even remembered to go downstairs and turn out the light in the study. But just now, when she had taunted him, blatantly mocking his authority in her life, a cold fury had swept through him. On his ship, no one would dare treat him in such a manner.

Was cold fury better than hot? Probably not. Not when he remembered what came next.

He had pretty much threatened her bodily violence; even if it was only a swat. Self-disgust gripped Riel, making him feel sick. He should knock on her door right now and apologize.

Still, she had behaved like a belligerent adolescent ever since they'd first met.

It didn't matter. She was his friend's daughter. He should have been more patient.

Lucinda could try the patience of a saint.

Riel tried to remind himself that he had *not* raised a hand to her. Above all things, he had kept his self-control. A victory over the young man he'd once been.

But none of those facts quieted his conscience. He had all but threatened her. Shouldn't he apologize?

His curled fist hesitated a quarter of an inch from her door.

Lucy had finally agreed to behave herself. She had agreed to stop testing him at every turn. It wasn't so much himself that Riel was worried about, but his great-aunt. If Lucy acted like a willful hoyden while he was gone, it might send his frail aunt over the edge. She could collapse—or worse, the stress could fatally weaken her heart and she could die.

Riel lowered the fist he had raised. No. Lucy had promised to behave now. If he apologized, she might take it as a sign of weakness. Then the battle would begin afresh.

Finally, she had given him a measure of her respect. Yes, inspired by fear. And while he did not want Lucy to fear him, perhaps this was the only way it could be—for now. He hoped it might be the first step to build a better relationship. First, mutual respect, and then, someday, perhaps trust and friendship.

He remembered when he'd been a new recruit on the Barbary ship. He had received many a lashing, but the selfish child had been quickly scourged from him. He'd grown up fast.

Riel would never lay a finger on Lucinda, but if it took an unspoken threat to make her toe the line while he was gone, so be it. He would not allow his great-aunt's health to be endangered.

Lucinda wasn't a child anymore, and it was time she grew up.

Chapter Eight

"MISS?" *A LOUD RAP* sounded on the door.

Lucinda moaned, and buried her head further under the covers, blocking out the unwelcome daylight, and the rude pounding upon her door. She had barely slept, and was exhausted.

"Miss!" Effie's voice came again.

Lucinda flung back the covers. "It is barely daylight," she cried out. Flopping back, she smashed the pillow over her head. She squeezed her eyes shut and searched for a comforting tendril of sleep, but all had fled. Last night's events stormed in like a flood. Her defeat. Her humiliation.

Her plan had failed. None of it had turned out the way she had hoped. True, Riel had barbarically threatened her, when she'd pushed him beyond endurance. But he had not snapped. It spoke to his character—the character her father had seen in him. She had been wrong about his plans to steal from Ravensbrook, too. That was a relief, although he still hid secrets from both herself and the Royal Navy. Did it matter? She could do little about any of it.

Now he would wield a scepter of authority over Ravensbrook and her life for two years. While in her heart she still didn't want a guardian, it was time to accept her father's wishes with grace. To make him proud of her.

Depression licked at her spirit. Why get up? Riel didn't need her presence at the solicitor's in order to sign his dastardly papers.

His barbaric threats returned to mind. She had never seen Riel behave with anything but complete control. Part of her didn't think he would have carried through with his threat to swat her last night. The other half remembered the dangerous glint in his black eyes, and wasn't so sure.

Perhaps she should go to the solicitor, like he'd requested.

Lucinda pushed the pillow from her face. Ever more depressed, she muttered, "Come in."

Effie rushed in, wearing a relieved look. She carried fresh water and a towel. "It is seven-fifteen, Lady Lucinda. Lord Iveny has ordered his carriage brought 'round. He asked that you arrive within twenty minutes."

Barely time to dress, and certainly no time to eat.

"I am sorry, miss. I tried to wake you earlier, but could not." Worry rounded Effie's green eyes.

Lucinda managed a smile. "It's not your fault. I'll wear my hair in a simple style today."

Whom had she to impress? She felt like she was about to ride to the guillotine.

With barely a minute to spare, Lucinda reached the main hall. Riel stood waiting, his hands clasped behind him. Today he wore a superfine dark blue jacket, a white linen shirt, sans cravat, as usual, and fawn breeches. Each item met the height of fashion, but somehow those fine clothes could not mask the rawness of the man beneath. A civilized veneer, as she'd accused last night. And beneath, a barbaric pirate. At heart, he must be one. His behavior last night had conclusively proven it. Although he had not snapped, he was clearly a dangerous, ruthless man.

His black hair looked wet, as if freshly washed, and was of course bound in its usual tail. Lucinda couldn't mask her faint frown. "I am here, my lord."

His dark eyes found hers and a flash of what—uncertainty? regret?—glimmered. He bowed slightly. "After you."

Wilson opened the door, and Lucinda descended to the carriage, her head held high and shoulders squared. She would do what she must. Father had wished it. It was the only thought that made palatable this carriage ride to end her freedom.

Riel entered the carriage after her. A small jerk, and they were off. Lucinda looked out the window so she wouldn't have to look at him.

"You are angry with me." His deep voice was quiet.

"I would rather not speak, if you don't mind, my lord."

More silence elapsed.

"I will leave for London directly after signing the papers. I should be back in a few months."

Colorlessly, she returned, "As you say," and continued studying the countryside.

"Lucy..." She stiffened, and he said no more.

The rest of the carriage ride to Mr. Chase's house transpired in silence. At least Lucinda had achieved that small victory. She would be polite to Riel, but he could not make her speak. If he wished for a conversation, he could speak to himself.

Mr. Chase greeted them with cheerful enthusiasm. "All is well, this fine morning?" he asked brightly.

Lucinda said nothing. Riel spoke instead. "It feels warm already."

Lucinda took the chair offered, and twisted her fingers in her lap as Mr. Chase pulled a thick folder from a drawer. "After a few signatures, you can be on your way, Lord Iveny," he said with a jolly smile.

Lucinda directed a hard, unhappy look at Mr. Chase. Could he not see how miserable she was? Did he not see that he was joyfully allowing a pirate to gain control of his old friend's estate?

Father, she thought silently. *Why did you do this to me? Now it will never be undone.* Riel would dictate her life, rule her future, and even approve—and therefore actually *choose*— the man she would marry. Her entire life looked bleak and dark. Starting now, to forevermore. She bit the inside of her lip.

In helpless frustration, she watched Riel sign his name to endless reams of paper. When Mr. Chase asked for her own signature on a few papers, she blindly signed them, not knowing what they were about. Legal gibberish, she was sure. All consigning her to a future of the darkest hell. Perhaps she was being a bit melodramatic here, as Mrs. Beatty had often chastised in the past, but at that moment, to Lucinda, it seemed like the darkest truth.

"That's it, then." Beaming, Mr. Chase shook Riel's hand and bowed over her own. "If you have any questions, I am here, but I'm sure all will run smoothly."

He *hoped* it would, Lucinda thought darkly.

Riel walked beside her to the carriage. "Thank you for signing without a fuss."

She flashed him a hot, feral glare. He actually flinched in surprise. "You have won, Mr. Montclair. Must you rub my nose in it?"

He followed her into the carriage. She averted her gaze to the window once more.

"Lucy."

She gritted her teeth.

"Please look at me, Lucy."

She turned, the movement stiff, eyes glacial. "What do you want of me now, my lord?"

He held her gaze for a long moment, as if searching for the right words. At last, "It is good I am leaving. When I come back, perhaps we can make a fresh start."

Lucinda looked away. Hopelessness slid through her, and she involuntarily swallowed. "I do not know why you wish for that."

"I want an amicable relationship between us."

"You may wish for the moon and the stars, Mr. Montclair, but they will be denied you."

He said no more. The journey to Ravensbrook had never lasted longer.

Once home, Riel lifted his bag into the carriage and he gave Sophie a warm hug and kiss goodbye. "I will be back soon," he promised. "Do not exert yourself."

"Don't worry, my boy." Sophie affectionately touched his cheek. "I will be here when you return."

Riel's dark eyes found Lucinda's. To her surprise, he took her hand and bowed over it. "Lady Lucinda. Until we meet again." For one short, alarming moment, the warm, rough texture of his fingers scorched into her flesh and imprinted upon her mind. The next moment, he climbed aboard his carriage.

A flick of the reins and the carriage rolled down the drive. Heart beating unnaturally fast, Lucinda clasped her tingling hand close. Why did everything about that man burrow under her skin like a splinter? Why was she watching him go?

Goodbye and good riddance. Isn't that what she should be thinking?

Sophie's hand touched her arm. "Come inside, child." She gave Lucinda a warm smile. "Shall we have some tea?"

     ✎ ✎ ✎ ✎ ✎

Fall, 1812

Three weeks stretched into three months, and then more. Riel's duties with the Royal Navy prevented him from returning home, and Lucinda was glad, except for one thing—Sophie longed to see her great-nephew. Daily, she expressed hope that he was all right. Sophie tried to hide it, but her worry increased with each day that passed with no word from Riel. Lucinda wished Riel would write his aunt a letter.

July and August passed quickly, and Lucinda and Sophie grew to be close friends. Lucinda loved spending each morning on the terrace with Sophie, talking about every topic under the sun. The older woman seemed like the grandmother she had always longed for. Lucinda's had passed away long ago.

Sophie often reminisced about her gardens at home. Ravensbrook's plot was small and ill-attended. Lucinda's mother had lavished love upon it when she was alive, but it had been minimally tended over the last thirteen years. When Sophie rhapsodized about the different flowers in her extensive garden at Iveny, Lucinda suggested renovating the garden at Ravensbrook. Of course, by then it was late July, but with the help of the gardener, they selected and planted a few flowers that would grow well into the fall. They planted beautiful beds of flowers in Lucinda's mother's old garden, as well as about Ravensbrook's front steps. The beautiful blooms cheerfully welcomed all who came to visit.

They planted the purple-belled foxglove, too, for one day Sophie let it slip that the leaves she stirred into her tea were from that plant. It was a remedy discovered and championed by the late Doctor William Withering of Birmingham General Hospital. It was believed to help those with heart problems. Sophie said her own doctor had pooh poohed it, but Sophie felt certain it was one of the reasons why she had cheated death for the last eight years.

Lucinda and Sophie were enjoying the lingering fruits of their labor when Riel's first and only letter came. It was a cool, mid-September day, but Lucinda and Sophie sat on the terrace drinking pink lemonade and exclaiming over the hardy little flowers that still bloomed now, early into the chilly fall.

"Madame, a letter." Wilson bowed over the parchment for Sophie.

"Why…" Sophie glanced up in surprise and her blue eyes twinkled with delight. "Whoever could it be from?" Wilson bowed again, and retreated.

Lucinda smiled, for Sophie often received letters from Iveny. Most were from old friends, wondering when she would come home. She was sorely missed at tea parties and all social events. Lucinda wasn't surprised, for in three short months she had grown to dearly love the older lady. Sophie was fun, ever positive, and imparted occasional pearls of wisdom that Lucinda pondered while going about her other duties.

Sophie turned over the letter and saw the wax seal. She went very still, and then pink suffused her wrinkled old cheeks. "Riel!" Hastily, she slit it open and began to read. The packet consisted of several sheets of paper.

Lucinda watched, feeling emotions she couldn't name. Was Riel returning to Ravensbrook? With Mr. Chase's help, she had just begun to manage the petty cash, and she wanted to learn more. She wanted to prove to both herself and Riel that she could run Ravensbrook just fine on her own. When he returned, would he strip that job from her?

Sophie rapidly scanned the parchment, and then the hope in her eyes dimmed and her shoulders slumped. "He can't return home yet. The Navy has ordered him on another mission. Dangerous, no doubt, for he says nothing about it." Sophie turned the page over, but it was blank. She sighed. "That boy."

"So, no word when he will return?" Lucinda asked with cautious hope.

"You may read it." Sophie offered it to her.

Lucinda eyed the dark, bold handwriting and quickly shook her head. "No. Thank you."

Sophie carefully folded the letter, and fixed Lucinda with a sharp look. "We've never spoken of it, for I felt it was none of my business. But will you tell me what happened between you and my nephew before he left?"

Lucinda looked away for a moment. How could she tell her friend—and Riel's great-aunt—that she and Riel didn't get along? "Riel and I don't see eye to eye."

Sophie waited patiently.

"He swept in from nowhere, with letters from Father that he was to take over my life, be my guardian, take care of Ravensbrook's finances. Everything. It was a shock, and I was grieving, and I'll admit I didn't respond well at first. And then..."

"And then the shock wore off, and you still didn't want him to rule your life?"

"Yes. If you knew...if you knew the things I believed about him, and how I behaved. Not to mention the things I did to try to drive him away..." Lucinda sighed. "I'm embarrassed to tell you."

"Then don't. Can you put it behind you?"

"I've accepted that Riel will be my guardian." After he'd threatened her into submission. That old irritation simmered, but she tried to dismiss it. She hadn't been entirely blameless in the incident, after all. "I want to control my own destiny, Sophie. I want to choose my husband, but Riel has ultimate veto over that. Honestly, I don't like it. I can make my own choices. Good choices. Unfortunately, I know he won't agree with me. We're just different people, Aunt Sophie."

Sophie sat silently for a moment. "Riel is a reasonable man, Lucinda. If you fall in love with a young man you've met at a Season, I'm sure Riel will agree to the match. Just tell him how you feel."

"Every time we talk, we end up fighting."

"It's good he's been gone, then, so you two could cool off. Perhaps you can start afresh when he returns."

Lucinda looked away. "That's what he said before he left. The problem is, I don't think we'll ever get along. He's like a splinter under my skin. I want to work him out, but he won't budge."

Sophie smiled. "He is strong-minded."

"That's an understatement," she muttered.

"So are you, if I may be so bold to say so," the older lady said. "Butting heads is not a bad thing. My beloved Charles and I did it all the time. What is important is treating each other with respect. It sounds to me like you might have behaved imprudently when Riel was here last."

Lucinda looked down. "Yes. You could say that."

"Then behave like the sweet young lady you are when he returns. Riel is a good man. He'll listen to your wishes and treat you with respect. Do the same for him. He'll take good care of you. You need only trust him."

And that was the crux of the matter. Lucinda wasn't sure how far she should trust Riel Montclair. Although she knew for sure—and was relieved—he wasn't a thief, the rest of his life remained a closed, shadowy book.

How much did Sophie know of her great-nephew's past? Was she aware of the secret he still hid from the Royal Navy? What about the dark something she sensed from his past? Perhaps they were the one and the same secret.

If Sophie did know his secrets, she undoubtedly loved him enough to overlook them all.

Crowning all of these uncertainties, however, was the fact that Riel Montclair disturbed Lucinda deeply, every time she saw him. And she wasn't sure why, dark secrets aside.

"I will try," she told Sophie now. "But I cannot promise roses in winter."

"An interesting analogy." The older lady eyed her. "But you will try?"

After a moment, Lucinda said, "Yes." A difficult admission, but wasn't she almost eighteen now? Time to put the past to rest. And time to fully accept that Riel would be her guardian, and the trustee of Ravensbrook. That wasn't to say she *wanted* him to be her guardian. But it was high time to move forward. To grow up and accept what she could not change. She just didn't know what her future, with Riel in her life, might look like.

"Good." Sophie pulled another sheet from the packet. "He included a note for you, too."

He did? Fingers suddenly trembling, Lucinda accepted the folded parchment. Her full name, *Lady Lucinda* was penned across the front in a bold script. Riel had written to her. For what purpose?

She flipped the edges open.

August 16, 1812

Lucy,

I know you hate it when I call you Lucy, but I cannot think of you by any other name, for it is how your father always spoke of you.

I do not like the circumstances under which we parted. I do not want enmity between us. When I come back, I would like to start again, if you will allow it.

I remain, ever yours,

Riel

Odd flutters beat in her breast. She took a steadying breath and refolded the parchment. Riel had asked again for a new start. Would she allow it? What might that relationship look like?

A flush warmed her skin and she placed the note on the table. What was wrong with her? Why did peace with Riel feel far more dangerous than war?

"Well?" Sophie spoke up. The bright blue eyes looked shrewd.

"He wants a fresh start, as we were talking about."

"And will you give it to him?"

Lucinda willed her pulse to settle back to a normal rate. Perhaps she'd been out in the sun too long. She gave a small nod. "I will do what I can." It was all she could promise.

September and October passed, and on October 29th, before nudging into cold, drizzly November, Lucinda turned eighteen. Mrs. Beatty fussed mightily over this special birthday, and she turned it into a delightful celebration by preparing Lucinda's favorite meal of chicken, mashed potatoes and lemon cake. A few close friends, including Lucinda's oldest friend Amelia, who had been visiting northern England during Commodore Hastings' funeral, came to share in the celebration. Sophie gave Lucinda a book on gardening, which Lucinda received with delight. She missed the absence of her father keenly on that day, but the presence of both Amelia and Sophie helped to diminish the pain.

November slipped into December, but no further letters arrived from Riel. Lucinda sensed that Sophie was beginning to fret about her great-nephew's safety again. Rumors circulated every day of ships down, and men lost. Could Riel and his ship become one of those casualties? Or had it already happened, and they hadn't yet heard?

❧ ❧ ❧ ❧ ❧

December, 1812

With the advent of cold weather, Sophie suffered more breathing attacks, which left her gasping for air. Coughing spells always brought on these frightening episodes. Sophie told Lucinda that the cold weather exacerbated her bronchorrhoea every year. The attacks scared Lucinda to death. Sophie's blue face and her short, panting breaths sped Lucinda's heart up to a panicked crescendo. The spells often happened when Sophie walked about the house.

A particularly bad spasm happened in mid-December. Lucinda had steered the gasping Sophie to a comfortable chair, but as much as Sophie leaned back with her eyes closed, the fast trot of her breathing didn't slow. Her face slowly turned purple, and Lucinda began to weep.

"Mrs. Beatty!" she cried out. "Mrs. Beatty, come quickly!"

The housekeeper ran out of the kitchen, swiping floured hands on her apron. "What is it, miss?" And then she saw Sophie. "La, Lady Sophia!" She pressed the thin, birdlike hands between her own worn, capable ones. "We're right here with you, my lady. Don't fret. All will be well."

Gradually, Sophie's breathing slowed to normal, and her face lost its bilious hue. Instead, it looked gray and wan.

"I'll fetch tea," Mrs. Beatty said at once, and bustled back to the kitchen.

Sophie lifted her hand, and let it flop back down. It was clearly too much of a strain for her to complete the action. "I wish to lie down. Lucinda. Would you fetch…"

"I certainly will. I'll be right back." Lucinda called for Effie, who ran for her strapping young man from the stables. Henry carried Sophie as gently as a butterfly to her room. Sophie's maid, who had been given the morning off, returned shortly thereafter and tucked up the old lady into bed. The doctor arrived, and left looking serious. He said she needed complete bed rest for two weeks. He also recommended that Sophie hire a nurse.

Lucinda crept back in the late afternoon to see how Sophie fared. To her relief, Sophie sat propped up against pillows, sipping tea.

"Oh, my goodness, I'm so glad you're all right," Lucinda exclaimed, and impulsively ran and carefully hugged the older lady. "I was so afraid…"

Sophie smiled. But up close, Lucinda saw that gray still tinged her face. Worry beat a staccato rap against Lucinda's ribs. "The doctor said…perhaps a nurse would help."

"No nurse!" Sophie snapped sharply. "It would feel like an angel of death hovering over me all the time."

Lucinda bit her lip. Tears formed in her eyes. Sophie reached for her hand and patted it, her expression softer. "Don't fret, child. I'm too ornery to die yet. Besides, I told Riel I'd be here when he returned, and so I shall." The familiar frown pinched her brows, and Lucinda felt a sudden, intense surge of irritation with Riel. Why hadn't he written to his aunt again? How could he allow her to suffer worry like this?

"I'm sure we'll hear from him soon," she said instead, and changed the subject. "Doctor Greer said you're to have complete bed rest for two weeks."

"Pooh," Sophie said promptly. "Perhaps a day. Maybe two. Life is too short to waste lying abed, closed off from the world. No, thank you."

"But he's a doctor. Don't you think he knows best?"

"I'm sure he *thinks* he knows best. But I've learned doctors don't know every blessed thing. I've proved a dozen wrong. According to them, I should be lying in a coffin by now. No. I'll keep living life as I see fit."

Lucinda smiled. "I hope I have half your spunk at your age."

A bit of Sophie's old sparkle twinkled back. "You're on your way, child. I think you and I are more alike than you think."

Lucinda was glad her friend was doing better. But soon it would be Christmas. Sophie had said nothing, but it was easy to guess she wanted Riel home for Christmas.

At least he could send a letter!

Riel, where are you?

Lucinda had never thought she'd do it, but right then she winged a prayer heavenward that Riel would come home soon. Solely for his aunt's sake, of course.

❧ ❧ ❧ ❧ ❧

December 23, 1812

Impatience bit into Riel as he watched the snowy country-side slowly roll by. The Navy's missions had taken far too long. And still they had scheduled another operation for after Christmas. Napoleon's forces had retreated from Russia and been decimated on their return journey home. The Royal Navy wanted to press the advantage during this opportune time. Just Riel's luck that the *Tradewind* was one of the fastest clippers in the world. Perfect for spying and firing on enemy ships.

The Royal Navy paid him well for his trouble, but Riel unfortunately did not have the option to say no to their "requests." Either he complied, or else the *Tradewind* would be impounded. Riel wouldn't allow it. At least this way, the Brits were pleased with his service, and less likely to go poking into his past, looking for reasons to seize his ship.

Soon the war would be over; at least, Riel hoped so.

He'd felt anxious leaving both Lucy and Sophie on their own for so long. He was supposed to be Lucy's guardian, but instead he'd been skimming the Portugese coast, playing war games with his old homeland. *Bonny, give it up,* he thought grimly. *Enough already.*

Would he find all was well when he reached Ravensbrook? Was his aunt in good health? He knew winter was the worst time for her. And what of Lucy? Would she give him a fresh chance to be a part of her life?

Riel hated how he'd left her. Furious with him. Humiliated. He hated that he'd made her feel such things. When he reached Ravensbrook today he hoped he'd find the glimpses of the Lucy he'd seen before that last, disastrous confrontation; a caring young woman who'd been concerned for his aunt before she'd even met her. A young woman capable of deep love and loyalty, evidenced by her wretched grief for her father and the affectionate, considerate way she spoke with Ravensbrook's staff. He looked forward to her feistiness, too.

But no more tests. No more battles. Riel was weary of both, and hoped Ravensbrook might be a place of rest for him during the next year and a half. He'd been uprooted so many times in his life; from France, and then from ship to ship. Iveny was a home, but he still saw it as Sophie's. And the townhouse in London felt like an empty shell. Fool that he was, part of him longed for Ravensbrook to be a true home for him. A place where he could gather his strength before venturing back into the world.

A harsh chuckle caught in his throat. A useless fantasy, unless a certain blond spitfire decided to share Ravensbrook with him.

Riel dropped his head against the back wall of the carriage. No. He was likely leaving one war zone and entering another. Perhaps he should rest for the battle ahead. Still thirty minutes to go.

Chapter Nine

LUCINDA STOOD on a ladder, hanging the last of the delicate, glass blown ornaments on the fragrant Christmas tree. Late afternoon sunlight glinted in the large room, reflecting off the snow outdoors. Sophie was taking a nap, and Mrs. Beatty put the finishing touches on supper. Tomorrow would be Christmas Eve.

She tied the last ornament to the branch and surveyed her work. Glass baubles of red, yellow and blue shimmered on the tall, perfectly formed fir tree. A delicate angel of gold leaned forward, her wings outstretched, as if trying to peer down into the family's Christmas and see what it was all about.

More Christmas items, carefully saved, year after year, decorated the room. An ancient porcelain nativity, which had been her grandmother's, rested on a small secretary. Golden candlesticks flanked it. Christmas greenery, along with red bows and mistletoe, decorated every corner of the parlor, morning room, dining room, study and ballroom. Already Wilson had laid a fire in the grate and its warmth licked through the parlor.

Lucinda loved Christmas. Like a child, she still expected bright, wondrous things to happen. It always seemed like anything was possible at Christmas time.

She returned her attention to the tree. It looked perfect...except one glass horse was crooked. Carefully, she adjusted it, and then smiled.

"It is beautiful."

Lucinda froze. That deep, accented voice. Her heart set to bumping so fast she felt it might hammer right out of her chest. She turned so quickly that her foot slipped on the ladder. With a cry, she wobbled, and in that moment Riel dropped his bag and lunged forward to catch her.

She fell hard against him, but he didn't stagger. Hard muscles rippled against her, and in that moment she felt the raw strength of him, holding her as if she were a feather.

"Riel." Warmth scorched her cheeks, and he allowed her to slide down so her feet touched the floor.

Dark eyes glimmered down at her and the faintest suggestion of a smile tugged at his lips. "Lucy." The one word was surprisingly gentle.

She stepped back. "What...what are you doing here? We received no note. Your aunt has been so worried!"

"My mission ended. I thought I would get here faster than a letter."

For some reason, Lucinda couldn't stop herself from scanning every inch of him. She'd forgotten how very big he was. His broad, muscular shoulders filled out his superfine black jacket, and as usual, his cravat-less white linen shirt left the strong, tanned column of his throat exposed. Dark gray breeches accented the lean cut of his hips.

Further warmth scorched Lucinda's face and she jerked her gaze back to his face, in a heartbeat taking in his black hair, still pulled back in that barbaric pirate tail, his eyes, such a dark, dark brown, and the faint stubble at his jaw.

Lucinda drew a quick breath and stepped back another foot. Why couldn't she form a coherent thought? At last, one flew to mind. "Your aunt will be relieved to learn you are safe."

"And what of you, Lucy? Or do you still hate me?"

Lucinda licked her lips. She did not hate him. But he did unnerve her, as he had done from the beginning. She lifted her chin. "I am ready to begin anew, if you are."

He smiled, and she almost didn't recognize him with laugh lines crinkling from his eyes and a groove dimpled into his cheek. "Truce?"

"Provided you give me no reason to regret it."

He laughed. "Feisty Lucy. I have missed you."

He had? Lucy watched him pick up his bag. How like him to carry his own baggage. Well, he must, since he had no valet. An unconventional man, but she had known that from the beginning. It was one of the reasons why their rapier clashing of wits was so invigorating...and so maddening. She never knew what to expect from him.

He headed for the door.

"Dinner is at six," she offered.

Riel grinned over his shoulder, and butterflies took wing in her stomach. She heard his boots clomp up the steps.

Lucinda sat down hard on a nearby stool. What in the world was wrong with her? It was as if she hadn't seen a man—any man—in months.

Well, truly, she hadn't. At least, no eligible men. But *Riel* certainly was not eligible.

Good thing she and Sophie had planned a big Christmas party for tomorrow night. It had been too long since she'd socialized with others of her own age. A few young men she knew would come, and while Lucinda was still too young to enter the marriage mart with any serious intent—since her father had requested she wait to marry until she was twenty—Lucinda could certainly have fun in the meantime. And fun she would have, dancing with *those* young men.

It had been months since any sort of gaiety had entered her life. Months since her first Season in London. Christmas might prove to be very exciting indeed.

ക ക ക ക ക

After Riel unpacked, he went in search of his aunt. He passed Lucy, hard at work in the study, arranging evergreen bows on the mantle. She'd drawn her lower lip between her teeth, and she looked very serious about her task. He smiled to himself, remembering her manner of greeting him home. Falling into his arms.

He grinned, knowing it wouldn't have been her choice of greeting at all. But the satisfaction he'd felt, holding her small, soft body against him for that one moment, while she stared up at him with those big blue eyes, kicked through him again. He'd felt completely certain in that moment that Lucy did not hate him at all. Her eyes had roved over him afterward and pink had touched her cheeks. Something about him had set her back on her pretty little heel.

Riel chuckled. Maybe Lucy had not intended to greet him warmly, but he felt warmly greeted after all. The few days he could spend at Ravensbrook should prove interesting.

He knocked on his aunt's door.

"Who is it?"

Did Sophie's voice sound more weak and quavering than before? He cleared his throat. "It is Riel."

A gasp and a clatter sounded. Then a rapid shuffle and the door flung open. "Riel!" His aunt flung herself into his arms and he held her tight, feeling the short, gasping breaths that shuddered through her thin frame.

"Aunt Sophie," he said gently. "You need to sit." Without waiting for her to protest, he scooped her up and carried her to a comfortable chair. He pulled up another beside it so he could sit and talk to her.

To his surprise, Sophie slapped his hand the instant he sat down. "You naughty, irresponsible boy! I've been worried sick about you."

"I'm sorry, Auntie," he said softly. "I've been at sea for the past few months. Mostly off the coast of Portugal."

The bright blue eyes glimmered with tears. "Still, you naughty boy. Worrying an old woman."

"How are you?" His stern expression urged her to tell the truth.

She fluttered her hand. "My health is no better, no worse. I don't wish to speak of it. Tell me about you. Are you well? Have you seen Lucinda?"

He smiled. "I have."

His aunt's gaze sharpened. "And does that smile mean peace exists between you at last?"

"One step at a time, Auntie."

"She's a fine girl, and I count her one of my dearest friends now. Don't you dare hurt her. I know how callous you can be sometimes."

"Has she told you tales of my wicked deeds?"

"No. Are there more?"

Sophie knew about his past, and thought of it the way Lucinda's father had. He felt grateful for Sophie's blind love and support, although he knew he didn't deserve it. "Lucy might think so."

"Put it in the past. She's agreed to give you a fresh start."

Riel nodded. It confirmed what Lucy had already told him. "She told you that, too?"

"Well, she said she'd try. And that's the best anyone can do."

Riel smiled faintly. "The next few days should prove interesting."

"*Days?* Gabriel Montclair, don't tell me you're leaving in a few days."

"Spies say Bonaparte's forces have retreated from Russia. They suffered grave losses. We must press to the finish."

Sophie twisted a ring on her finger. "Are you in danger, out on those wild seas?" she asked bluntly.

Riel didn't want to answer. He didn't want to worry his aunt still more.

Sophie swatted at his hand again. "Stop looking at me as if a dash of truth might do me in. Always give me the truth, no matter what. Promise me."

"Yes. It is dangerous. But *Tradewind* is one of the fastest ships in the world. You have nothing to worry about."

"I'm not a fool. I can see the truth, even when you hide it."

Riel smiled and said softly, "I'll be fine, Auntie. Don't worry."

Sophie nodded. "Help me to the dining room. Supper's about ready. Then I want you to tell me all about your adventures."

කියි කියි කියි කියි කියි

Lucinda dressed with care in her favorite lemon and cream dress for dinner. The mourning period for her father was over, and she was glad, for she was sick to death of the dismal black. Bright, fresh colors suited her far better, and they lifted her spirits as well. And as far as mourning her father—she always would. It made no difference what color she wore.

"You look beautiful this evening, miss," Effie said with approval. The maid loved to arrange Lucinda's hair just so, but usually Lucinda didn't want to take the time required to achieve Effie's works of art. Tonight she did. She wanted to show Riel how much she had matured. How sophisticated and grown up she was, at long last. She wanted to make it clear she was an adult now, and fully capable of running her own life.

Lucinda looked in the mirror at her long blond hair swept up in curls and coils, with tendrils kissing her cheeks. Thanks to Effie, she looked older than her eighteen years. Maybe she even looked twenty; the effect she had wished to achieve. "Thank you, Effie."

Lucinda slowly descended the stairs to the dining room. So many conflicting emotions continued to churn in her about Riel's return. First was the alarming way he'd caught her in the parlor. And how she'd felt in his arms. Lucinda refused to think long on that. He had startled her, that was all. Fright from her fall had scrambled her brain.

Riel, for all the polished veneer of civility he wore, was not a man with whom to trifle. It remained to be seen if peace could exist between them. She'd try, as she had promised Sophie, but if he vexed her, or made unreasonable, autocratic demands, she would be unable to help the consequences.

Sophie and Riel already sat in the dining room. Riel sat at the head of the table, with Sophie on his right side. Lucinda chose to sit on his left, across from Sophie. His presence sent prickles of awareness dancing down her skin.

This would not do, not at all. Lucinda focused on smoothing her napkin across her lap.

"Isn't it wonderful, Lucinda?" Sophie exclaimed, patting Riel's hand. Her eyes sparkled as they hadn't in months. "Our dear boy is home!"

Lucinda cast an uncertain glance at her guardian. Riel was hardly a boy. Instead, every inch a man.

His calm, level gaze met hers, and a hint of a smile curved his mouth. "I think Aunt Sophie still thinks I am four years old."

"Pooh," Sophie retorted with a smile. "But you're just as precious to me now as you were then."

Red touched Riel's blunt cheekbones.

Delighted, Lucinda said, "What was he like as a boy? Always into scrapes? Playing with frogs?"

Riel smiled, and Sophie laughed merrily. "I only visited him once, before the French Revolution started. He was four, and cute as a bug with his black hair and mischievous twinkle. He was forever running off into the forest, catching bugs, and digging ditches to see the water run by. His parents had a pond and he floated boats made of leaves and bark across it. Even then the sea ran in his blood, I suppose. His grandfather—my brother—was a sea captain in England long ago."

Lucinda asked Riel, "So you always wanted to go to sea?"

"After my father lost my home in that poker bet, it seemed the only thing to do."

"Didn't you have relatives you could go to?"

"I felt ashamed. Because of the French Revolution, we'd lost our title. My father lost our land. I wanted to prove I was a man and could make it on my own."

"And so you did."

After the briefest hesitation, he raised his glass to his lips. "And so I did." A shadow blackened his gaze, and then it vanished.

Lucinda wondered about that dark look. What events from his past could still shadow his present? What secrets was he hiding? The ones he didn't want the Royal Navy to discover?

"Has Lucinda told you?" Sophie chirped up. "We're having a big bash tomorrow night. We thought Christmas Eve would be the perfect day, since people will want to be home on Christmas day."

"A party?" Riel glanced at Lucinda.

"A ball," she corrected.

He sent his aunt a frown. "You haven't exerted yourself, have you?"

She fluttered a dismissive hand. "Of course not. Lucinda and I planned everything together, which was the best part. Then I let her and Mrs. Beatty do all the real work."

Riel returned his attention to Lucinda. "Mr. Chase approved the funds?"

"Of course." A bit of irritation prickled. "I'm not irresponsible."

Mildly, he said, "I did not mean to imply you were."

Lucinda fell silent, and fingered her fork. Riel was barely home and already he was asking questions and clearly distrusting the wisdom of her decisions. It bothered her, and it hurt.

"You know, Riel—Mr. Montclair—Ravensbrook has survived just fine without you here. We'll manage just as well when you leave again." Lucinda dared to push it a bit further. "You *are* leaving, aren't you? When might that be?"

Sophie stared at her; probably shocked by her atrocious manners. Lucinda's gaze tangled with Riel's dark one.

He took a while to respond. Then, quietly and softly, he said, "Shall we rekindle the war, Lucy?"

"No. But please respect my decisions. Mr. Chase and I have handled things just fine for the last six months. I want you to trust that between the two of us, we might possess a brain that equals yours."

He said nothing for another long moment. Finally, "I was not trying to disparage your decisions, Lucy. But it's my job to make sure Ravensbrook's money is spent wisely. You'll forgive me, but I have not been able to check the ledgers in six months. I have no idea what is going on."

Confronted by his calm logic, Lucinda's ire deflated. She even felt foolish. "Of course." She bit her lip. "I'm sorry."

He smiled a little. "In answer to your question, I leave the day after Christmas."

"So soon?" she blurted, and then could have bitten her tongue. It wasn't like she wanted him to *stay!*

"The Navy has assigned another mission for my ship."

Tartly, Sophie said, "Why don't they use their own ships?"

"They're running thin, what with the war with the Americans and the war with France going on at the same time. *Tradewind* is a clipper, and one of the fastest ships in the British fleet. She can easily dart in and out of coves and spy on enemy ships. The Navy has rigged her up with additional cannons."

"For all purposes she's a war ship."

"Yes."

"You'll be forced to fight the entire war." Comprehension and sick acceptance wobbled in Sophie's voice.

"Yes."

"Why?" Lucinda said. "You're not a commissioned officer. *Tradewind* is your ship. How can they force you to fight?"

"I want to defeat Napoleon, too."

"That isn't the whole story." Lucinda felt this truth clear to her bones.

Riel gave her a level look, as if trying to decide how much he would tell her. Finally, he said, "If I do not comply, the Navy will look for any reason to impound my ship. Seize it, in other words, and use it until they are finished with it. Even then I might not get it back."

"But that would be stealing!"

Riel shrugged. "They'll look for any infraction I might have committed and use it to their advantage."

"Any infraction?" Lucinda jumped on that interesting tidbit. "And would they find a reason to seize your ship?"

Again, that indefinable pause. Again she sensed that dark something in him, indicating that all was not as it should be with Riel Montclair. Maybe something from his past...or from more recent history. Riel's edginess now, added to his first mate saying they didn't want to raise the Navy's suspicions, combined to make Lucinda very suspicious indeed. What could Riel be hiding that he didn't want the British government to discover?

"Will you tell me?" she pressed. Lucinda could read nothing in that black gaze, and because of it, guessed he would not tell her the full truth now.

"I am a French citizen," he said at last. "What better reason could they have to impound my boat?"

A good reason, indeed. But again, it wasn't the full story. Lucinda wasn't sure how she knew this, but her intuition rarely led her astray. That same intuition told her Riel would reveal no more. Not now. Maybe not ever. For now she would accept it, but Lucinda vowed that someday, somehow she would discover Riel Montclair's deepest secret.

Perhaps this knowledge would give her the ability to gain some measure of control over her life—not that she wished him harm. She didn't. But what if, down the road, she needed some sort of leverage over him? For example, if he refused to let her marry the man she wanted. Knowing Riel's darkest secret might give her the ability to ensure her future happiness.

The underhandedness of her tentative course of action did not sit well within her, but on the other hand, the thought of gaining this greatest, most ultimate control over her life beckoned like the sweetest treat. One way or another, Lucinda would find out the truth. Then she would choose how to best use that information.

ન્જ ન્જ ન્જ ન્જ ન્જ

After supper, Riel helped Sophie back to her room. Before he left, she put a quelling hand on his arm. "She can read you, Riel."

"Lucy?"

"Yes, Lucinda. Of whom else would I be speaking?" Sophie said impatiently. "She knows something is not right."

Riel knew very well what she meant. Lucy's pointed questions about his past weighed heavily upon his mind.

"She knows no facts. I want it to stay that way."

"Why? Don't you trust her? Do you think she would notify the authorities?" His aunt sounded indignant.

"I don't want to start the war again," he said grimly. "She still doesn't want me to be her guardian. I can see it. I won't give her ammunition to force me out of her life."

"You're making a mistake. You should be honest with the girl. Better now than later, when it can come back to bite you."

"No. I will not." Riel didn't say it, but he didn't want Lucy to look at him with contempt in her eyes. He had gained her respect. He didn't want to lose it. And he also must fulfill his promise to Peter. The truth would give Lucy leverage to railroad him out of her life. He could not allow that.

ન્જ ન્જ ન્જ ન્જ ન્જ

The next morning Lucinda awoke to sunshine sparkling off the snow and bright blue skies. Christmas Eve! And a party to anticipate this evening.

She sprang out of bed, but a glance at the clock told her it was only half past eight. Effie wouldn't arrive until nine. Well, for once she could dress herself and grab a crust of bread from Mrs. Beatty's larder. Still much needed to be prepared for the ball tonight. Lucinda could not loll about in bed, waiting for the clock to mark the slow passing minutes until nine o'clock.

After donning a simple cotton frock of light blue and lace, Lucinda brushed her hair until it shone, and then left it lying in long waves down her back. There. Presentable. She nodded at the mirror and went in search of breakfast.

Lucinda perched on a chair in the dining room, nibbling on cold, leftover potatoes, when Riel arrived. He wore his jacket, and the scent of fresh air came with him. Evidently he had been up for some time. "Where have you been?" she inquired.

"I retrieved the ledgers from Mr. Chase." He poured himself some tea, which Mrs. Beatty had just brought out, along with a tongue cluck of disapproval at Lucinda for eating cold food.

"He's already up?"

"Yes. Last summer he mentioned he often gets up at five. Since I don't have much time to check the ledgers, I took a chance he might be up early this morning."

"I've been keeping the petty cash," she said with some pride.

"Have you?" With a surprising smile that relaxed his features, he sat across from her. "Mr. Chase has taught you well, then."

"I hope so." Lucinda decided to broach a subject she'd been thinking about for several weeks. "The Season is only a few months away. I'd like to know what monies are available to me. I need to commission a few dresses made before I go to London."

"I will figure that out for you today."

How agreeable he was! Lucinda decided she might like this relaxed, smiling Riel. She smiled, too. "What else have you planned for this day?"

"I will ride the grounds and see how the tenant farmers are faring."

Lucinda felt proud that she could tell him she'd ridden out only last week. She relayed a full report of a roof that needed fixing, and assorted other odds and ends the people of Ravensbrook needed. One woman needed extra money to pay for a doctor's care, for she was about to give birth. Mr. Chase had already provided that money.

Respect and approval gleamed in his eyes. "You have done well, Lucy."

Warm pleasure flushed her cheeks. "Thank you."

"If you like, I will figure out the money for the dresses now."

Lucinda felt surprised. He exited from the room, but soon returned with a blue ledger and a parchment. While she finished her meager breakfast, washed down with hot tea, Riel did quick sums on the extra paper. Then he pushed it across the table to her. He'd circled a tidy amount, prefixed by a pound sign.

Lucinda didn't know if the amount was a lot or a little, or even how many dresses she could buy with it. Of course, she knew the cost of the black dresses the modiste had made for her mourning period, but they had been simply designed gowns—not the latest fashion.

"Is it the same amount as last year?" she asked, trying to make a comparison.

To her surprise, Riel rose and angled his large body into the chair next to hers. Her heart beat faster, overwhelmingly aware of his close presence. He smelled clean, of warm, baked sunshine, and again she felt the raw power of him, carefully controlled, as always.

He pushed the blue ledger before her. His tanned hand rested next to her own. "See. Here is the amount from last year." His warm breath touched her cheek.

Goosebumps prickled down her arms and Lucinda's palms felt suddenly clammy. What was wrong with her? *Stop it!* she told herself.

The party could not come quickly enough. She glanced at the book and focused her thoughts. "So the amount this year is less, because of the mourning dresses."

"Yes."

Lucinda supposed she would have to make do with what-ever the money would buy her. Last year she'd bought twelve new gowns. Perhaps this year she could buy only eleven. Disappointment lodged in her throat.

Absently, Lucinda scanned the other entries on the ledger. She realized the page appeared to be totals of last year's expenses. The cost of her wardrobe, the expense of food—the amount of which surprised her a great deal—as well as the wages for Mrs. Beatty and the other staff. Her jaw dropped. "Is this how much Mrs. Beatty is paid each *year?*"

Riel glanced at the page. "Yes."

"But…" It must be a mistake! "But how can she live on that? My dresses for the Season cost six times her yearly salary!"

"True," Riel agreed with a surprised, but faintly approving look. "But she lives here. She pays no expenses for food or lodging."

"Still. It doesn't seem right." Lucinda felt guilty now for the apparently extravagant amount she'd spent on dresses last Season. And just moments ago, she'd felt disappointed she could only acquire eleven gowns instead of twelve! How many dresses could Mrs. Beatty buy with her meager funds?

Riel's gaze held hers. "What do you want to do about it?"

Lucinda blinked. "I can *do* something?"

"You are the mistress of Ravensbrook now. You can suggest an increased salary for your staff."

"But…" Lucinda's mind swam with the enormity of this idea…and the responsibility. "But where would that money come from? Isn't all the money used up each month?"

"The crops brought in a little extra last year, and trims can be made here and there."

"Trims?" Lucinda wasn't sure if she liked the sound of that.

"Cut back on frivolities. Buy fewer dresses this Season, and give the extra money to your staff. Or give Mrs. Beatty and a few others a Christmas bonus, instead."

While Lucinda did not like Riel calling her wardrobe a frivolity, she considered his words. It did seem unfair that she should have so much, and her devoted servants, so little.

"If I were to give Mrs. Beatty a bonus, how much do you think would be appropriate?" she asked at last.

His gaze held hers. "You are serious."

"Yes. Mrs. Beatty has been more than a housekeeper here for the last thirty-three years. She's been a mother to me, too. She deserves far more than she earns."

"Have you any others to whom you would like to give bonuses?"

Lucinda named a handful of others, including Effie and Wilson, the butler.

Riel suggested an equal bonus for all, but Lucinda disagreed. Heads close together, they dickered out appropriate allotments for five of Ravensbrook's oldest and most loyal staff. Lucinda's dresses for the Season dwindled to eight.

Agreement finally made, Riel leaned back. "You have surprised me, Lucy. In a good way," he added, when her eyebrows climbed.

"You believed me to be rich and spoilt, and completely selfish?"

"I am happy to see that you are not."

It felt like a backhanded sort of a compliment. Lucinda wasn't sure whether to feel insulted or proud. "Remember, you know little about me, Mr. Montclair. Let this be the first of your many lessons."

A smile glimmered. "I have learned many already."

"I thought we agreed to forget the past."

He regarded her, still faintly amused, and his eyes intensely black. "I await you to teach me how wrong I have been."

Warmth flushed her skin. "Then prepared to be schooled, Mr. Montclair. I have much to teach you."

He chuckled. "Never will any of your lessons be dull, will they, Lucy?"

She flounced to her feet, suddenly finished with the conversation and the flush searing her skin. "Enough of the games. I have business to attend to, for the ball is only hours away."

"Leave a dance for me."

Lucinda couldn't help but frown. How like him to autocratically demand a dance, instead of asking for one nicely, with an ample helping of humble supplication! "If I lack for partners I will gladly squeeze you in. If not..." She shrugged.

Riel only smiled, clearly unperturbed, which made Lucinda frown a little harder. She would make sure her dance card was filled up, and speedily. Riel Montclair might think he had a right to dance with her, just as he had the right to rule her life and run Ravensbrook, but he was wrong. At least in this small matter, Lucinda would teach him that she was in charge of her own destiny. And her destiny did not include a dance with a certain supremely confident, raven-haired pirate!

"Good day, Mr. Montclair." She spun on her heel and left him to enjoy his breakfast alone.

A quiet chuckle followed her out. With a flare of indignation, Lucinda wondered if he'd ruffled her on purpose. She felt doubly determined to deny him any dance this evening.

Chapter Ten

CANDLES SPARKLED in the chandeliers in the ballroom, and punch filled the deep crystal bowl. Delicious Christmas confections adorned the buffet table along the wall, as well. Lucinda could hardly wait to sample them. Mrs. Beatty had baked up a storm all week. It was eight o'clock, and already guests streamed into the house.

"Hello!" Lucinda greeted her oldest and dearest friend, Amelia, and her parents. "I haven't seen you in ages! How have you been?"

Amelia rolled her eyes to the ceiling. "Bored," she said drolly. "At least until dear Jonathon came to visit."

Before Lucinda could ask who Jonathon was, a tall man with fashionably trimmed chestnut hair stepped forward and bowed over her hand. "Lady Lucinda," he said in a smooth drawl. "Amelia did not say how beautiful you are."

Lucinda smiled, quick to see how very handsome he was, with dark green eyes and classical features. And he was dressed to the minute in the very latest fashion, she noticed. "I am pleased to make your acquaintance, my lord." Clearly he was titled. It seemed a safe assumption to make.

"He's my second cousin once removed, the Duke of Warrington," Amelia informed her. She patted her mousy brown hair, scraped back into a tidy bun. At least, it was tidy for now. Amelia was prone to outrageous mishaps, and rarely did she survive one evening without her dress spotted or her hair caught by a passing gentleman's cuffed sleeve as he raised his arm to sip champagne. Unlikely though it was, this scenario had played out on several occasions.

"I didn't know you were related to a Duke," Lucinda teased her friend.

"If only I could be a duchess, then perhaps all of my worldly troubles would vanish." Meaning her unlikelihood of catching a husband, Lucinda knew. Amelia believed herself too tall and plain. She did not see herself as the witty, clever girl she was, but Lucinda firmly believed the right man existed for Amelia. Someone who would recognize her for the treasure she was.

She took her friend by the arm. "Come, Sophie will want to speak with you again. She's become my dearest friend over the last several months—next to you, of course." A step away Sophie sat, chatting with Lady Humphrey. Lucinda introduced Amelia's parents and Jonathon.

Sophie smiled. "I'm so pleased you could come to the ball. Lucinda has told me all about you. It's good that young people could come and liven up Ravensbrook."

Amelia's parents joked a little about being considered "young people," and chatted with Sophie.

Amelia plucked at Lucinda's arm. "Where's your beastly guardian? I'd love to meet him." Amelia and her family had been on holiday during Lucinda's father's funeral.

"Doubtless he's about somewhere," Lucinda said dismissively.

"What does he look like?" Amelia pressed.

Lucinda sighed. "He's hard to miss. He's big, with long black hair, like a pirate. His manners are frequently as atrocious."

Amelia snorted with delight. "He sounds a peach. Let's find him."

"Before you go," the Duke of Warrington spoke behind them, and Lucinda turned, embarrassed that she'd rudely ignored a duke. "If you would be so kind, Lady Lucinda, I would love the honor of a dance later this evening."

Lucinda promptly extended her dance card. "Take two slots," she encouraged, and then realized how that sounded. "I mean," she said hastily, "only if you wish, of course, your grace." She'd been on a tear all evening, cajoling dances from all the young men she knew. Four slots remained, and she was determined to avoid Riel until every last one was taken.

The Duke smiled and wrote on her card. "I would be pleased to accept two from the most beautiful lady in the room...besides Amelia, of course." Amelia rolled her eyes at this. "And please call me Jonathon." His wonderful eyes held hers, telling her he truly meant his words. Lucinda flushed, and felt a little giddy. Clearly he was the most highly titled man in the room—besides Riel, if one could count his French title—and Jonathon found her attractive. With a smile, he moved away, weaving his tall, well-formed body through the guests, heading in the direction of the punch bowl.

Lucinda gave a low squeal. "You do *not* have a duke for a cousin."

Amelia smiled. "I do, and he's as nice as he looks, too. Not that I know him all *that* well. He's one of the distant relations that show up for Christmas and the like every five years or so."

"Still."

"Show me your pirate."

Lucinda's nerves prickled up and she knew Riel stood right behind her. She tucked her dance card up her sleeve and turned with a smile. "Well, aren't we fortunate? Here he is now."

Amelia's eyes widened a bit, and then narrowed when she turned and saw Riel. She extended her hand. "I am Lady Amelia."

"Riel Montclair, Baron of Iveny, at your service." He bowed over her hand.

Amelia flicked Lucinda a glance, eyebrow arched. "It seems Lucinda led me astray. You are well mannered."

He smiled. "I am pleased someone thinks so."

Lucinda took Amelia's arm. "We were just heading to the punch table."

Her friend refused to budge. "You've been so eager to fill up your dance card, Lucinda. Perhaps Lord Iveny would care to take a dance."

Lucinda shot daggers at her friend. "No, Amelia. Mr. Montclair is..."

"Fortunate to catch you with slots still remaining. It would also be my pleasure, Lady Amelia, if I could sign your card, as well."

"Well." Amelia offered a crooked smile. "I would be pleased, too. Thank you, Lord Iveny."

Riel signed for one of Amelia's dances and while he did so, Lucinda edged away. When Riel offered Amelia a compliment on her gown, Lucinda crept further afield, and then darted for the punch table, abandoning her friend. With a trembling hand, she poured punch into a crystal glass. Goodness. That had been a close call. Two more slots to fill. Whom could she apprehend next?

She scanned the room, noting that Riel still spoke to Amelia. Good. It gave her more time to find her next unwitting dance partner. Her eyes lit upon a friend's twin brother. So what if he was only sixteen? He would do. With a grin, she made haste for Timothy.

Blond-haired Timothy reluctantly signed for a country dance; reluctant only because he couldn't dance well, he told her. Otherwise, he'd be pleased to dance two dances with her, he vowed. His milk chocolate eyes shone with puppy-like adoration.

One to go. Lucinda skirted a clump of elderly matrons and hugged the edge of the ballroom, looking for her next victim. From this vantage point, she could see that everyone enjoyed themselves enormously. A success, then. She and Sophie could feel proud.

Sophie had given her wisdom on all the little elements that would make the party a smashing success—crystal glasses, the lightest confections, the best music, and beautiful linens. Everything had been polished until it shone; chandeliers, the wooden floor...everything. Ravensbrook had never looked so grand, and everyone seemed to be loving it.

However, Lucinda sighed now with frustration. Surely there were more eligible young men! Where was Harry, the eldest son of an earl who lived on the other side of the village?

Maybe his cough had returned.

With a frown, Lucinda stood on tiptoe and scanned the room. Plenty of old men. Strike those.

Her dance card was plucked from her fingers. "One slot left, I see," Riel said, and with bold strokes claimed the last dance.

Lucinda gasped with outrage. "I don't remember being asked, Mr. Montclair! Is this how nobility behaves in France?"

"It is how a pirate behaves." He smiled, showing his teeth. "And that is what you think of me, isn't it? Your friend Amelia has been most forthcoming."

The traitor. "You have always known what I think of you. It's been no secret."

"Until the waltz, Lucy." And then he was gone.

Lucinda frowned down at her dance card. Filled now, to be sure. If only she could strike through his name. And he'd taken the waltz! The closest, most intimate dance of all. It was still considered scandalous by some. And it was the last dance of the night. He did want to get on her last nerve. He was deliberately trying to irk her! She growled beneath her breath.

"I see Lord Iveny found you." Amelia peered at Lucinda's dance card.

"Thanks so much. Did you steer him to me?"

Amelia smiled. "You really have a thing for him, don't you?"

Lucinda choked on a gasp. "I do not have any *thing* for him. He drives me absolutely up the wall and down the other side."

Amelia grinned. "He can't be all bad. He's put a definite sparkle in your eyes."

"A sparkle of rage," Lucinda informed her. "For a far more pleasant sparkle, I would look upon your cousin, the Duke."

"Have you any suggestions who might sign my dance card? The pickings look slim tonight."

"Try Timothy. He signed mine."

Both Amelia and Lucinda burst into rueful giggles. "You must be desperate," Amelia said. "But so am I. Wish me luck." She made her way over to young Lord Fenwick.

❧ ❧ ❧ ❧ ❧

The Duke of Warrington was a sublime partner. He whirled with Lucinda through the steps of the Scottish reel, his movements smooth and graceful. Her heart pounded quite deliciously by the end.

He led her off the dance floor. "I'm parched. How about you?"

Lucinda agreed that she could use a sip of punch, and so he crooked his arm, which she happily took. After pouring a splash into each cup, he looked down at her with a surprised, considering smile. "You are an unexpected treasure to find in the wilds of the country. Had I known you were here, I would have wrangled an invitation to visit my relatives much sooner."

Flattered, Lucinda wondered if he truly meant those words, or if he was a rake of the first order. Amelia had said she didn't know him that well. And how old was he? Likely about twenty-four. She sipped her drink to cover the uncertain flutters his words caused within her. "Do you often make it to the ton for the Season, Duke?"

He cast her a wicked, charming smile. "Call me Jonathon. And I live in London. May I be so bold to call you Lucinda?"

Goodness, he was smooth, and moved so very quickly. Lucinda knew she was still inexperienced with men, and wondered what seasoned girls might say to him. She offered a calm, hopefully sophisticated smile. "I would be pleased if you would."

"Good." He grinned still more. "Would you like to go somewhere and talk for a while?"

Unease flickered through her. "Well..."

"Lady Lucinda's dance card is full." Riel spoke from behind her. "She would not like to disappoint the next gentleman in line."

Much as Lucinda felt a bit of relief at Riel's intervention, she also felt a smidge of annoyance. However, she would not snipe at Riel in front of Jonathon, for she had no wish to appear like a child before the very handsome Duke of Warrington. Instead, she affixed a serene smile upon her lips. "Jonathon, have you met my guardian, Riel Montclair, Baron of Iveny?"

"Can't say that I have." Jonathon offered his hand, and the two men shook. It seemed a bit firm on both parts, if the white knuckles were to be believed. "I'm the Duke of Warrington. Call me Jonathon."

The Baron stiffened, ever so slightly. "Riel."

The two men eyed each other for a long moment, and then a puzzled frown flickered across Jonathon's features. "Have we met before...Riel?"

Beside her, Lucinda sensed the palpable tension in Riel's large body. A glance up revealed no expression on his face, however. "I doubt that, Duke. I do not move in the circles of the London gentry. I own a ship and spend most of my time on the sea."

"Oh." The tiny frown lingered, then cleared. "I must have you mixed up with someone else."

But who? Lucinda had never before met a man as distinctive as Riel. Truly, he was one of a kind. Perhaps in the past Jonathon had met someone with similar features. Perhaps. But she couldn't forget the way Riel had stiffened. Had he recognized Jonathon? If so, why would he deny it?

The next man on her dance card arrived to claim the quadrille, and with reluctance she bid farewell to Jonathon.

"Until our next dance," he told her with a mischievous twinkle.

The rest of the evening whirled by in a merry jumble of dances. Lucinda was pleased to see that her friend Amelia did not lack for dance partners. Riel danced with her twice, as did Jonathon. She also noticed that Sophie appeared to be having a wonderful time talking to new friends. Lucinda stopped by a number of times to see if Sophie needed anything, and spent a few minutes chatting with her until the next man came to ask for his dance.

Lucinda suffered through the country dance with young, clumsy Timothy, then another thrilling twirl about the room with Jonathon. Afterward, servants extinguished a few lights, and older people shuffled for the door. It was time for the last dance. The waltz. Riel's dance.

Lucinda saw his dark head move across the room and felt like a mouse about to be pounced upon by a cat. Couldn't she escape? Must she suffer one dance in his arms? She cast a quick, longing glance toward the exit.

Amelia appeared by her side. "You're not going to run out on your last dance, are you?" she said with a sharp, amused glance. "If anyone has reason, it would be me. I hear young Timothy smashes toes."

"He does," Lucinda agreed ruefully. Thankfully, the smarting had eased several dances ago.

"The Baron is a fine dancer," Amelia said. "I think there's more to him than meets the eye."

How well Lucinda knew this! "He's owns another title, actually...in France." She wasn't sure why she felt the need to tell her friend this.

"He's French?"

"Half French and half English. He chose the English title because the French Revolution abolished all aristocratic titles." At Amelia's arched, inquiring brow, she elaborated, "He would be the Duke of Montclair."

"A Duke in your very own house. And you felt so impressed with Jonathon."

"Jonathon is different," Lucinda said defensively. "Riel... I don't think either title means anything to him."

Amelia watched him zigzag closer. "I believe you are right. The Baron is his own man."

Was that a sparkle of admiration in her friend's eyes? Lucinda felt an uncomfortable twinge of alarm. "You don't find him...interesting, do you?"

Amelia smiled slowly. "I will leave that fascinating man to you."

Lucinda felt disconcerted. "That is not what I meant at all!"

"Isn't it?" With a knowing smile, Amelia glided across the floor. "It's time to collect my last dance from young Timothy."

Where was Riel now? Lucinda glanced back and forth, still flirting with the idea of making her escape, when she felt a hand on her elbow.

"You are not planning to stand me up, are you, Lucy?" The deep voice stirred her nerve endings.

"I thought I might take a breath of air."

"It is snowing."

"It is?" Lucinda shivered, despite herself.

The band struck up the strains of a beautiful waltz.

"Lady Lucinda." Riel extended his hand, and reluctantly, she took it. It felt warm and strong, and a bit calloused, too. The next moment she was in his arms, with one hand clasped in his and the other resting on his shoulder. The fine fabric of his tailored jacket could not hide the hard muscle beneath. Her heart beat erratically. Upon her waist, Lucinda felt the imprint of each of his fingers. They seemed to sizzle into her flesh.

The man unnerved her. More so, it seemed, the closer she got to him.

Riel led her with unexpected grace across the dance floor.

"You dance well, for a pirate," Lucinda told him, feeling the need to jar the uncomfortable closeness between them.

He chuckled. "Perhaps I am not the thorough barbarian you believe me to be."

"Oh, you are. Of that I am sure, Mr. Montclair...your titles of Baron and Duke not withstanding."

"Sophie told you."

"Of course. Do titles mean so little to you?"

He remained silent for a few moments. "They are not what make a man. Character, honor and integrity do."

"And you possess the full measure of each?"

His half smile looked surprisingly self-deprecating. "I try, Lucy. But I know you'll believe what you will. You seem to prefer to look upon me as the devil incarnate."

"I do not." Lucinda felt aghast.

"Then how do you see me? Not with favor. You have made that clear from the first day we met."

Lucinda searched for words to describe what she felt for the man who held her so close that she felt very aware of every point where their bodies connected, and of his dark gaze that tangled with her own, demanding her full attention.

"I think you are wonderful to Sophie." Lucinda admitted. At the same time, she didn't want to go overboard and stroke his all confident ego, either. "But to me...your manners leave much to be desired."

He pulled her a fraction closer as they went into a turn. Lucinda's heart beat faster as she caught a waft of the clean scent of his skin. The warmth of his body seemed to seep deep into her pores.

Riel said in a quiet, low voice, "And are your manners perfectly impeccable?"

"What?" Flustered, Lucinda couldn't seem to remember their topic of conversation.

His midnight eyes narrowed, and his lips twitched. "You are not wool gathering, are you, Lucy?"

Lucinda flushed. "No. I...I am thinking on matters of other import."

"Such as?"

She grasped for a new topic. "Such as why Jonathon thinks he's met you before. And you became tense when he asked. Why?"

He smiled. "How quickly you change the subject."

"Answer my question."

"If I have met Jonathon before, I do not remember him."

He told her the truth; she could see it in his eyes. Then why had he stiffened when Jonathon asked if they'd met? Perhaps he felt wary of anyone who might know some corner of his dark secret. "What are you hiding, Riel Montclair?"

His hooded gaze looked contemplative. "So little trust between us. Perhaps we should focus on the present, and your future. That is all that is important to me."

"The past does not matter?"

"All that matters is I will see you safely married. And then you need never see me again."

His statement hit her like an unexpected blow. "You eagerly await that day, as well?"

"I look forward to the day when we can finally have peace between us."

"I have not been fighting you."

"No? You still do not want me here. You don't want me to be your guardian. It's written all over your face. You ran away so I could not sign your dance card."

"But you pursued me and signed it anyway!" she returned with asperity.

"Are you displeased?"

Her face warmed, and she found she could not meet his eyes. "Of course I am displeased. I am forced to dance with a pirate. What girl could want that?"

"Not you, Lucy?"

Her eyes finally met his. Cheeks warm, she bit her lip. "If I must, I can endure the horror of it."

He drew her close as the waltz slowed to a stop. In her ear, he said, "Good night." His warm breath fluttered inside that delicate instrument, and then abruptly he turned and was gone.

Lucinda stood still, trembling, and watched his broad back disappear into the crowd.

க் க் க் க் க்

Riel could not sleep for long hours after retiring to his room. He paced the chamber, feeling restless and edgy. It disturbed him, more deeply than pleased him, that Lucy still clearly disliked him. Hadn't he come to Ravensbrook expecting more battles with her? And yet it had not started out that way at all.

His mind replayed the way she'd involuntarily greeted him. His insides tightened, thinking of it. Their conversations had been civil, too, for the most part. And he'd enjoyed her feisty confrontations. He'd begun to think she might like him a little, and it had felt good.

But when Lucy had stated that dancing with him was a horror she could barely tolerate, it had cut, like the flay of a cat-o-nine tails.

Lucy did think of him only as a pirate. Beneath contempt.

Riel shoved a fist against his temple, feeling the old condemnation struggle for control in his soul once again. And the old doubt, too, tried to slither in like a snake.

Truly, was he little more than a pirate? At heart, was he no more than the failure he'd been all those years ago? He had been unable to save anyone then. Only Peter Hastings had saved his sorry hide from the gallows.

Peter had reassured him that God had forgiven all his sins when Riel had asked for it. Most of the time Riel believed it, but other times, like now, the guilt, anger and grief for what had happened, and what he'd done, welled up, tormenting him over and over again. His past would forever deny him a true life. It would deny him a future, and keep him forever alone.

Riel knew it wasn't just because of Lucy that the old feelings were rising up and threatening to swallow him. In fact, he could count on one hand the number of times that had happened over the last several years.

It was because of Warrington.

Surely the man had never seen Riel before; if so, surely Warrington did not remember him. Riel did not remember

Jonathon. All those years ago, the present Duke would have been a boy; perhaps thirteen. But that name...that name Riel knew all too well. That name had almost signed his death warrant. That name had begun all of this misery.

He sat on the edge of his bed, clenched knuckles digging into his scalp, and struggled against the old feelings of guilt, impotent fury and worthlessness. He forced himself to remember how far he had come. More men than Peter believed him to be a man of honor and integrity now. It was the man he wanted to be. The man he intended to be.

He could not change the past. Hopefully Warrington knew nothing about it. If he did, Riel's life as he now knew it would end. He would be unable to fulfill his promise to Peter. He would be unable to protect Lucy.

That could not happen. He would not allow it.

For now, Riel would face the future one day at a time. So far, all was well. As long as Jonathon did not remember, Lucy would be safe.

In a low, harsh voice, he prayed, asking God for the ability to protect Lucy until another could safely take care of her. Then he would go, and Lucy would be pleased to finally be rid of him.

Riel tried to ignore the burn of pain he felt. In truth, it did not matter what Lucy thought of him. He had a job to do, and a promise to fulfill. And he would fulfill it, no matter the ultimate cost to himself.

❧ ❧ ❧ ❧ ❧

Lucinda had hurt Riel's feelings. She had suspected it last night, but it became clearer on Christmas, which dawned as a bright, sunny day.

Lucinda had never thought she could possibly touch Riel's feelings. He always seemed so strong and detached from the world around him—and from her. But last night, when she'd told Riel that dancing with him was a horror she could barely endure...it had cut him somehow.

She had *said* it. But she hadn't meant it. Not at all. In fact, it had been a lie; the ultimate tongue-in-cheek irony, and the complete opposite of how she truly felt. She'd said it only to protect herself. And to push him away. She had succeeded.

Lucinda watched him now, and she felt bad about how she had hurt him. Riel seemed unusually quiet and reserved this morning.

They had all gathered in the parlor around the Christmas tree. Snow sparkled outside, reflecting cold winter light into the room. Lucinda had purchased presents for Sophie, of course, and for the staff. In addition, the staff bonuses had already been received with exclamations of gratitude. But she had nothing for Riel.

Only two presents remained. One for her, and one for Sophie. Both from Riel.

"Open yours first," she urged Sophie.

As eager as a child, the older lady ripped at the fine gold paper with her well-manicured nails. "Oh!" Mouth rounded, Sophie pulled out a light blue, fluffy confection. A shawl, they discovered, when she shook it out. Sophie pressed it to her cheek. "I love it, Riel. You dear boy! It's cashmere, isn't it?"

"Only the best for you, Auntie." He kissed her cheek and she kissed him back, and then she promptly arranged the shawl about her shoulders.

"It's perfect. Just what I need." Aunt and great-nephew looked to Lucinda next.

Her package felt light, and just the shape of Sophie's. A careful ripping of paper revealed a lemon yellow shawl, which felt as soft as a kitten. Tears of pleasure stung her eyes. "Riel! Thank you."

He nodded, and gathered up the bits of paper.

"I...I'm sorry," Lucinda said. "I have nothing for you."

He barely glanced at her. "It is all right."

"It's not."

He stopped what he was doing and gave her a long look. "It is not."

As if sensing the undercurrent in the room, Sophie rose to her feet and shuffled for the door. "I'll be in the kitchen, fetching a cup of tea."

When she had gone, Riel slowly lowered his big frame onto the couch beside Lucinda. "What did you mean?"

Unexpected tears prickled her eyes. "I'm sorry."

"Why? Because you think you hurt my feelings?"

He referred to last night, Lucinda knew it. "Didn't I? I'm truly sorry. I didn't mean to hurt you."

"You hate me. At last I understand that. Do not apologize for how you feel." He looked away, but not before she saw a flash of vulnerability, deep in his eyes.

One of her comments had finally hurt him. And she was sorry. "No, Riel. I didn't mean what I said last night. And I don't hate you, either."

He glanced back with a frown. "You do not?"

The truth must be spoken, but it was hard to get out. Lucinda didn't hate him, but she didn't want him to rule her entire life, either. How to say that? And he disturbed her. But she certainly couldn't tell him that! She licked her lips and whispered, "No."

Riel regarded her steadily, but still with a faint hint of disbelief. "If you don't hate me, then what do you feel for me?"

She didn't know!

Lucinda managed to say, "I respect you. I believe you can be gentle and kind, because you treat your aunt that way."

"Do you still want me gone, Lucy?"

Didn't she? Why didn't she say "yes"?

Because she wouldn't mean it. Not entirely. It was an alarming admission to make to herself. While she did want to be in charge of her own life, she didn't particularly want to see the back of her unwanted guardian, either. Lucinda felt confused. Nothing made sense.

So she struggled for more words. "I...I appreciate how you intervened with Jonathon last night. He was going a bit fast, and for a minute I didn't know what to do. I would have managed," she hastened to make plain, "but it made it easier for you to be the ogre. That way I didn't have to reject him."

"I'm glad you're wise enough not to go anywhere alone with Jonathon."

Indignantly, Lucinda returned, "I would never go anywhere alone with a man!"

"Is that a promise? In case I miss some of your coming Season?"

"Of course."

"Good."

"You may not be back for the Season?" Lucinda again felt a curious sense of disappointment. Tomorrow he would leave. When would she see him again? More importantly, she told herself, how would it affect her Season in London?

"I do not know. Sophie will chaperone you as best she can. I will need to ask you to curtail your activities to those she is well enough to attend."

Lucinda felt a stab of disappointment, and then an idea flashed to mind. "Amelia said she and her mother are going down for a month. What if Lady Carlisle chaperones the events Sophie cannot make?"

He nodded. "I will accept that." After a moment, Riel spoke again, slowly. "If Sophie's attacks get no better, you may not be able to go to London at all."

"But I must. How else will I meet new people?"

A log collapsed in the fireplace, sending a shower of sparks into the screen.

"You mean a potential husband." He stood abruptly and headed for the poker.

"No. Father didn't want me to marry until I'm twenty. That's over a year and a half away. I'm not ready to find a husband, and then pine for him until I turn twenty."

"No?" Amusement twitched his mouth, and for the first time that morning, tension seemed to relax from his broad shoulders.

"Of course not. I want to have fun. I'm tired of being stuck here at Ravensbrook." Lucinda became aware that she might sound like a spoiled child. "I mean, I love it here, and Sophie has made it even more fun, but I want to go somewhere different. Do something new."

"I can understand that."

"It's why you love the sea," she guessed.

"Yes." He replaced the poker and paced back. "I think Sophie wants to return to Iveny. She puts on a brave front, but she feels ill."

Lucinda nodded with understanding. "She wants the comfort of home and her friends." It was exactly what Sophie needed. Why hadn't she seen it?

"I'll need your help to convince her it is all right to go home."

Riel needed her help? Lucinda stood up too, and shut away the lick of depression she felt at the thought of her friend leaving. Of being alone at Ravensbrook. "Do you think I will manage well enough on my own?"

"Will you?" His dark gaze held hers. It seemed like a test, and Lucinda stiffened her spine. Isn't this what she wanted—freedom, and the chance to prove to Riel that she could run her life without his intervention? "Of course. Mrs. Beatty and Wilson are here. I'll be fine."

"I am placing my trust in you, Lucy. Do not disappoint me."

"What sort of trouble could I get into here, in the dead of winter? There's nothing to do!"

"You will obey me about the Season? If Sophie cannot go, neither will you."

"I will go with Amelia and her mother." One month in London would be better than none.

Riel looked down at her. Unreadable emotions flickered through his black eyes. "I feel like I am shirking my word to your father. I am the one who should be here, watching over you and taking you to London."

"I've told you before that I need no guardian. Let me prove it to you."

He growled and thrust a large hand into his hair. It looked smooth, scraped back into that tail. Lucinda wondered if it was. She stood still, watching the play of emotions over his blunt, angled face, and the thick bunching of muscles under the deceptively civilian veneer of his superfine jacket. He was a big man, and he was strong. She remembered the feel of him, dancing with him last night, and her cheeks warmed.

"You may go with Amelia, as long as the Carlisles don't stay with Warrington." His dark gaze focused on her once more, and then unexpectedly dipped to run over her flushed cheeks. She drew an unsteady breath, and willed herself to stop standing there like a ninny, staring at him. His gaze drifted to her mouth, and then rose to meet hers.

Lucida blushed again, feeling warmer. "Very well. Shall we speak to Aunt Sophie now?"

He stared at her for another moment, as if trying to comprehend the reason for her blush. Lucinda wished for nothing less. She didn't want Riel to gather any misconstrued ideas.

"Are you coming?" Gathering up her skirts, she turned and swept from the room. Time to convince Sophie to return to Iveny.

ళ ళ ళ ళ ళ

When Riel readied for bed that evening he felt satisfied with the day's accomplishments. Sophie had reluctantly agreed to return to Iveny, and Lucy had agreed to abide by his rules concerning her upcoming Season. He'd also written a note to Lady Carlisle.

Riel wanted to be present for Lucy's time in London, but knew it was unlikely. It bothered him, for he'd promised Peter he would protect her at all times. Was he skirting his duty in order to protect his ship?

Logic told him she would be fine. Lucy had sworn she did not want to become involved with any men during this Season. Knowing this, Riel felt relatively certain the wolves would circle her, biding their time until next year.

Lucy had also agreed to be chaperoned, and had sworn she would spend no time alone with any young men. Riel did trust her, although he did not necessarily trust the young bucks of the ton. Warrington would be there, and Riel distrusted him; for more reasons than were perhaps fair. At the very least, he felt certain the man was a rake. Lucy, sweet, innocent and beautiful, would be choice prey for a man like Jonathon.

Fury surged in him at the thought. His fists clenched, and Riel forcibly ordered himself to relax.

No harm would come to Lucy. It would not. Riel tried to shut his mind to the thought of someone closing in on her with the goal of despoiling her innocence...of hurting her. His heart pounded harder, and his jaw hurt from clenching it.

He needed to be there. Much as he tried to convince himself that Lucy was in no danger—that it was only his past and his promise to Peter rising up to warp his mind—it didn't help. Riel felt a sick feeling in his gut. Lucy would be easy prey for a felon.

He strode to the mirror and forced himself to look himself in the eyes. They looked black and fiercely wild. Slowly, he relaxed, willfully focusing into the present.

The past was done. Desalt and the other man were dead. Lucy was in no danger like Pen had been. Maybe it was a good thing Riel would miss Lucy's Season. Ever since seeing Warrington, the past had flamed up, again and again haunting him. He might not be as objective as he'd like to be. In fact, he just might find trouble where none existed. Never did he want to make a mistake like that again.

Lucinda would be in no danger under Amelia's mother's eagle eye, nor under Sophie's, either. And, more importantly, Lucy had no intention of getting serious about any young man this year. So the potential danger would be minimized.

Next year would be the dicey one. Riel hoped for Bonaparte's defeat by then. Even if not, Riel would watch Lucy like a hawk every minute of next year's Season. Even if it meant losing his ship.

 familiar ₰ ₰ ₰ ₰ ₰

After Riel left for his ship and Sophie left for Iveny, each day at Ravensbrook seemed to stretch out into unbearably long and empty hours. Lucinda missed the chats she and Sophie had enjoyed over tea each morning in the conservatory. Mrs. Beatty was willing to talk if Lucinda lingered in the kitchen after breakfast, but afterward, the housekeeper attended other chores about the mansion. Lucinda felt very alone.

She cajoled Mr. Chase into teaching her more about Ravensbrook's accounts, but even that took up little of her day. Lucinda missed having someone to talk to.

She even missed Riel. Quite against her will, she remembered again and again how he had said goodbye to her, that day after Christmas. Of course, first he'd told Sophie goodbye in the parlor.

Afterward, Lucinda followed him outside to his carriage. She'd told herself it was because she wanted a breath of the crisp, fresh air.

After tossing his large bag into the carriage, Riel had turned to her, looking larger than ever in his black greatcoat. The blunt angles of his face seemed sharper that morning, his eyes blacker, his mouth sterner.

"Will you write?" she found herself asking. Then hastened to add, "So I will know when to expect your return."

"Will you write to me, Lucy?"

An unexpected flutter trembled through her heart. "If you would like me to, I will."

"I would." His quick response and the directness of that black gaze unnerved her.

"Very well, then."

"So agreeable." His lips curved, faintly mocking.

Their relationship had leveled out yesterday, and Lucinda was glad. Now she said pertly, "You are a difficult man to please. Do you wish for sugar or spice?"

He smiled then, a full one. "I like both, in equal measures."

Her heart pounded unexpectedly fast. Feeling slightly daring, she extended her hand. "Then here is the sugar, Mr. Montclair."

His warm fingers closed around hers, and to her shock, he raised her hand to his mouth. The touch of his lips warmed her skin like fire. He lowered her hand a little, but still held it. "And the spice?"

Lucinda's face felt hot, and she tugged at her hand. "Release me, or I will show you!"

He chuckled, and released her. "There is my Lucy. I will miss you."

Lucy felt quite unable to say anything at all. His Lucy? She was not *his* Lucy! Except, why did she watch his carriage until it disappeared into the forest? Why did her life feel so empty without him in it?

She was bored, that was the problem, Lucinda told herself as the days crept by from January to February to March. She spent occasional afternoons with Amelia and other friends, and while those times were fun, it didn't remedy the despondency in her spirit.

She did not miss that maddening man. He hadn't even had the decency to write her one letter! She'd posted two. Both newsy tidbits, but nothing of a personal nature. One she'd carefully signed, "Your obedient servant, Lucinda." The description made her snort with laughter, and she felt certain he would catch the irony she intended. If he received them. If his ship had not sunk, and he was not at the bottom of the sea.

Lucinda tried not to dwell upon these stomach turning possibilities. He was fine. He was Riel, larger than life, and in command of every situation. No one would dare fire upon his ship. ...Would they?

Lucinda wrote weekly to Sophie, too, and Sophie replied nearly as often. Her handwriting looked spidery, and sometimes shakier than others. She claimed she was fine, but little hints told Lucinda that all was not as it should be. Once, Sophie mentioned the doctor had been out twice in one week. One time she mentioned lying abed and being bored to tears. Lucinda worried about Sophie's health. And she wondered if Sophie would be able to make it to London for the Season.

Lucinda finally wrote Sophie in the middle of March, when she was so bored one day she couldn't stand it any longer, and asked if she might visit Iveny for a little while.

That was when Sophie wrote her the truth. She was not well enough to receive visitors, and she would be unable to make it to London.

Chapter Eleven

May, 1813

ON MAY 1ST, Lucinda packed up the new dresses the village modiste had made for her, along with various cases, valises and her reticule, and traveled with Amelia and her mother to London. She was excited to finally be able to go, short as the Season would be for her, but she still was worried about Sophie. At least Riel's great-aunt felt well enough to invite Lucinda to stay for a week after her visit to London was over. Lucinda had quickly and gratefully accepted.

Lucinda and the Carlisles arrived at the rented townhouse on a warm London afternoon. Amelia's family, while titled and owned land in the country, was not rich. One month of renting a townhouse in London was all they could afford. Lucinda had offered to pay for her room and board, but they would not hear of it.

Amelia was terribly excited that Lucinda could stay with them. On the night of their first ball, she exclaimed, "I'm so glad you're here! We'll have such fun. And maybe some of the young men who flock to you will grant me a dance, as well."

"Pooh," Lucinda said. "You'll have your own string of suitors, just begging for dances."

Amelia rolled her eyes to the ceiling. "Please. In a perfect world, that may be so, but we both know the truth. I can bear it. Now tell me, who do you think will be there tonight?"

The girls giggled over possible lists of attendees while Effie and Amelia's maid, Betsy, finished their upswept hairdos.

Amelia wore a deep purple creation that complemented her light brown hair, while Lucinda wore aqua blue. She hoped the village modiste had truly made the silk gown in the latest fashion. If not, then Lucinda intended to order several additional new dresses during her stay in London.

"Girls!" called Lady Carlisle. "We're ready to go."

The Marquis of Elderidge's house overflowed with fashionably dressed people.

"Lady Victoria told me this is *the* ball of the Season," Lady Carlisle whispered as they made their entrance. "Everyone who is anyone will be here."

"What a coup," Amelia said under her breath. "And perhaps arriving late in the Season will deliver us a useful advantage."

"What do you mean?"

"By now they're likely bored with one another. We are fresh faces. Fresh fodder for the rumor mills. Look." She nudged Lucinda's shoulder. "They can't help themselves."

Lucinda noticed the elderly matrons staring at them. They sat in chairs with their backs to the wall. Carefully coiffed gray hair jiggled as they bent their heads to one another, whispering assiduously.

Despite herself, she giggled. "You are awful, Amelia. But perhaps you are right."

"Ladies." Lucinda immediately recognized that smooth tenor and whirled.

The Duke of Warrington was just as handsome as she remembered. He wore a crisply tailored, chocolate tailed coat, and buff breeches with highly polished shoes. He bowed over their hands, but lingered over Lucinda's. His green eyes looked deeply into her own. A flash of mischief lurked in them. "Now the Season may begin."

Lucinda blushed, but beside her, Amelia snorted. "We're wise to your tricks, cousin. Save your practiced charm for the dimwitted ladies."

"It is not flattery when it is the truth, cousin. Lady Lucinda, may I be the first to sign your dance card?"

"Of course." She hoped she sounded polished and sophisticated.

"May I be so bold as to take two?"

"I would be pleased, your grace."

"Jonathon," he rebuked softly. "And may I still call you Lucinda?"

Lucinda smiled, trying to appear both worldly and confident. She wasn't certain how well she pulled off the fiction. "Of course."

A swarm of young men soon descended upon Lucinda and Amelia. Some were tall, and some short. Some were nice looking, some merely foppish. A few fumbled over their tongues in their eagerness to sign Lucinda's dance card. Many signed Amelia's, as well. A faint blush tinged Amelia's cheeks when a stocky, but good looking, blond young man asked to sign her card before he asked to sign Lucinda's. Lucinda felt pleased for her friend.

The evening twirled away in a delicious progression of sparkling lights, sumptuous food, and unending dance partners. Lucinda was relieved to discover that her modiste had done her proud. The aqua silk gown matched, to the minute, the highest fashion.

Lucinda had never enjoyed herself more. It was just what she needed after the long, uneventful months at Ravensbrook.

The Christmas ball flitted through her mind. So did the man who had claimed the last dance. Riel was not in London and she was glad, she told herself. She did not miss him. Not at all.

Lucinda forced the image of her dark guardian from her mind.

Of all the men she danced and chatted with that evening, she liked Jonathon the most. He had a sharp wit—cutting, sometimes—but he was always unfailingly courteous to her. He'd claimed the supper dance, so Lucinda sat beside him during the evening meal.

"This is not your first Season," he said. With excellent manners, he cut a bite of meat.

"No. I was seventeen last year, but halfway to eighteen. My father agreed I could come early with a friend of mine."

"And now you are a beautiful young lady, fully grown."

A blush warmed Lucinda's cheeks.

"Where is your saber rattling guardian this eve?" The Duke asked casually, but Lucinda sensed his sharp interest.

"He is on his ship, fighting the French."

"I understand he is half French."

"Yes. How did you learn that?"

Jonathon cut another portion of meat with swift, deadly slices. "I have my sources."

Lucinda eyed him with caution. "Why are you so interested in the Baron?"

"I want to be sure you are properly cared for. That is all. If he is absent, perhaps I could be of assistance. I would be happy to warn off any threatening tigers."

Lucinda smiled. "And who would save me from you?"

He chuckled sharply, as if her question caught him by surprise. In that moment, his teeth vaguely resembled fangs. "How right you are. But I will sheath my claws to assist a maiden in distress. I plead on my honor that you may trust me."

Now his teeth merely looked normal again. Lucinda decided she was becoming fanciful. "Thank you, my lord, but Lady Carlisle is chaperone to both Amelia and to myself."

"And what if a young man tries to whisk you into the garden? Will Lady Carlisle beat him with her reticule?"

"No. But I would kick him. I assure you, my father taught me how to inflict grave bodily harm upon a man."

Jonathon chuckled again, but with clear delight now. He raised his glass. "Lady Lucinda, you are a rare treasure. You will enlighten this boring Season no end."

"Thank you...Jonathon." Lucinda felt more at ease now. She had drawn a line and the Duke had laughingly agreed to toe it. *See, Riel,* she mentally told her absent guardian. *I don't need you after all.*

The rest of the evening passed quickly and enjoyably. Only one thing disturbed Lucinda. Although she had no desire to choose a husband this year, none of the young men she danced with came close to fitting the bill. Some appeared to be in love with themselves, and talked ad nauseam about their card games and other exploits, some were tongue-tied—perhaps she should give them another chance—and others appeared to be dandies or rakes, and again, full of themselves.

Perhaps she'd judged them too harshly. Still, the only man capable of providing interesting conversation appeared to be Jonathon. It pleased Lucinda to dance the cotillion, the last dance of the evening, with Amelia's cousin. The evening ended with laughing good humor.

On the carriage ride back to the townhouse, Lucinda said to Amelia, "Well? Did you find any interesting men? What about the blond one?"

"Oh, he was nice. He even asked for another dance after my card was filled. Perhaps next time." Eyes glowing, Amelia looked out into the night. "What about you?" Her voice sounded dreamy.

"Not so lucky, I'm afraid. I found fault with all of them, except for Jonathon. Perhaps I am too picky."

Amelia turned with an arched brow. "Do *not* get caught up on Jonathon. He is a rake of the first order."

"I know you're probably right. But the others seemed...I don't know." Lucinda sighed.

"Boring?"

"Yes."

"What are you looking for?" Now interest sharpened her friend's tone.

"I don't know. A man capable of talking of matters besides cards or fencing would be nice."

"You want an interesting man. A strong man?"

That description instantly brought Riel to mind. "No."

Amelia smiled. "Of course not. Then who do you think you want, then?"

"I don't know. Perhaps I'm being too particular. Maybe I need one of those card playing men, after all. They'd happily live at their club, and I'd run Ravensbrook as I see fit."

Amelia snorted. "And what of love? Doesn't that enter your marriage equation?"

"Love would be nice. But I must be practical."

"You want a man you can boss around?"

"Must you be so vulgar, Amelia?"

"I am asking a question. Do you want a man you can lead around by the nose?"

Lucinda gasped at her plain speaking friend's nerve. "I don't know. I'd never thought about it before."

"Choose one of those men *only* if you want to be bored for the rest of your life," Amelia advised. "For me, I would go for the spark."

"Spark is a bundle of trouble and maddening to boot. In fact, I would sooner tie a stone around my neck and jump in the middle of the lake," Lucinda retorted at once, knowing her friend referred to Riel. "I will allow no man to rule me, Amelia. Never will I submit to one of those bossy, arrogant creatures. Of that, you may be sure."

"Mmhm." Amelia had the audacity to grin. She gazed out the window again, doubtless dreaming of her blond-haired Prince Charming. Probably he was all goodness and light, contrasted with a certain pirate's black charm.

Amelia believed Lucinda felt a spark of attraction for Riel. Her friend couldn't be more wrong.

Lucinda crossed her arms and left Amelia to daydream of happily-ever-afters with her prince. Real life would never be so simple, but Lucinda did not say so. She didn't want to crush her friend's naive, romantic dreams.

ક્ષ ક્ષ ક્ષ ક્ષ ક્ષ

May whirled by. Still Lucinda received no letter from Riel. To be sure, she no longer expected to receive one. How would the post find her in London, at the Carlisle's rented townhouse? Besides, if Riel returned unexpectedly, he would likely dock in London. Perhaps one day he would arrive out of the blue and crash her wonderful party.

Lucinda told herself not to think about her guardian. In fact, so far, Riel's guardianship was working out just fine. He was never present! It was all working out for the best.

Lucinda enjoyed every tea party, every fête, every supper and ball. Amelia did, as well. Lucinda thought she spied stars in her pragmatic friend's eyes. Either those, or tears. The blond young man—Fredrick—paid Amelia intermittent attention. When he spoke to Amelia and danced with her, Lucinda observed him to be attentive and charming. At other times, especially when he was talking to another girl, he behaved as though Amelia were invisible. Frequently he looked right through Amelia when walking by with another girl on his arm. Lucinda had never witnessed her friend feeling such wide mood swings; by turns elated and then despondent.

"If you ask me, he's too much trouble," Lucinda told Amelia in late May. They sat in Amelia's room. Only a week remained of their stay in London.

"But he truly likes me. When we are together, I can see the affection in Fredrick's eyes," Amelia sighed, with her elbows on the window ledge. She gazed—moonily, in Lucinda's estimation—outside. The street lamps cast warm light into the dark streets.

"He is not constant. It's like he wears different personalities for different people. Maybe he does like you," Lucinda conceded, "but he doesn't treat you as well as you deserve to be treated."

"As Jonathon treats you?" Amelia's tone sounded cutting. Clearly, Lucinda had hurt her feelings.

"I'm sorry, Amelia. But yes, like Jonathon. He's always charming and a complete gentleman. Never does he ignore either you, or me."

"At least Fredrick is not a rake."

"Isn't he? Amelia, he chats up every girl in the room." Lucinda bit the bullet and spit out the hardest words she'd ever needed to say. "He has even tried to flirt with me."

Amelia flew to her feet. Her gray eyes hardened to stormy ice, and she trembled. "Get out, Lucinda."

"I did not..."

"Get out!"

Tears stinging her eyes, Lucinda fled from the room. She hadn't meant to hurt Amelia, but she had spoken the truth. She wanted to shake Amelia free of the strangling web Fredrick wove about her friend's heart. Clearly, he was stringing Amelia along. Lucinda believed it would please Fredrick if every girl in the room fell in love with him. But clearly, Amelia refused to see this truth.

Lucinda didn't want Amelia to be angry with her, but she didn't want to apply platitudes to salve her friend's ego, either. Amelia deserved a nice young man, and Fredrick wasn't one. But how could she make Amelia see that for herself?

The days wore on. Amelia behaved in a stiffly polite fashion toward Lucinda. At parties, she boldly tried to claim more of Fredrick's attention. Lucinda detected contempt in the blond man's eyes. Did Amelia see it? If she did, she made no mention.

Two nights before they were to go home, a horrifying scandal broke. It reduced these dramas to the petty standing they deserved. Terror swept through the gentry of London.

Chapter Twelve

TENSION KNIT Riel's muscles tighter, and his temper shorter, as May arrived and slowly dragged by. His heart told him he belonged with Lucy. An ineffable sense of unease nagged at him, accusing him that he was not where he had promised to be...protecting her.

Why did he feel like some dark presence encroached upon her, even now?

Riel threw himself into the multiple tasks necessary to captain his ship and accomplish the Royal Navy's commands. He pushed *Tradewind* harder, faster, and demanded the impossible from his men. On several occasions, he reduced the Royal Navy's Lieutenant Commander aboard his ship to silence by roaring at his men to comply, and be quick about it.

Riel didn't like himself, but he needed to return to London, and now.

At long last, the Lieutenant Commander appeared satisfied with the intelligence they had gathered, and Riel set aloft his fastest sails and scooted for home. His gut told him it could be too late. His heart prayed it was not...and he prayed for Lucy's protection.

Again and again he swore to himself that next Season he would not leave her side for one moment. Was she all right now? She had to be.

During that swift passage from the French coast to London, Riel read and reread his letters from Sophie and Lucy. Worry for his great-aunt bedeviled him, too. He knew she had been unable to travel to London, and so he knew Lucy lived with the Carlisles now.

Only reading Lucy's letters eased the knot in his stomach— and then only for a few moments. They made him smile. Clearly, she had tried to write prim and proper missives, but she couldn't prevent her feistiness from sparkling through. He especially liked the way she'd closed her letters. His humble servant? His *obedient* servant. Riel chuckled softly at that thought, imagining the wicked gleam in her eyes when she'd penned it.

He missed her; and more than he had expected.

Spray hit his face now as *Tradewind* leaped and plunged through the waves, heading for London. Soon. He estimated docking by six that night.

Not soon enough for him. Not soon enough at all.

He climbed below to finish preparations so he could leave the ship the instant she docked.

But it was seven o'clock before Riel finally leaped free of his ship and strode for downtown London. He had no idea where Lucy might be, but he had a few contacts. It shouldn't take long.

"Extra, extra!" chirped a grubby newsboy on a street corner. "Special edition, guv'nor."

Riel glanced down at the paper and stopped dead. Black headlines screamed, "Debutant Raped and Battered."

Riel ripped the paper from the unsuspecting lad. "When did this happen?" he roared.

Fright widened the boy's eyes. "Don' know, guv'nor. I canna read."

Riel fished coins from his pocket—double the price of the paper. "Keep the change," he mumbled. Striding fast again, he flipped it open and read,

A well-heeled debutant of the ton was abducted
Wednesday night and raped. The dastardly attacker
blindfolded the helpless woman. When finished soiling
the lady of high station, he released her to wander the
dark streets of London alone, hands tied, and
blindfolded with a silk scarf. The kindness of strangers
returned her home. Constables report the girl's clothes

were soiled, and her mind apparently broken when they
attempted to interview her. She could not tell them
where she had been, nor who had taken her. For the
protection of her family, the lady's name has been
withheld.

Panic clamped like a vise around Riel's heart. Was he too
late? Had Lucy been attacked and raped?

Where was she? He broke into a run. If Riel didn't know for
certain that two people were long dead, he would think this was
a repeat of Morocco, twelve years ago. Not as deadly, but just as
evil.

A predator of women stalked London.

Why hadn't he listened to his gut? Why hadn't he been with
Lucy? He'd broken his promise to her father. He had failed yet
another innocent woman.

Riel ran faster, his breaths tight and nearly choking his
lungs.

Please let her be all right! Please.

He would do anything...*anything* to learn that Lucy was
safe.

✎ ✎ ✎ ✎ ✎

Lucinda and Amelia sat close together at the sparsely
populated ball. Lucinda tried to ignore the trickle of fear sliding
through her nerves. Is was the last ball they could attend this
Season. Surely the rapist wouldn't show up here, of all places.
The legendary Bow Street Runners must be hunting him by
now. This logic didn't relax the unease she felt.

Lady Carlisle had not wanted to come, but both girls had
insisted. When the butler and footman had agreed to guard
their carriage with a gun and an ancient sword, Lady Carlisle
had reluctantly capitulated.

Now Lucinda wondered if they should have bothered. Few
people had come; at least, so far. And those who had arrived
exclaimed in low voices about the horrific scandal. That poor,
poor nameless woman had been plucked from a ball such as
this only two days ago. A ball Lucinda had attended, which
made it all the more alarming.

"Strolling in the garden, no doubt," whispered some.

"Just what she deserved," whispered others.

Lucinda felt appalled. What woman deserved to have a man force himself upon her? Or to be dumped to wander the pitch black streets alone? She shuddered, and rubbed her calf, to which she'd strapped a butter knife with a narrow pink ribbon. If attending high society functions proved to be a dangerous sport, she would be prepared.

"What are you doing?" Amelia whispered. At least now they were talking.

Lucinda lifted the edge of her skirt an improper few inches. "I'm prepared," she hissed. "If a man wants to come after me, he will lose choice body parts."

"With a butter knife?" Amelia snorted. Unexpectedly, she hugged her.

Lucinda hugged her back, and tears threatened. When she pulled away, moisture glistened in her friend's eyes, too.

"I'm sorry, Lucinda, for the snit I've been in. I was petty and jealous."

"And I'm sorry for doubting if Fredrick cares for you."

Amelia shook her head. She dabbed her nose with a hanky. "No. You were right. Look. There he is. He's been here thirty minutes, and still hasn't acknowledged me. I'm afraid you were right about him."

Lucinda didn't want to be right. She wanted her friend to be happy. Unfortunately, Fredrick was not the man to accomplish that goal.

Jonathon arrived soon after, and twirled Lucinda away. More people crowded in as dusk deepened to nightfall. In fact, now it looked as if the ball might be better attended than any other function to date.

People probably wanted to gossip, Lucinda uncharitably guessed, as she danced with a dandy. Or old dowagers wanted to count heads and guess who the fallen debutant might be.

A loud disturbance registered near the entrance. Women gasped, and heads turned.

"An invitation, sir," bleated the butler.

But the man, a tall, black-haired one, dressed in a rumpled black jacket and partially unbuttoned shirt, strode unhindered into the room.

Shocked, Lucinda's dancing feet stilled.

Riel!

He swiftly scanned the room, looking...looking, and then she felt—like a lightening bolt through her body—when those black eyes found her. He headed for her, his pace fast and deliberate, plowing through all the people in his path. His bristled jaw needed a razor, his skin was tinged gray, and his black eyes burned.

Lucinda's heart fluttered into her throat and she stood frozen, unable to look away from the man advancing upon her.

"Riel," she gasped, when he was within two steps.

Now one step separated them. "Lucy!" It was a deep, harsh growl. "*Lucy.*" Now an agonized rumble. His strong hands gripped her arms. "You are all right?" Those black, scorching eyes scanned her from head to toe, and then returned to her flushed cheeks. "You are all right," he asked more quietly, but just as urgently.

Lucinda licked her suddenly dry lips. "I...I am fine, Riel. When did you return?"

As if suddenly realizing everyone stared at them, he tugged her arm, leading her toward the wall for privacy. He ignored the tiny, irritated throat clearing of her dance partner.

Lucinda sent a hasty, apologetic glance backward, and hurried along in Riel's fast wake. "Where are you taking me? What has gotten into you, Riel?" Finally, she stopped and dug in her heels. "Tell me this minute what you are about, dragging me off like this."

He spun to face her, so near to her that every nerve ending jumped in awareness of his close proximity. He had never seemed so large, or his eyes so black. He smelled of the sea, as if he had just left his ship.

"Why are you here?" she whispered.

"I am here because you are here, Lucy." An unknown emotion roughened his words.

"When did you arrive?" For the life of her, she could not stop staring at him, and made no effort to increase the space between them.

"An hour ago. And I came directly to find you."

Her throat closed under his intense, dark appraisal. What was he thinking? Why did her heart beat so fast? "Why?" she asked finally, faintly.

"Because I was worried!"

"You were worried? About me?" A warm emotion filled her up, so full it bubbled over. She smiled. "Really?"

"Yes, Lucy." His calloused palm cupped her jaw, but his touch felt gentle, belying his rough, raw appearance. Deep emotions roiled in his obsidian gaze, and her mouth felt suddenly dry. In that moment, Lucinda felt completely and utterly cherished.

She licked her lips. "I am well, as you can see."

His hand dropped. "When I saw the paper... *Lucy,*" he said in a low, vehement voice. "What are you doing at this ball?"

She felt momentarily bewildered. "Dancing? At least until you arrived."

"Truly." He sounded grim. "Then you have earned yourself a close companion for the rest of the night."

"What do you mean?"

"What do *you* mean, exposing yourself to danger? Attending a frivolous ball?"

Her temper flashed, evaporating the more tender emotions she had felt just moments earlier. "I am chaperoned. The butler and footman are armed."

Musicians struck up the waltz, and a gentleman appeared to Lucinda's left. "I believe I have this dan..." He faltered when impaled by Riel's black, dangerous stare. Without a word, the man melted in the direction of the punch table.

Riel claimed her hand and pulled her into his arms. His dance steps were not as smooth as last time. In fact, they seemed jerky, and tension thrummed through the thick, hard muscles beneath her fingertips.

She felt indignant with the liberties he presumed. "You are a barbarian," she hissed. "I will not dance every dance with you!"

"You will not need to. I will watch you every minute. And you may be sure each of your dance partners will know it."

Lucinda gasped. "You beast." And here she'd been all a flutter for an alarming minute, actually glad to see him! "The high seas have not improved your social skills."

"I care nothing about wagging tongues, Lucy. I care only that you are safe."

"Well, I am, and you are crushing me in your arms!" An exaggeration, but he had anchored her too close to his large body.

He allowed another fraction of an inch to ease between them. His dark eyes glittered down at her. "You are so unhappy to see me, Lucy?"

Unfortunately, she had been too happy to see him! Lucinda knew she should feel relieved that he'd so quickly resumed his dictatorial guardian role—that way she'd remember exactly who he was. Instead, disappointment licked through her.

"How can I be happy when you rush in and give me a tongue lashing? Then you yank me into your arms and begin dictating the rest of my evening. Which of those charming behaviors would you like me to applaud?"

They danced in silence for long moments. Finally, he said, "Shall we begin again?"

Lucinda bit her lip. "We have started over too many times to count, Mr. Montclair. Perhaps we need to accept that the road before us is rough. I see no peace in our future."

"Montclair again." He seemed to relax infinitesimally. "Moments ago, I was Riel."

He baited her. Lucinda turned her chin away, refusing to look at him.

The music slowed, indicating it would stop very soon. To her shock, Riel had the gall to pull her closer to him. She felt his warm breath slide into her hair. In a low voice, he said, "I thank God you are safe, Lucy. Know that is the *only* thing important to me."

And then he released her into her next partner's willing arms. But he was never far from her, not for the remainder of the evening. His watchful gaze followed her and the young men with whom she danced. Even Jonathon noticed.

"Your guardian has returned with a vengeance. If his eyes were knives, I would be flayed to bits by now."

"He doesn't approve of me being here. Not with what happened." It seemed inappropriate to speak of the scandal with a person of the opposite sex; and a Duke, to boot. Although she'd had no problem arguing with Riel about it.

Toward the end of the evening, she sat with Amelia and her mother for a moment to rest. Amelia wore a frown, and studiously avoided looking at one quadrant of the room.

"Has Fredrick been beastly again?" Lucinda asked with sympathy.

"No. He keeps asking me to dance, and I keep refusing."

"Good for you."

"He wants to confuse me. I won't allow it." Amelia pinned Lucinda with a sharp gaze. "On the other hand, there is no question what the Baron thinks of you."

Lucinda frowned at once. "He is an unmanageable pirate. A boor of the first order."

Amelia smiled. "Not the way I see it. He crashed the ball and charged straight for you, mowing down everyone in his path. Very dramatic, if you want my opinion."

"I do not. Besides, he made it clear he thinks me a ninny-headed fool, coming to a 'frivolous ball'—his words—with a rapist on the loose. He chewed my ear off for the first five minutes."

"And for the next five?"

"I chewed his ear off," Lucinda admitted.

Amelia looked to the ceiling, as if imploring God for wisdom. She shook her head. "You're deceiving yourself, if you think that's all it's about between you two." With that cryptic remark, she fell silent, and watched Fredrick approach out of the corner of her eye.

Riel appeared, and with a bow gravely asked Amelia to dance. She accepted with a happy smile. Lucinda twirled away with her next dance partner, and Fredrick was left standing alone, looking displeased. Poor boy, Lucinda reflected with no pity. Now he would have to find a new victim.

❧ ❧ ❧ ❧ ❧

Riel accompanied the Carlisle coach to their townhouse, and then spent a moment talking to Lady Carlisle before signaling for a carriage. Lucinda wondered what the discussion had been about, but told herself it didn't matter. She didn't care if he returned to his ship and she never saw him again.

A lie, and she couldn't deny it. The fact disturbed her.

The next afternoon, Lucinda attended her last tea party, and then it was time to pack up. Effie did most of the work, but Lucinda chose the items she'd need for the trip to Iveny, and the maid packed these last bits into two trunks. The Carlisles had agreed to drop Lucinda off at Iveny for the promised visit to Sophie on their way home. It was out of their way, but it could not be helped.

On Sunday morning, Lucinda joined her trunks and valises in the parlor and watched the Carlisle footman pack up the carriage.

"That's it," he said, picking up Amelia's last valise.

"What about my things?" Lucinda said.

The footman didn't hear, but Amelia, just entering the room, did. "Didn't Mama tell you?" A wicked glint lurked in her eyes. "The Baron has offered to drive you to Iveny, since he's going there himself."

Lucinda's brows drew together. "Why is this the first I've heard of it?"

"Would you have been happy to learn of it sooner?"

"No."

"Exactly my point. You tend to react rather dramatically to anything to do with Baron Iveny."

"That is true," Lucinda admitted with chagrin. "But I wish you'd told me, Amelia."

It would have been even better if Riel had consulted her about the driving arrangements. Instead, he'd managed her like a child, as if she possessed no thoughts of import on the matter.

"I'm sorry. Will you forgive me?"

Lucinda sighed. "Of course." She felt vaguely disgruntled that the Carlisles must have believed she'd pitch a histrionic fit regarding Riel driving her to Iveny. Why else delay telling her the truth? Was her behavior toward him so untoward?

Perhaps so, she realized with further discomfort. Well then, time to change matters. Time to prove to everyone, including Riel, that she was a mature young woman.

She reminded herself of this yet again when Riel pulled up in his black carriage minutes later. Irritation still simmered in her, although she could not fully explain why. He leaped with quick agility from the carriage, and took the steps up to the townhouse two at a time.

With a determined smile, Lucinda advanced toward her guardian, who darkened the doorway. She dropped him a curtsey. "Mr. Montclair. How pleased I am to see you this morn."

His lips twitched, and he offered a half bow. "As I am to see you, Lady Lucinda."

"Such manners," Amelia said with an arch grin. "Perhaps hope exists for the two of you."

Lucinda bit her tongue, but continued to smile.

Goodbyes were said, and tears shed, although Lucinda and Amelia laughingly reminded each other they only lived a quarter day's drive away. Lucinda invited the Carlisles to dinner when she returned to Ravensbrook. With this satisfactory arrangement, they waved goodbye. Effie left with the Carlisles, for Lucinda had promised her a week's vacation after the Season. Effie wanted to visit with her family and her sister's new child.

Iveny was a full day's journey from London, and Lucinda applied herself to working a small tapestry. Needlework was not her choicest occupation, but it beat quarreling with Riel, which she disturbingly wanted to do. Clearly, if she wanted to become a serene, mature young lady, she should avoid speaking to her cavalier guardian altogether.

After replying with a polite smile and monosyllabic words to his initial attempts at conversation, he sent her a narrow look and then, to her satisfaction, left her alone. He spent the morning reading *The Times*.

As she absently worked the tapestry, Lucinda wondered how Sophie fared. In her letters, Sophie had insisted that she would feel better once the weather warmed up, and Lucinda hoped she was right. She wanted nothing more than to find Sophie as chipper and full of life as she'd been when she first arrived at Ravensbrook, almost a year ago.

They stopped for lunch at a small coaching inn named the White Hare. Lucinda observed it to be clean, and after she had refreshed herself, joined Riel at a table near a low burning fire.

Bread and a cup of tea awaited her. "Thank you. Have you ordered for me, as well?"

"Did you want me to?" Those black eyes looked amused, and a touch guarded.

Argumentative words leaped to her lips. All morning they had simmered, much as she had tried to ignore them and beat them into submission with fierce pricks of her embroidery needle.

Why did she still feel so perturbed? After all, it made complete sense for her to ride with Riel to Iveny. That did not bother her. What bothered her was that Riel had not discussed the matter with her at all, or even informed her of the new plans. Instead, he'd ignored her and made arrangements directly with Lady Carlisle; as if Lucinda were a parcel to be juggled until a convenient means of delivery was found. She felt managed and ignored. It bothered her, although she did not completely understand why.

The sarcastic attitude she'd fought all day unfortunately won the battle for her tongue now. "Does it matter, Mr. Montclair? It's your nature to take command of every situation, is it not?" She didn't give him time to respond. "I assume you know which morsels would most please my palate."

"Lucy," he growled.

"What?" Her eyebrows arched.

The waitress arrived, and Lucinda ordered steak and kidney pie. She folded and refolded her damask napkin lying on the table until Riel ordered a pork roast and the waitress left them. Then Riel's large hand covered hers. "Lucy."

Shock rippled through her—mostly because a lightning bolt seemed to sear from his skin to hers.

"How dare you..." Ineffectively, she tugged to free herself.

"Lucy." His grip tightened. "I want peace between us."

Lucinda's face burned as she imagined the others at the inn staring at them. Perhaps...horror of horrors...presuming them man and wife! She hissed, "Unhand me at once."

"Listen to me."

Lucinda kicked his boot. A flush rose on his cheekbones. Never before had she created that desired effect. Finally, she might win one of their confrontations. "If you will be brutish, so will I," she warned. "Now, unhand me."

His black brows drew together, and his other hand captured her free one. "I want to speak, not fight, Lucy."

She jerked discretely at her captured appendages. Mortification arose. Now people *were* staring! "You are making a spectacle," she snapped.

He watched her for a moment, his frustration and incomprehension clear. He could not understand why she disliked being manhandled? Let's see how he liked it.

Lucinda kicked his shin hard beneath the table. "I do not like being groped, Mr. Montclair. Release me at once. Before more people turn to frown upon your behavior."

A dangerous glint hardened those black eyes. "You have not seen a spectacle, Lucy. Would you like me to make one?"

She gasped, and her cheeks flushed hotter. Who knew what depravities lurked in his black, barbarian's heart? She could well imagine a pirate like him throwing her over his shoulder and mounting the stairs, as if to the rooms above, just to mortify her into submission.

"I hate you!" she choked out. "I hate you with every fiber in me!"

He released her hands, and she instantly tucked them into her lap and refused to look at him. Tears burned in her eyes, but she refused to let them fall, either.

The waitress arrived with their meals and Lucinda poked at the steak pie with her fork. Her stomach growled, so she swallowed the lump in her throat and forced down a few bites. Iveny was still hours away. She would not starve in the meantime, simply because this man chased away her appetite.

"Lucy," he said after a while.

"You have no respect for me. Kindly leave me in peace."

They finished the meal in silence, and returned to the carriage. Riel made no attempt to speak to her, and Lucinda told herself she was glad. She swallowed the welling lump in her throat, pressed her nose to the window and watched the countryside roll by. Riel, to her surprise, fell asleep.

As the carriage bumped over the country road, Lucinda cast occasional glances at him. Asleep, he looked younger, and more vulnerable. The strong lines of his cheekbones and jaw looked softer.

Lucinda abandoned looking out the window and studied him more closely. Gray shadows smudged beneath his eyes, and weary lines bracketed his mouth. He looked exhausted, simply and plainly, and her heart went out to him.

She had not asked how his mission with the Navy had gone. In fact, she had asked nothing about him at all. Instead, everything, from the time he'd erupted into the ball until now had been about *her*. Riel being worried about her. Riel watching her every dance partner like a hawk. Riel arranging to drive her to Iveny himself. Riel saying he wanted peace with her.

And she had deliberately taken offense to every real and imagined transgression he had committed, and attacked him for it.

Was she truly so ungrateful for his concern for her? Was she only concerned about herself and her own wishes? Or did she want to *find* reasons to argue with him?

The last explanation was correct, she finally admitted with a deep sigh, and looked out the window again. He needled fearfully under her skin. But she had pushed things too far at the inn. He'd only wanted to speak to her, but she had escalated it into a battle. She had acted like a spoilt brat. And all because she'd felt ignored in the travel arrangements.

Not her proudest moment. And a complete failure in her endeavor to become a mature young woman.

With an indrawn breath, Riel sat up and glanced out the window.

"Are we almost there?" Lucinda asked quietly.

The sleep bleary eyes focused on her and hardened, evidently remembering their latest fight. "Yes." And then, after long moments, he said, "I want to speak to you, Lucinda."

Lucinda. He was angry, surprise, surprise.

"Let me speak first," she said. He opened his mouth, but she said, "Please."

He acquiesced with a nod.

"I'm...I'm sorry." It was harder than she had thought to offer these words of reconciliation. Part of her *did* want war with him, she realized. It erected a wall between them. A wall behind which she could protect herself.

Her mind flashed to the ball, when he'd cupped her jaw so gently. Riel made her feel things she didn't want to feel...not for him. She drew a quick, unsteady breath. The feelings scared her, but they were no excuse to behave like a child, or a shrew.

"I'm sorry I started that silly fight. And I'm sorry I kicked you. Twice."

A little of the tension relaxed from his big frame. "You said I don't respect you. Why?"

He remembered, and had thought about it. Surprised, but pleased, Lucinda carefully chose her words. "You take liberties, and you don't ask. Like taking my hand at the inn. Or stealing a dance at the ball. Or arranging for me to come with you to Iveny, but you didn't even speak to me about it. I feel like my wishes mean nothing to you."

He sighed. "I am sorry, Lucy. I haven't treated my men any better this past month."

"Why not?" she asked softly.

He shoved a hand over his slicked back hair. "Because I've worried myself sick over you. I've failed both you and your father. I was not with you, where I had promised to be."

"I was fine. Lady Carlisle chaperoned me."

"A predator would not be thwarted by Lady Carlisle. I knew...I had a deep feeling you were in danger." Silent moments ticked by. "Your father asked me to protect you from the wolves, Lucy. And that is what I intend to do. Next Season, I will be your chaperone. You will live in my house, and you will go nowhere unless I am with you."

Her father had asked Riel to protect her from the wolves? What a strange request. It also explained Riel's fierce protectiveness at the ball. He thought he'd failed his duty. And he was afraid she had been hurt.

Duty. It explained his overbearing behavior then, and his autocratic words now.

A curl of unhappiness slid through her.

"I am not a fool, Riel. Did you think I would go off alone and make myself a target for a madman? And what if he's caught by next Season?"

"I will protect you, Lucy. Accept that now."

"I understand that you feel responsible for me," she said softly. "And I understand the promise you gave my father. But understand me, too. I do not want to be treated like a child. Discuss matters with me. Don't order me about. I'm nearly nineteen. Next year, with any luck, I'll be married. I am a grown woman, Riel. Treat me as one."

His gaze flickered over her face, and then brushed over her dress. Warmth touched her cheeks when those dark eyes met hers again. "All right, *chéri*. I'm sorry. I will treat you as an adult. As long as you behave like one."

"You will see only the very best in me from now on, Riel Montclair," she promised. And then doubt arose. "How long before you return to your ship?"

He chuckled. "Two weeks. Are you up for the challenge?"

"I am always ready for any challenge you throw my way."

He laughed aloud. "Now I am glad to be home, my feisty Lucy."

She smiled, and a bit of joy sprang free in her spirit. For now, they had come to an understanding. Peace for two weeks was possible. Right?

Chapter Thirteen

SOPHIE GREETED THEM at the door to Iveny, leaning on a cane. Her bright blue eyes sparkled as merrily as ever, but to Lucinda, she looked much older. Her skin looked translucent and papery, and the hand that touched Lucy's cheek felt dry. Lucinda hugged the older lady carefully, not wanting to throw her off balance.

"I am so glad you could come, my child. And Riel." Sophie turned her cheek for his kiss.

"You are well, Auntie?" His dark eyes scanned her with affection, but also with the same apprehension Lucinda felt.

"The warm weather has almost cleared up my cough, and I am as right as rain. Hilda has tea set for us in the parlor. Come."

Lucinda followed Sophie, and her gaze scoured the grandeur that was Iveny. White marble floors, old tapestries on the walls, and heavy wooden furniture in each room. Iveny exuded wealth and opulence. It was certainly far grander than Ravensbrook, and probably much older. And she had been worried that Riel might want Ravensbrook. A laughable idea now. He already owned a far better estate.

Lucinda poured tea for each of them. "The flower beds along the drive are gorgeous, Aunt Sophie."

Sophie smiled, and then coughed. It sounded low and congested, and alarm tightened around Lucinda's heart. Hadn't Sophie just said her cough was almost gone? At least a horrible coughing spell did not beset the older lady now.

After dabbing her mouth with a hanky, Sophie said, "I asked Henry to plant snap dragons this year. They are impertinent little flowers, aren't they? Popping and blooming bits at a time, or all at once, just as they've a mind to."

"I'm thinking about planting pansies this year." Lucinda was glad Sophie's cough had quieted. "What others do you think would do well, especially for that shady area near the terrace?"

"Azaleas are a good year-round plant. Perhaps I could come help you choose others. Perhaps some roses."

Lucinda set down her tea cup, surprised. "You want to come to Ravensbrook?"

"I would like nothing better." The old lady's eyes snapped. "Ravensbrook...and the company," she patted Lucinda's hand, "were most agreeable for my health and spirits last year. I'm thinking you can bring me to Ravensbrook, Riel, when you drive Lucinda home."

"You are sure, Auntie? It is a long trip..."

Sophie swatted his arm. "Am I senile? I know what I'm about. And I want another trip to Ravensbrook. But this time I'll return to Iveny in October. Perhaps after your birthday, Lucinda."

Joy welled up and Lucinda flung her arms around the older lady's neck. "Oh, Aunt Sophie! I'm so glad you'll come. Ravensbrook isn't the same without you. In fact, it was quite dull after you left."

Pleasure pinkened Sophie's cheeks. "Well, then. It is decided. Are you up for it, Riel?"

"Of course, Auntie. I wish only for you to be happy."

"Good!" Sophie coughed again, but only for a moment. "Now, while you are here, I have a few things I'd like you to look into, Riel."

Sophie listed a number of minor repairs that needed to be accomplished, and Riel agreed to complete these tasks, as well as check through the accounts.

"That will keep him out of mischief," Sophie twinkled at Lucinda. "Perhaps tomorrow I could show you my rose garden."

"I would love that." Lucinda slid a glance at Riel, who sipped tea out of a dainty cup. It seemed out of place in his large hand. The white of the porcelain contrasted sharply with his skin, revealing how very dark the sun had bronzed him. A raw vitality emanated from him; a stark contrast to his aunt, who looked so small, white and frail. Sophie's health was not as good as she wanted them to believe, but at least she seemed happy. Both she and her nephew possessed the same indomitable spirit.

Without thinking, Lucinda smiled at Riel. "I think I will be happy here."

After the barest hesitation, he offered a slow smile in return. It relaxed his features and warmed a place deep inside of her. "I hope you will, Lucy. Nothing would please me more."

A bubble of joy rose up and burst, spilling warm, golden sunshine over her soul. It felt good...perhaps too good. Lucinda wondered if peace with Riel might prove to be dangerous after all.

≪ ≪ ≪ ≪ ≪

Riel spent the next week tending to the many chores left delinquent during his long absence. He actually needed weeks to set everything in order, but did not have it. Soon he would have to return to his ship.

He spoke to Sophie's solicitor, accountant and various tradesmen he trusted to get the jobs done. He left the butler, a capable man, a list of items that needed to be finished, and felt certain that in time they would be completed.

He saw little of Lucy that week, except for at the supper meal. Every now and again, Riel wondered if she avoided him on purpose. But it didn't matter. He often saw her outside with his aunt, laughing and talking about something or other. Lucy's company did his aunt a world of good. Now more color thrived in her cheeks than when they had first arrived, but her cough was no better. At times it sounded so congested he wondered how she could breathe. One morning he took her aside and asked if she had the consumption. That was when Sophie told him the truth.

"No. It is bronchorrhoea. In addition, the doctor says I have dropsy, which means a failing heart. He approves me taking foxglove, but even that has its limits. I am getting worse, and nothing can be done about it. In the meantime, I will live life as I see fit."

"Auntie." Grief tightened his chest, but Sophie patted his arm.

"I've lived a long, full life, Riel. And I've been blessed to have you and Lucinda in my life. What more could I want?" She gripped his arm. "And do me a favor. Don't tell Lucinda. She's happy, and I want her to remain so. She's barely had time to deal with her father's death. The last thing she needs is to worry about an old woman like me."

Riel agreed, but Lucy was no fool. She knew something was wrong. She often eyed Sophie with a frown when his aunt wasn't looking.

Lucy rode a brown mare from the stables almost every day, too. The wind whipped color into her cheeks, and she looked beautiful. Riel wanted to ride with her, but found no spare minutes for leisurely jaunts.

The last night arrived, and Sophie and Lucy's cases were packed up in Sophie's coach. The three of them would ride in his carriage for Ravensbrook. By rights, it should be a two day drive, but Sophie wanted to make it in one. It may be more tiring, but they could rest all the next day.

When Sophie retired after supper, Riel went in search of Lucy. Part of him wanted to know if she had been avoiding him, after all. They had barely spoken all week. He missed her more than felt comfortable. And he'd missed their spicy confrontations, too.

The library door stood ajar, and in the corner of the room a lamp glowed on her bright hair. Lucy sat curled up in a deep chair near the window, obviously lost in a book.

He eased down on the arm of her chair, and she blinked up, startled. A flush kissed her cheeks. "Riel," she said softly.

He smiled. "Are you enjoying your book?"

"Yes. I'm trying to finish it before we leave."

"You could bring it with you."

"Oh." Obviously, this thought had not occurred to her. "Then perhaps I will retire." Closing the book, she rose to her feet.

"We'll leave early tomorrow."

"I know. Thank you." She stared at him for another inexplicable moment, and then said, "Goodnight, Mr. Montclair."

He did not like her sudden formality. "What happened to Riel?"

"It's improper, don't you think, between guardian and ward?" She slipped past him. "I will see you tomorrow."

Disturbed, Riel watched her go. He preferred their arguments to this prim and proper cool shoulder. Peace it was, as he had wished.

Maybe he did not want peace. He rose and strode after her. Maybe he did not want peace at all.

৵ ৵ ৵ ৵ ৵

Clutching her book, Lucinda hurried out of the library. What a close call! Her heart had fluttered most alarmingly when Riel had sat on the chair arm and loomed over her.

For her own peace of mind, she'd endeavored to avoid him all week. It hadn't been hard, as he'd been so busy. She still could not forget that tender moment at the ball, nor that slow smile he'd given her when they first arrived at Iveny. Both still unnerved Lucinda to no end. She found herself blushing every time he entered the room now. That would not do at all! So she'd avoided him. It seemed the most prudent thing to do. She slipped toward the staircase.

Bang! Bang!

A sudden pounding came at the front door, and the butler hurried into view, his night cap perched atop his head. Snatching it off, he drew himself to his full, short height, and with flourish opened the front door.

"An accident!" screamed a woman. "Fetch someone! Come quickly!"

Lucinda dropped her book on the stair and bolted for the front door. Riel reached it ahead of her. His deep voice sounded soothing and authoritative. "What happened?"

"The wagon overturned. Please, come quickly!"

Grabbing a lantern, Lucinda followed Riel and the butler into the pitch black night.

"See? There!" sobbed the woman. "My son. My *son!*"

A huge wagon lay overturned on its side, half in the ditch. The dirty white horse had managed to scramble to its feet, and stared at them with wild, rolling eyes. Under the back wheel Lucinda saw a leg. Horror choked off her breath.

Moments ago, she'd been reading in peace—at the same time this wagon had crashed. The same moment this woman's son may have died.

It did not seem possible. How could peaceful ignorance exist in tandem with tragedy?

"What happened, ma'am?" the butler asked.

"Oh, please, help him!" sobbed the woman.

Riel had already reached the large-timbered, massive wagon. But what could he do? It would take a small army of men to lift it off the still form lying beneath it. A small boy, Lucinda saw as she hurried closer. Perhaps eight or ten. His face was white, and his leg twisted at an awkward angle beneath the heavy wooden wagon.

Riel knelt beside the boy, and his large hand gently touched the boy's neck, checking for his pulse.

"He's alive," he reported. "But in shock. We'll need a doctor, and quickly. George, send a stable lad."

The butler ran toward the stables.

"But the wagon," Lucinda gasped. "How will we get it off of him?"

"I will lift it. Lucy, help the woman pull the boy out."

Before she could protest, Riel had stripped off his coat and shoved his sleeves up his arms. "Are you ready?"

"Yes. *Yes!*" cried the woman. "Please hurry."

Riel squatted a bit and with a grunt, slowly lifted the great, heavy timbered wagon as if it weighed no more than a large trunk. But the cords in his muscular forearms bunched and rippled as he waited for them to move the lad.

The boy moaned as they moved him, and his mother sobbed. Riel lowered the wagon again, carefully, after the boy was free, and then ripped off the boy's pant leg and examined the twisted limb with his fingers. "Broken in several places. He will be more comfortable inside, but it will hurt if we move him."

"We'll stay here," the mother decided, and Lucinda ran to the house for blankets and another lantern.

Long minutes stretched until the doctor arrived on his horse. He set the leg, amid the boy's pathetic screams of pain. Riel and the stable lads managed to right the wagon, but one wheel was broken. Finally, the doctor, boy and mother—the latter two upon a horse—moved down the lane toward the home of the little family. It turned out the woman's daughter was giving birth and that was why they'd been speeding down the lane in the night.

Lucinda felt shaken by the ordeal. She carried the lanterns, and Riel carried the extra blankets inside. The grandfather clock chimed midnight as George put them away and bid them goodnight.

Lucinda found her book lying on the step where she'd left it. "It's scary to realize how quickly something like that can happen."

"An accident?" Riel's gaze slowly scanned her face.

"Yes. I thought all was well. I was reading my book...and...and a tragedy happened just outside our door." Her lips trembled. "Sometimes I wonder what I was doing when Father died. Was I reading a book? Drinking tea? Laughing with my friends, all the while he lay in agony, dying?"

He said nothing.

Unexpected tears slipped down her cheeks. "I don't want that, Riel. I don't want the people I love to die, and not be with them!"

"What do you mean?"

"I don't know. I don't *know!*" she gasped, overcome with small, dry sobs. "I think of that poor girl in London. No one knew. She was all alone." More tears crept down her cheeks.

"Lucy." His arms closed around her. His strong, steady heart beat beneath her cheek.

She wept, not sure why she felt such agony of soul. "When...when Sophie dies I don't...don't want her to be alone!" She hiccupped and burst into fresh tears.

"Lucy." He held her tighter.

"I don't want to be alone either, Riel," she wept. "I don't want to be alone anymore."

"Lucy, you're not alone."

"Not right now, I'm not. But when Sophie leaves... I'm just selfish. I'm so selfish, Riel!"

To her gasp of surprise, he scooped her up into his arms. Frightened, she flung her arms around his neck. But he carried her with ease up the stairs. She felt the broad, powerful strength of him, and the thick muscles rippling beneath his linen shirt. He'd never put his jacket back on. One portion of her mind told her this was inappropriate. She should not be in his arms.

But she felt so safe.

To her further shock, he kicked open the door to her bedchamber and carried her inside. He lowered her to the bed. His brown eyes looked impossibly dark in the dim, flickering light of the candle.

"You are tired, Lucy. You need to rest."

His face was so near her own that she could touch it, if she had a mind to. She did. As if observing someone else, Lucinda watched her fingers rise and touch his stubbled jaw. It felt prickly and rough. Tentatively, she ran her fingers over it, feeling the texture.

His eyes closed briefly. "Lucy," he growled. He liked it. She could see he did by his fierce, tortured expression.

Suddenly shocked by her actions, Lucinda snatched her fingers away. "I'm sorry," she whispered.

"Sleep, Lucy." And then he was gone.

◈ ◈ ◈ ◈ ◈

Riel's response to Lucy's touch had been visceral and completely inappropriate. He lay awake far into the dark night, trying to force it from his mind.

At dawn, he'd found a thin excuse for it. He'd had little time for female company over the last few years, thanks to his unending responsibilities with the Navy. And he'd had none at all since becoming Lucy's guardian.

It did not matter. Lucy was his ward, period. The feelings he'd battled all night would die a quick death. Lucy deserved someone far better than he. He would be careful around her now—until all returned to normal.

As the sun crested the horizon, Riel dressed with quick efficiency and thought over Lucy's emotional outburst, too. He didn't want to think about Sophie dying, but it was clear his silence about his aunt's fatal health problems provided little comfort for Lucy. She knew something was terribly wrong. She feared Sophie would die, just like her father had. And so Sophie would, too, but no one knew when.

Pain gripped his heart. He didn't want Sophie to die, and he certainly didn't want her to die alone. He felt comforted and grateful that Lucy felt the same way. Coupled with Lucy's heartfelt cry that she didn't want to live alone after Sophie left Ravensbrook for Iveny again; Riel saw only one solution to both problems. He would talk to Mr. Chase about it first. Then he would present Lucy with a choice...a chance to take charge of her own destiny. He smiled. She would like that.

❧ ❧ ❧ ❧ ❧

By neither word nor action did Riel act like anything untoward had happened between them last night. Lucinda wondered if he had forgotten it, or if he'd dismissed it, thinking she was overwrought and had behaved irrationally. True enough on both counts.

She felt both ashamed and mortified, thinking about the way she had touched his unshaven jaw. The memory still burned into her fingers. She told herself this morning that she was grateful that Riel now treated her with reserved efficiency while footmen loaded the last of the trunks into Sophie's carriage. Then all three of them, plus Sophie's maid, settled into Riel's carriage and they started off. Lucinda would not think too closely on why Riel's detached politeness bothered her.

After a while, Riel decided to ride outside with the coach-man, and then Lucinda was able to relax more fully and chat with Sophie. The carriage seemed bigger without him in it, and the air more easily filled her lungs. As always, he disturbed her, and she was less sure than ever what to do about it.

They arrived at Ravensbrook in the dark, and everyone fell into bed, exhausted. The next day, Sophie's cough rasped terribly, and she could not get out of bed. Lucinda attended her, frequently popping in and out of her room to help her take sips of tea, to plump her pillows...anything to help ease her discomfort. It wrenched Lucinda's heart to see Sophie's dear face blue from the effort of trying to breathe, and to see her lying there looking so frail and weak. It didn't seem possible that she could gain the strength to overcome the horrible turn in her health, but amazingly, she did. After a few days, she sat up, drank her tea unassisted, and then, with Riel's help, she spent the mornings in her favorite spot on the terrace.

Relief eased into Lucinda's heart with each positive stride in Sophie's recovery. One day before Riel's scheduled departure, Lucinda found him in the library, frowning over the ledgers.

She hadn't seen much of him over the last few days, for he'd been riding thither and yon over the entire property, taking matters in hand. He hadn't been to Ravensbrook since Christmas, and it may be months before he returned again. Clearly, he wanted all to be in order before he left.

"Riel."

Riel looked up and a faint smile flickered. He rubbed his temple with his thumb. "Sophie is well?"

"She's fine." Lucinda came closer and noticed the dark smudges beneath his eyes, and the weary grooves etching the corners of his mouth. "Have you slept?" Then she blushed, realizing how inappropriate the question might sound. "You look tired."

"I am tired. I leave for my ship tomorrow, and I still have much work to do."

She moved closer, and noticed the uncharacteristic roundedness of his shoulders, another indicator of his exhaustion. He'd been pushing himself without relief since leaving his ship—at both Iveny and Ravensbrook—to ensure that all was in order. He'd surely driven himself relentlessly on his ship, too. And he'd return to still more work.

"Show me what to do," she said softly. "I want to help you."

"You have enough to do with Sophie. I plan to talk to her about hiring a nurse."

"Don't. She can't bear it."

The dark brown eyes regarded her. "Then all of the work will fall to you and her maid."

"I know. It's all right. And she's fine. I want to help you."

"Has Mr. Chase been teaching you more of the ledgers?"

"Yes."

"You have done a good job."

Pleasure warmed her heart. She moved closer, so now the desk edge bumped into her skirt. Lucinda touched the smooth, polished surface with her fingertips. "I'm ready for more responsibility. Will you give it to me, Riel?"

He pulled the Queen Anne chair close to him. "I have a list I've been meaning to go over with you." When she had settled beside him, his dark gaze pinned hers. "You will see it done?"

"Of course." She felt a tiny bit offended. "I have more than two thoughts to rub together in my head."

He smiled. "I know you do. But it's important a few of these jobs be completed by the end of summer."

"All right." Eagerly, she leaned forward and Riel explained in detail about each of the items on the list. Lucinda made notes so she would remember what he had said. All the while, she felt very aware of his close proximity, and the clean, spicy scent that was uniquely Riel. His tanned fingers moved over the parchment, pointing things out to her. She scanned his face as he spoke, and she realized she was trying to memorize every line, every angle...the exact color of his dark brown eyes...everything about him. Soon he would be gone, and she didn't know when—or if—she would ever see him again.

The last thought stabbed through her heart. Lucinda knew his work was dangerous. Much as he unsettled and even irked her sometimes, fear twisted in her heart at the thought of him being injured...or dying like her father had done.

Lucinda blinked back hot moisture and bit her lip as Riel finished his list. "Uh huh," she said, although she hadn't heard the last words he'd said.

He sent her a sharp look. "So meek, Lucy. So amenable to everything I've told you to do."

Lucinda stared at him, wondering if he meant to vex her. "Have you missed your daily tongue lashing, Mr. Montclair?"

He smiled. "You are wool gathering. I just told you to help Mrs. Beatty wash the dishes each night."

She gave him a mock glare and quickly wiped away a tear that wobbled over her lid. "I will be glad to see the back of you. You may be sure of that."

His smile faded. "Lucy..." His gaze followed the bright tear drop shimmering on her finger. More quietly, he said, "Are you crying over me?"

Lucinda stood, and brushed away more irksome tears. "I told you I can't wait to see the back of you. Why would you ask such a silly question?"

He stood, too. With a rough finger, he lifted her chin up, and his eyes traced the path of her tears. "At last we have peace, Lucy?"

"Until you return and begin bossing me during my next Season," she managed to retort.

"I will come sooner, if I can."

She swallowed hard. It would be a long time before she saw him again, and Sophie would leave at the end of October. So long to be alone. Why had she ever wanted to live at Ravens-brook by herself? Yes, she wanted to captain her own destiny, but Lucinda had discovered she did not like living alone. Sophie's bright presence and Riel's overwhelming vitality filled every corner of her home. When he was not there, she felt lonelier than she had ever felt before.

"Try not to get yourself killed," she told him.

"You eagerly await my return, and my unending demands during your Season?"

"I'll be relieved when I don't have to worry about you dying anymore."

"You care, Lucy?"

Her face warmed, but she didn't look away. "Perhaps. We have become friends, haven't we, Baron?" A testing of their relationship lived in those words. Also a small admission of how much he meant to her. She could barely admit the full truth to herself.

"Friends." He smiled a little. "I believe we are that, Lucy."

Lucinda smiled, but felt it was high time to change the subject. "Sophie is doing better. Do you think it will last?"

He watched her for a minute, as if considering his response.

She stepped back. "Your silence tells me the truth. How long have you known? Why haven't you told me?"

"Sophie didn't want to worry you."

"I'm already worried! I'm not stupid. I can see she's worse than last year. What is wrong with her?"

"Dropsy." When she stared at him without comprehension, he elaborated, "Her heart is failing, and is filling with fluid. So are her lungs. It's only a matter of time."

Lucinda's face crumpled. "No!"

"I am sorry." Pain etched his features. He felt the anguish deeper than she did, of course. It was his beloved aunt, after all.

"I'm so sorry, Riel." She sat down, her legs feeling shaky. "What can I do for her? Will she go any time?"

"Probably not soon. This winter may be her breaking point. It's always her worst time." He lowered his large frame onto the couch beside her. "I have a proposal for you."

She eyed him uncertainly. Apparently, it must be a request, so she could choose her response. "What is it?"

"I talked to Mr. Chase. He has agreed to keep all of Ravensbrook's accounts from November through next Season...should you decide to move to Iveny with Sophie in October."

"I could do that?" Cautious joy filled her. "Sophie wants me to come?"

"It would make her very happy. And me, too, to know you are there to watch over her."

"But what about Ravensbrook and the staff? Someone must keep watch over its affairs."

"I think with Mr. Chase, the new accountant he's hiring, Mrs. Beatty and Wilson working together, Ravensbrook will fare just fine."

"But it's for so long... But I don't want Sophie to be alone, either. I know she has her devoted staff and her friends, but..."

"No family."

"I'm not exactly family, am I?"

"To Sophie, you are."

Tears blurred Lucinda's eyes. "I feel honored that she thinks so."

"You are wonderful to her, Lucy. She told me you're like the granddaughter she never had."

Lucinda swiped the tears from her eyes. "I love her, too."

"You can give joy to her last months. If you won't do it for her, do it for me."

Riel would view it as a personal favor? Of course, Lucinda would move to Iveny for Sophie's sake alone. But she must explore this interesting avenue just a bit further. "Riel. Are you saying you would owe me? Of course I would do it for Sophie. But if you would be in my debt, too..."

His serious expression relaxed. "Any favor you wish. Just name it, and I will give it to you."

She smiled. "A valuable commodity. I will hold it until the perfect moment."

He smiled. "So it is agreed?"

"Of course. Thank you for thinking of it, and for arranging it."

"You are welcome, Lucy."

She stared at him for a moment, surprised by their amicable meeting of minds. "I never thought this day would come."

"That you could talk rationally with me?"

"That we could agree on anything," she returned with asperity. "Typically, you run over my wishes like a bull in a pottery shop."

"It is the difference between you waving a white flag or a red flag."

Surrender, in other words. With a snort of exasperation, Lucinda leaped up. "That has earned you the end of peace, Mr. Montclair!"

He chuckled and rose. "Your father would be proud of you, Lucy. I am proud of you, too."

Why did his praise warm her from the inside out? Why did she care what this pirate thought of her? And yet she did. She respected him and looked up to him, she realized with a flutter in her spirit.

"I will be in the garden if you have further requests to make of me, Mr. Montclair. Good day."

His maddening chuckle followed her out.

At last she had voluntarily acquiesced to his wishes. Her wishes too, she was honest enough to admit. Now she could spend the winter with Sophie. Neither of them would be alone. She felt grateful to Riel for arranging that neat solution to both of their problems.

If only her semi-amicable relationship with Riel could last through next Season.

Unfortunately, that seemed unlikely, especially if the rapist wasn't found. So far, no more crimes had been reported, but the Season wasn't over yet. One thing was for certain; if the rapist wasn't caught, and if she knew Riel at all, he would be on full alert next April, and certainly at his most overbearing and obnoxious.

If so, and if she wanted to live her life on her terms, and pursue the young men she wanted to pursue, then she'd definitely have her work cut out for her. Riel would likely become an unmanageable pirate if any suitors came sniffing too closely. That would prove quite unhelpful, for Lucinda felt determined to find a suitable husband next Season. She'd turn twenty soon after. Then Riel could go his way and her life would finally be her own again.

Depression slipped through her. It sounded perfect. The future she had always dreamed about. Then why did she feel so unhappy?

Chapter Fourteen

MUCH AS SHE TOLD HERSELF she was glad to see him go, Lucinda felt a thick lump in her throat when Riel finally drove off the next morning. No kisses on her hand this time. Just a quick climb into the carriage and he was off. It seemed like he couldn't get away fast enough.

...Although he *had* hesitated by the front door and looked down at her for a long, inexplicable moment before leaving. "Goodbye, Lucy," he'd told her in a faintly rough voice, and then descended the steps to his awaiting carriage.

Ravensbrook seemed empty without Riel. But Lucinda was happy that Sophie continued to feel good—at least, for the most part. Although Riel's aunt suffered more frequent, intense attacks than last summer, they passed quickly. The warm, unusually dry summer seemed to improve the older woman's cough.

They talked for hours about possible new plants for the garden, and then Sophie suggested Lucinda might plant a few rose bushes. Lucinda agreed to try one and see how it fared.

One morning, when Sophie felt particularly well, and her cough only occasional, they traveled to the village to choose a rose bush. It was late in the season for planting, but Sophie insisted it would survive just fine.

"Best yet, we'll see what color the blooms are," she said happily. Clutching her cane, the two traversed the small rose garden. Sophie lit upon a butter yellow rose.

"It's perfect!" she cooed. "I have long wished to find one just this shade."

Lucinda smiled. "Then let's take it."

They planted the rosebush with the gardener's help, and after the first few sickly days, it rallied and burst forth into brilliant blooms. With a gleam in her eye, Sophie proclaimed herself quite satisfied, and Lucinda promised to buy more roses next year.

Summer fled by. Damp, rainy weather set in and the days grew colder. Late October and Lucinda's nineteenth birthday arrived before she knew it. She invited Amelia and a few other friends over to enjoy a small party. Sophie's worsening cough prevented the older lady from attending, which was a dark blot on the occasion.

A letter for each of them arrived from Riel, too. Sophie was thrilled, and Lucinda read hers over and over again...short as it was. It simply said,

Happy birthday, Lucy. I will deliver to you a present of your choice when I return. May your day be as bright and beautiful as you are.

I remain
Ever yours,

Riel

His words warmed her. He thought her bright and beautiful? Better than a tantrumming, spoilt brat! Maybe he believed she'd grown up at last. Although Lucinda still didn't think she needed a guardian, she missed Riel. His absence left an aching void in her heart. How that could be when he irked her so much, she could not fathom, but there it was. Perhaps she was lonely, and wanted more people to talk to. In any case, now Riel owed her both a present and a favor. She would be a rich girl indeed when he returned.

However many long months from now that might be.

At the beginning of November Sophie's cough dramatically worsened, and they traveled to Iveny. Content, Sophie spent most of her days wrapped up in a blanket in the conservatory.

Lucinda made sure the fire always burned, for the warmth seemed to help Sophie's cough.

The days slowly passed. November slipped by, and then it was Christmas. Letters arrived from Amelia and Riel. Riel could not come home, but he mentioned the end of the war appeared in sight. Lucinda hoped so.

Amelia sent a newsy letter, and excitedly wrote that she and her mother planned to spend the entire Season in London. It would be Amelia's last Season, and her parents had decided the expense would be worth it. Amelia also mentioned, with many exclamation marks, that young Timothy Fenwick and his twin sister would attend, as well. In late March, both would turn eighteen. "Imagine all the sore, stomped toes! Miss you, but April will be here before we know it."

Perhaps the time would fly by for Amelia, but it did not for Lucinda. Sophie's health took a dramatic turn for the worse in January, and she could not get out of bed. Worried, Lucinda spent most of her days with her, reading to her, helping her eat, and just spending time together.

As Sophie grew grayer and sicker, so did Lucinda's spirits. Sophie's bright eyes dimmed, and Lucinda wanted to weep. Where was Riel? He needed to come home. Now. Before it was too late.

In February, she wrote a letter in care of Command Headquarters in Portsmouth, urging Riel to come home at once.

ക്ക ക്ക ക്ക ക്ക ക്ക

The long months at sea passed quickly for Riel; at least, for the most part. The days were full of daring sorties with the French, zooming close to spy on locations, and then fleeing from cannon fire. *Tradewind* suffered a wound to her upper deck. A repair fixed at sea.

They anchored at various small ports as the Lieutenant Commander directed, so the intelligence they gathered could be ferried to appropriate command centers. Never once did they dock in Portsmouth, although Riel did receive the letter Lucy sent—but not until March. The news weighed on his spirit. He longed to be home and see his great-aunt. And Lucy. He missed his feisty ward more than he'd ever dreamed possible. His heart ached when he thought of her, which was often.

And he was weary. Long days and nights at sea, combined with the unremitting stress and fear of discovery, meant Riel did not sleep well. When he did, especially on those darkest nights, he dreamed of Lucy.

In those dreams she always came as she had that day in the study at Ravensbrook, when he'd been exhausted and wondered how long he could drive himself without rest. She came as an angel to offer comfort to his tormented soul. Her smile applied the balm of peace to the stress he felt running in the shadows with the enemy each day, and flirting with the truth...seeking it, and finding it, as was his job. Searching out French locations and following clippers to their hideouts. A deliverer of spies and messages. Cloak and dagger. Secrets and truth. Much like the truth in his own soul that he wanted to keep hidden.

How long before someone discovered that secret at last? How long before he was exposed as a killer? He'd been afraid Warrington might expose him last Season. If not him, then someone else.

Darkness lived in Riel's soul; a blot that would never leave. Didn't it say somewhere—perhaps in the Bible, as he'd learned as a boy—that all hidden truths would be exposed? One day, his black secret would be uncovered. Lucy would find out. This certainty became stronger as the days stretched into March, and when the stress of his job and worry for his great-aunt felt like a sword through his soul.

Lucy still came to him in his dreams then, offering sweet comfort...but in the middle she always learned the truth of his past. Always her lovely face contorted with the contempt and condemnation he deserved. And always she fled from him, leaving him desolate and alone.

Forever alone. Riel woke from the dreams sweating and cold. Despair and hollow acceptance grew that one day the nightmare would come true. One day he would lose Lucy forever. But first, he would deliver her to a man worthy of her...who would enjoy her fire. Who would love her with his whole heart, as she deserved. Then, when he'd completed his promise to her father, it wouldn't matter if Warrington or someone else exposed his past.

Riel tried to fill the empty ache inside him with work, and more work, day and night. And he cherished the dreams when Lucy came to him and he could have her all to himself for a little while. Before the wolves tore her away from him forever.

One wolf, however, would never get his teeth into her. Warrington. As the time grew closer to the Season and the end of his work with the Navy, Riel grew more resolute on this point. He didn't trust Warrington, and never would. And his decision was based on more than what had happened in Morocco. That brother of a viper would never touch Lucy.

Chapter Fifteen

April, 1814

ONE MORNING in early April, Lucinda read to Sophie from the book of Proverbs. Sophie sat propped up by pillows all hours of the day and night now. It was the only way she could breathe. Her ankles and feet had swollen to three times their normal size, but the quilt covered them from view, protecting her fragile hold on dignity. The foxglove plant did not work as well anymore. And if Sophie took more, she felt nauseous and didn't eat. So Riel's aunt had decided to continue her original foxglove regimen. The alternative would only hasten her death.

Right now, Sophie's eyes flickered open and she appeared to be listening. This encouraged Lucinda to read on. When she paused to turn the page, Lucinda heard the front door close, and then the butler's voice in the hall. Then the rumble of a deep, accented voice.

Lucinda bolted to her feet. Riel!

She ran out of the room, Bible still in hand.

Riel. In the flesh, talking to George, the butler. Lucinda went very still and her eyes drank him in. Joy and relief washed through her. He stood larger than life. As always, bigger than she remembered. Still, he wore his black hair in that tail and a cravatless white linen shirt. His tan pants cut lean lines down his strong legs and his superfine, dark blue jacket emphasized the broad, muscular power of his shoulders.

In a flash, Lucinda remembered every time she had been close to him: dancing with him, and when he'd carried her up

Iveny's stairs, holding her close. She remembered the raw strength of him. The determined, unbending, indomitable force that was this man, her guardian.

Breaking out of her involuntary trance, she flew toward him. At that moment, Riel saw her. Those black eyes shot through her with the force of a cannon.

Her steps faltered, her heart thumping. "Riel." No other words came to her mind.

Without a word, he strode for her. A frown knit his brows together.

Lucinda stopped, confused, as he approached. Why was he frowning? Then he shocked her still more when he cupped her face with his big, calloused hands and his black gaze scanned every inch of her features. Her heart fluttered in her breast.

His warm hands felt comforting.

"Lucy, what have you done to yourself?" Concern rumbled in his deep voice.

She relaxed a bit. "Nothing. I've just been sitting with Sophie..."

"All the day, every day? Attending to her every need?"

"Yes."

Anger flashed. "Lucy."

She frowned back. "This is a fine greeting, Riel Montclair!"

"You look white and exhausted. Like death." His voice scraped like rough velvet.

She gasped and pulled free. "I do not!"

"You have not been taking care of yourself." His knuckles gently brushed her cheek.

Lucinda relaxed again and allowed her gaze to tangle with his dark one. He cared for her. At last, she understood him a little. That was why he behaved like a boor sometimes. She offered a tiny smile. "I missed you too, Riel."

A smile gentled the straight slash of his mouth. "And I you, Lucy." He leaned close and dropped a kiss on top of her head. "But you must take care of yourself."

Heart fluttering, Lucinda pulled back. "Sophie's worse. She requires a lot of care."

Determination steeled his features. "It is enough, then. I will hire a nurse for her."

"No!"

He strode toward Sophie's room. "How is she? I received your letter and came as fast as I could." He stopped in the doorway to his great-aunt's room. Shock, followed by anguish, contorted his features. Just as quickly, he masked it and knelt beside the bed. "Aunt Sophie." His tanned fingers enfolded her small, withered scrap of a hand.

Sophie's eyes opened and a spark flared to life—one Lucinda hadn't seen in weeks. "My dear boy," she whispered. "I...knew it must be you when Lucinda ran off like that."

Riel glanced at Lucinda, but she could not read his expression.

A paroxysm of coughing seized Sophie's frail frame. Tears burned in Lucinda's eyes by the time it finally quieted. Each time it happened she feared that Sophie would not recover, or that the fluid in her lungs would deepen so much that she would suffocate to death.

That helpless fear skewered worry through Lucinda again and again all day long, every day. The grief she felt, knowing she could do nothing for her friend but spend time with her was intolerable. This past winter, Lucinda had begun to pray more than ever before in her life; for Riel's safety, and for Sophie. If Sophie could not recover, she prayed that her last weeks would be happy, and that she would die in peace, surrounded by those she loved. At last, Riel had arrived home safely. One prayer answered so far.

"Do not speak." Riel's voice sounded rough. "Know this. I am home for good, Auntie. The war is over, and the Navy is finished with my ship."

Sophie smiled and raised her hand a fraction, grasping for Lucinda's, which she quickly held tight. "Lucinda has taken the best care of me. I am glad you're home, Riel. We both are."

Riel spoke a little about his long missions, and then Lucinda felt she should leave the two alone to visit. Quietly, she excused herself and retreated to her room to splash water on her face. Did she truly look so awful?

One look confirmed she did. Her eyes looked wide and sad, and her skin pallid. And she felt exhausted. She hadn't slept well in ages. Although Sophie's rooms were located downstairs, her cough woke Lucinda again and again, all night long, and knotted her heart with worry and fear. Sophie would not allow

Lucinda or her maid to attend to her at night. She said they needed their rest. True. But Lucinda still could not sleep.

Now that Riel was here, perhaps she could take a nap. Lucinda stretched out on the cotton quilt and instantly fell asleep.

✸ ✸ ✸ ✸ ✸

Riel joined Lucinda, who felt much refreshed, for supper. "It is arranged," he said. "Sophie has agreed to hire two nurses."

"Two?"

"One for the day and one for the night. You need your rest, Lucy."

Lucinda felt relieved. The nurses would know what to do for Sophie—more than she did, that was for sure.

After a swallow of wine, Riel said, "It's not necessary to hover by her bedside every minute of the day. It is not healthy."

Lucinda trembled with quick temper and slapped her napkin down on the table. "Says who? You?"

"You have done too much. Sophie's sickness is killing you, too." The gentleness of his voice undid her, and tears spilled down her cheeks. They came all too readily these days.

"I can't bear to see her suffer like this, Riel. I want to do something to help her feel better, but I can't. All I can do is talk to her or read to her."

"Continue to do those things, then. But take time for yourself, too."

Lucinda picked at her food. "Is the war truly over?"

"It is only a matter of days."

"Thank goodness."

"You are happy to have me home?" That dark gaze held hers, and she sensed a deeper question there. One she was not certain how to answer.

She *was* happy he was home. More glad, perhaps, than she wanted to feel. He still unnerved her more than she liked. And certainly, she still knew none of her enigmatic guardian's dark secrets, either. But she would speak the truth.

"Yes. I'm relieved you weren't killed or injured. And I'm glad you're here...to help me with Sophie."

"It has been a heavy responsibility. Thank you for taking such good care of her, Lucy."

"I would do nothing else," she said quietly.

"Your father would be proud of you. You have developed into a caring and selfless young lady."

"At last you admit I've matured? That I no longer need a guardian?" Her spirit quickened. She enjoyed baiting him. In fact, she had missed him terribly, she realized with a pang in her heart. She was so glad he was home.

He smiled, too, surprising her. "You need a protector. And I will be yours." Riel forked a bite of meat into his mouth.

"Jonathon calls you my saber rattling guardian."

"Good. Then he will keep his place," he said grimly.

Lucinda frowned. "I need to collect suitors, not scare them off."

"I will separate the wheat from the chaff."

"*I* will do that, thank you. I will choose my own husband." Then a thought that had been tugging at her heart for some time spilled out. "But perhaps I should wait until next Season to find a husband. I can't leave Sophie here, suffering and alone, while I go off to dance and flirt at frivolous fêtes and balls."

"You surprise me more every minute."

"That I have finally grown up?"

"Sophie wants you to go to London."

Lucinda blinked with surprise. "Did she tell you that?"

"Yes. She's afraid you will refuse to go. She asked me to insist, and to convince you to do so."

"But..." Tears sprang to her eyes. "I can't leave her here alone. I won't!"

"It is her wish."

"No. I will not."

Riel remained silent for a moment. "I do not know if she is well enough to transport to London."

"We do not need to transport her. I just said I will stay here. And that is the end of the matter." Lucinda bit off a crust of bread. Riel could not force her to go to London, and well he knew it.

"I will speak with Sophie about it."

Lucinda said nothing. In her mind, the battle was finished. For once, she would have her way, and Riel could do nothing about it.

❦ ❦ ❦ ❦ ❦

The next morning, Lucinda found Riel in Sophie's room. Their heads were close together, and they appeared to be deep in conversation. She stepped back. "I'm sorry. I'll come back later."

"No." Riel said. "This concerns you. I was just about to tell my aunt of your stubbornness, Lucy."

Sophie glanced from one to the other of them.

"Auntie, Lucinda refuses to go to London. She wants to stay with you."

A flash of tired spunk sparkled in Sophie's eyes. "Then pack up my paraphernalia. I'm going to London."

"No, Aunt Sophie! I am happy to stay here."

Weak and sick as she was, Sophie set her jaw in a stubborn line. "It is my last wish." She fixed Lucinda with her bright blue eyes. "Do not deny an old lady her dying wish."

"But you're comfortable here. And the move cannot be good for your health!"

Sophie coughed, long and painfully. Then, "What difference does it make? I am going to die, Lucinda. I would rather do it with you and Riel close by." She coughed for an excruciatingly long minute. Each sharp, wheezing cough felt as painful to Lucinda as a nail piercing her own heart.

Sophie continued on, as if uninterrupted. "And knowing you are enjoying yourself...will make it all the more palatable for me. You can come and tell me...all of the ton doings every day. It will cheer me considerably."

After this long, halting speech, Sophie coughed for another long minute, and turned an alarming purple. Helplessly, Lucinda stared at the obstinate older woman.

At last she said, "If you insist, Aunt Sophie."

"I do. Now, you and Riel arrange it all. I need to rest."

Lucinda kissed Sophie's forehead, and followed Riel out. After the door closed, she crossed her arms and glared. "*Now* are you happy? This trip will be the death of her. I just wanted to stay here and keep her company!"

"She wants you to go to London. Aren't her wishes important?"

"Of course. But she can't risk her health. I'll go, if she insists, but it would be best if she stays here."

"Did you not hear her? She has made up her mind to go to London. By now you should know that when Aunt Sophie makes up her mind, there is no changing it."

How well Lucinda knew this. She frowned at him. "Like a certain nephew of hers."

He smiled. "Exactly. Pack up. We'll leave day after tomorrow."

"But I have no new dresses!" Still, Lucinda dug in her heels.

"We will commission several made the moment we reach London. They will be my birthday gift to you."

Lucinda blinked. An extravagant birthday gift, and highly inappropriate, too. "It's not fitting for a man to buy a woman a dress...unless she is his wife." She then blushed hotly. Why had she said such a thing, and why did she blush so? It mortified her, but she glared at him, trying to hide it.

"I am your guardian. It is my job to see that your needs are provided." A faint grin tugged at his lips.

Aggravated, she said, "And you care nothing about social mores, do you? Pirate that you are!"

"I am a barbarian through and through, Lucy. It is the man I have become, and the man I will remain." His own man, in other words, and one who refused to be swayed by society's persnickety rules. A dangerous man, then, for Lucinda never knew what to expect from him.

"Finally, you admit it." Frustrated beyond measure, she impulsively goaded, "Will you also admit to the deep, dark secrets of your past?"

His muscular shoulders stiffened slightly. "The past is of no concern to you. Only your future matters. And I will happily guide your steps until you find a man worthy of you."

"Hmph. We will see about that."

Riel smiled. "Yes, we will." He turned on his heel and left her there, steaming.

Must he always have the last word? Not in the final, ultimate battle, Lucinda determined. She would choose her own husband. Riel's qualifications for "suitability" would not stop her from marrying the man she loved...a man of her own choosing.

And one thing was for certain. That man would be nothing like Riel Montclair. Her husband would be kind and caring, and eager to grant her every wish. This was the type of man she desired. All bossy, arrogant men would be struck from her list.

Chapter Sixteen

LONDON WAS ALREADY in a social whirl when they arrived in mid-April. News of Napoleon Bonaparte's recent defeat added an air of gaiety to the entire town. Lucinda felt relieved, because it meant Riel would not need to sail on any more dangerous missions. He would not leave again, and she was glad. For Sophie's sake, of course. And the Silk Scarf Rapist had not struck since last year. All of London had relaxed and now enjoyed the entertaining Season.

Lucinda found Riel's townhouse to be large and comfortable, and she loved her room, decorated in creams and lace with accents of pale yellow. Fresh yellow daisies filled a vase on her dresser. A similar bouquet graced the dresser in Sophie's room, which was decorated in crisp whites with sprigs of blue. It suited her to a "T."

The trip had been difficult for Riel's great-aunt, but she seemed no worse now than at Iveny. Lucinda was grateful for that, too, and she found herself looking forward to the first tea party, which would be late that very afternoon. Amelia and her mother would attend, as well.

First, though, Lucinda had an appointment this morning with the modiste. As she'd decided to order all of her gowns at once, the appointment would take some time. Of course, Sophie couldn't come, so it was just Riel and Lucinda in the carriage...most improper, of course, but Effie had a stomach bug, so there was no help for it.

Lucinda felt very self-conscious as Riel opened the door for her to enter Madame Batiste's modiste shop. It seemed most inappropriate for him to be there—as if he were her husband. In truth, that's what she feared Madame Batiste would think.

The modiste's initial greeting alarmingly confirmed this fear. The stout woman wore her black hair upswept in an intricate, tangled do. Her glasses dangled from a cord around her neck and bumped against her ample bosom as she hurried forward to greet them. "Madame, Monsieur Montclair. *Entre, s'il vous plaît!*"

French had been one of Lucinda's better subjects at Miss May's, so she understood Madame Batiste all too clearly. Her face flamed. "*Non,*" she said quickly. "Monsieur Montclair..."

"Is happy to help my lady choose her dresses," Riel interjected smoothly, and directed a surprisingly charming smile at the modiste.

Madame Batiste beamed. "But of course. And you have need of how many gowns, my lady?" she fixed black, beady eyes upon Lucinda.

"Eight," she said faintly.

"Bon. Sit, sit." She hurried through a dark doorway.

Lucinda sat beside Riel on a small wicker bench. Her face felt hot, and she hissed, "Why did you let her think that we're...we're..." She couldn't say the word.

"I believed it would make you feel more comfortable."

"More *comfortable?*" Lucinda edged away from his large, disturbing body. "Yes. I am truly comfortable now, pretending a great pirate like you is my husband!"

"I fail your requirements?" She did not care for his smile. He enjoyed this, the wolf!

"I believe honesty is the best policy."

"As do I. But you do not wish to endure Madame Batiste's disapproving glances and wagging tongue throughout this entire ordeal, do you?"

"Of course not. But..."

"I will tell her I am your guardian, if you wish. Madame Batiste..." That good lady had returned. "Lady Lucinda would like to make one thing quite clear..."

"Yes!" Lucinda interjected quickly. "I want no black or brown colors. They are drab, and I despise them." She felt Riel's amused glance, but ignored him.

"Of course, Madame." Madame Batiste elevated her nose. "I would not dream of such colors for your complexion. You are best suited for blues and yellows and pinks. All in the pastel hues, of course."

"Of course," Lucinda said. She had never met a modiste so certain of herself. To believe her airs, she'd just arrived from the fashion capital of Paris. "What gowns are fashionable this Season?"

The modiste and her helper presented an array of plates showing different gowns. Afterward, the French modiste drew Lucinda's attention to a few sample gowns on display in her shop. Several appealed to Lucinda, so Madame Batiste urged her to try them on. She said she would tuck them up with pins so Lucinda could see what they'd look like, fitted to her form.

Lucinda did not like the first one she tried on, but Mrs. Batiste nodded in approval of the second. Pins prickled from her lips as she nipped and tucked the garment to fit Lucinda. At last, she nodded with approval. "Show your husband, Lady Lucinda. I am sure it will please him."

Lucinda couldn't very well say she didn't care what her "husband" thought. She'd taken the easy route, and chosen a lie of omission. This would be her punishment for her sins, then; parading her entire wardrobe before his untutored, pirate eyes. What did he know of fashion?

Holding her head high, she exited the dressing area and swept in state before Riel. "What do you think?"

She didn't think he would pay the slightest attention. Clearly, fashion meant little to him. Yes, he seemed to possess several fine new jackets, but the rest of his wardrobe remained the same. Tan pants, white linen shirts, and black boots.

To her surprise, Riel's eyes raked down her form, as if inspecting a potential new scow. Nerves prickled up over her skin...over every place his gaze touched.

"The lines become you," he told her, and his dark eyes met her own. A flare of heat scorched her at the barely veiled compliment. "Perhaps gold would suit for this dress. It looks like an evening gown."

"Exactly as I thought!" crowed Madame Batiste. Her lips curled into a smug, cat who'd found the canary smile. "You are lucky to have a husband with a keen eye for what suits you best. Come. Try another gown."

Lucinda tried on six gowns, and approved six plates. She liked ten in all, but Riel praised eight the most highly. Although she wasn't sure why she craved his approval, she narrowed her choices to the eight they both liked. Riel said little while she discussed colors and fabrics with the modiste. He seemed satisfied with the gowns she had chosen, and that seemed to be enough for him.

Madame Batiste appeared extraordinarily pleased with the large order, especially when Riel paid half of the amount immediately. She escorted them from the shop with a beaming smile and a promise that the first would be ready in a few days.

Lucinda felt pleased with her purchases and bounced into the carriage with a dreamy smile curving her lips. She imagined wearing her new gowns to the upcoming balls and fêtes.

"You will capture the eye of every eligible bachelor in town," Riel said. He sat across from her, with his long legs stretched out before him. His black boots just missed the edge of her gown, and Lucinda's heart thumped once, hard, in her breast. Why must his close presence always affect her so?

"The more suitors, the better," she returned. "I want to find a husband in the next few months."

Silence elapsed. "Then I will have my work cut out for me."

"What do you plan to do?" A tiny frown furrowed Lucinda's brow. "I will do all of the work. I will dance and chat with them to see who is most suitable for me."

"But I must check their backgrounds. You do not want to be pursued only for your money, do you?"

Taken aback, she said, "I am not rich, Riel. Remember, I've seen the accounts. Why would you say such a thing?"

"You see only the stipend your father's trust pays the estate each month."

She blinked, confused. "What are you saying?"

Riel named a sum that the bank held on her behalf, as well as investments and other properties her father owned. "It will all be yours when you marry, Lucy. It's my job to make sure you marry a man not only worthy of you, but a man competent to run a vast estate like Ravensbrook."

Lucinda gasped. "Truly, Riel? All that money will be mine when I marry?"

"Yes."

She tried to digest this new, overwhelming revelation. Now she understood why Riel felt so responsible for her, and determined to honor his oath to her father.

"Thank you for telling me. I will keep that information in mind while I search for my husband.

"That is why I will help you choose. You will have no second chance if you choose wrong the first time."

"I will listen to your opinion," Lucinda agreed. "But know this, Mr. Montclair. *I* will choose my husband. Not you."

"I will approve of him, or you will not marry."

Hard-headed, as always. Lucinda sent him a narrowed look, but pressed her lips together and said nothing. Words held no sway over Riel Montclair. Actions would prove her ultimate victory. Then Riel would finally comprehend that she was the captain of her own fate. Not him.

⚜ ⚜ ⚜ ⚜ ⚜

Lucinda's first gown, a light blue, silk organza confection with silver threads, was ready in time for her first ball of the Season. She had enjoyed several tea parties, but she disliked sitting still for long periods of time at those affairs. She'd much rather dance. And far more possibilities for husbands lurked at the balls. Heaven knew, she needed to find an acceptable man within the next few months. At least, she did if she wanted Riel Montclair out of her life by her twentieth birthday. And she did, of course.

Butterflies danced in Lucinda's stomach when they arrived at the ball. This was the Season she'd looked forward to for her entire life; the sparkling one, where she'd at last meet her perfect man and fall in love. Now only to find him.

"Isn't it marvelous?" Amelia said. "Look at all the new people here this year." She looked pretty in a lavender satin dress with lace appointments. Several men had already signed Amelia's dance card.

Lucinda had tucked her card up her sleeve. She'd rather choose the men she danced with this evening. That meant flitting to the ones she most wanted to become acquainted with, and demurely batting her eyelashes. Perhaps it wasn't proper, but was definitely more fun. She felt encouraged by all the new faces, too. Perhaps she'd find her future husband this very night!

"Come with me," she hissed. With a tug at Amelia's arm, she scooted in the direction of a tall young man neither had seen last year. "Get your card ready."

With a wry smile, Amelia trotted in her wake. "What would the Baron think of your behavior now, Lucinda?"

"Does it matter? He's outside talking to a shipping magnate." She planted herself in front of the new young man. "La." Lucinda fluttered her fan. "Oh! I beg your pardon. I thought I had made your acquaintance last year. Please, do excuse me!"

The young man grinned and bowed. "But I am pleased to make your acquaintance now. I am the Earl of Hart, Donald Tinsley."

Lucinda charmingly introduced both herself and Amelia, and secured that fine gentleman's signature upon both of their dance cards.

"See?" she giggled, and hurried on. To her surprise, a male hand plucked the card from her hand.

"Aha!" The Duke of Warrington's green eyes laughed down at her. "You have left only six dances for me, Lady Lucinda. I assure you, that will not be enough."

"Jonathon!" With pleasure, the breath caught in her throat as she gazed up at the charming rake she hadn't seen in a year. As always, his chestnut hair was styled in the latest fashion, and his tailored clothes impeccable. "You may take two dances, if you so insist."

"Two?" He *tsked* over that, and signed his name with flourish to her card, and then Amelia's. Then he cupped Lucinda's elbow. "If I may steal your friend, cousin?" And then he steered her to the punch table. "Where have you kept yourself this past year?" he asked, filling a crystal cup.

"I've been mostly at Iveny with Aunt Sophie. Her health is not good."

"The Baron's aunt? Is your charming guardian in attendance this year? Or will you require my protective services again?"

"I am here, Warrington." Riel's deep voice commanded their attention, and a small frown furrowed Jonathon's brow.

"Splendid. Then I may relax and enjoy Lucinda's company. Our two dances this evening will be a start."

"Have you any slots left, Lucy?"

"A few." Reluctantly, she handed her card to Riel, who signed his name. To the last dance, she noted with a touch of exasperation. Thankfully not a waltz this time, but rather a quadrille.

Jonathon eyed Riel. A pensive expression narrowed his eyes. "Are you sure we didn't meet years ago, Montclair? Seeing you again, I feel certain you're familiar to me."

Tension stiffened Riel's large frame. His assessing—perhaps wary—gaze settled on Jonathon. "Not likely. I've spent most of my life at sea."

"Where?" The cruel twist to Jonathon's mouth indicated he knew that he'd made Riel feel uncomfortable.

Did he relish it? Lucinda felt disturbed, for it seemed so. Certainly, there was no love lost between the two men. Riel disliked Jonathon for some unknown reason, and Jonathon clearly resented it.

Riel shrugged. "All about. The Mediterranean, Italy, Spain."

Jonathon shook his head. His eyes glinted a cold, dark jade. "Perhaps somewhere else."

"I think not." Riel's cool voice sounded final.

Lucinda glanced from one to the other, and wondered about the strange tension thrumming from Riel again—like the last time Jonathon had asked that same question. Had Jonathon indeed seen Riel before? But where? And why would the idea disturb Riel?

"Perhaps you are right." Jonathon glanced at Lucinda, and his usual charm chased the darkness from his eyes. "Would you like a glass of punch before the dance begins?"

"Perhaps a sip of water." Jonathon cut between herself and Riel, and with a light touch at her back directed her to the crystal pitcher filled with water. Lucinda felt it was a rude dismissal of Riel, and sent him an apologetic look over her shoulder. He watched Jonathon, his black eyes hard.

Her first dance partner claimed her hand soon after, and then more young men, including the questionable Fredrick from last year, asked to sign her dance card, and she allowed them. Evidently Amelia had decided to give Fredrick another chance, too, for she presently danced with that young man. Fredrick had gained a little weight over the past year, and the beginning of jowls softened the jaw line of his handsome face.

Jonathon claimed the supper dance. Lucinda was happy to see he'd returned to his usual, thoroughly charming self.

At the end of the meal, she brought up the question that had been bothering her all evening. She didn't want to resurrect the previous unpleasantness, but she did need to know the truth. "Do you truly think you've met Mr. Montclair before?"

"I do." Jonathon frowned. "But I can't recall where. I haven't visited any of the places he listed."

"He sailed the Barbary Coast, too," Lucinda said, finishing her sorbet. "I think he was only seventeen then. It was a long time ago."

"Truly?" Jonathon's brows shot upward. "I lived in Morocco with my parents when I was thirteen. My father was a foreign diplomat. Perhaps I saw him there." His eyes narrowed and hardened, as if trying to see into the past.

Lucinda wondered why Jonathon kept insisting he'd seen Riel before. It sounded so...unsavory. As if Jonathon desired to remember something unpleasant. Her brow wrinkled. Surely Jonathon was mistaken. He must be remembering someone else. Riel was honorable. He'd never take part in anything evil or distasteful. Would he?

Jonathon looked up and saw the expression on Lucinda's face. "Come now," he said, and his thinned lips relaxed into a smile. "I'm sure it is nothing. The music has begun. Shall we dance?"

With a relieved return smile, Lucinda took his arm. *See, it's nothing,* she told herself. Jonathon remembered nothing, because there was nothing to remember.

Lucinda enjoyed herself thoroughly at the first ball of the Season, and danced with quite a few new young men. While most seemed pleasant, many of them seemed more interested in talking about themselves than asking questions of her. However, a good number expressed hope that they'd see her at the next soirée. With this, Lucinda had to be content. To her count, perhaps five men might be interested in her.

A few of the foppish dandies from last year attended, of course, but she'd already ruled them out. She'd give her new prospects a good chance, she decided. It was their first ball, too. Perhaps they were nervous. Next time they might be more relaxed and ready to talk about new topics.

However, despite her determination to give her suitors the benefit of the doubt, so far none of them matched the image she'd begun to sketch in her mind of the man she most wished to marry. Handsome would be nice, of course. And besotted with her would be even better. That way he would be eager to please her, and amenable to all of her wishes. Yes. That would be the perfect sort of man. She had no doubt she'd fall in love with him the instant she met him.

One thing Lucinda did know: she did not want an authoritative man, or a hard-headed, stubborn one, either. Certainly not a man like Riel Montclair, who at this very minute strode toward her to claim his dance...the last dance.

The moist palms of her last partner released her, and she reluctantly stepped into Riel's arms.

For a few moments they danced without speaking. Unfortunately, the silence made Lucinda focus upon other things...such as how different Riel felt from her last dance partner, and from most of the others she'd danced with this evening. Instead of limp holds and clammy hands, strong, hard muscles rippled beneath her fingertips. He held her securely, with sure confidence. Instead of scanning the room for the next female he wished to dance with—or worse, the gleam of the lecherous ones who'd like to take a stroll in the garden—his steady gaze never left her.

She lowered her eyes under the intensity of his direct appraisal. Thankfully, the dance required that they split apart for a few moments. All too soon, they came back together.

He said, "I see you have danced three times with Jonathon. You allowed him an extra slot?"

"Of course. He is a fine gentleman. He knows how to treat a lady."

"And I do not?" They twirled apart, and then back together.

"We both know how you would treat me, if given the chance." She referred to his threat two years ago to swat her.

He smiled. "I am glad I've not had to take you in hand."

"You would not dare lay a finger upon me."

"I am glad you've conducted yourself like a lady these last two years so I would not need to do so."

Her hand dropped from his shoulder and she jerked to free herself from his touch. Of course, he did not allow it. Alarmingly, he tugged her a fraction closer, instead. His dark eyes gleamed down at her. "You are a grown woman now. I'm proud of the lady you have become."

She ceased struggling. The man always kept her off balance. How was that? Even after knowing him for two years— of course, he'd been gone much of the time and beyond that, she had avoided him whenever possible. And Sophie had provided a welcome barrier, too. "Do my ears deceive me?" she inquired. "Was that a compliment?"

He smiled, but it looked slightly mocking and warning at the same time. "Do not prove me wrong."

"What great trust you place in me."

"I know you well, Lucy. Do not forget it."

"Soon your threats will have no bite, for I will be married. Then you will have to find a new chatelaine to order about."

"I have learned my lesson. No more wards for me. You are enough for any man to handle. I would not willingly submit to that noose of responsibility again."

Lucinda felt a prick of hurt, and said tartly, "If not a ward, then a servant to order about. Men like you need to have power over someone. It is what makes you feel a man."

Anger flickered in his dark brown eyes, and tension tightened the thick cords of his shoulders. She became aware, yet again, of what a powerful man he was. Her head only reached his chin. She'd seen him lift a whole wagon without help in order to free the leg of the boy who had been crushed beneath it. His hands were big. They felt hard on her waist now, but they had gently tended the boy as he examined his wound.

Several times, those hands been gentle on her. A faint, alarming warmth stole through her at the memory.

"You know little of me as a man, Lucinda." He released her when the music whispered to a close. The end of the ball.

"And one last thing," she said. "Please stop signing for my last dance. I'd prefer to leave it open for a special, eligible suitor of my choice."

Those black eyes narrowed. "Do you mean Jonathon?"

"I mean any man. Except you, of course." Perhaps that was terribly blunt and rude, but she needed to get her point across.

A muscle tightened in his jaw. Before he could argue with her, she said, "It is not seemly. A guardian should not claim the last dance. It is inappropriate. People might get the wrong idea."

"And what idea might that be?"

Lucinda frowned. How neatly he'd trapped her into this uncomfortable corner. "You know."

"Explain it to me."

Her face heated. "The last dance is special. Surely you know that. It is to be reserved for the gentleman I hold in the highest esteem." Whom she was interested in, in other words.

"A gentleman chooses where to sign the card. Not the lady."

"Yes, well..."

He continued smoothly, with a small smile she did not care for, "You fear that by claiming your last dance I am sending a message to every man that you belong to me."

"Exactly!" Her cheeks felt hot—no doubt they were dreadful spots of color that made her look as if she'd tippled heavily of the alcohol-laced punch this evening. "I do *not* belong to you, Riel Montclair."

"You are under my protection and authority. I want to make that clear to everyone. Most especially your special gentlemen."

Anger glowed in her bosom. "You are a power hungry brute, Mr. Montclair. Perhaps I will not allow you to sign my dance card at all!"

He blinked, as if taken aback. Good. "And furthermore," she flashed, "I would sooner dance twelve times with Timothy Fenwick, who smashes toes, mind you, than *once* with you. You may not have another of my last dances, Baron. And if you sign for it, I shall scribble it out."

"Lucy." Contrition flickered.

Good! She spun away and marched off. Let that set him back on his heel. Let him suffer for his arrogant proclamations. Never mind that she'd just attacked him like a shrew. Lucinda shut her mind to this stab to her conscience. Riel Montclair must learn that he could not arrogantly rule her life.

ക്ക ക്ക ക്ക ക്ക ക്ക

When Lucinda told Sophie about the ball the next morning, the elderly lady's eyes sparkled for the first time in days. She pushed herself more upright on the pillows.

"It sounds...lovely." Sophie's low, raspy cough wheezed for a minute. Then, "You found nice young men to dance with?"

"Ye...es." Lucinda could not help the lack of enthusiasm in her voice.

"What was...wrong with them?"

"Nothing," Lucinda said quickly. "They were fine. It will just take time to become better acquainted. Then I can make up my mind about them."

"A wise choice." Sophie coughed again, but briefly. To Lucinda's hopeful ear, she actually sounded better today. "And Riel? Did he...behave himself? I know...sometimes...he maddens you."

"We madden each other, I think." Lucinda remembered dancing in his arms last night, and how unsettled she'd felt. And the way she'd instinctively used words to push him away, yet again. And of course the fight they'd had. She was sorry for the harsh words she'd said. She did not, however, want him to feel that he had the right to lay claim to any dance that he wished. No. She'd drawn the line and he must toe it.

"I don't know why I behave as I do with him," Lucinda admitted, plucking at the coverlet.

Sophie coughed long and low for a few minutes, but fluttered a dismissive hand at the water Lucinda offered her. "Tell him, then."

"Tell him what?"

"Apologize." Sophie's eyes looked bright. "If you truly regret the way you treated him."

Did she regret it? In some ways yes, and in others, no. He wasn't innocent in the matter either, she reminded herself. "I'll try to behave with more decorum in the future," she promised Sophie.

"Which behavior do you regret now, Lucy?" The deep voice behind her scattered a prickle of nerves down her neck.

She glanced up at him. "Must you intrude upon a private conversation?"

"I apologize. If you would like, I will return later."

So amenable. Most unlike him.

Sophie patted the coverlet beside her.

Riel dropped a kiss on Sophie's cheek, and perched his big frame on the edge of the bed. Disturbingly, his knee brushed Lucinda's and she surreptitiously edged hers away.

"Lucinda was just telling me about the ball," his great-aunt said.

Riel's gaze found hers. "Did she tell you that she has already acquired a dedicated suitor?"

"Really?"

For a moment, Lucinda didn't know whom he meant, and then she laughed. "Oh. Do you mean Jonathon?"

"Yes. The Duke of Warrington seems taken with you."

"The Duke...of Warrington?" Sophie's voice quavered, and she glanced quickly at Riel.

Lucinda said, "Yes. Remember, you met him at the Christmas party at Ravensbrook last year."

"Yes. But I didn't...make the connection for some reason." Sophie glanced back at Riel with a faint frown.

Now Lucinda frowned at the two of them. "Is that name familiar to you, Sophie?"

The older woman opened her mouth, and then shut it again. Riel, on the other hand, regarded Lucinda steadily, with a grim set to his mouth.

Lucinda pressed, "Jonathon said he knows you. You know him too, don't you?"

"No. But the family is familiar to me."

"You make them sound so unsavory. Tell me why."

"I know nothing about Jonathon. But his brother was an undisputable rake." Riel seemed to retreat to a place far within himself.

Sophie patted Riel's arm. "You two go on. I need my rest."

With another kiss on her cheek, Riel followed Lucinda from the room. Once they were out and the door closed, Lucinda said, "Her cough seems a little better today."

"But she seems weaker. Never has she asked me to leave so quickly. She was tired."

Lucinda was not so sure. "I think she wants us to talk. That way I can apologize for a few of the things I said last night. But," she was hasty to make clear, "know that I still do not want you to take command of my dance card again."

Riel stopped at the head of the stairs. "You want to apologize to me?"

"I don't *want* to apologize to you. But perhaps I was a bit...harsh in my summations of your character last night." That he was a power hungry brute, for example.

He smiled, relaxed against the wall, and crossed his arms. He regarded her with some amusement. "Tell me more. This is a rare moment. I must soak up every syllable."

Lucinda frowned. "You are the most maddening man. I have no wish to stroke your enormous ego any further."

He chuckled, inflaming her temper still further. Tilting her chin, she swept down the stairs.

Unfortunately, she moved so fast that her toe caught in the hem of her skirts and she tripped. She flailed for the banister, and then pitched forward and tumbled down the stairs.

Chapter Seventeen

PAIN BIT INTO Lucinda's hips, legs and arms in that brief, wild spin...until her head slammed into the banister. Bright sparkles of light danced behind her eyelids. A great shout assaulted her eardrums.

"Lucy!" Boots thumped on the stairs.

"Are you all right?" The voice rumbled near her now, and her eyes fluttered open to see Riel's dark, concerned face inches from her own. "Are you all right?" he asked again, and she became aware of his great hands running over her arms.

"I...I am fine." She winced, attempting to sit up. Steadying hands helped her.

"Any sharp pain? Broken bones?"

"I...don't think so." Gingerly, she tested each limb. They seemed to work, although twinges of pain made her bite her lip.

"Good." To her shock, Riel swept her up into his arms and carried her downstairs.

She clutched at his neck. "You must stop doing that."

"You are afraid I will drop you?"

"No." Lucinda knew he would never drop her. She felt secure in his arms. Riel would always keep her safe; of this, she felt very certain. All of a sudden, she couldn't remember why she kept pushing him away.

It alarmed her, and she clutched him harder as weak tears of reaction threatened. She pressed her face into the hollow of his throat and tried to gain control of herself.

Gently, he set her down on the sofa in the parlor and sat beside her. "You are crying." With a tender frown, he brushed the drops away.

His gentleness was her undoing, and more unwanted tears spurted down her cheeks. His fingers stroked her hair, and the sensation felt soothing and comforting.

"You are bleeding," he said in a low voice. "Stay here."

She dried her face with her sleeve. When he returned with a warm wash cloth and other necessary items, she sat quietly, and allowed his gentle ministrations.

"It is only a small cut," he told her.

Lucinda felt his calloused fingers in her hair and his warm breath on her temple.

An odd part of her wanted to close her eyes and soak up the sensations. And so she did. She liked the sensation of him touching her, she realized with a slow thrum of her heart. Alarmingly, she liked it very much indeed.

Lucinda felt a sense of loss when Riel's fingers fell away. "Finished."

She glanced up at him, feeling shy and suddenly vulnerable. His gaze caught hers, and scanned it, as if trying to search deep into her soul.

She wet her lips and offered softly, "Thank you."

"You are welcome, Lucy." His black gaze fell to her mouth, and for a heartbeat she had the insane notion he just might kiss her.

Her pulse quickened. Did she *want* him to kiss her?

A flush warmed her cheeks, and hastily, she looked away. Was she crazy? She did not want Riel Montclair to kiss her!

After a hesitation, he rose to his feet and Lucinda felt bereft.

"I will have the housekeeper send in tea," he said in a harsh voice. He strode from the room.

Lucinda watched his broad back move down the hall and wondered what had just transpired. The fall must have addled her brain. For still she stared after Riel as if she could not drink in every inch of him fast enough.

Again, the truth whispered up from her soul. Her guardian was devastatingly handsome. She liked every line of him—the breadth of his muscular shoulders, his trim hips, the blunt, at times harsh angles of his face. Those direct black eyes and those big hands that had touched her again so gently.

Lucinda put her hand to her forehead. It felt decidedly warm. She must be coming down with a bug. Either that, or she was losing her mind.

Riel Montclair was an irksome, maddening man. Tender feelings for him were not only delusional, but self-destructive. Perhaps she did need that tea...and a nap. That should set the world to rights again.

⋙ ⋙ ⋙ ⋙ ⋙

Riel had wanted to kiss Lucy.

After telling the housekeeper about the tea, he walked out the back door and into the warm sunshine. He headed for the street, walking fast.

Riel had wanted to kiss Lucy, and he still did. It was no use trying to deny it. Or trying to deny why he wanted to lay claim not only to her last dance at the balls, but every other one, as well. His feelings for her had deepened in a wholly self-destructive way. No longer did she only inhabit his dreams. A safe place, because it was unreal, and easily dismissed as the fantasies of an exhausted mind. Now, not only did he still dream of her, but Riel spent much of his day in the same house with her, near her. Smelling her floral scent on the stairs, hearing her talk to Sophie...sharing supper with her every day. No longer could he deny that he savored each of these links to her. Lucy was a feisty, warm and beautiful woman. He liked everything about her.

Riel knew he was becoming too emotionally entangled with her. His job was to find her a husband. Period.

Certainly a position for which he could never apply.

Riel walked faster, trying to shove his unwanted feelings deep into his soul. To exorcise them, for they would only bring him pain.

Lucy did not want him in her life. Over and over again, she had made that abundantly clear. And if—or when—she discovered the truth of his past, she would spit him out for good.

Riel had known for some time that he needed to back away from her, but he couldn't manage to do it. He liked firing her up. He liked holding her in his arms during that last, most special dance.

Riel allowed his thoughts to go no further. Lucy was not the woman for him. No reputable woman was. His past dictated that he must spend the rest of his life alone.

As far as Lucy was concerned, Riel was her guardian, and that was all. His first and only duty was to see her married. And to protect her from wolves like Jonathon.

His fists clenched, glad to think about a less disturbing topic. That rake wanted to penetrate her life. *Three* dances at the ball. Riel had wanted to grab him by his fluffy cravat and order him to step off. Except Jonathon would have looked at him with amusement and turned to Lucy for validation to stay.

Lucy liked the miscreant. But Riel would not trust the man. Not for one moment. Especially after the way Jonathon had baited him last night. The other man relished his unease. Cruelty lurked in him...better hidden than with his brother, but clear just the same.

Riel didn't like a few of Lucinda's other suitors, either. Particularly the one named Fredrick. He'd noticed Amelia dancing with him, too. What did the two see in him? He was a jowly, spoilt mama's boy, at best. And at worst...long days at sea with the worst of humanity told Riel that Fredrick could possess a vicious side.

If Fredrick coerced more than one dance each evening with Lucy, Riel would discourage that suitor, too. Choosing to dismiss him with less provocation would raise Lucy's ire, and she'd likely dance with him all the more, just to spite Riel.

How, then, to discourage Jonathon, whom he felt was the worst of the lot? Unfortunately, unless Jonathon made a misstep, or Riel found proof that he was a rake of the first order, he could do little. But he would watch the wolf every minute, that was for certain.

Woe to the rake if he laid an inappropriate hand upon Lucy, or tried to lure her into the garden. Riel's fists tightened, relishing the thought of dusting that self-satisfied, aristocratic nose until it spurted blood.

Meanwhile, Riel would bide his time. And he'd ask Lucy to favor him with her last dance each evening. Riel couldn't deny that he wanted it for purely selfish reasons. But it did make a statement, too. One he wanted Jonathon Warrington to heed. Riel was guardian over Lucy, and Warrington would have to come through him to get her.

の の の の の

More tea parties, soirées, fêtes and balls whirled by. Lucinda enjoyed them all. Riel had humbly asked if she would allow him a dance at one ball, and at the next he again asked for the last one. She wasn't sure why she gave it to him. Especially since she wanted to spend as little time as possible with him. That one, wild moment last week when she'd wanted him to kiss her continued to haunt her, and that would not do. It would not do at all.

Jonathon continued to sign for two of her dances each night; one of which often included the supper dance. She continued to grant the stocky Fredrick one dance, and Timothy often asked for one, as well. The two young men always signed Amelia's card, too. She was glad her friend's dance card was almost always full.

So far, Fredrick had behaved himself, but it did seem that he danced a might too closely to her friend tonight. Unseemly. She'd also noticed Fredrick lurking at the punch table for long stretches while others danced. Was it because he couldn't get a partner? Or because he enjoyed the spiked punch too much?

While Lucinda enjoyed herself, and nightly discovered new ways to encourage interesting conversational paths with her dance partners, it was turning out to be more work than she'd expected. All of the men loved to talk about themselves. Only a few asked about her interests. She found this frustrating. While she did need a husband, she didn't want a self-absorbed bore. Where was her dream man? This evening, one man had preened the entire dance, another sniffed constantly, and another droned on and on about topics of no importance to her at all.

Boring, boring, boring! Where were the exciting men? She averted her eyes from Riel, who danced across the room with a redhead. True, he agitated her. But she wanted romance, not disturbed feelings.

Why hadn't she found her future husband yet? Where was the heart stopping romance? *Why* hadn't she fallen in love?

As usual, Jonathon was the best candidate of all, but right now he danced with a pretty brunette—a Lady Annabelle, she believed—who laughed up at him. Lucinda could not feel jealous. It was just the way Jonathon was. He was as a bee to honey. All women loved him. No wonder she liked him, as well.

Currently, she danced the cotillion with young Timothy Fenwick. Only once had he stepped on her toes this evening. She scanned his face. He wasn't bad looking in a tall, blond-haired, puppy dog sort of way.

Frustrated with her lack of prospects so far, Lucinda blurted, "Do you find it boring?"

His brows flew up and he accidentally stomped on her toe. "Sorry!" His ears turned beet red. Steps jerky, he directed them both back into the rhythm of the dance. "Boring? Do I find what boring?"

"All of this." Lucinda sketched a dramatic hand about the room. "You are a man." Well, barely. "You probably don't look on balls as women do. But I've been to six balls this Season, and five last, and it is always the same. I dance with the same men. Those men talk about themselves, and then we switch partners and it begins again. Where is the excitement?" she implored, not really expecting an answer.

Lucinda struggled to ignore the truth. She did feel prickles of excitement—but with only one man—Riel.

What if he had kissed her the other night?

Lucinda shivered and then blinked, horrified. Had she lost her mind? She must scourge all thoughts of her guardian from her head.

Timothy offered a small smile. "I try to step on one less toe each night. That's all the excitement I can master right now."

Timothy was a nice young man. So earnest and awkward, and sweet, too, really. What would he know about romance, or the things her friends in the finishing school had squealed over after lights out? Certainly, none of those things were happening to her. Of course, they did not happen on the dance floor, but out in the garden.

A plan so wicked that Lucinda almost stamped on Timothy's toe raced across her imagination in living color. She nearly gasped with horror...and delight.

What better way to banish Riel utterly from her thoughts? Not to mention learn if the excitement she'd always dreamed of could exist? It would infuriate Riel, to be sure, but did he need to learn about it?

And Timothy would be the perfect choice to fulfill this most illicit of endeavors.

Impulsively, Lucinda fluttered her hand before her face. "La, I am so hot. Do you find it warm in here?"

"Yes. Why don't they open the windows?"

"The matrons are afraid of the night airs. They fear taking ill, because then they might miss the next soirée. And all of the juicy gossip, too."

He snorted.

The music slowed, and Lucinda tugged on his arm. "Will you come with me? I'd like to take a stroll in the garden, but I'm afraid to go alone."

"Well..." One brow raised a bit. Clearly uncertain, he glanced across the room to where his mother and sister sat.

"Only for a moment. Please," she cajoled, and felt like a wicked, wicked girl as she did so. Knowingly luring him to a slippery path.

"All right," he agreed at last. "But only for a moment."

She grinned. "Thank you." Taking the arm he offered, she accompanied him out the French doors to the garden paved with stones. It was a large garden, and thick groves of trees bordered the winding pathways. Lucinda urged him toward a dense clump.

Timothy said, "It's a bit chilly. Do you want your wrap?"

"No." Lucinda did not feel cold at all, for apprehension and excitement washed by turns through her, leaving her feeling both warm and cold at the same time. Once they were hidden among the trees, she stopped and folded her arms.

Timothy uneasily glanced back at the French doors, which were still barely visible. "Perhaps this isn't the best idea. If someone saw us, they might get the wrong impression."

"No one will see us." Lucinda crept further back into the foliage. With a frown, he edged toward her. "Timothy, I'll tell you the truth. I asked you out here for a reason."

"A reason?" Uncertainty edged those few syllables.

"I want to conduct an experiment. An *experiment* only, so don't get any other ideas."

"What sort of an experiment?" He sounded suspicious, as well he might.

"Have you ever kissed a girl, Timothy?" She felt quite certain he hadn't.

"No. But..."

"Would you like to?"

In the semi-darkness, a blush darkened his face. "Lady Lucinda, I do not think..."

"We've known each other all of our lives, Timothy. Right?"

"Yes..."

"And we can trust one another."

"I thought so, but..."

"Timothy! All my life my friends have giggled about...*kissing,*" she said in a low voice. "I want to know what all the excitement is about. Dancing is fun, but over and over again, it is boring. I want to know if that's all there is to romance. If that's all there is between a man and a woman. Don't you?"

He hesitated, and she could tell he struggled to choose the right thing.

"Just one kiss," she begged. "And only for a second, if that's all you want. I just have to know."

"One?" Uncertainty roughened his voice.

"One. And please don't think I have a thing for you, Timothy, because I don't. You're safe. That's why I chose you." And almost like a brother, but she didn't say that, for fear of offending him.

"One kiss, and we'll forget it ever happened?"

"Yes! Exactly."

Still, he hesitated a moment more. "We shouldn't. But maybe just once won't hurt."

"Good!" Excitement and apprehension prickled through her nerves. She swiped perspiring palms across her dress and took a hesitant step toward him, at the same instant he took one toward her. She giggled, and he chuckled nervously. He looked down at her, as if gathering the courage for what he must do.

Perhaps she should make the first move, since she was the older woman. Lucinda tilted her chin and pursed her lips. She wasn't sure if this was how it was done, but it seemed as good a start as any.

Chapter Eighteen

RIEL SAW LUCY head out to the garden on young Timothy Fenwick's arm. Depositing his dance partner into the arms of the next on her list, Riel slipped outdoors.

Lucy's bright yellow skirt flashed to his left, and he followed quietly. Did he want to catch them in the act?

The act of doing what? Lucy had shown no interest in that young pup.

At last he spotted them, through the branches of a low tree. Lucy and Timothy stood toe to toe. Shock swept through Riel. His heart began to pound in slow, heavy beats in his chest. Timothy stooped toward Lucy and awkwardly bumped her nose.

Riel couldn't seem to move, but his hands clenched into fists.

Another clumsy adjustment, and then Timothy kissed Lucy.

Hot emotion seared Riel. Jealousy. He couldn't deny it. A fist closed around his heart. How dare that young villain? He'd teach him a lesson, and box his ears, too!

Timothy jerked back, his face flushed, and clearly embarrassed. Disappointment flickered across Lucy's face.

"Perhaps...perhaps I'd best be going," Timothy said, and bolted.

Tense with possessive rage, Riel watched him go, trying to make sense of what he'd just seen. And then the truth hit him.

He relaxed. Timothy wasn't the aggressor. Lucy was. Why didn't that surprise him?

Lucy had snared the boy in one of her impulsive schemes.

Why? Did she long for excitement? Riel smiled then, a thin one, and his heart kicked faster in a grim sort of anticipation. If she did, he'd be glad to provide it. In fact, an equally impulsive take-down might be just what Lucy itched for.

ৰ্ড ৰ্ড ৰ্ড ৰ্ড ৰ্ড

Lucinda felt disappointed as she watched Timothy flee. Her first kiss. It had felt moist and tepid. What was exciting about that? Especially after risking her reputation to sneak into the garden to do it.

"Was it worth it?" Riel spoke behind her.

Shocked, she spun. "Have you been spying on me?"

"Watching over you is my job."

"Well, even though it is none of your business, the kiss was quite...nice."

Riel smiled, and his teeth gleamed white as he moved out of the shadows. "Nice. I hear no conviction in your words, Lucy."

"It was perfectly pleasant," she insisted. Or, it would have been if one enjoyed kissing a warm wash cloth. Surreptitiously, she wiped her lips with the side of her hand, pretending to yawn.

"So, young Timothy failed to impress you." Something intensely dark and dangerous simmered in his black eyes, belying his calm words.

"Young? His ability to kiss has nothing to do with being young. It was perfectly adequate."

"Adequate. I would feel I'd failed, if a woman found my kisses adequate."

Lucinda rolled her eyes to the heavens. "What do you know of love?"

"Love? You are in love with young Timothy?"

"What if I am? What do you know about that finer emotion? I've noticed you never dance with the same woman twice. And who knows how many affairs you've had in the past."

"Perhaps I have not found the right woman."

"Keep searching," she mocked. "And then maybe all of your practice kisses might do you some good!"

Riel moved closer; a large presence in the moonlight. "Was that a practice kiss with young Timothy, Lucy? An experiment?"

Lucinda struggled to deny it, but would not lie. "What if it was?" she said at last.

"So, you plan to sneak out into the garden with other men, and compare their kisses."

"No!" she gasped, shocked, despite herself. "I'm not a hussy, Riel. How dare you think that? Not that it's any of your business, but Timothy was my first kiss."

He moved closer, and his face fell into the shadows. "Your first kiss. Was it all you had hoped?"

Lucinda looked away, wishing he would leave her alone. It made her feel uncomfortable, how close he was. A raw, palpably dangerous emotion radiated from him. Butterflies danced in her stomach. "It was not quite what I expected," she admitted. "Perhaps I should take a page from your book and find another person to kiss, so I can compare."

"Perhaps a man of experience." Surprisingly, he did not object to her outlandish suggestion.

She stared at him. "You agree I should find another man? An...an experienced man and...and compare his kisses to Timothy?"

"I would have to approve the man. I must be sure you are safe."

"Why don't you just lurk in the garden and spy on us?"

He ignored this. "Do you agree, then, to this course of action?"

Lucinda felt acute trepidation. "Well, I..."

"Come with me. Look through the window. We will find the perfect man for your experiment." Hand cupping her elbow, he urged her to a floor-to-ceiling window which afforded a perfect view of the swirling, dancing aristocrats inside. Lucinda felt very aware of his warm, calloused palm against her skin. Her heart beat faster when she realized how close he stood beside her. The fine cloth of his broadcloth jacket whispered against her arm, which he still hadn't released.

His deep voice rumbled above her, "I see several of whom I would approve. What about Colonel Farley?"

Forcing her thoughts from his touch, Lucinda gasped out a laugh when she spotted portly Colonel Farley dancing by with the widow O'Hare. He must be sixty, if a day, and he still sported a full head of whitish yellow hair, including long, bushy sideburns. He pranced gaily from one foot to another, obviously enjoying himself, while poor Mrs. O'Hare hopped faster, trying to save her toes from being smashed.

"No, Riel. I will *not* kiss Colonel Farley."

"Then let's find you another eligible bachelor. Hmm. How about the Marquis of Silverlake?"

Lucinda giggled. "Even worse!" The Marquis reminded her of a cartoon caricature—tall and skinny with a beaky nose and receding black hair. Odd, to boot, if tales could be believed.

"I see you are discerning, after all."

"Of course I am!" She felt insulted. "It must be someone nearer my own age. And nice looking would be a plus. What about Jonathon? He's six years older than me and I'm quite sure he's experienced. I'm sure he would be happy..."

"Not Jonathon." Riel's voice sounded harsh.

She glanced at him, surprised. "Why not? He and I are friends, and..."

"He has too much experience."

"But isn't that the point?"

"Jonathon is a rake."

"He is not!"

"Lucy," he said more gently. "I must approve of the man, or the experiment is off."

"But you are only choosing old men! I would sooner kiss a fish."

"A man nearer to you in age, then, and safe."

"Yes," she agreed. "But experienced."

"I can think of one. Is ten years too much of an age difference?"

"No." Lucinda's heart beat faster. That was the span between herself and Riel. "No...that would be fine."

"You agree to kiss this man, no matter who he is?" He drew her back into the shadows, away from the window.

"As long as he doesn't have buck teeth, or smell like a toad."

"You are sure?" He tipped her chin up with his knuckles.

"Yes." She swallowed hard. "Who is he?"

"Me."

Her heart charged faster. "I will not kiss you!" she scoffed, jerking free of his touch. "You...you're my guardian and you annoy me no end. Not to mention," she hastily added, "it would be inappropriate."

"You have my offer. It is for one time only. How else can you conclude your experiment?"

"I...I don't know," she said breathlessly. "I don't think that's such a good idea."

"Why not?"

Why not, indeed? She was crazy to even consider it! But hadn't she wondered what his kiss would feel like? And perhaps he was right. Maybe he was the perfect choice. Older, but not too old. Experienced, but not a rake. She knew she could trust him, if nothing else.

Feeling as though she teetered on the edge of a cliff, she suddenly made up her mind. "Very well, then. Kiss me."

"You are sure?" he asked again.

No, she wasn't sure. Not at all. But she wanted him to. "Yes," she said faintly.

One broad hand cupped the side of her jaw, and his thumb gently stroked the skin of her cheek. Lucinda's mouth went dry as her gaze tangled with his dark one. Slowly, he came closer and her lips tingled in anticipation. His breath fanned those delicate nerve endings for an impossibly long moment, then, whisper soft, his firm lips touched hers.

Lucinda's heart jerked at the warm contact. She heard a sweet roaring in her ears and then his mouth moved over hers.

Timothy hadn't done this, she thought incoherently. Moments...or perhaps long minutes later...she felt a gentle nip on her bottom lip. When her lips parted in a soft gasp, he took the kiss far deeper than she'd ever believed possible. Lucinda whimpered at the velvet sensations, and her knees went weak. More sweet, intense moments passed as Riel demanded more, and she gave what he desired. Mindlessly, she gripped his shoulders for support. Fire shot through her as he claimed these liberties. Her head spun and she sensed, just out of reach, a place of stars and colors and light that only he could take her. If only she surrendered to him.

She *wanted* to surrender to him.

But she couldn't. Hadn't she fought all of these years not to surrender to his power over her?

But she wanted...

He put her from him, and bewildered, she stared up at him. Riel's dark eyes looked as black as midnight, and his breaths sounded harsh. "Was that better than Timothy?" he said roughly.

Lucinda struggled to remember who Timothy was. "It...it was longer," she managed to say tartly, at last.

Riel chuckled then, deep in his chest. "Better than adequate?"

"If you are waiting for praise, you will not receive it. Somehow, Mr. Montclair, I suspect you have far more experience turning girls' heads than you have let on."

"Perhaps it is the woman who has turned my head."

Confused, and heart fluttering, she eyed him. "What do you mean by that?"

"Never mind, Lucy. You have concluded your experiment. I trust I will not find you kissing young men in the garden again."

She would certainly not be skulking in the garden with *him* again. Nor would she kiss him again! She had just discovered that he possessed the power to disturb her far more deeply than she'd ever dreamed possible. Perhaps it would have been prudent never to find out.

She inclined her head. "I have concluded my experiment. You may rest at your ease."

He smiled. "Never do I rest at my ease with you, Lucy."

Chapter Nineteen

IF LUCINDA HAD WANTED to find excitement, she had found it; in the arms of Riel Montclair.

Lucinda gave Riel a wide berth after their improper, sizzling kiss. Every time she saw him now, her heart bumped and skittered, and all she could think about was his warm lips on hers.

It was most improper...but she had agreed to it! And now she must live with the consequences, which were alarming. She felt more excruciatingly aware of him now than ever before. Each time she brushed by him on the stair, and even worse, each dance in his arms, was exquisite torture. Riel continued to ask for her last dance, and she irrationally continued to give it to him. More balls, tea parties, fêtes and soirées passed by as May melted into June.

At the same time, Sophie's health began to slip. Although the glorious days were bright and sunny, her cough grew no better. The doctor possessed no words of encouragement. When Lucinda asked what could be wrong, he raised his hands and shook his head. Lucinda tried not to set much store by his obviously gloomy outlook. Sophie had never put much stock in a doctor's opinions. Always she'd confounded their dreariest predictions.

But now she didn't. Day and night, Sophie sat propped up so she could breathe, and she never left her bed. Although her feet were covered, Lucinda saw they were more swollen than ever, and Sophie's racking cough kept her awake late into the night. It hurt Lucinda, listening to those painful coughs and gasps for air and she often cried herself to sleep. During the day, she spent every minute she could with Sophie, either talking with her, or reading from the Psalms in the Bible, which Sophie had requested.

If that wasn't enough, the Silk Scarf Rapist struck again in early June. London had been lulled into a false sense of security, since the rapist had not struck for an entire year. Newspapers screamed that the vile criminal had abducted and raped another debutant, and abandoned her to wander the dark streets of London alone, hands tied behind her back, and blindfolded with a silk scarf.

Worse, Lucinda was acquainted with Lady Annabelle, the victim. Horror filled her heart, and she could not seem to stop imagining what had happened to the other girl. How terrified she must have felt, and how alone.

The morning after the crime, Riel stopped Lucinda in the hall.

"You heard what happened."

"Of course." The news had broken last night, and this morning Lucinda felt like a wreck after listening to Sophie cough all night. Plus, terror had crawled through her, thinking of poor Lady Annabelle. She'd been abducted in the park. No one had seen her vanish, and she'd been gone for ten long hours. "No one is safe anymore."

"I am glad you understand that." The harsh lines of Riel's face softened as he looked at her. "Then you will agree to go nowhere alone. Everywhere you go, I will be with you."

"I never go anywhere alone now," she felt it necessary to point out.

"Lucy."

"Fine. I will accept your close presence wherever I go." Then she blushed a little. What was she saying, *close* presence?

"And no more escapes into the garden."

Now her cheeks burned. "I learned my lesson last time, believe me."

She could not read his expression. "So, you agree?"

Lucinda crossed her arms. "Yes. For once I will meekly follow your every dictate. You may rest at your ease, Mr. Montclair."

Now he did smile. He leaned forward and his lips brushed across hers in the briefest of caresses, shocking her. "Thank you, Lucy."

Heart racing, she watched him stride down the hall. She crossed her arms tighter against herself. However, she still felt the warm imprint of his lips upon hers, and the pleasure of it stole her breath. She liked his touch and his kisses entirely too much. She should have slapped him, of course. Except he'd surely meant the kiss as nothing more than a chaste caress. She knew this, but her heart irrationally longed for it to mean something more. She inhaled deeply, for the faint scent that was uniquely Riel lingered.

Her guardian was a good, honorable man. Even gentle and kind, too, when it suited him.

These involuntary admissions made her bite her lip as she watched him disappear into the kitchen. An insane part of her wanted to run after him, to take his arm and talk to him...about anything. She wanted to spend more time with him. For they spoke little in the townhouse anymore—almost as if he'd been trying to avoid her during these past few weeks, as well.

Had she lost all good sense?

Lucinda turned on her heel and headed upstairs. Riel was a dangerous pirate, she told herself, trying to drive some logic into her brain. A man like him did not belong in her life. Didn't she feel certain he still concealed a dark, deadly secret?

Lucinda didn't want to believe that anymore. She didn't want to believe it at all.

Riel let himself into Sophie's room a few minutes later, cursing himself for kissing Lucy again. He'd tried to avoid her these past few weeks, and just now, when she'd agreed to follow his directions so he could keep her safe, he'd felt so grateful that he'd kissed her.

No. That wasn't entirely true. He'd kissed her because he'd wanted to. He'd taken the flimsy excuse of a chaste, approving kiss and run with it. At least this time he'd had the sense to end it before taking it too far.

"Riel." Sophie's raspy whisper drew his attention to his aunt, who sat propped up against the pillows. Her nightgown looked fresh and clean, and decorated with little sprigs of bright blue embroidery, but the crisp garment couldn't improve the gray cast to her skin, nor draw attention away from her sunken cheeks. Her eyelids slid halfway closed.

"Auntie." He took a seat beside her and took her frail hand in his. "How are you feeling?"

"Don't...waste...breath. What is wrong...with you...and Lucinda?" She exhaled Lucy's name in a long slur.

Riel tightened his grip. "We are fine."

"Riel." Sophie's eyes widened into a glare and then relaxed again. "Tell...truth."

"I kissed her, Auntie. Twice." Riel stood and paced. Her silence meant she wanted to hear more, so he told her. All of it.

To his surprise, a smile ghosted Sophie's lips, and a faint sparkle brightened her eyes. "That's...wonderful."

"No, it's not, Auntie," he said grimly. "I'm not fit for any woman. Least of all Lucy."

Sophie frowned gently. "Have...you still...not forgiven...self, Riel?"

Riel gripped the back of his neck with one tense hand. "How can I? A man is dead because of me."

"It's...more than that." Sophie sucked in a long breath. "Tell me."

Sophie had neither the time nor energy for him to dissemble, and Riel didn't want to. He needed to confide in someone. His feelings were eating him alive. Before he could speak, Sophie fluttered her fingers. "Sit...Make me tired... watching you."

Riel did as she asked, and again enfolded his great-aunt's hand in his. He gently stroked the back.

"I'm afraid, Auntie. I'm afraid that someday I will do it again." At last, he spoke his deepest fear. "That I'll lose my temper and kill someone in a rage."

Shock flickered across Sophie's features. "Never! Was special...circumstance." She coughed and choked and gasped.

Riel's heart thundered with heavy, apprehensive beats until she quieted. Then he continued the conversation, as he knew she wished. "No, Auntie. I lost control. Rage consumed me. It might again."

Sophie's hand gripped his. "Has it...since then?"

"Never."

Sophie squeezed his hand. "And...it won't...again. Forgive self...Riel."

Riel dipped his head and gazed at the woven rug on the floor, not wanting even Sophie to see the film of moisture covering his eyes. "I can't."

"You've...asked God...to forgive you." Sophie gasped for breath for a moment, and determinedly pressed on. "Is your...judgment...of yourself...more right than his?"

"No, but..."

"God has forgiven you. You...must, too." Sophie closed her eyes, and struggled to catch her breath.

Riel thought about what she'd said. It made sense, but it was difficult for him to accept. At last, he said, "I will try, Auntie. But I'll never be good enough for Lucy. You see only the good in me. She sees the worst."

Sophie's eyes fluttered open. "You're a foolish...boy." She drew a long breath, and disturbingly, a faint rattle sighed through it. "Do you...love her?"

"No!" The denial came deeply and vehemently. He abruptly stood and paced again. "I cannot, and I will not be that foolish, Aunt Sophie. No future is possible for Lucy and me. You have a gentle, understanding heart, but if Lucy found out the truth she would hate me. And she'd look at me with rightful contempt."

Sophie's jaw set in a stubborn line.

Riel kissed her forehead. "Do not look at me like that. We both know I'm not fit to be her husband."

Tears glistened in Sophie's eyes, and she gripped his hand with a shadow of her old strength. "Forgive self, Riel. Life...too short...for regrets."

Riel would regret forever that one black day thirteen years ago. It had delineated his life thus far, and would continue to tarnish his future. He was too much of a realist to pretend otherwise.

But when Sophie looked at him, her old eyes bright with tears, a part of him softened. "I'll try," he said, with another gentle kiss on her brow.

But how? How could he forgive himself? He could never accept what he had done. Even worse, what if he snapped, and did it again? He could never rest at his ease or get close to anyone—especially Lucy—as long as that possibility remained in his black heart.

Chapter Twenty

A few days later

LUCINDA HAD ANTICIPATED the masquerade ball for weeks. The thought of dancing with mysterious, masked men had thrilled her. Instead, when she slipped into the ballroom that evening, she found the masks gave the ball a sinister feel, what with a rapist on the loose. Was he one of the gentry? In what costume might a rapist clothe himself?

Lucinda stood near the wall, watching the doings through her gold mask on a stick. Tonight she wore the gold silk gown for the first time, and if anyone asked, said she was Marie Antoinette.

She spotted Timothy Fenwick, who wore a knight's armor with a sword at his hip. Since their aborted kiss in the garden, he had steered quite clear of her. Lucinda supposed she deserved it. But she'd also noticed that since the kiss, Timothy had gained a new boldness. He asked many girls to dance, and frequently signed Amelia's card twice.

Perhaps her improper advance had not ruined him, after all.

She involuntarily searched for Riel. It took only a second to find him, for she always possessed an innate sense of his location.

Riel had come as himself. A pirate. He wore a white linen shirt, open below the throat, and it sported loose sleeves, cuffed to a band about his wrists. He also wore a wide belt, a wicked looking dagger, black breeches and his usual black, battered boots. He only lacked an earring.

He certainly did not lack for female attention. Lucinda couldn't help but notice the bevy of women eyeing him as if he were the first course...or perhaps dessert. The bolder of the bunch fluttered their dance cards beneath his nose. She averted her eyes from the trollops circling him, even now.

"Lucinda." Jonathon stood at her elbow. His smile curved below his black mask. He'd arrived as a bandito, and looked very dashing, too, dressed all in black, with a saber at his hip. "You look lovely."

She fluttered her eyelashes, trying to look her part— although she wasn't quite sure how Marie Antoinette had behaved. "Why, *merci,* Jonathon."

"May I sign for the first dance?"

"Of course." Lucinda became aware that Riel watched them. A faint frown drew his brows together. He'd prefer it if she never danced with Jonathon at all. Perversely, she offered Jonathon a bright smile. "I hope you'll wish to sign for more than one dance."

Jonathon grinned wolfishly, showing his teeth. "If I could, I would steal you from all others, Lucinda, and keep you for myself. However, with your guardian glaring at me as he is, I will content myself with two. May I have the supper dance again?"

Lucinda grinned. "I would be very pleased." She did not imagine the frown lowering Riel's brow as Jonathon took his time over signing her card.

Next, Fredrick stepped up. "May I have a dance, as well?" He sounded faintly surly, but she allowed him to sign, too.

Abruptly, he turned and headed for Amelia, whose brows twitched together. At that moment, Timothy stood by her side. Faintly, Lucinda heard Amelia tell Fredrick, "I told you 'no.' Now leave, if you please." Fredrick whirled and stormed off.

Jonathon had apparently noticed the same scene. "It appears Fredrick has lost the favor of my dear cousin."

"He dances a bit too close from time to time."

"He is a knave," Jonathon said. "Amelia is better off without him. As would be you."

Lucinda glanced at her card. Fredrick did make her feel uncomfortable. Perhaps she should stop dancing with him, too. "Well, it's just one dance." Then she saw the one for which he'd signed. The waltz! It was bad enough to endure that barely appropriate dance with Riel. But Fredrick? She bit her lip. "I suppose I will endure."

The music struck up, and Jonathon led her onto the dance floor. Lucinda quite forgot all about Fredrick as the night whirled away. At least she forgot about him until late in the evening, when he arrived to claim his waltz.

Fredrick pulled her quickly into the whirling throng and held her much too close. She smelled alcohol on his breath and wrestled to maintain a proper distance between them. Jonathon was right. She'd been foolish to let Fredrick sign her dance card again. No wonder Amelia had denied him a dance. In point of fact, she couldn't remember Fredrick dancing with many people at all during the last few weeks.

Now she knew why.

Fredrick stepped too quickly to the music. Lucinda dragged her feet a little, trying to slow him down, but he paid no attention. He hustled her toward the far corner of the room. Fury blazed in his small, pebbled eyes and he gripped her hand too hard. He ground out, "Why won't your friend dance with me?"

"Loosen your grip, sir." Lucinda was tired of fighting the devil. "In fact, release me at once. I am finished with this dance."

"Not until you answer my questions."

Lucinda twisted her hand, trying to free it, but Fredrick only squeezed harder. The bones in her hand squished together, turning her skin white. Pain skewered up her arm and tears sprang to her eyes. "Stop at once! I will not answer until you behave with decorum."

He jerked her closer, and growled in her ear, "Why won't Amelia *dance* with me?"

His breath smelled quite unpleasant. Of alcohol and stale kidney pie. Lucinda gritted her teeth. "Because you are a lout!" She stamped hard on his toe. Unfortunately, he wore boots and she, only thin satin slippers.

Now his fingers pinched deep into her waist, and she involuntarily cried out in pain.

He snarled, "You two tramps think you're above me. Is that it? You think I'm dirt beneath your fine shoes."

He was hurting her. Blood pounded in Lucinda's head, and fear tainted her bravado. He'd steered her near the door to the garden. What did he intend to do? How could she escape him?

If only she could reach the butter knife she'd strapped to her shin! But lacking all other recourse... No help for it. Lucinda must employ the method her father had taught her to disable a man. She hauled back and kneed him in a most tender location.

Her thick skirts and petticoats likely softened the blow, but Fredrick still blanched and doubled over. Unfortunately, he did not loosen his grip. He recovered quickly and continued to drag her toward the garden door.

"Stop!" Lucinda dug in her heels. Unfortunately, the loud music and even louder chattering voices swallowed up her cry.

The door drew closer and closer. A tall, dark form stepped in their path.

"Release her," Riel said through his teeth.

Relief shot through Lucinda.

After an indecisive moment, Fredrick thrust her free and she staggered into Riel's hard, solid body. "Keep your trollop," Fredrick spat. "No doubt she is soiled goods." His narrowed, pig's eyes glared at her. "Or if she isn't yet, she will be soon."

Fear curled in Lucinda's stomach.

Hatred blazed from Fredrick's eyes, and she pressed backward, unconsciously seeking Riel's protection. His hands curled around her arms, securing her close against him. He said, "Is that a threat, Fredrick?"

The stocky blond man took a step backward, evidently not liking the look on Riel's face.

"She's fast and loose. You know it and I know it, Montclair. Girls who wander about in gardens ask for the most base of attentions."

In a flash, Riel put Lucinda behind him and had Fredrick by the cravat. He jerked the younger man up on his toes. Fredrick's eyes fluttered wildly, and then narrowed with malice. "Release me!" he sputtered.

"I will release you when you understand one thing. Unless you like pain, you will steer clear of Lady Lucinda."

"You're threatening me bodily harm?"

"I am promising it." Riel smiled. "And I also promise I will relish administering it." He jerked Fredrick up a notch higher. "Is that clear?"

Purple flushed Fredrick's face. "You will regret humiliating me. Both of you will!"

"I have not heard your answer." Riel's knuckles were white at the other man's throat.

"I will not offer her another dance. You may be sure of that."

Riel released Fredrick with a thrust, which sent him staggering back two steps. "I will hold you to it."

Fredrick strode away, shaking with palpable rage. Others who had stopped dancing to watch the interchange began to whisper among themselves. A few ladies tittered, which likely did not improve Fredrick's disposition.

Lucinda found herself trembling. Riel turned to her, and his hard look softened. "Are you all right, Lucy?"

"I...I'm fine."

"You do not look fine." Riel took her hand and led her to a vacant chair near the wall. He saw her seated, and when she refused a glass of punch, sat beside her.

Arms crossed, Lucinda watched Fredrick lurk near the alcoholic punch bowl across the room. "He's horrible."

"Forget him, Lucy." Riel's voice brought her attention back to him. "You are safe, and I will make certain you remain that way."

"Thank you, Riel." Tears prickled her eyes, but she blinked them back.

"You are sure you do not want a drink?" He put his hands on his thighs, as if ready to rise immediately to do her bidding.

"No." She put her hand over his to forestall him. "I'm fine." Then she realized what she had done. His hand felt very large beneath hers, and she felt the firm texture of his skin and the few short dark hairs that roughened the back of it.

"I'm sorry!" she whispered, snatching it back.

"You have not offended me, Lucy."

"But it is most inappropriate."

The black eyes smiled a little, holding hers. "I think we are beyond trivialities like that, don't you?"

"It is not right for us to become too close."

"We are bound together by your father's covenant. We are...bound...to become close."

Lucinda looked down, remembering their stolen kiss in the garden, and the chaste one in his house the other day. Alarmingly, she wanted to feel his arms around her again, holding her close to him. And she'd like to experience another of his kisses, too.

Hot color burned her cheeks, and she looked quickly away, hoping he would not notice. The music whispered to a halt, and matrons gathered up their wraps. Was it already time to go?

The band struck up a new, lively tune, and Riel's hand closed over hers this time. "I believe this is my dance."

"Of course." Lucinda stepped into his arms a trifle too willingly. She relished the feel of being near him...of feeling his muscles play beneath her fingers, and she enjoyed the sure touch of his hands upon her, minimal as that contact was. They glided effortlessly together, and the soft strains of the music wove around and between them, seeming to knit them together as one.

Was Riel holding her a little too closely to him? Lucinda did not care. In fact, unable to help herself, she edged the barest fraction nearer. A whiff of the clean, masculine scent that was Riel filled her senses. The fine linen of his shirt felt thin, compared to the jacket he usually wore, and touching his shoulder felt almost as if no barrier existed between her fingers and his bare skin at all. Confusion and a flame lit inside her at the thought.

What was wrong with her? Had she lost her senses? She had felt none of this when dancing with other men, not even Jonathon.

Here, at last, was the magic and the excitement she craved. But it was with Riel. Her heart pounded faster, and for a second, she imagined the impossible...if Riel were her suitor. The breath caught in her throat. If he pursued her, would she deny him?

No. She felt his warm breath at her temple, and for one wild, fierce moment, she longed for him to be the man to court her. For him to be the man who pursued her with his whole heart, and with all of the strength and determination that were only Riel.

Lucinda shifted in his arms as panic slid through her. What was she thinking? She couldn't have these kinds of feelings for him!

"Lucy?" He frowned. "Are you all right?" He looked over her head, apparently scanning the room. "Did you see Fredrick?"

Fredrick? That disagreeable young man couldn't be further from her thoughts. Instead, the tall man before her filled every corner of her mind and heart. "No," she whispered, and pulled back the instant the music stopped.

Riel watched her with a concerned, quizzical expression. That couldn't be helped. Better that, than let him know what she'd truly been thinking.

"I...I believe I am tired. I would like to take my leave now."

He inclined his head, still obviously trying to figure out what was wrong with her. He extended his arm. With grace, she accepted it, and felt the hard muscles of his forearm through the fine cloth. Lucinda said her goodbyes, and walked beside him for the door and down the steps to the lamp lit street. She felt intensely aware of the man at her side.

Fredrick bumped her arm hard, on the way down the stairs, and Lucinda almost felt grateful for the flash of rage she felt, for it turned her mind away from her disturbing guardian.

Fredrick disappeared into a carriage. The horses clopped down the street. A new thought entered her mind, and her eyes narrowed. Those women who had been abducted...had they spurned their suitors? Had they been raped by a malicious, rejected man such as Fredrick? She would put nothing past that man. Malevolence lurked in him. Fredrick was a man to watch.

❧ ❧ ❧ ❧ ❧

A few more weeks whirled by, and once again, Lucinda tried her best to avoid Riel. Her burgeoning feelings for him would not do. In the mornings, when he came down for breakfast, she wanted to linger and talk to him. She did not. At supper, when he tried to engage her in conversation, she was polite, but left as soon as was decently proper.

She did *not* have any sort of romantic feelings for Riel Montclair. She needed to find an eligible man to marry, and fast. And her disturbing guardian was certainly not him.

At this rate, the Season would end before she found a husband.

Sophie didn't talk much anymore, but one afternoon she patted Lucinda's hand and urged her to come closer. In a breathy whisper, she said, "Have...you...fallen in love...yet?"

Lucinda's mind flashed to Riel, but she struggled to banish that errant thought. She shook her head. "I don't know what's wrong, Sophie." She thought back over the past two months. A few young men had shown interest in her in the beginning, but now, for the first time, Lucinda realized they had all faded away. She frowned. Even that nice Earl of Hart she'd met at that first ball.

"You...are frowning."

"I'm thinking. A few men seemed interested in the beginning, but I haven't danced with them in weeks. They've been at the balls, though. I've seen them."

"Perhaps...they've found...another young woman?"

"Maybe. But all of them? I don't understand it."

"Has...Riel...scared them off?"

Momentarily taken aback, Lucinda considered the odd question. "I don't think so. He did threaten Fredrick, but Fredrick is frightful. As far as the others...I don't think so." At least, she hadn't seen Riel glowering at any of her suitors. But he *had* deliberately warned Jonathon off on multiple occasions over the last two years. To no avail, thankfully. Persistent Jonathon was well accustomed to having his own way. Riel didn't scare him.

Sophie patted her hand. "The right one...will turn up."

But Sophie's comments made Lucinda think. During dessert at supper that night, she asked Riel, "Do you find it strange that few men are pursuing my hand?"

He relaxed back in his chair. "Have you shown them the cut of your tongue, Lucy?"

"No!" She sent him the frown he clearly desired. "Sophie asked if you've scared them off. Have you?"

She could not read his black gaze. "What purpose would that serve me? You remain my responsibility until you marry."

"What if I never marry?" she asked, just to be difficult.

"Then we will grow old together."

Disconcerted, she pushed her dessert plate away. "Then I had better make my selection soon. A man of your age may soon find his choices dwindling."

"I will never marry."

This statement took Lucinda aback. "Never?"

Riel remained silent.

"Why?" she pressed, feeling both surprised and a little bewildered.

With a restless movement of his shoulders, he looked out the window. "The sea is in my blood. It is where I belong."

Lucinda couldn't believe it. Warmth lived inside Riel. And tenderness. He'd shown both on numerous occasions to both herself and Sophie. "Don't you want a home? Or children..." Her voice faltered.

She'd been about to say he'd make a wonderful father. Warmth burned her face when those dark eyes held hers. Pain lurked in them. "I will never have a family or a home. The sea is where I belong."

Unexpected pain sliced through her. "How you must itch to get back, then."

He did not deny it. Sophie had said the sea had called him from a young age. Its siren song must be strong indeed, for him to forever swear off home and hearth. Who could possibly match the great, restless mistress of the sea? Anguish licked through Lucinda.

Blinking quickly, she said, "Then I had better marry soon, so you can speedily return to your first love."

Riel's fist clenched. "It is the way things must be, Lucy."

Why, then, did pleading soften his eyes—as if he silently begged her to understand something deeper? But what? Why would he possibly say words that weren't true?

"Then I must find a man to marry soon," she managed. "Perhaps Jonathon will ask for my hand and give us both what we most urgently desire...a severing of our inconvenient relationship." Lucinda bit her lip. Did she truly mean what she had just said? No. Not at all.

"Jonathon is not the man for you."

Lucinda blinked in further surprise. This was the first time Riel had voiced a blunt objection to her relationship with the Duke.

"Riel, you will not interfere in our friendship." Especially since Riel clearly would never pursue her for himself. He loved the sea. She should feel grateful that he'd skewered her fledgling fantasies. He was all wrong for her, anyway. She'd known that from the start.

"If I discover proof he's a rake of the first order, I will end your friendship."

She gasped at his pure, high-handed gall. "Jonathon is not in the least bit unsavory! He is above reproach, unlike you! He's lived as a gentleman his whole life. You've lived as a pirate for half of yours. You know nothing of what it means to be a gentleman."

"I know what it is to be a man. An honorable man. Your Jonathon will measure up to my standards, or you will cut him from your life."

"I will *not*."

His lips straightened into a thin, grim line. "We will see."

Balling her hands into fists, Lucinda exclaimed, "What will you do? Forbid me to see him? It will not work. What's more, I will lose all respect for you!"

"Lucinda."

She jumped up and fled from the room.

Chapter Twenty-One

AT THE BALL the next night, Lucinda refused Riel's request for a dance. For one thing, she could not stand the torture of being in his arms, nor the ache of being near him. For another, she'd thought more about why so few men pursued her. It might be because Riel kept staking claim to her last dance. Maybe. Intentionally or not, Riel was sending them the wrong message. She needed to find a husband.

Really, only Jonathon pursued her, and much as she'd argued with Riel about it, she did not anticipate Jonathon asking for her hand in marriage. She just resented Riel's high-handed temerity in threatening to cut off their relationship.

Riel could think about that while she danced her last dance with Jonathon later this evening.

"A frown is creasing your lovely brow," the Duke of Warrington said now, as they danced the first waltz of the evening. He leaned close and whispered in her ear, "Perhaps in lieu of a dance, you will stroll with me in the garden."

Lucinda's heart beat more rapidly. It was tempting, if for no other reason than to confound her guardian. She glanced across the room. He danced with a tall, slim brunette who pressed a little too closely to him. Lucinda looked away. Soon she would be freed of his guardianship. She tried to ignore the anguish that squeezed her heart at that thought. He loved the sea. Fine. She must get on with her life, as well.

Tonight, she'd taken bold measures to ensure it. Lucinda had renewed her acquaintance with Donald Tinsley, the Earl of Hart, and would dance with him twice later on. He'd seemed quite pleased that she'd sought out his attention.

She looked up at Jonathon. "I'd best not. The Baron may call you out."

Jonathon's eyes narrowed. "He doesn't like me, and hasn't since the first."

"He thinks you're a rake of the first order. If he finds proof of it, he's threatened to cut you out of my life."

"Really." Jonathon's lips thinned. "We will see about that."

Lucinda squeezed his shoulder. "Don't worry, Jonathon. I won't let that happen. We're friends, and we will remain so, because I wish it. Riel has little say in the matter."

Jonathon smiled. "You are both feisty and beautiful, Lucinda. No wonder no other woman attracts me like you do."

"You are a flatterer," she retorted with a laugh. "But I appreciate your kind words."

"You think I don't mean it?" For once, Jonathon actually looked serious. "I have met no other woman who has held my attention for as long as you, Lucinda."

"I will take that as a compliment. I think."

Jonathon laughed, and pulled her a little closer as they approached Riel. Lucinda lifted her chin as they sailed by. Riel Montclair must learn that he was not lord over her life. And as soon as she married, she would be freed from him forever.

She need only find that right man. Certainly, he was not Riel Montclair. Once again, she tried to ignore the ache of pain in her heart.

Lucinda also tried to block from her mind the image of her guardian's black eyes watching her. A part of her did feel like she belonged to him...that she should heed his words. Well, she would, if he was reasonable. If not, well then...

The ball progressed as all others through supper and dessert, and then more dancing continued. The partnering of the players varied, though, like colors on a loom. Lucinda had warned Amelia to steer clear of the malevolent Fredrick, but Amelia had already come to that conclusion on her own. Right now, her friend danced with young Timothy Fenwick. Was that the second time this night?

Lucinda took a breather as the dance ended, and Amelia headed for the chairs as well. Lucinda noted Timothy gazing after her friend like a lovesick puppy dog.

"Is Timothy courting you?" Lucinda asked as her friend sat, waving her fan before her damp face.

Surprised uncertainty flickered in Amelia's eyes. "I don't know." A small pause elapsed. "He's gained two inches this past year." She glanced at the tall, blond-haired young man, who now danced with a pretty red-head. "He still sometimes looks like a mournful puppy to me."

"Does he still smash toes?"

"Once or twice every dance." Amelia glanced ruefully at the dried patch of spilled punch on her dress. "Perhaps we are a matched pair."

After the dance, Timothy approached and asked a bit hesitantly if Amelia would like a cup of punch.

"Thank you." Again, Lucinda noted the uncertainty in her pragmatic friend's eyes. "I would love one."

With a quick grin, Timothy hurried away.

"He's kind of cute with you," Lucinda offered.

"Do you think so?" A frown touched Amelia's brow, and then eased. "Tell me all about your latest suitors."

"I don't have any to speak of. Jonathon is certainly not serious. I've danced twice with the Earl of Hart. He seems nice."

"What of the Baron?"

"*Riel?*" Pain crept into Lucinda's heart. She didn't want to dwell on her conflicted feelings for her guardian. "I've told you he drives me batty. Did you know he threatened to cut Jonathon out of my life? Yes, that's right. He said he will, if he finds proof of unsavory, rakish activities. The gall of that man."

"I think you should be careful of Jonathon, too."

Surprised, Lucinda said, "But he's your cousin."

"Riel's right. Jonathon is a rake."

"Well, I don't expect Jonathon to ask me to marry him, if you're worried about that. It's just that Riel can be so...frustratingly bossy. It maddens me."

"Even if he only wants what's best for you?"

"Even then."

Timothy returned with Amelia's drink and Lucinda excused herself, on the pretense of an important errand. Really, she wanted to see what might develop with her friend's unlikely romance with young Lord Fenwick.

"Lucy." Riel appeared by her side. She would have kept walking, but he captured her hand. His easily dwarfed hers, and his palm felt warm and calloused. Her mouth suddenly went dry and her heart beat faster. She attempted to free herself, but he didn't allow it. "Walk with me."

"Why?" she hissed, having no choice but to walk fast at his side. "You are behaving most inappropriately, as usual."

To her shock, he opened the door to the garden. Lucinda dug in her heels. "I am *not* going out there with you again. Perhaps you think me a woman of easy virtue..."

"Lucy." The single word stilled her protest. But she couldn't be alone with him. He disturbed her too deeply. Not only that, but she'd had enough of his dictatorial decrees, too, she reminded herself again.

All the same, she followed him to the edge of the rose garden.

Still, he did not release her hand. Her temper bubbled. "Will you kindly unhand me? I am tired of being dragged thither and yon."

"I am sorry, Lucy." He released her.

"You're sorry? For what? Dragging me out here?"

"I'm sorry I threatened to cut Jonathon out of your life last night." The words sounded rehearsed...and forced. As if he didn't want to say them, but knew he must.

Surprised, she crossed her arms. "What made you see the error of your ways?"

"Lucy," he growled. "I know I was unreasonable. I am sorry." A few moments ticked by. At last, more quietly, he admitted, "I don't like it when you're angry with me."

"You care what I think of you?"

His hand swiped at his black hair in that tail; a frustrated movement. "Of course I do."

This was a new development; a turning point in their relationship. He'd just allowed her to see that she held power over him, too. An equaling of the playing field, at last. "You do?" she said softly.

"Will you forgive me?"

"Of course. If you will forgive me, too, for avoiding you and being a bit cold tonight."

Tension eased out of his broad shoulders. "Of course. Do you still have a dance to give me?"

"I have one right now."

It felt cool outside, compared to the hot crush of bodies indoors. Strains of music drifted outdoors. A waltz, of course.

"Will you dance with me? Here?" he said quietly.

It was vastly inappropriate. But what about their relationship had ever been ruled by etiquette? She moved into his arms and felt like she'd come home. Her hand slid up to his shoulder, and he pulled her close enough that her cheek could rest on his chest. Much nearer than proper. But she liked it. In fact, she relished it.

The strains of the melody strummed through her heart, and tangled with the strong thump of his heart in her ear. This was where she wanted to be. In his arms forever. All of their silly snits and arguments over the years fell into perspective at last.

They were their first, tentative steps of courtship. At least, for her that was true. She didn't know what Riel felt for her. But now she understood why she'd shoved him away so strenuously for so long. She'd fought this quiet certainty that she'd completely and irrevocably lose her heart to Riel Montclair.

A sob gathered in her throat as this alarming truth swelled, filling her heart completely. She loved him. She'd fallen in love with her strong, immovable, maddening, honorable guardian. The man whose first love was the sea.

How had it happened? Why him? He met none of her specifications!

Well, he was tall and handsome...

Stop it! Didn't she want a man who would let her rule her own life? An agreeable man, not an authoritative one. A civilized gentleman, not a pirate. A lord of the manor, not a ship's captain! A future between them was impossible. He'd never give up the sea to court her.

But what if he would? A shiver ran through her at the thought.

"Are you cold?" Riel asked, against her hair.

"No," she whispered. Her foolish fantasies must go. Riel did not intend to marry...not ever. This fact sliced into her soul. Further proof that her feelings were fruitless and self-destructive. Perhaps...maybe if she ignored them, they would go away.

"Lucy." He pulled back. His black eyes held a faintly quizzical look. "Are you all right?" Then he frowned and brushed her cheek with his fingers. "You are crying! Why?"

Lucinda drew a quick breath. Never could he know what she had been thinking. She pulled away. "I believe the dance has ended."

"What is wrong?" Concern deepened his voice.

"Sometimes we want...what is simply impossible."

"Do you mean Jonathon?" His voice roughened.

Jonathon couldn't be further from her mind. But maybe it would be best to let him think so. "I'm glad you changed your mind about him. I will be sure to tell him."

"Lucy." He touched her arm.

"I'm chilly, Riel." She had felt warm in his arms, but now she felt cold, alone and heartsick. "Will you see me inside?"

"Of course." He offered his arm and they walked inside. Lucinda held onto the moment for as long as she could. All of her life she had wondered with whom she would fall in love. Now she knew.

How could her heart choose a man who would never be hers?

Tears glimmered again, but she swallowed them back.

Enjoy the moment, her soul whispered. *Enjoy every minute you have with him, for soon they will be gone.*

Chapter Twenty-Two

ANOTHER WEEK crept by. Sophie could barely speak now, and lay blue and quiet most of the time. Lucinda still read to her. It seemed to be her only comfort. Grief grew in Lucinda's heart for the friend who was quietly slipping away, and for the man she could never have.

She continued to spend most of her time with Jonathon at the dances. Riel didn't like it. His features stiffened when they twirled by him, but he said nothing. She did catch him shooting Jonathon a glare, jaw clenched, from time to time.

"Your guardian doesn't think I possess honorable intentions toward you." Jonathon said one evening.

"Do you?" Then Lucinda felt bad. "I'm sorry. But he's under the impression you're a rake. It's an impression I share, if I must be honest."

Jonathon bowed over her hand. "Lady Lucinda, I am finished playing the field."

"You are?"

He lifted her fingers to his lips. "Perhaps it is time I settled down."

"It is?" Lucinda could not seem to stop her inane questions. But she stood transfixed. Could Jonathon possibly be saying...?

"Perhaps it would help if I state my intentions to your saber rattling guardian."

"Perhaps it would." Lucinda felt faint.

"Then I will call round at the earliest opportunity." Sea green eyes held hers as he bestowed another kiss upon her knuckles. "Would that please you, Lady Lucinda?"

Lucinda pulled herself from her stupor. Would it?

Then, "Of course!" She wanted a husband, didn't she? If she couldn't have Riel, then Jonathon was the best of the lot. And he wished to marry her? It seemed beyond the realms of possibility that a first-class rake would give up his idle pleasures to chain himself to her.

"Are you certain?"

He smiled. "I have never met such a charming, spirited woman, Lucinda. You have quite captured my heart."

"Oh. Well...thank you." Lucinda felt tongue-tied. Shouldn't she be saying something else? Like pledging her undying devotion to him, too? The words stuck in her throat, but Jonathon didn't seem to notice.

He released her hand at last. "I will speak to the Baron now and set up an appointment to speak to him. Soon all the ruffles will be straightened out, and your guardian will no longer need to protect you from me."

Lucinda nodded. Jonathon strode in Riel's direction.

A proposal. She'd just received her first—and *only,* she reminded herself—marriage proposal. She should feel elated. And indeed, her heart pumped alarmingly fast. But whether it was from joy or panic, she could not tell.

ఆ ఆ ఆ ఆ ఆ

Jonathon called at Riel's townhouse two days later. When Lucinda saw his carriage pull up, she impulsively sprinted for Riel's empty study. Would Jonathon truly ask for her hand? What would Riel say to him?

Heart thumping, she hid behind a long drape in Riel's study. Perhaps this wasn't her brightest idea, but she couldn't bear the thought of waiting outside the door, biting her nails. Wasn't this about her? Didn't she have a right to hear it all?

These logical justifications did little to soothe her conscience, but Lucinda didn't move from her hiding place. She waited, nerves jumping, for the men to enter. She still wasn't sure how she felt about Jonathon's proposal...if indeed that was the purpose of his call today.

Of course it was. Biting her lip, she listened as the men's boot steps entered the room. The door clicked closed.

She peeked around the edge of the curtain. Jonathon stood with flowers in his hands, facing Riel, behind the desk. Stiffly, he said, "I'm not sure if Lucinda has mentioned the reason for my visit this day."

A moment of silence. Lucinda frustratingly could not see Riel's expression, for he stood with his back to her. "No. Lady Lucinda has brought nothing to my attention."

"I am here to humbly request her hand in marriage."

Riel moved to the side of the desk. His stiff, broad shoulders and his jerky first step were the only indicators of his emotions.

"You may not have Lucinda's hand, nor any other part of her." His voice sounded flat, without expression.

Red suffused Jonathon's neck, and rose to his cheeks. "You have no right to refuse me!" he snarled. "I am a member of the aristocracy. I have a title, land, and wealth. What do you have, Montclair? This townhouse, and a little ship, bobbing in port."

"This is about Lady Lucinda. I am her guardian, and that is all the authority you need to understand."

Jonathon clenched his jaw. "You hate me, Montclair. You have from the beginning. Why?"

"You are a rake, Duke. Is that not reason enough?" Riel turned now, and Lucinda saw that his eyes were hard.

"It's because I remember you, isn't it?" Jonathon lashed out, like a feral cat advancing upon its prey. "Lucinda mentioned you'd been in Morocco thirteen years ago. So was I. I remember you from Tangier, don't I?"

Riel's face closed. "I have been many places, Duke. The locations are unimportant."

Jonathon's fingers crushed the flowers he held. "We will see about that, Montclair. We will see!" With a swift turn, he exited from the room. The front door slammed, and reverberated throughout the entire house.

Riel's white-knuckled fingers gripped the back of his chair.

Lucinda slipped from her hiding place, not particularly caring that it revealed her shameless eavesdropping. "Riel! Why?"

"Lucy." His shoulders straightened. "You were spying."

"Of course. Are you surprised?"

A smile glimmered. "No."

"Why won't you let me marry Jonathon?"

"I will not," he said harshly. "And that is the end of it."

"It is not the end until you tell me why!"

"He is a rake, Lucy. What more do you need to know?"

Lucinda fisted her hands. "Who else am I to marry, then? No other suitors have knocked on my door. And Jonathon says he wants to settle down."

"A leopard cannot change its spots."

"Such as you? Once a pirate, always a pirate? Who are *you* to judge anyone?"

"I will be the judge of Warrington," he said in a low, vehement tone. "And he will never be good enough for you!"

"Then who is? How many other suitors have you scared off?"

His fingers fisted. "Lucy. I'm not trying to be unreasonable. I'm trying to protect you."

"*You* are the one from whom I need protection, Riel Montclair. Your job is to deliver me to a suitable husband, but you just sent one right out that door. Tell me why! And don't tell me it's because Jonathon's a rake. Rakes are a pence a dozen in London, and any number of them settle down and get married. I want the truth!"

"Lucy." He said no more.

"I thought so. Stiff-necked and unreasonable to the end." She left the study and slammed the door behind her. It felt good. For a moment.

She dashed to her room, overcome with tears. Riel would deny her every happiness. He'd never offer her himself, and now he'd just denied her the one man who did want her.

Lucinda collapsed onto her bed and clenched her pillow in helpless, hopeless anger and grief. She felt achingly alone. Perhaps she would remain so for the rest of her life.

❧ ❧ ❧ ❧ ❧

Riel paced the study like a caged lion. Lucy hated him, but he'd live with that pain. At all costs, he must protect her from that viper, Warrington.

The Duke would marry Lucy over Riel's dead body.

His mind returned to Jonathon's threats. He'd been in Tangier, Morocco thirteen years ago. The same year Riel had been there. The same year he'd killed Desalt.

What if Jonathon had witnessed the trial aboard the British Naval frigate, *HMS Endurance*? What if he spread those facts throughout London?

Riel did not care if others learned about his past. It was old news, and settled in that foreign port. And thankfully, the Brits no longer wanted to find a reason to seize his ship, since the war was over. The news would, however, ruin his reputation if it spread about the *ton*.

Riel paced, trying to think. He cared nothing for the *ton* or its whispering gossip mills.

But he did care what Lucy thought. He couldn't bear to see the disgust and contempt in her eyes if she learned the truth. That fear had haunted his nightmares ever since winter. He couldn't take the thought of it actually happening.

Lucy trusted him now. Although she was angry at him for the moment, she liked him—he could tell by that soft look in her eyes when she smiled at him. And he could tell by the way she kissed him.

Riel's gut twisted, thinking about that stolen kiss in the garden. The kiss he'd taken much too far, unable to stop himself. Even now, weeks later, he continued to think about that sweet kiss with uncomfortable frequency, as well as the chaste one he'd purloined in the hall not so long ago.

Riel didn't want any other man to touch Lucy. And he'd recently realized how mercilessly he'd grilled each of her suitors all Season long...and unconsciously chased off every one.

All except for Jonathon, the worst of the lot. A predator, his instincts told him, but he couldn't prove it. He'd bet his ship that the man wanted to use Lucy, and spend all of her money on his idle pursuits. Then he could keep his own fortune intact for his heirs.

Riel clenched his fists. Jonathon was a worm; he felt it in his bones, and not just because the Duke was a Warrington, either. Riel would lay down his life to protect Lucy from that snake. Jonathon would never have her.

Nor would any other man.

Then the truth hit him like the swing of an unfettered sail boom to the head.

Riel wanted Lucy all to himself. Because he loved her.

Chapter Twenty-Three

THE SEASON twirled on, including the latest of the unending balls. Lucinda felt heart weary and sick of them. She didn't want to pretend to look for a husband anymore.

This evening, all the players were present: Riel, Jonathon, Amelia, Timothy...and even Fredrick. Lucinda had managed to avoid Riel completely for the last two days, including meals, which she requested be brought up to her room. He frustrated her beyond measure. She loved him, and yet couldn't have him. And while she wasn't entirely sure she wanted to marry Jonathon, Riel had stripped that choice from her, too. Why did she have to fall head-over-heels in love with that maddening man?

And why was he so set against Jonathon? Besides the rake issue, of course. Something more fueled Riel's palpable dislike of the man. But what? Was it something to do with Riel's past? Something Jonathon might know about?

It made little sense to her. But at least Riel had not requested to sign her dance card this evening. He seemed to understand she would refuse him flat out.

Lucinda danced the waltz with the Earl of Hart now, and she scanned the room, looking for Jonathon, her next partner. He'd claimed two of her dances, as usual. He didn't appear to be giving up, despite Riel rejecting his marriage proposal for Lucinda. She felt grateful for his constancy. At least Jonathon cared enough about her to continue on as friends.

She spotted Jonathon leaning against the wall, sipping punch. A frown disturbed his handsome brow. Unusual for him. So was the fact he wasn't dancing. What was he thinking about?

Her gaze continued to scan the room, and she spied Riel. He stood with his arms crossed, watching her. A frown pulled his brows together, too. She averted her eyes, and glanced in another direction. Yards away, Amelia danced with Timothy Fenwick again.

Lucinda felt a hard bump on her arm, and Fredrick strode by, heading for Amelia. An ugly scowl contorted his face. The scent of alcohol drifted to her nose.

Donald guided her steps toward the opposite side of the ballroom, but Lucinda tipped her chin left and hissed, "This way." She urged him after the dissolute Fredrick. Obligingly, the handsome young man swept her in the direction she wished to go. Lucinda stood on tiptoe so she could see more clearly...and gasped.

Fredrick's meaty fist gripped Amelia's arm, and he yanked her from Timothy. Amelia staggered sideways, and Fredrick shoved her so hard she fell to the floor. In the next breath, Fredrick hauled back and punched young Fenwick dead in the nose.

"You rat!" Amelia leaped up and snapped her fan across the brigand's face. Fredrick flinched, and seized her arm again. He forced her to stride with him toward the exit. Meanwhile, Timothy wore a dazed look, and pressed his fingers to his bleeding nose.

Amelia slapped Fredrick again, but the blond man's meaty hand squeezed her arm harder, turning it white. Amelia cried out. Lucinda gasped. Suddenly, Timothy appeared out of nowhere and clipped Fredrick on the jaw.

With a snarl, Fredrick turned on him. Fear flashed across the younger man's face. Fredrick swung for him, but Timothy side-stepped and clobbered Fredrick's eye this time. Timothy punched him again and again, with amazing speed, and blood spurted out of Fredrick's nose. Another punch made him double over with a moan of pain.

Men, including Riel, advanced on the fighting pair and pulled them apart. Fredrick, clearly the worse for wear, sagged on the arms of those who had rescued him. "You'll pay!" he spat. The charge seemed to include everyone in the room. "I'll call you out. I will kill you!"

"I'm better with a blade," Timothy said, swiping his bloody mouth. Incredibly, he smiled. "Tell me the time and the place."

Fredrick's eyes narrowed, and his face turned a bilious purple. "*Trash,*" he spat at Amelia, and then, for some unknown reason his gaze fixed upon Lucinda. "*Trash!*" he screamed. Riel and the others dragged him to the door, and bodily threw him out.

Amelia rushed to Timothy. "Are you all right?"

The dance had stopped by now. One matron lay slumped on the floor in a dead faint.

"I'm fine," Timothy said with a sheepish smile. "I'll clean up. I must look a sight."

"No." Amelia raised a hand to his face, but quickly lowered it. "Thank you."

Timothy disappeared in the direction of the washroom, and Lucinda joined Amelia at the wall.

"Timothy is your knight in shining armor!"

"Yes," Amelia said softly.

Lucinda didn't want to pry into her friend's feelings. They might still be too new to share. Instead, she said, "I think he likes you."

Amelia nodded. "It's flattering." Her cheeks flushed. "But he's so young."

"He's grown up, and he's filling out nicely," Lucinda pointed out. "And think about this; perhaps in a year or two he'll master his dancing, and his charm will attract all the girls. Best to lay the groundwork now, Amelia," she advised with a small smile. "In case you might be interested later."

Timothy reappeared with a clean face, and Amelia glanced at Lucinda, her eyes suddenly bright. "I might. I just might at that."

❧ ❧ ❧ ❧ ❧

Lucinda managed to avoid Riel until supper the next day. When she came down to request that another tray be sent to her room, she found her guardian in the kitchen speaking to the cook.

Lucinda silently waited for him to leave.

He turned to her. "I want you to dine with me this evening."

Instead of arguing in front of the cook, she followed him into the dining room. There she stopped. "I would like to dine alone."

"You are behaving like a child," he said, pouring a glass of wine.

She frowned. "Better than a close-minded, dictatorial pirate."

"I know you won't believe me, Lucy, but I refused Jonathon with only your best interests in mind."

"Tell me then, once and for all, why you hate him so. And leave out the part of him being a rake, if you please. That excuse has worn thin."

"Sit with me, Lucy. Please."

With a faint huff of a breath, she did as he asked, just in time for the first course to arrive. Both tucked into the succulent roasted asparagus and bread.

"You won't answer me, will you?" she asked after a while, when he said nothing.

"I care about you, Lucy."

The words felt like an unexpected punch to her heart. "You do?"

"You deserve an honorable man, and one devoted only to you."

"Jonathon is devoted..."

"Jonathon cares only about himself."

"You don't know him! You've judged him from the first."

"Do you truly want him, Lucy? Are you in love with him?"

The question caught her off guard. With that direct black gaze holding hers, as if able to read into her soul, Lucinda floundered. "I...I think he is a fine man. And certainly no one better has asked for my hand."

Riel would never ask for her hand. If only he would.

"Do you love him?" he pressed.

Lucinda didn't know what to say. She did not love Jonathon. She loved this recalcitrant man before her. But since he would never want her, she would have to settle for second best. "Would you change your mind if I did?"

He sipped his wine. "Perhaps."

Lucinda felt a sick flare of victory. "Well, know this. I care about him, and I want to marry him."

A loud noise suddenly pounded from the front of the house.

Riel immediately strode from the dining room. Lucinda followed, after wiping her mouth with her napkin.

George swung open the door to reveal Jonathon. Fury flashed when Jonathon's gaze landed upon Riel. "Montclair," he gritted through bared teeth. "I would like a word with you."

Riel stiffened, and for one second Lucinda tasted his fear; an emotion she'd never sensed in him before. The next moment, it vanished. "Of course. In my study."

Chapter Twenty-Four

LUCINDA PACED the hall, biting her lip. She could hear nothing. She'd tried to press her ear to the door, but had heard only a low rumble of hard, unfriendly voices.

Unexpectedly, the door wrenched open and Jonathon stalked out. "I will tell *all* of London," he snarled over his shoulder.

Riel appeared in the doorway. His tanned face looked pale. "Tell whomever you wish. It's old business, and settled long ago."

Jonathon whirled on him. "I will tell Lucinda."

If possible, Riel grew paler still, and his hand clenched the door frame. "Tell her," he said in a low, rough voice.

"I will." Jonathon turned to her.

Lucinda's gaze flickered between them. A horrible, sick feeling swelled within her. All of a sudden, she did not want to hear what Jonathon had to say.

She licked her lips. "Wait. I do not..."

Jonathon gripped her arm. It hurt. "You *must* listen. You must learn what manner of man your guardian is. Then you can decide if he's worthy of your respect."

"You're hurting me," Lucinda said faintly.

"Sorry." Jonathon removed his hand. "But the truth must be aired now." His green eyes looked like frozen chips of ice. The hostile glance he sent Riel glittered with cruel triumph.

Riel stood like a statue in the doorway. He said nothing to discourage Jonathon's proclamations.

Lucinda didn't *want* to know what Jonathon was talking about, and yet she had to know. If Jonathon knew an important truth about Riel—important enough that he insist she listen— shouldn't she discover what it was?

With apprehension, she said, "What...what is it, then?"

"Perhaps you should sit down."

"No." Lucinda's mouth felt dry. "Tell me now, please."

"Very well." Jonathon glanced at Riel, but made no effort to hide the anger and the glee in that one hard look. "I've said several times that I thought I remembered Montclair. I could not remember from where, though, for the life of me. And then, last night, after watching that brawl between Fredrick and Fenwick over Amelia, the feeling became stronger. This afternoon, after a short nap, the memory finally snapped free. I saw him thirteen years ago in Tangier, Morocco. Aboard the British Naval frigate, *HMS Endurance*."

Lucinda glanced at Riel. "I didn't know you were in the Navy."

"He wasn't," Jonathon interjected. "He was on trial, and my father was the judge. I came with him to work that day. I heard the charges against Montclair, and he confessed to his crime. Murder."

Lucinda's mouth fell open. "*Murder!* No."

"Yes. He killed a man and he should have swung. Some pansy Captain of the Royal Navy took pity on him and got him off, more's the pity. Captain..."

"Hastings," Riel said quietly.

Lucinda's gaze shot to his. "*Father* set you free?"

"I didn't deserve freedom."

"So it's *true?*"

"Yes," he said flatly.

She couldn't believe it. She staggered back a step. Instantly, Jonathon cupped her elbow and led her to a nearby bench.

Lucinda, however, could not remove her eyes from Riel. "You *murdered* someone?"

He said nothing; just watched her, his face devoid of expression.

"You killed someone," she whispered. Lucinda's world began to crumble. The stones of their relationship, so carefully built, collapsed about her, one after another. Trust in Riel. Respect. Hero worship, from time to time. Love.

A sob choked her throat. From the beginning, she had suspected he harbored a dark secret. But she'd had no idea how dark or depraved it could be.

Riel was not the man he pretended to be. He never had been. She'd fallen in love with a murderer. A *murderer!*

She averted her face, unable to look at him.

"I would like a word with Lucinda," Jonathon shot over his shoulder, and knelt beside her.

Riel remained where he was, as if frozen to the spot, and said nothing at all. He appeared to be in a state of shock.

"Lucinda." Jonathon wiped at her tears. "Lucinda, listen to me. See the manner of man your guardian is? He says he wants to protect you from me, but perhaps it is you who needs protection from him."

Lucinda bit her lip, trying to control her shuddering breaths.

Softly, Jonathon said, "I know this is a shock to you, but listen, you don't have to remain under his authority. I will rescue you. If you'll give me your hand in marriage, I will be a devoted husband. You will not regret marrying me for one single day."

But how could she? Nothing had changed. Riel was still her legal guardian, and he'd forbidden the marriage. Or did Jonathon want her to run away with him?

"I...I do care for you, Jonathon." But she did not love him. She loved a certain raven-haired pirate. A *murderer*. Again, the devastation of it ripped through her. What a fool. What a fool she was! She'd *known* from the beginning he'd hidden something from her. Yet she'd turned a blind eye to this truth. She'd believed she had been wrong.

And yet she'd been right all along.

The last tiny, illogical hope that she'd nurtured, deep in her heart, that maybe, someday, Riel might want her, vanished. Riel was a murderer. A criminal. And completely unacceptable as a husband.

Anguish suffocated the breath from her lungs. She could never marry him. *Never.*

More tangled thoughts tumbled through Lucinda's head. She had to get him out of her life, and at once. Not only because he was a murderer, but because she loved him. She couldn't spend another minute with him, or her heart would break, more deeply and painfully every day. So she must marry immediately, so he'd leave immediately. And Jonathon seemed as good a choice for a husband as any.

Jonathan said in a low voice, "Are you all right, Lucinda?"

"Yes." She drew a shaky breath. "I would be happy to marry you. But how?" she whispered. "Riel still doesn't approve."

"It doesn't matter." Jonathon whispered now, too. "Come away with me. We'll get a special license. If we're discovered before the marriage, Riel will have no say in the matter, for we'll spend a night alone together. Then he'll have to agree to the marriage."

This plan made complete sense to Lucinda. Out of the corner of her eye, she saw Riel finally move out of the study doorway. She could not look at him. She felt sick inside, as if someone had dug out her heart and left her alone to bleed and die. "Yes." She licked her lips. "When should we go?"

ৰ্তী ৰ্তী ৰ্তী ৰ্তী ৰ্তী

Riel felt uneasy as he readied for bed that night. What a hellish evening. Earlier, at dinner, Lucy's blue eyes had flashed fire when she'd insisted she wanted to marry Jonathon. The pain of that wrenched through him again, but it meant little compared to what had happened later.

Lucy had finally learned he was a murderer.

Again and again, the shock and horror in her eyes damned Riel to the darkest pit of hell. She'd barely looked at him after that. But she'd spoken plenty to Jonathon.

Lucy had retired to bed the instant Jonathon left, and that fact raised Riel's suspicions, too. His gut told him something was wrong—besides Lucy hating him with all of her heart now. But what?

Riel stayed up until midnight with the half-formed idea that she might try to sneak out. If so, he'd stay up and catch her. It didn't happen.

Where would she go if she did? And with whom?

Jonathon. Tension gripped Riel's heart now, as it had ever since Lucy discovered the truth, and she and the Duke had whispered together afterward.

He stripped off his jacket and hung it over the chair back. He wouldn't put it past Jonathon to formulate a plan to make Lucy his own. Then Riel would no longer hold authority over her life. She would be at the mercy of that viper.

Frustrated, Riel sat down hard and yanked off his boot. If only he possessed proof that Jonathon was a two-faced weasel. Of the very same stock as his brother.

Riel's fists clenched hard, remembering the self-satisfied sneer Jonathon had sent him before exiting this evening. Riel had wanted to cuff him then, and longed to punch him now.

Fury simmered through his veins like a hot, mindless song. He had succumbed to its seduction long ago. He would not now. This time, he'd keep a level head. Riel would find out what Lucy plotted. Tomorrow would be soon enough.

Riel pulled off his other boot and chucked it to the ground.

Suddenly he was on his feet, striding for the door. He had to make sure Lucy was all right. Deep in his gut, he felt that something was wrong. Once upon a time, he had failed to listen. This time he would not ignore it. He'd check and make sure she was still there. And if he woke her up, better yet. They could talk tonight.

Riel ignored the civilized whisper that said it was improper for a man to enter a woman's room while she slept. His other half—his barbaric half—would not listen. By all that was holy, Riel told himself, he was her guardian, and he would make sure she was safe.

He rapped once on her door.

Silence.

Of course. She was asleep. He'd look in, just to make sure, and relieve the knot of unease in his chest.

Riel pushed open the door. As his eyes adjusted to the dim room he saw Lucy's bed, and the lump upon it. So, she was there.

Riel never knew what made him stride over and twitch back the bedclothes. A corner of a pillow peeked out. For a second, he couldn't believe his eyes, and then, with one savage jerk, he ripped off the entire quilt.

Gone! Lucy was gone.

Chapter Twenty-Five

LUCINDA'S HEART POUNDED after her nocturnal climb down the trellis outside her window. Jonathon waited for her below, his arms open to catch her if she fell. Of course, she didn't.

Jonathon had already caught the valise she'd tossed down to him.

Lucinda cast a backward glance at her guardian's townhouse, which lay silent and dark, except for a light in the study. Riel was still up, but unaware she'd finally escaped from him at last. After tonight, she would be freed from him forever.

Once, that had been her dearest wish. But no more. Tears ached in Lucinda's throat at the impossibility of it all, but she swallowed them back.

A few hours earlier, she'd almost abandoned her impulsive plan to marry Jonathon. Once the shock of learning the truth had worn off, she'd at last thought of Sophie. How could she possibly leave her dear friend now, while Sophie fought for her life? She could not. Then Lucinda realized she could come back and spend as much time with Sophie as she wanted, after she married Jonathon. Jonathon wouldn't mind.

Somehow, Lucinda would manage the pain of seeing Riel during that time, too. She could not leave bear to leave Sophie during her remaining days or weeks; not for longer than this one night. And she had no intention of doing so, either.

"Come," Jonathon urged, tugging at her hand, and with one final look at Riel's house, Lucinda ran after him to the waiting carriage.

Heart beating rapidly, she settled into Jonathon's carriage. It seemed surreal that she was on her own. Unfettered. Free finally to make all of her own choices. Free of Riel.

A hot tear rolled down her cheek, but she quickly dashed it away. She'd made the right choice. Now her fate rested in Jonathon's hands. He was a true, civilized gentleman.

She'd made the right choice.

Jonathon sat silently, too, as the carriage rolled through the dim London streets. Perhaps he was tired. It was late. Lucinda didn't feel much like talking, either.

"Where are we going?" she ventured after a little while.

"The Drury Inn, on the edge of town. I've arranged the special license, and we can be married tomorrow." It was hard to hear Jonathon's voice, and an odd timbre seemed to resonate through it. Lucinda dismissed the thought. The carriage was small, and the cobbles of the street outside magnified noises, distorting all normal perception of sound.

Jonathon did not seem to want to talk, so Lucinda fell silent, too. Her heart felt heavy, and she struggled not to think about Riel. She peered out the window at the dark, gloomy streets of London. Depression licked through her spirit. She remembered the girls who had been left to wander the streets alone, after being attacked by that madman rapist. She shivered. How lonely it must have been for them. How horrifying.

"Are you cold?" Jonathon's voice came out of the darkness. "I have a rug if you need it."

"No. I'm fine. Thank you." Some part of Lucinda's mind wondered why Jonathon made no move to sit beside her...although in truth she didn't care. Maybe he believed it would be improper, since they weren't married yet. And Jonathon was every inch the gentleman. He would pursue the honorable path until their vows were said.

She turned her eyes away from the black, vaguely menacing streets of this unfamiliar section of London. Clasping her hands in her lap, Lucinda drew a quiet breath to settle her nerves.

I'm doing the right thing, she told herself again. Riel would not charge after her and interrupt her plans. By morning, when he realized she was gone, she and Jonathon would be married. So then why did she feel so nervous and unsettled?

Perhaps because it was so late, and dark. And while she was with familiar Jonathon, the dark carriage was foreign, and so was the inn they approached. And the future stretched out, a dark unknown as well.

Lucinda forced her mind to positive thoughts. Of course, the inn would be of the highest caliber. Of this, she had no doubt. Perhaps once she entered her room and slipped into slumber on her comfortable bed she would feel better.

Yes. That's all she needed. But her heart told her that nothing would make her happy except for Riel. Yet how could he ever provide happiness for her? He was a murderer. Again, the knowledge choked her. Lucinda struggled to push it from her mind.

After long minutes, the carriage finally rolled to a halt.

"My lord." The driver opened the door. Jonathon jumped down, and took her hand to help her out.

It was too dark to make out much of the Drury Inn. But it looked like a solid structure, and a lamp burned in one window. She followed Jonathon inside. The driver carried their luggage behind them.

Once indoors, her spirits perked up slightly. At least fresh flowers festooned the check-in counter, and lace curtains bedecked the windows.

The large innkeeper looked a bit surly, though. The bald man shoved the book toward Jonathon to sign.

"Is the room prepared as I ordered?" Jonathon asked.

"Yeah." The man flicked Lucinda a beady glance. "Up the stairs, second door on the right."

"Thank you."

Room? Had Lucinda misheard? Perhaps it was a suite of rooms. Keeping quiet, she followed Jonathon upstairs, and he unlocked the door.

Lucinda's steps faltered in the doorway. It was not a suite of rooms. It was *one* room, with a massive four-poster bed smack in the center. A fire, flanked by two wing chairs, burned in the hearth. Apprehension uncurled within her.

She waited until the driver deposited their bags and exited before speaking. "Jonathon? We're not married yet. What is the meaning of this?"

"You trust me, don't you, love?"

After a moment, she said, "Yes."

Jonathon smiled. "To forestall your guardian's attempts to tear us asunder before we are wed, it must look as though you have been compromised this night." He pulled off his gloves and placed them on the dresser.

Lucinda's heart beat faster. "I understand that, but..."

"Tsk tsk," Jonathon waved a finger. "I promise I will be a complete gentleman. That chair by the fire will be my bed this eve."

Lucinda felt a whoosh of relief, followed by uncertain guilt. "But won't that be uncomfortable?"

"For one night I will survive. I will merely dream of tomorrow."

Lucinda would not think about tomorrow night. She could not. "But...but how will I dress?"

"I will leave you for a few minutes. Perhaps I'll take a stroll outside. You are tired and want to rest now, I am sure."

"Yes. Please."

"Very well. Let me get a warmer jacket." Jonathon opened his large valise and pulled out a folded great coat. "Be back soon." And then he was gone.

Lucinda sat abruptly on the bed. It all seemed like too much, too fast. Was she truly ready to marry Jonathon? It seemed wrong to be here with him. She loved Riel.

But Riel was not the man for her.

This truth didn't quiet the doubts pummeling her heart. Was she doing the right thing? Or had she made an impulsive decision because she'd been devastated to learn the truth about Riel?

Tears burned in her eyes, and Lucinda bit her lip. She was well rid of him, she reminded herself. More tears formed in her eyes and ached in her throat.

Jonathon was the man for her. He was a Duke. An upstanding gentleman. And at least he was wealthy, so she knew he wasn't marrying her for her money. He was also handsome, charming...and could have any girl in the world. But he had chosen her. And he was willing to risk scandal to have her. Lucinda should feel honored by the depth of his devotion.

Her heart felt hollow when she thought about Riel again. If she couldn't have him, any man would do. And Jonathon was better than most.

Lucinda quickly disrobed and pulled on her night rail. Neatly, she packed all her things away. Effie would be proud.

She stood in front of the dresser mirror, and pulled the pins from her hair. A few fell on the dresser, and one bounced into Jonathon's open bag. While running a brush through her blond tresses, Lucinda slipped her hand into his valise to find the errant pin. It was not on top, so her fingers dug down through his clothing to find it. She felt momentary embarrassment to touch his personal items, but told herself she was being silly. Soon he would be her husband.

Nausea gripped her. She gripped the dresser to steady herself. *Stop it. It is going to turn out fine.*

Under control again, she knelt and resumed her search for the pin. Lucinda did not feel the hard, slender pin, but rather silky textures. Curious, she lifted a corner of the garment. A scarf? She pulled it out, and then noticed another one beneath it. Several more lay tucked into the bottom of his valise.

Scarves? Red, yellow, and blue ones. Designs mottled the bright colors. Jonathon had four. What in the world? And then her fingers touched something else entirely. It felt rough and fibrous. Rope. Lucinda pulled out a loop and stared at it. Her heart thumped. Why would Jonathon carry scarves and rope in his bag?

Certainly they weren't ordinary items for a man to possess.

Only one man might carry such things. Her heart pounded faster as she tried to push the thought away, even as it slid into her mind.

The Silk Scarf Rapist.

But Jonathon could not be that fiend!

Could he?

The doorknob rattled, and Lucinda surged to her feet. It opened. Too late, she realized she still held the red scarf in her hand. Jonathon slipped inside and locked the door behind him.

No sense hiding it. Lucinda had to know the truth. With trembling fingers, she lifted the scarf. "What is this?"

Jonathon turned, and his pleasant expression faltered. His lips thinned. He strode toward her and plucked it from her fingers. Anger shimmered, and his slender fingers suddenly looked bony. His knuckles turned white. "It has nothing to do with you."

Lucinda felt sick. *He was not denying it.* Could he truly be...the one? Surely she must be flying to ridiculous conclusions. "Why...why do you have scarves in your valise?"

Jonathon shut the case and locked it shut. "They are not for you." His green eyes glittered, looking dark and unfathomable. And that's when she knew the truth.

Her voice trembled. "Why not? Will you save them for another girl? Or perhaps for after we are married?"

"It is not what you think. They are gifts."

Too little, too late. "And the rope? Is that a gift, too?"

Jonathon's face contorted. "I like you, Lucinda. You are not a part of it, I said."

Quiet, deadly fear slid into her soul. "I am now," she whispered.

Jonathon clenched his fists and a visible change came over him. A cold mask shuttered the windows to his soul. "Accept what I've told you, or you will leave me no choice."

Terror curled like tentacles around her heart. "You will rape me?"

"Agree to silence, or I will be forced to do far worse."

Lucinda gasped.

"Marry me and agree to keep my secret, or..." Jonathon wound the silk scarf around his palms.

Lucinda trembled and wished for her butter knife. She stepped backward. "Why?" she demanded in a shaking voice. "Why would you commit such monstrous deeds? You have everything! A title, wealth, land...and you can have any woman you want. Why...why succumb to such depravity?"

"A man who has easy access to everything becomes bored, Lucinda." He advanced toward her, the scarf stretched taut between his hands. "The thrill makes the pleasure more...acute."

Lucinda gasped, and backed up still more. "You are mad! Why...how could you even think of such depravity?"

Jonathon smiled. "My brother was my hero. I have not mentioned him to you, have I?"

"You...you have a brother?"

Jonathon grimaced. "He was murdered. But not before I saw his way with women. I was thirteen, and quite impressionable.

It stuck with me, and over the years I have learned how right he was. Forbidden fruit is the sweetest."

He stood toe to toe with her now, and Lucinda felt the silken scarf upon her neck. She had to keep him talking. She had to think of a plan of escape.

"Then...then the girl you raped last year was not your first?"

Jonathon chuckled. "Of course not, my love. But the others were low born girls. Quite feisty, too, some of them. That's one of the reasons why I like you so much, Lucinda." Quick as a wink, he swirled the scarf down and secured her wrists together.

Lucinda struggled, horrified, but Jonathon only hauled her up against his hard body and kissed her. She jerked her jaw right, and spit on him.

Jonathon's smiling eyes glittered down at her. Softly, he said, "And so the sport begins." Before she knew what he was about, he dragged her to the four-poster bed and tied her wrists to the post.

He loomed over her. "Now. Will I need my ropes, or will you behave?"

Panic beat a staccato rap through her heart and soul. Using every ounce of her strength, Lucinda tried to fling her body off the edge of the bed, but she wasn't fast enough. Hard hands bit into her, forcing her back, and Jonathon straddled her.

Lucinda bucked and twisted. Horror and fear seeped into every corner of her mind. And then he leaned forward, crushing her with his full body weight. Moist lips kissed her.

Desperately, she jerked her chin left and right but could not escape him. Lucinda felt like she was suffocating. She felt like she was about to be swallowed up by a dragon from the very pit of hell.

Help me! she prayed incoherently. *Send Riel.* Oh Riel, where was he?

For the barest second, Jonathon pulled back; perhaps to gather breath to stoke the fires of hell in his soul, and Lucinda screamed out, "Riel!"

Jonathon chuckled. "Your blackguard of a guardian will not save you now. I am the one you should be pleading with. My name should be upon your lips. Say it," he urged softly. "I want to hear you say my name."

"You are insane! Go to the devil."

"Say it now," he whispered. "Or I will make you scream it later."

She felt his hands upon her, and it was more than she could bear. "No. *No!* Riel!" she sobbed out. "*Riel...*"

∽ ∽ ∽ ∽ ∽

Panic thrummed through Riel, but with methodical swiftness he searched Lucy's room, looking for any clue pointing to where she might have gone.

Nothing. Except a valise had vanished, as had several of her new dresses.

He shoved a despairing fist at his head. "Lucy!" he growled. Terror clawed at his heart. "Where are you?"

He ran downstairs and called for his carriage. George, sleepy though he was, quickly saw to it. Outside, clouds obscured the full moon. The dusky night felt ominous and still. Riel gave the driver instructions. They couldn't have gone far. At least, Riel prayed they hadn't gone far. During the short ride, he prayed to God that he'd find them before it was too late.

When the carriage slowed, Riel sprang out and sprinted up the steps to the Warrington mansion. With a heavy fist, he pounded upon it. "Open up now!" he roared. "Be quick about it!"

A butler eventually peered out. A disdainful frown wrinkled his brow. "Here now, sir. It's the middle of the night. If you would be so good to return tomorrow..."

Riel put a shoulder to the door and shoved his way inside.

"Here, now!" the man bleated. "Come back at once, sir!"

But Riel sprinted up the stairs. He'd been here once before, and had a good guess where Jonathon's rooms might be. He burst inside. Empty. He ran to the dressing room and washing room. All neat as a pin and empty. Swiftly, he checked the table top. No notes. Nothing. Frustrated, he sent a final glance around the room, and then barreled past the butler and a footman, who had just reached the master suite.

"I sent for the constable!" the butler exclaimed in a querulous voice. "You will pay for your misdeed."

Riel lunged down the stairs and burst into Jonathon's library. A clue must be here, somewhere. Quickly, he pawed through the papers on the desk and in the drawers. A paper poked up out of the trash bin, and he snatched it out. Times were written on it; as if Jonathon had figured out to the minute the best time to snatch Lucinda. Two hours ago, by the look of it. And he'd scrawled the name of an inn. The Drury Inn, on the outskirts of London. And the name of a church and time for tomorrow.

Crumpling it in his fist, he elbowed past the butler and footman again and tore for his carriage. Two hours had passed. Was he too late? He roared instructions to the driver.

Would he make it in time? Anguish tormented Riel, as scene after scene of what Jonathon might be doing to Lucy flashed through his mind. He had no proof the Duke was the Silk Scarf Rapist. But his heart told him that Lucy was in grave danger. Had he failed a woman for the second time in his life? Riel could not bear the thought. *Please God, not Lucy. Please, no!*

Many long, excruciating minutes crept by as his team galloped through London. With every passing moment, tension coiled around Riel's heart like a tight watch spring. Anger and fear churned in him. Images from long ago tortured his mind. Images that, if he was right, could be happening again right now. Finally, the carriage slowed.

Riel hurtled out of the carriage before it stopped moving. A burly man stood at the inn's door, closing up, but Riel shoved his way inside. "Tell me the room number of a recent arrival. A man and woman," he commanded. "The woman has blond hair."

The bald man's beady eyes narrowed. He whipped out a knife. "You'd best be on your way, mister."

"She has been abducted!" Riel said through his teeth. "I am her guardian."

"As I said," the man lifted his knife. "Ye'd best be on your way."

Riel's fist shot into man's throat. With a gurgle, the inn-keeper sank to the floor. Without a backward glance, Riel headed for the desk. Which keys were gone? Half of them, it looked like. He'd have to pound on all the doors.

Riel took the stairs three at a time, and at the top he hesitated, feeling faintly dizzy. It all seemed like a sick dream. It was just like before, except there were no screaming women. No open door. Lucy. Where was she?

And then he heard a blood curdling scream.

Lucy! Heart pumping, he charged down the hall. Again he heard a cry, and this time he knew it was Lucy, for she cried out his name. A wealth of terror rang in every syllable. Riel hit the door with his shoulder and it splintered like matchsticks.

He saw Lucy on the bed with that maggot, Warrington on top of her.

Fury tore through Riel...so intense he momentarily lost all rational thought. He had no recollection of crossing the room. Only of snatching the snake off of Lucy. A red haze enveloped his mind, and he punched Jonathon's surprised face as hard as he could. He saw another, nearly identical face. It belonged to a dead man.

Riel slugged Jonathon again, and blood spurted from his nose. And again and again, he hit him. Jonathon made one attempt to rally and punch back, but Riel's years on the high seas, straining with sheets and the tasks of sailing a ship, endowed him with a strength the other man had no hope to match. Four more punches, and Jonathon collapsed on the bed, unconscious. Riel wanted to keep hitting him. To obliterate the scum who had hurt Lucy...who had hurt Pen.

Breathing hard, he staggered back a step. No. He could not. He would not kill another man.

"Riel," a tiny voice whimpered. Lucy. At last he focused upon her and then collapsed on his knees beside her.

Lucy stared up at him with wide, terrified eyes. Her wrists were tied to the post, and her ripped, thin cotton night rail was bunched about her knees. Tears filled her eyes and slipped down her face. "Riel, I knew you would come."

With a groan of anguish, he made short work of releasing her wrists. "Lucy." He groaned again and pulled her to him. "Lucy," he whispered in her hair, and then held her tight. No other words were needed.

❧ ❧ ❧ ❧ ❧

Lucinda clung to Riel and wept. He had saved her from Jonathon.

The last minute replayed through her mind in slow motion. Again, she experienced the relief that had swept through her when Riel bashed down the door. And then fear of another kind drove into her heart, for a feral snarl contorted Riel's face, making him look like a savage beast. He'd ripped Jonathon off of her and pounded hard, heavy blows into his face. Cartilage crunched as Riel smashed Jonathon's nose, and still his flying fists did not abate. In that moment, Lucinda knew Riel could easily kill Jonathon with his bare knuckles. For moments, she had actually feared for the Duke's life.

But Riel staggered back when Jonathon fell back on the bed, unconscious. The mindless fury eased from his face, and Riel's gaze fell on her. The next moment, he crumpled beside her and pulled her into his arms. *Riel.* Her protector. She felt safe in his arms.

And she still, foolishly, loved him. She loved a murderer!

Lucinda wept harder. But wasn't Riel a different man now? An honorable one.

Right now, for this one moment in his arms, none of that mattered. She held him tighter, and felt his raw strength as his heart pounded against hers. He buried his face in her hair, and she felt his warm breath on her neck.

This was where she wanted to remain. With Riel, forever. She loved him.

She loved him with her whole heart. Lucinda gasped out another sob and pressed her cheek into his neck. His rough whiskers gently scraped against her skin.

She loved him. She loved this man, who had driven her mad from the start and whom she'd pushed away for two long years.

And yet she'd almost given her life to another.

Horror trickled in. What a fool she'd been, running away with Jonathon! Impulsiveness had nearly killed her. And all because she couldn't face loving Riel, and knowing she couldn't have him.

Maybe it *would* be torture for Riel to remain in her life for a while longer, but she shouldn't have run from him, or her feelings, either.

More tears slipped down her cheeks. Tears of despair...and of relief, for right now she was exactly where she wanted to be. In Riel's arms .

"Lucy." His low voice rasped. Riel pulled back, and his dark eyes looked tortured. "Lucy, are you all right?"

Gulping, she gave a quick nod.

"He didn't...he didn't..." he said roughly.

"No."

"Thank God." Relief eased his features, and he held her tightly and securely in his arms, as if unwilling to let her go.

A groan behind them made Lucinda jerk around. "Riel!" Terror struck to her soul. "He's waking up!"

Riel's features contorted into a dangerous scowl. "We'd better find a way to restrain him. Besides my fists."

Lucinda leaped up. "He has a rope in his bag."

"Leave that for evidence. I'll use a sheet."

Chapter Twenty-Six

RIEL HANDED JONATHON over to the authorities, and a Bow Street Runner and several constables scoured the Duke's mansion and carriage. They discovered enough evidence to put him in jail. Riel, as well as the rest of the London, was relieved to witness the end of the Silk Scarf Rapist's reign of terror.

And Riel felt a grim satisfaction that after punching Jonathon into unconsciousness, he'd possessed the self-discipline to stop hitting the snake. Riel's latent fear of losing control, and again mindlessly killing someone in a rage, at last began to evaporate. Finally, healing unfurled in his soul.

Lucy was another story.

Riel was fiercely glad he'd saved her from that monster. God willing, never again would a Warrington harm a woman.

Once they got back home, however, the full reality of the situation hit Riel.

Yes, Lucy was safe, but nothing had changed. She had run away from *him* that night. She'd been shocked to discover his past murderous sin, yes, but she'd chosen Jonathon. She'd wanted to marry that rat. She'd said so, before she learned of Riel's monstrous deed.

Lucy did not want him. All of their squabbles should have proven that to him. All the ways she'd pushed him away over the last two years should have made that abundantly clear. But foolishly, Riel had believed something deeper had developed between them. He had fallen in love with her, and hoped she might love him, too.

How wrong he'd been. Lucy had not only been willing, but eager to marry Jonathon.

Pain knifed through Riel's heart. He loved her so much. If he thought he had the slightest chance now, he would pursue her, and perhaps even beg her to consider him, even though he knew he was unfit for her. But Lucy did not want him. She never had. And now she saw him as a murderer.

It was time he accepted reality.

He should feel happy. After all, Lucy was safe. He'd saved her from the wolf, like he'd promised Peter. Now he must only stand by her side until she married...much as that thought cut like a blade.

And so Riel shut himself in his study all week long, hoping it would ease the pain. It didn't. And so he made a decision. After Lucy's Season ended, he'd take another voyage on the *Tradewind*. Living with Lucy at Ravensbrook would prove more torture than he could endure.

❧ ❧ ❧ ❧ ❧

This last week in Riel's townhouse had felt strange to Lucinda.

Sophie, although peaceful, was weaker still. Lucinda and Riel had agreed not to tell her about Jonathon's attack upon Lucinda. They didn't want to upset her, or compromise her frail health. Lucinda spent every minute she could with Riel's aunt, reading, or just talking. Grief gripped her heart as Sophie's health failed.

Lucinda had skipped most social events. They held no appeal. Amelia said people were starting to speculate about her absence. So tonight she would finally attend her first ball since the incident. Although no one would know about the foolish choices she had made, Lucinda could not forget them.

Riel was quiet, too. He disappeared into his study for long hours every day. When he wasn't there, he was with Sophie...and only when Lucinda was absent. He only emerged from his self-imposed exile to escort her to those very few social events. And there he remained distant and silent.

Lucinda didn't understand the distance between them, not after the way he'd dramatically rescued her, and then held her in his arms long afterward.

It had seemed like he cared for her. So why had he avoided her all week?

Lucinda tried to tell herself it was for the best, but it bothered her, and she could not let it go. Was he still angry that she'd run off with Jonathon? Because she'd defied him?

If so, surely he would confront her. But he didn't. So it had to be something else.

She stopped him, one day on the stair, with a quick touch on his arm. He looked at her hand for a long moment, and she dropped it. A blush warmed her cheeks. With those dark, unreadable eyes upon her, it was hard to think.

"Is something wrong?" she asked.

"You are well. What more can I wish for?" He seemed detached, but otherwise hard to read.

"You're angry with me. Is it because I ran off with Jonathon?" Her heart stuck in her throat at the bold question—the crux of the problem between them, she knew it.

"You followed your heart. Sometimes our hearts betray us." His black eyes held hers. What was he trying to tell her?

"So you're not angry with me?"

"No. I am not angry with you." He brushed by her, and continued up the stairs to Sophie's room.

Apprehension gnawed inside her. Something was wrong. Clearly, Riel did not want to speak to her. But why?

Even Amelia, dancing a scandalous number of dances with young Fenwick at the ball that evening, noticed Riel's cool manner.

"What's happened between you and the Baron?" she asked as they sat together, taking a breather between dances.

Amelia had been shocked to learn that her cousin was the notorious rapist, but over the last week she had come to her usual level-headed equilibrium about it. Lucinda could not. The horror of that night played over and over again through her dreams.

"It's complicated," Lucinda said now. She wished she could talk to her friend about it, but there were too many secrets... and not all were hers to share.

"Is he angry with you?"

"I don't know. Things aren't right between us. I'm not sure if they ever can be again." For Riel was still a murderer. Self-admitted. By rights, he should not be escorting her all over London, but Lucinda could not, and would not, reveal his secret to the authorities. And so he would remain her guardian in this complicated game.

"Jonathon tried to force himself on you, didn't he?"

Lucinda blanched. "Don't ask me what happened."

"It's clear on your face. And Riel's the one who bashed in Jonathon's nose."

"Yes," she said, looking down at her hands.

"Why don't you talk to him?"

"I've tried. He doesn't want to talk to me. There's nothing left to say."

"The looks you give each other speak volumes."

"I don't want to talk about it."

"You're miserable, and so is he. Talk to him," her friend urged.

Lucinda swallowed. "Why? What's the point?"

"The point?" Amelia rolled her eyes, and then pushed her, for Riel appeared a scant few yards away. "Baron," she called. "Lucinda has an empty slot she would like you to fill."

Riel strode closer, as tall as ever, with his hair still in that pirate's tail. His black eyes burned into Lucinda like coals. "Is that your wish, Lady Lucinda?"

That was another thing. He'd begun to call her by her full title. It annoyed her. With a chin tilt, she stood. "Yes. I would be honored."

Riel offered his black clad arm. She took it, and followed him to the dance floor. And then she was in his arms, dancing a country dance. His steps were smooth and polished. Every inch the gentleman Baron...or a Duke. Nothing of the pirate. Or was there?

His eyes glittered down at her. "Why did you want to dance with me?"

"I realized I never thanked you."

His steps faltered. "For that night?"

"Of course for that night."

They danced in silence for a moment, twirled apart, and then together again.

Stiffly, Riel said, "I am sorry the man you loved betrayed your trust."

Lucinda felt a flare of shock. Riel believed...? But then, she'd let him, Lucinda remembered. Now she must put that lie straight, at least.

"I don't love him. I never did." An unknown emotion flickered in those dark eyes. "I..." She caught her lower lip between her teeth. Lucinda couldn't say that she'd been desperate to flee from her feelings for Riel. And that she'd been a fool. "I believed no other man would ask for me. I thought he was my only choice."

They spun apart, and then found their way back to each other.

"You believed that eloping with Jonathon would be more pleasant than enduring another year under my care?" An edge bit through his voice.

Lucinda blinked back tears and looked down. Yes. More pleasant than a year of anguish, living close to the man she truly loved, but could never have. A man unfit to be her husband, and worse, one who had no desire to pursue that position. Wasn't the sea his first love? What a sorry, impossible mess it all was.

Riel's grip tightened on her, and she felt the tension simmering inside him.

Another parting, then whirling together again. Lucinda hated the ever increasing distance between them. Desperately, she blurted, "Why are you so angry? And why have you been avoiding me?"

"Your opinion of me is clear. I will fulfill my duties as your guardian, but you will not be forced to endure my presence any more than is necessary, Lady Lucinda."

Something snapped inside of her. "Stop it!" With a glare, she stomped on his toe.

Shock, and then a spark of the old Riel flared to life. "Stop what, exactly?"

"Call me *Lucy*. You always have. Why stop now?"

"You want me to call you Lucy?"

Tears filled her eyes. "I want you to be the man you were before I learned your horrific secret."

"I am still that man."

"How can you be?" she burst out. "You *killed* someone," she whispered. "How can I forget that?"

His fingers at her waist tightened. "As I wanted to kill Jonathon that night," he said in a low voice. "But I did not."

Lucinda tried to make sense of this apparent non sequitur. "The man you killed...was he a rapist, like Jonathon?"

"No." The single word bit out. "He was innocent of any crime except for greed."

Lucinda guessed more must lay behind the story than Jonathon had revealed. "What happened? Will you please tell me?"

"It will make no difference. I'm still guilty of murder."

"I want to know. I must know, if you are to continue as my guardian. I need to know if I can trust you or not." Of course, Lucinda already knew she could trust him. She just wanted to know the complete truth for herself.

His dark head dipped closer to her own. "You are ready to leave the ball?"

Her heart fluttered faster. "Yes."

"Then come." Like a matador with a cape, he strode for the exit.

"Baron!" Their heads swiveled at George's voice. What was he doing in the ballroom? "It is Lady Sophia. She asked me to get you. I fear..." His white face and pinched lips told the story.

Within minutes they boarded the carriage and headed home. Silent tears slipped down Lucinda's cheeks. She prayed they were not too late...she prayed Sophie would not pass this eve.

≪⃛ ≪⃛ ≪⃛ ≪⃛ ≪⃛

They found Sophie breathing shallowly, and looking as gray and weak as a kitten. She greeted them both faintly, and indicated she wanted to speak to Lucinda alone.

Once Riel left, Sophie gripped Lucinda's hand with alarming weakness. "Tell Riel...what...feel for him."

"But I don't..."

Wise old eyes looked into her soul. "Don't lie...to a dying... woman. It's clear...what you feel."

"But he killed a man. You know that, don't you, Sophie?" Lucinda whispered.

"Yes. The man...was...responsible..." Sophie gasped for breath. "...for the death...of a girl...a friend of Riel's."

"But..."

"Riel...must tell you. Promise me...one thing, Lucinda."

"Anything." Tears burned.

"Do not...mourn for me. I go...to a far better place. Smell flowers...live...love. Now...is your time, Lucinda. Don't waste...a precious moment. Promise me."

Lucinda nodded, blinded by tears. "I love you, Sophie."

"And I...love you." Sophie smiled. It was a glimmer of her old bright one. "Know nothing...could make me happier...than you...and Riel...overcoming...barriers between you." Her breaths quieted, and her spurt of energy evaporated. Sophie whispered, "Call Riel."

"Riel!"

Riel immediately entered, and Sophie clasped his hand. "Stubborn boy," she whispered. "Forgive...self. You are...worthy of...far...more than a dukedom. You deserve...every happiness. Pursue what...you most want...don't let...anything stop you."

Riel glanced at Lucinda. "I will do all I can."

Sophie's eyes fluttered closed. "Good. I...will rest now."

Sophie slipped quietly away in the night. Both Lucinda and Riel were there, and even the doctor. He said her heart just stopped beating. A peaceful passing, and for that, Lucinda was grateful. She'd been so afraid Sophie would suffocate on the fluid in her lungs. What an awful passing that would have been.

But now she was at peace.

Chapter Twenty-Seven

Mid-July, 1814

FOR LUCINDA, the Season was over. She said goodbye to Amelia and her family and rode with Riel and Effie to Iveny, where the funeral was held and Sophie buried.

Lucinda wept off and on for days. It didn't seem fair that God would take her father, and then her best friend. All within two years. The pain seemed more than she could bear. One small comfort was knowing Sophie had been at peace about it. In fact, Lucinda believed toward the end Sophie had rather looked forward to heaven. To seeing her beloved Charles, and living in a place where no more sickness, death, or pain existed.

Sophie lived in a far better place than the misery in which Lucinda now lived.

A few days after Sophie's funeral, Riel took her home to Ravensbrook.

"I am taking the *Tradewind* on a merchant voyage," he told her on the night of their arrival.

Pain blistered in Lucinda's heart. She whispered, "You're leaving?" Here it was. The beginning of the end. He would return to his mistress, the sea.

"I will be back." His dark gaze offered no more.

Lucinda couldn't bring herself to ask when he'd return. "When do you leave?"

"Tomorrow morning."

"Oh." Wasn't this for the best? Perhaps during his absence she would forget the impossible, insane love she felt for him.

That confounding love continued to grow every minute she was with him. If he left, perhaps the torment in her heart would heal.

Perhaps, eventually, she would find another man. She couldn't imagine it. Certainly, she'd never fall in love again. Not ever. It hurt, horribly, but life wasn't fair, was it? Not to her father, not to Sophie. Not to herself.

"What...what of Ravensbrook's accounts?"

"You can pay them, Lucy."

She raised surprised eyes to his. "You believe I'm capable?"

"I believe you can do anything you set your mind to."

She licked her lips and made a decision. "Good. Then tell me, once and for all, what happened all those years ago. Why you murdered that man."

Riel rocked back on his heels. "You still want to know?"

"Of course I do. Sophie told me there's more to the story. I want to know the full truth, Riel. Before you return to your first love, the sea."

"The sea is not my first love, Lucy." His gaze held hers.

Surprised hope flickered. "Then why did you say you want to spend the rest of your life at sea?"

"I am not fit for any other life." He must mean because of the murder he had committed. Was that why he'd chosen the sea? Not a love, then, but a prison.

"Come sit with me on the terrace."

Outside, she sat in Sophie's favorite chair, and Riel sat in Lucinda's. His gaze sought hers. "Are you sure you want to hear this? It's a gruesome tale."

"I'm sure." It didn't matter anymore, what he had done. Not to her heart. She loved him. But her mind still needed to know the full truth.

Riel began, "As I told you, I crewed on a ship to the Barbary Coast. You were right—it was a pirate ship. The men on it were hard, greedy and selfish. After I was initiated, a bond knit us together like brothers. At least, I believed so.

"I became friends with a lad named Pen. He was about my age, but small in size. We both worked the sails, and Pen was as nimble as a monkey. When I was seventeen, we docked in Tangier, Morocco for a few weeks to sell our gain and to take on supplies and water. I learned something then that changed my life forever."

Lucinda shifted in her chair. A horrible fascination glued her attention to his words. And sickness plagued her, too, knowing she was about to learn how Riel had killed someone.

Riel stood and paced.

"I went below deck to grab my boots to go into town. I saw Pen, then, changing his clothes...*her* clothes, I realized in shock. I don't know how she'd kept it a secret for six months on that ship. Anyway, she turned and saw me and begged me to keep her secret. I told her it was too dangerous. She had to get off the ship. If any of the men found out..." Riel shook his head, and looked far away, as if into the past.

"She refused, and we argued, loudly. She jumped off the ship, onto the dock. I tried to follow her, but the first mate, a man by the name of Desalt, stopped me. I could tell by his grin that he'd heard us arguing. He knew Pen was a woman. I warned him off, but he just laughed at me."

Riel remained silent for a moment. "I tried to follow Pen, but I couldn't find her. Stupidly, I stayed out late, drinking. It was dark when I got back to the ship. Pen wasn't back. Desalt wasn't there, either. I slept off the alcohol, and the next morning Desalt was back. Pen wasn't. I asked if he'd seen her. He gave me a greasy smile and said, 'Make it worth my while, an' I'll tell you.'"

Riel clenched his fists at the memory. "I was scared. He could have done anything to her. But whatever he'd done, it had lined his pockets. I watched him all day. At dusk he left the ship, and I skipped duty to follow him."

Lucinda listened with bated breath. So far, it didn't sound like a tale of murder. Rather of a young man worried about his friend. When Riel didn't speak for a long time, she scanned his face. It looked tortured.

At last he said, "I..." That one word sounded guttural, and he cleared his throat. "I followed him." Riel's voice grew unnaturally quiet. "He entered a house in the worst section of town...a brothel, I could tell. As he went in, a man came out. A tall aristocrat, who looked self-satisfied. He fiddled with his cravat, tweaking it as if he were some preening bird. He wore a top hat, he had dark hair, and he was young; I guessed about twenty-four. He looked out of place. It didn't look like an establishment for an aristocrat."

Riel drew a breath, as if girding himself to go on. "After Desalt went inside, women started screaming. Upstairs, it sounded like. I ran in and up the stairs. Three or four women stood in a doorway, shrieking. One fainted. I ran inside and stopped. I couldn't believe my eyes. Pen lay on the floor, half dressed...like a tramp. And...and blood was all over her." His voice sounded thick, now. "Desalt was shaking her, yelling at her. She didn't move, so he put his hands around her throat and throttled her, and screamed even louder."

Riel gripped the table, as if for support. "Something inside me snapped. I launched at him and dragged him off her. I punched him again and again. I couldn't stop. All I saw was blood...Pen's blood...and Desalt's." He drew a long, shaky breath.

"Desalt fought me back. He swung a chair at me. I grabbed it and yanked him forward so hard his head cracked on a dresser. It sounded like a gunshot. He fell to the floor and didn't move.

"Soon after, men in British military uniforms swarmed into the room. Your father was there, Lucy. He asked what had happened. Only one woman spoke English. I was in shock, and held Pen in my arms. I couldn't speak. Desalt was dead. Pen was dead. The soldiers carted me off to their ship. Captain Hastings wanted to sort matters out with the British consulate, since all of the people involved were English. Well, I was half English, but that was close enough. He didn't want trouble with the Moroccan government."

Riel sat down and buried his head in his hands. "The Duke of Warrington was the Consul under the British Consul-General, James Matra, at the time."

Lucinda gasped.

"He wanted me to hang for murder—for both Desalt's and Pen's. Preferably on the British warship. But he'd accept turning me over to the Moroccan government, or extraditing me to London to swing. He wanted to prove to the Sultan that the English are tough on their own.

"Captain Hastings spoke on my behalf, but I didn't understand why. I'd talked to him in the brig and tried to tell him what had happened. I confessed to killing Desalt. I signed my own death warrant by admitting it, but I was ready to die. I had killed a man in a violent rage. Desalt had not even harmed Pen. She was dead when he arrived." His voice broke. "I killed an innocent man."

Lucinda could keep silent no longer. "He was *not* innocent! Desalt had obviously sold Pen into prostitution. The customer he forced upon Pen killed her. Desalt was as guilty as the actual murderer!"

"No. It was my fault. I should have tried harder to find Pen that first night. But I got drunk, instead." Self-disgust roughened Riel's voice. "I failed her, and then I killed a man."

Lucinda waited, knowing there was more.

After a moment, he continued. "I burned to know who had killed Pen. In my gut, I thought it was that aristocrat I'd seen. While Captain Hastings pled for leniency for me, I sat in a cabin packed with people; news people, Moroccan officials, and the ghoulish and the curious. I saw all sorts of people...and then I saw him. The man who had left the brothel that night. He wore no top hat, but I knew him. I shouted, 'That's him!' He didn't even flinch. His lips curled into a sneering smirk, just like they had night.

"The warped bastard!" Riel said now through his teeth. "One of my shipmates heard me. He asked what I meant, and I told him.

"The trial progressed, and I fully expected to hang the next morning. But somehow—I'll never know how, or why—Peter took the Consul aside and convinced him to let me go. Then he spoke to Sultan Mawlay Sulayman's men. I'll never know what your father said to any of them. But I was a free man. Peter advised me to leave Morocco immediately. He arranged for me to set sail on an English ship the next morning. Before we sailed, my friend from the pirate ship stopped by and told me the aristocrat was dead. They'd jumped and killed him in the street the previous night. He was the son of the British Consul, the Duke of Warrington. Jonathon's older brother."

Stunned, Lucinda said, "So Jonathon did recognize you. He must have been at your trial."

"Yes. What he doesn't know is that I'm responsible for his brother's death, too."

"What?"

"I named him to my friend. I knew what could happen. Even worse, he could have been innocent."

"But he wasn't."

"No. My friend coerced a confession from him. He was guilty, all right. And he hadn't given Pen the money he'd promised Desalt, either. That's why Desalt was so upset that night, and why he attacked Pen."

"What an awful story!" Lucinda felt sickened. What an awful brother Jonathon had had. What a horrible influence upon an impressionable young boy.

Riel stood again. "So you see, I am a murderer. Twice over. I am responsible for the deaths of two men."

"They were both awful men. Criminals!" Lucinda jumped to her feet. At last, she felt relieved. Riel was guilty of nothing. "Jonathon's brother deserved to hang. But he never would have stood trial, not with his father as Consul, and peer of the Consul-General. Justice was served, Riel."

"Perhaps. But Desalt is dead. I killed him with my own hands. He was a greedy swine, but he didn't deserve to die."

Lucinda did not agree. "It was an accident, Riel," she said softly, and placed a gentle hand on his arm. "You didn't mean to kill him. He cracked his head on a dresser. The dresser killed him!"

A ghost of a smile touched Riel's lips, but soon vanished. "I would have beaten him to a bloody pulp. Murder was in my heart."

"Rage. Not murder," she said. "And grief for your friend." She felt the tension in his arm, and the tight control under which he always held himself. Now she understood why. And she realized that grief still consumed him...and guilt did, too; for being unable to save Pen, and for killing the scoundrel Desalt.

"Riel." She moved to face him. Her gaze ran over his features. His eyes looked as black as pitch, and the blunt lines of his face were taut with self-condemnation. "Riel," she said again, and touched his cheek. "My father did not think you were guilty," she whispered, "and neither do I."

Disbelief flickered. "You don't?"

"No, Riel. It's time to forget the past. Think instead about the man you have become."

"You see value in me?" He sounded vulnerable.

She gave a breath of a laugh. "Do I see value in you?" She loved him! "You are the most honorable man I've ever met. My father was right about you."

"So you will allow me to stay in your life, as your guardian?"

"I won't chase you away, if that is what you are asking."

"It is all I am asking...for now."

Her heart beat faster when she looked up at him. But she could read nothing on his face except for a smile. "Then you will leave tomorrow?" Disappointment lodged in her heart.

"I promised suppliers a shipment."

"All right." He was a ship's captain. It was his life. At least it wasn't his first love. Hope unfurled. So much had happened in the last few weeks. Perhaps she needed to give herself time to grieve for Sophie, and to come to grips with what Jonathon had done to her. She needed to heal. Learning the secrets of Riel's past finally put to rest all of her doubts and fears. He was honorable and fair...the man she'd always hoped and believed him to be. And he would return to her.

But still she did not know what he felt for her.

"When will you be back?"

"By your birthday, Lucy. Will that be soon enough?"

Three long months. "Of...of course."

His gaze ran gently over her face, as if trying to memorize every detail. "Let's go over the ledgers together."

◈ ◈ ◈ ◈ ◈

Riel left early the next morning, before she was up, as he'd told her he would when they'd scoured the ledgers together the afternoon before. She'd enjoyed every one of those quiet minutes, working at his side, and feeling the occasional brush of his arm, and inhaling the clean masculine scent that was just Riel. Sometimes, when she leaned close to him, he would pull away after a moment, as if determined to put distance between them

It hurt. Lucinda did not understand him at all. But then again, everything about her life had been pretty muddled for the past few months. It might be best that he'd decided to leave for awhile. She repeatedly told herself this as she went about the daily tasks of Ravensbrook in the months that followed. Perhaps by the time he returned, she would have her head on straight.

Lucinda still suffered through nightmares which replayed the night Jonathon had tried to rape her. She awoke gasping with fear...and always before Riel rescued her. Why?

The days passed slowly. Lucinda felt terribly alone, and she hated it. She missed Sophie, and grieved for her friend as she tended the garden they'd planted together. The little rose bush bloomed hardily, as did the other plants.

The summer slowly slipped into late August, and Amelia invited her to stay for a week at their house. Lucinda enjoyed that happy time. She also noticed that Timothy Fenwick came to call more than once.

"He's sweet on you," she giggled to Amelia one day. They sat on the wide swing which hung from the Carlisle's largest oak tree.

"Perhaps I'm sweet on him, too. He does have a charm about him."

"A cute, puppy dog charm."

Amelia said nothing, and Lucinda felt instant concern. Perhaps her friend had taken her comment the wrong way. "You know I like Timothy, Amelia."

Her friend pushed off with her toes, and they started swinging again. "I know you do. I must say, I never thought I'd fall in love with a younger man."

"You're in *love*?" Lucinda squealed and hugged her. "Oh, Amelia! I'm so happy for you!"

Amelia pinkened, and a happy smile lit her face, which was never less plain than now. "He's already declared himself to Father, but we've decided to wait until he's twenty, at least. Perhaps he will change his mind by then."

"Amelia! He will not. He is totally besotted with you, and you know it."

Amelia smiled again. "And what about you, Lucinda? Have you admitted yet that you're in love with the Baron?"

It was Lucinda's turn to fall silent. "I do love him," she admitted.

"I knew it all along."

"But so many things have happened between us. I was a brat for the first year, and then chased Jonathon...and then everything else happened." Lucinda had at last told her best friend everything that had happened in London...and about Riel's past, too. Amelia agreed with Lucinda. Riel was guilty of nothing at all.

"So you don't know how he feels about you."

"Why would he have any feelings for me? I was a shrew to him half the time, and the other half I pushed him away, and *ran* away. I've been such a fool, Amelia. And he left on this last voyage so fast I think he was glad to see the back of me."

"Are you sure?"

"I am sure of nothing with that maddening man! He drives me up the wall and down the other side."

"Did he say when he'll be back?"

"October."

"When at last you'll turn twenty. Didn't your father want you to wait until then to marry?"

"Yes. But I see no one in sight to marry. Perhaps I will turn into an old maid."

Amelia looked at her with sympathy and amusement. "Lucinda, come visit me after your birthday. Promise me."

Lucinda's brows furrowed in confusion. "Of course. Now, tell me again...when did Timothy actually propose?"

♦ ♦ ♦ ♦ ♦

October, 1814

The summer months passed with excruciating slowness for Riel. True, he'd promised a shipment to a longstanding, faithful buyer, but he also longed to be with Lucy.

Hopefully, the time apart would allow things to settle between them. Lucy had needed time after Jonathon's attack and Sophie's death to recover. And to process the revelation of his sordid past.

Riel still did not know how Lucy felt about him, but she did believe he was innocent of murder. That fact allowed the deepest wound inside him to begin to heal. Sophie had tried to convince him of the same thing for years, but Riel hadn't been able to accept her words. Instead, he'd felt consumed with guilt over his actions...and the fear that he might repeat them one day.

But he hadn't, not even in the one brief, blinding moment when he'd wanted to kill Jonathon.

At last, Riel allowed himself to accept God's forgiveness for his past sins. And at last he began to forgive himself. One day in his cabin, he dropped to his knees and in wonderment thanked God for his grace and forgiveness, and for the healing that finally soothed his heart.

And Riel hoped—perhaps foolishly—that Lucy might nurture deeper feelings for him. He remembered the tenderness in her eyes when she'd told him she believed he was innocent, and the vehemence with which she'd insisted he was an honorable man. Could she possibly love him?

The days of summer slid past on the high seas. Standing on the humming deck of the *Tradewind,* with the wind driving her at a fast clip through the choppy seas, cleared Riel's mind of all but one most important fact.

He loved Lucy, and he wanted her to be his wife. He needed her with a ferocity that shook him. Falling in love had never been in his plans, but if there was the slightest chance she might love him even a little...

When Riel got home, he would find his answers. He loved her, and he'd pursue Lucy until her smart, pretty mouth finally admitted what she truly felt for him.

October arrived, and so did the end of his successful voyage. Two days later, Ravensbrook's tall, three story stone structure loomed around the last copse of trees. Riel's heart beat faster. Lucy. At last, he'd see her.

Would she meet him at the front door, with her blue eyes soft and smiling?

He wanted nothing more than to gather her in his arms and hold her close.

He was almost home. Would he at last find a home for his heart, as well?

Chapter Twenty-Eight

THE CRUNCH of wheels on the drive made Lucinda hurry to her bedroom window. A groomsman ran up to the matched pair of blacks hitched to the black carriage. A familiar carriage. She gasped. Riel!

He was here! For some reason, she'd believed he would arrive on her birthday, still two weeks away.

Lucinda could not speed fast enough down the stairs. She peered out the front window. The carriage door opened without the driver's assistance. So like Riel. And then, as her heart skipped and bumped with joy, Riel vaulted up Ravensbrook's steps, his strides long and lithe, as if he couldn't wait to burst inside.

The butler opened the door with a bow and a flourish. "Lord Iveny." Wilson refused to speak to a nobleman without using his full title.

"Wilson." Riel's tall, muscular frame filled the doorway and his gaze immediately focused upon Lucinda.

With a trembling smile, she moved forward. "Riel." Once again, his sheer size, and the intensity that was only Riel, hit her heart hard, making it race.

Uncharacteristic shyness slowed her steps. She loved him. More than ever before, this certainty stabbed her with the force of a lightening bolt. She loved him with all of her heart, but what could a wonderful man like Riel possibly feel for her? A ward thrust upon him. An ungrateful one for that matter, and one who had caused him no end of grief over the past two years.

In two strides Riel closed the distance between them. He caught her hands and looked down at her, his dark eyes steady and curiously intent. "Did you miss me, Lucy?"

Words caught in her throat. She had, and too fiercely. "How...how could I miss a man as irksome as you?"

His slow, soft smile befuddled her. She felt lost... bewildered by that unfathomable black gaze of his.

Riel leaned forward and kissed her forehead. Not what she had hoped for, but it felt heavenly. His warm lips lingered, speeding up her heart so it pulsed through her body, making her short of breath. "I missed you, too, Lucy." He released her. "Now, what have you been about while I was gone?"

She immediately missed his touch, and that scandalous realization warmed her cheeks. "I must see about dinner. Mrs. Beatty must be warned to set another place."

�� �� �� �� ��

Later, after a hastily planned supper, for which Lucinda had asked Mrs. Beatty to prepare all of Riel's favorite dishes, her guardian leaned back in his chair. "You know how to refresh a man, Lucy."

Lucinda's cheeks warmed. "Thank you. I think."

He watched her, as if gauging her every response.

She frowned, willing her cheeks to cool. "Must you stare at me in such a manner? It is rude, as you know."

"Is it rude to want to memorize every line of your face? It is all I could carry of you on my voyage."

What was he *saying* to her? Her heart beat faster. "Kindly do not play games with me, Mr. Montclair. Would you like dessert?"

"I would like to walk in the garden with you."

"Now?"

"Now." He stood and dropped his napkin on the table.

When she stared up at him, he held out his hand. "Are you coming?"

She stood without his help. Her heart tripped dangerously fast. "Mrs. Beatty will not approve of us missing dessert."

"Will you not hold my hand, Lucy?" His gaze held hers.

"Of course," she said pertly. "Your wish is my command." With a quick breath, she looked at the broad, tanned hand he held out to her. She slipped hers into his, and his warm, calloused fingers closed around hers.

Heart bumping with questions, she accompanied him to the terrace, and then down the steps to the garden.

"The blooms are gone," he said quietly.

"It is fall. A time of death and decay."

"Necessary before renewal."

"Yes," she agreed.

"But even amidst death, hope blooms."

Puzzled, she looked up at him. "What do you mean?"

"Look." He pointed, and then she saw the tender yellow bloom on Sophie's rosebush. By rights, it was well past time for new blossoms. All the old ones had been deadheaded away. But this one furled open like the sun, infusing light and color and the hope of spring in the midst of the fall.

Lucinda knelt and dipped down to smell its sweet fragrance. Tears gathered in her eyes as Riel knelt beside her.

"Sophie and I planted this." A tear slipped down her cheek. "It's tenacious, just like she was."

His arms went around her and without a word, she crumpled into him. "Sophie's not gone, Lucy," he said, holding her tight. "I think that flower is to remind us, don't you?" She nodded wordlessly. When she at last pulled back, he offered her a handkerchief.

She dabbed her eyes and blurted, "I don't want to lose you, too, Riel."

He tugged her to her feet, which was a more comfortable position than kneeling on the ground. "Have your feelings for me changed, Lucy? You don't want to chase me off any longer?"

Lucinda smiled and sniffed. "It never worked, did it?"

"No. And it will not."

"Good." She felt relieved, but then bit her lip. "When do you leave again?"

"You already want to get rid of me?"

"No! Truly, you are an impossible man with whom to have a civil conversation."

"I want the truth between us, Lucy."

The truth? She was scared to tell him the deepest truth in her heart. What if he didn't feel the same way about her? And by rights, he shouldn't. Hadn't she caused him endless headaches over the past two years?

All the more reason for her to take courage in hand and take the first step now.

Slowly, she said, "All right. I'll tell you the truth. You've done an exemplary job as my guardian. No one could have done it better."

"Really? Exemplary?" A smile tugged at his mouth.

"Yes," she returned, lifting her chin a fraction. "And if you are quiet, I will pay you more compliments."

Surprise lifted his brows, but he remained silent.

"All right, then." Lucinda searched her mind for the best words to convey what she saw in this man, and a little more of what she felt for him. "I look up to you...and *not* just because you're bigger than me. Be certain of that. I've always respected you, Riel, much as I tried to fight you at every turn. You were a force to reckon with, and it maddened me, again and again, how right you were on *almost* every occasion."

She smiled. "I needed you to be reasonable and fair and strong, and you were. And I respected you for insisting that I heed your words. I knew you were looking out for my best interests all along, and I did listen, even though at times I kicked and screamed the whole way."

Something flickered deep in those dark eyes. "And now, Lucy?"

Her heart caught in her throat. "Now..." She swallowed. "Now I have discovered no other man compares to you. You have quite spoiled me for all others, Riel Montclair."

A faint smile tugged at his lips. "Does that mean all others will leave the picture?"

Her heart pounded unnaturally fast. "Yes. If...if you wish it."

"Lucy," he growled, and tugged her close to him. "If I *wish* it? Yes, I wish it. You are all I've been able to think about, night and day, for the last year and a half."

"I am?" A smile of pure wonder bloomed. "Truly?"

"Yes, you minx. You got under my skin from the first."

"Are you sure you didn't want to flay *into* my skin?" she asked slyly.

He smiled, and glanced down at the rosebush. "When I see that yellow rose, it reminds me of you."

"Of me? Because of the thorns?"

"No, Lucy. Because it is beautiful, like the sunshine you pour into my heart."

Riel thought of her like sunshine? "But what about all the maddening things I've done to you?"

He smiled. "The spice. But you are sweet underneath it all. The way you cared for Sophie all those months, and the way you care for me, and helped me to forgive myself..." His fingers brushed her cheek. "You make me feel whole, Lucy. You make me feel hope."

Lucinda didn't know what to say, but a soft, sweet emotion burgeoned inside her as she looked up at him.

Riel took her hands in his. "Lucy, I love you. That's why I wouldn't let another man have you. It's true. I scared all of your suitors away, although I didn't realize it until later. I wanted you all for myself." He watched her, his gaze vulnerable, as she had never seen it before.

She drew a shaky breath of pure joy. "Riel, you pirate," she whispered. "You stole my heart a long time ago."

Incredulity, followed by quiet, intense joy flickered across his features. "You love me?"

"*Yes.*"

"Then you will marry me?"

"Of course I will!" She managed to smile. "Although what I'll do with a bossy man like you, I don't know."

"Love me, *chéri?*"

Lucinda flung herself into his arms. "I do love you, Riel, with my whole heart."

It felt heavenly to be in his arms. After a moment, Lucinda's lips curved against his jacket. "I think Father and Sophie are pleased, don't you?"

"I think this was your father's plan all along."

Lucinda grinned. "He was a clever man. I'm glad he put you in my life—irksome though you have been from time to time."

"I do everything because I love you."

"I know," she said softly. "And I love you, too. I want only to be close by your side, from now to forevermore."

His eyes glinted down at her. "You don't think that will be dangerous?"

"I count on it," she said cheekily. "I can think of nothing more exciting than our passionate battles."

His black eyes burned a smoky color. "I promise you their resolutions will be most satisfying."

Her cheeks flamed. "Riel Montclair!"

"You do not want it?"

Her face flamed hotter. "I do. But you are a wicked, wicked man to suggest such things to my maidenly ears."

He chuckled, and drew her close against him so they touched at every point possible. "How soon will you be my wife, Lucy? I have waited far too long already."

Daringly, she wrapped her arms around his neck. "In two weeks, when I turn twenty? Will that be soon enough, my wonderful, honorable guardian?"

He shook his head. "Not nearly, my sweet Lucy."

She grinned. "Perhaps then tomorrow, my wicked pirate."

"Then a pirate I must be."

"I knew it from the first."

"As I knew you were a beautiful spitfire." Riel kissed her at last, slowly, thrilling her to her toes. "But I did not suspect you would steal my heart."

She smiled up at his handsome face, so very close to her own. Joy blossomed in her heart. "I love you," she whispered.

Never would either of them be alone again. Somewhere in heaven, she knew Sophie and Father were smiling.

"And I love you," Riel murmured. "Forever." He sealed his new promise to her with a kiss.

The End

Acknowledgments

I DEEPLY APPRECIATE the many people who have helped make this book possible. First, I'd like to thank my editor, Lori, for catching a number of typos, and for her brilliant idea to fix one plot point, when I was absolutely stuck.

Also, I am so grateful to my beta readers for taking the time (and on a time crunch this time around) to read and provide valuable feedback on this book. Suzy, McKenna, Betty, Briana, Kristy, and Jen, thank you so, so much! Each of you brought fresh, unique insights that I had never considered before. This book is so much better as a result of your help.

And always, thanks to my wonderful husband, Dale, who supports me and believes in me, no matter what. I am blessed beyond measure.

And to my wonderful kids: You work so hard, and you are so talented. I am so proud of you. Reach for the stars. Don't let anything stand in your way.

About the Author

JENNETTE GREEN HAS ALWAYS had a passion for writing. She wrote her first story over thirty years ago, and her first romance novel, *The Commander's Desire*, was published in 2008. It was awarded "Readers' Favorite Hero for 2009," and has received "Top Pick" and "5 Star" accolades from a number of review sites. Other books by Jennette include *Her Reluctant Bodyguard*, a Christian romantic suspense novel, and *Ice Baron*, a science fiction romance, packed with action and romance. These books have received awards such as "Top Pick," "Recommended Read," and "Reviewer's Choice Award" from popular review sites, and Ice Baron placed third in the science fiction category in an international ebook competition.

Jennette loves to travel with her husband and children, and particularly likes long walks along the ocean, dreaming up new stories.

She loves to hear from her readers.

Drop her a note at:
jennettegreen@jennettegreen.com.
Connect on Facebook:
https://www.facebook.com/JennetteGreenRomanceAuthor

Visit her website to discover new and upcoming books!
www.jennettegreen.com

CPSIA information can be obtained
at www.ICGtesting.com
Printed in the USA
FSOW01n2046080716
22551FS